I0762902

JUNE BABY

JUNE BABY

A Novel

SHANNON GARVEY

THOUSAND VOICES

x

RANDOM HOUSE

New York

Random House
An imprint and division of Penguin Random House LLC
1745 Broadway, New York, NY 10019
randomhousebooks.com
penguinrandomhouse.com

Hardcover ISBN 978-0-593-97990-7
Ebook ISBN 978-0-593-97992-1

Printed in the United States of America

4th Printing

First Edition

BOOK TEAM: Production editor: Jennifer Rodriguez • Managing editor: Rebecca Berlant • Production manager: Sandra Sjursen • Copy editor: Melissa Churchill • Proofreaders: Kimberly Broderick, Andrea Gordon, Catherine Sangermano

Book design by Debbie Glasserman

The authorized representative in the EU for product safety and compliance is Penguin Random House Ireland, Morrison Chambers, 32 Nassau Street, Dublin D02 YH68, Ireland. https://eu-contact.penguin.ie

For my mother, Chrissy,
who walked with me to the library,
who drove me to the bookstore,
and who listened to me talk about the
world of novels that felt so real to me.

It's easy to see the beginnings of things, and harder to see the ends.

—JOAN DIDION, *Goodbye to All That*

I am a collection of dismantled almosts.

—ANNE SEXTON

JUNE BABY

PROLOGUE

June 2013

The early June wind was warm and humid. It slid across Ruth's bare arms and cheeks as she cut through the air, coasting on her bike down the short hill away from town. Through a thin alley, down a sandy path to her right, she saw a spark of blue, and as she pressed her brakes and slowed to a stop, the ocean surrounding Block Island came into view. The rain had let up during the ferry ride over, and the sun was growing stronger. Dazed, Ruth watched small waves break upon the sand, and she wondered if she'd ever been this alone in her life.

She was seventeen. Her mother was dead, her father had put her on a boat and shipped her off to an island, and now she was meant to find a woman she had never met before and didn't know anything about—a woman named Diana.

Only an hour before, Ruth had been sitting in the passenger seat as her father, Joel, pulled his old Ford van up to the curb and parked across from the ferry dock in Galilee, Rhode Island. The smell coming off the fishing boats clashed with the coffee steaming out of the Styrofoam cup in Joel's hand, making Ruth's empty stomach turn. Putting her head against the glass, she stared out the car window as seagulls swarmed over a piece of trash on the sidewalk, squawking and pecking at the empty plastic bag as a light rain began to fall.

Joel cleared his throat and Ruth turned to her father. They hadn't spoken all morning. His eyes were puffy and faintly bloodshot, making the blue in them pop. He had shaved, and there was a bloody nick near his ear that was now dry and flaking. Paint stains speckled his canvas work vest.

Grabbing a grease-stained receipt from a McDonald's bag on the floor, he pulled a pen from his pocket, tested it on the corner of the paper, and wrote a name and number on the back of it. As she watched him write, Ruth wondered if he remembered the cellphone she had for emergencies was broken—a plastic brick at the bottom of her backpack—or if he assumed there would be a payphone on the island. Or if any of this had crossed Joel's mind at all, if he was concerned about sending her off without a way to contact her. He didn't seem it, and Ruth wasn't surprised. It wasn't that her father was intentionally reckless, but somehow she always ended up fending for herself when he was in charge.

It was hard not to feel like she was being ejected from her old life, from her family, but Ruth was resigned to it now, everything passing through her mind in a thick fog, her reactions slow. She had fought Joel at first, but she was tired of fighting now. If this was what he wanted, then fine.

"All right then," he said, handing her the receipt. "Off you go. If you can't find Diana, call me at work and I'll tell you how to find Sarah and Bill."

Ruth tried to remember the last time she saw her father's friends. She had a vague memory of running across their small backyard while the adults sat in low folding chairs, the smell of burning tiki torches and cigars coloring the air.

"Why can't I just stay with them?" Ruth asked. Her voice was almost breaking, and she dug her short fingernails into her palm to fight the emotion back. She didn't want him to see her cry.

"It's a good opportunity," he said, his voice robotic. "Get you out of the diner for a change."

"How do you even know this woman?" Ruth asked, staring down at the scribbled name and number—*Diana Beckett 401-885-0933*.

"Your mom worked with her—when she was on Block Island that summer. She's an artist. They were friends."

Ruth wondered if Diana had come to her mother's funeral, and then she pushed that thought away. There hadn't been many people there.

"Okay," Joel said. Unable to put it off any longer, Ruth stuffed the receipt in the back pocket of her jean shorts, opened the car door, grabbed her bag from the back seat, and headed out into the rain. Joel got out too, pulled Ruth's bike out of the van, and rolled it toward her.

"Let me know when you get settled," Joel said. He hovered as if to hug Ruth but didn't, and Ruth noticed then how tired her father looked, how drained of life, and she felt guilty for causing it. She was tired of being a problem, tired of her grief making him upset.

For a moment, she thought about asking him if she could stay. She'd get better, she wouldn't have to be a burden. But Joel cleared his throat again, the sound he made when he was uncomfortable, so Ruth took the handlebars out of his hands and walked toward the ferry.

Now on the island, standing on the side of the road, Ruth reached into her back pocket. The sun had come out again, but the receipt Joel had given her was wet from sitting on the ferry's rain-dampened bench for an hour. Pulling it out gently so that it wouldn't rip, she saw that the name and number had been mostly smudged off, so they were inscrutable, the blue ink having bled into the rest of the receipt.

"Shit."

For a brief second, Ruth considered getting on the next ferry back, biking home, and telling her father that his plan was off. But then the thought of sleeping in the house among her mother's things while Joel tiptoed around her, unable to handle her sadness, flooded her mind. The thought of the strained conversation, the thin walls, the smell of burnt toast creeping under the bottom of her closed door, of Joel's varying attempts to get Ruth up and out of bed—sometimes anger, sometimes tearful pleading—it all made Ruth feel like she was suffocating, even from this far away. She couldn't go back.

The limp paper fluttered in the breeze, and trying to make out her next move, Ruth looked around, spotting a wood-shingled library across the street. Painted tables decorated the lawn, and heavy hydrangeas spilled out foamy and blue from the breaks in a short fence. An older woman with thick, white hair clasped in a low bun was stretched, arms overhead, underneath an umbrella, cranking the handle so that it bloomed open and created a patch of shade in the grass. When she was done, she walked up the short path, flipped the sign on the door to OPEN, and disappeared inside.

Ruth crossed the street and leaned her bike up against the library, then opened the door and stepped into the dark, cool room. As her eyes adjusted to the low light, she smelled the familiar scent of old books and heard a fan buzzing softly in the background. The woman with the white hair at the front desk looked up from her computer screen.

"I was wondering if you could help me find someone," Ruth said, approaching the desk. Scooting her wheely chair closer to Ruth, the woman furrowed her eyebrows. Ruth felt any resolve she might have had earlier dwindle into desperation.

"What's your name?" the librarian asked.

"Ruth."

"You're looking for someone who lives here?"

Ruth nodded.

"The police might be better for that," she said, and Ruth stood there, crushing the receipt in her fist. She wanted it to disintegrate.

After a moment, the woman asked, "Who is it?"

"Diana, something. She's an . . . artist, I think?"

Ruth looked at the soggy paper and tried once more to make out Diana's last name and number. She felt stupid for knowing so little—like a small child lost in a supermarket, asking where her mom went. The thought made her chest squeeze while she tried to smooth out the paper on the countertop. The woman watched her, then leaned across the counter, picked the paper out of Ruth's hand, and held it away from her face into a weak patch of sunlight, looking down through her glasses.

"What is this?" she asked.

Ruth explained that her father had sent her to find this woman.

"He sent you with only this?" the woman asked, her eyebrows colliding in disbelief.

Ruth nodded again.

"How old are you?"

"Eighteen," Ruth said, and the woman pursed her lips, thinking. It was a lie. Ruth would turn eighteen in August, but she didn't want the woman to know she was a minor—she didn't want her to call the police and be sent back to her father.

Without saying anything more to Ruth, the woman picked up the phone next to her and started dialing.

"Diana?—It's Bonnie. Hey. No, everything's good. There's a young lady here named Ruth who's looking for you. Yeah. Does that ring a bell? Okay, hold on." Bonnie covered the receiver. "What's your mother's name?"

"Maggie . . ." Ruth replied and stopped. "Maggie Phillips? My dad, Joel, sent me."

Bonnie nodded.

"Joel and Maggie Phillips? Their daughter." There was a muffled response where Bonnie looked at Ruth straight in her face, still holding the phone up to her ear.

"Okay," she said. "Yup, will do," and she hung up.

Bonnie dropped the receipt into a wastebasket under her desk, ripped off a piece of notebook paper from a pad in front of her, and scribbled an address on top.

"You have a bike?" the woman asked.

Ruth felt herself nod.

"Okay. Diana said you can head straight over and to mind the holes in the driveway. It's a big hill, but you're strong, right?"

She handed over the paper and pointed into the distance, giving some quick directions that Ruth immediately forgot. She felt like she was on a carnival ride, the haze of motion and people washing over her. It stirred something within her, working against the numbness that had been holding her since her mother died. Taking the notebook paper, she thanked Bonnie and left the cool, quiet library.

Getting on her bike, she glided out into the road toward an empty intersection. The sun was beating against her face, and she needed to squint at the street signs before she checked the paper and headed up a steep street lined with grass and budding daisies that wobbled in the warm summer air.

As Ruth biked up the hill, sweat dripped from her face and arms. She often stopped to catch her breath and look at the large houses set back on their green lawns, the low bushes around them thick and lush.

It was hard not to think of her mother everywhere, to picture her during the one summer Ruth knew she had spent on the island—Maggie, in her youth, unencumbered by a husband or daughter, her cancer years away from her body or mind. Ruth had always imagined her mother's many tumors like shattered glass, the shards sprinkled across her body into the farthest corners, hard to find, impossible to clean out. Thinking about Maggie as she had been, Ruth could see it all happen in reverse. Like rewinding a movie, she could imagine the shards coming together, the glass falling upward until it was whole once again, sitting, benign, on the shelf.

Ruth could picture Maggie cresting the hill, just as Ruth was now, the ocean breeze cool against her hot skin—both of them unaware of what was to come.

As Ruth pedaled, she passed a man on a ladder painting the trim of a window. A small radio was on the stoop playing a song that her father loved. As she watched him paint, he reminded her of Joel. Worry ran through her. Who would check on him alone in the house? She wouldn't be there to scold him into putting out the late-night cigarettes or to shop for food that didn't come in plastic trays. Watching the man descend the ladder and crack a beer, worry faded back into anger. Ruth was angry that she felt the need to take care of her father even as he was sending her to a stranger, leaving her to grieve alone. It was the first time she had ever heard Joel talk about "opportunities" with her, and she didn't buy it. He just wanted her sadness out of the house.

Soon the road deteriorated into rocky sand, and she had to get off her bike to push through the thick patches until she saw a gap in the grasses up ahead. A sign hung from rusted chains attached to a post, and Ruth could read 53 Payne Road carved into the wood and painted over with black. She double-checked the piece of paper Bonnie had given her before turning her bike onto the driveway. Walking, she weaved the bike around potholes, a small dust cloud kicking up behind her until she reached the end of the driveway. A green archway of privet bushes, big enough that if Ruth jumped, she could barely touch the branches with her fingertips, deposited her onto a yard with a beach cottage overlooking a sprawling garden. There was a large beech tree with a swath of shade underneath it, a sliver of ocean hazy on the distant horizon, and a small shed with a blue door right at the edge of the property.

Ruth's face was hot to the touch, and her mouth was dry. She dropped her bike on the grass and slung her backpack off her shoulders. From a distance, Ruth could see shadows passing across the wire screen of the front door and could hear the sounds of kitchen items being sorted and drawers being shut. Approaching the doorway, Ruth stopped, preparing herself to knock, but before she could, the door opened with a peeling metallic squeal, and a red-haired woman with a deeply freckled face walked out onto the stoop. The woman stared at Ruth for a minute. Her eyes roamed over Ruth's face, stopping at every feature. Ruth felt herself starting to itch under the woman's gaze.

"You're Ruth," the woman said. It was a question posed as a statement. Ruth nodded.

"You're Diana?" Ruth asked, her voice raspy. The woman nodded.

Neither of them said anything for another moment as Diana studied Ruth.

"I'm sorry about your mom," she said, and Ruth was struck by how the woman's face fell as she said the words.

Ruth was about to ask her how well she knew Maggie but Diana abruptly brushed past her and started walking around the house, talking behind her as she went.

"The hose is the coldest, and you look like you need to stick your head under some water—submerge a bit."

Ruth followed, confused, and considered the shady garden. She nodded at the suggestion, starting to feel dizzy from the heat. Diana leaned down and cranked the rusty faucet. The hose became taut, and water flowed from its mouth into the scrubby grass. She handed it to Ruth and took the backpack out of her hand.

"I'll be out front when you're done," she said.

Ruth waited for Diana to round the corner before turning the hose on herself, soaking her hair in the cold stream and feeling the welcome pressure against her skull. The water ran over her burned skin and underneath her sweaty clothes—she didn't care. She had kept it together so far that day, but now that she was alone she unclenched her fists and began to cry, letting the hot tears get washed away by the flow of water as if they'd never happened.

Ruth thought of the fog, the heavy weight she'd felt loaded down by, how most of her days since school had ended were spent lying in bed, too tired to get up until it was time for her to go to work at the diner. She wasn't thinking about Maggie. Any thought she had felt too sharp, too close. She was protecting herself. Joel didn't understand.

The incident that had sparked everything started when Ruth finally left her bed to get water. As she went to open the fridge, she noticed all the notes that Maggie used to write for herself were gone. She snapped, growing more and more frantic as she searched in the kitchen drawers, in the trash, pulling everything out, letting it all spill onto the floor. When Joel got home, she screamed at him for throwing them out, for touching anything of Maggie's. She had no recollection of what she had said, but she did remember his tears, how silent he was, his large hands covering his face as he sobbed. Even when Ruth thought of it now, when she saw his horrified face in her mind, she was still angry at him. He was acting as if he had never cared, as if life was business as usual, and she wasn't going to forgive him for that.

Ruth sat on the back step for another moment, trying to push the uncomfortable memory out of her mind, occasionally drinking from the hose, taking her time.

When Ruth thought about her mom, her body ached, like it was folding in on itself. Since Maggie died, this sensation had struck Ruth where she imagined herself growing smaller and smaller, her insides crunching up against one another, everything squeezing together like it might combust, but it never did. There was no release.

What she hadn't told anyone, what she often denied even to herself, was that a small part of her felt relief that it was over—that she didn't have to watch her mom fade anymore, that the ache was better than those final days when the space between each of Maggie's breaths was longer and each rise of her chest was more and more shallow. It had felt as if the waves on the shore were going to stop and Ruth had no way of knowing what would happen then, realizing how much her life as she understood it depended on the rhythm of those waves continuing. What she couldn't say out loud was that she had needed to look away.

A breeze came over the yard, and Ruth looked up. The shadows of the leaves rippled jade green against the grass. She realized then how quiet it was. All she could hear was the flowing of the hose water into the grass, the shuffling of the leaves above her, and a mourning dove cooing somewhere nearby. It seemed to Ruth suddenly like a magical place—like a place in one of the books she used to love reading as a child. Back when she would hide away in a shady spot in her backyard, turning pages until Maggie came looking for her. The breeze ruffled everything again, and she took a deep breath. Standing, she wiped her eyes, turned off the hose, and headed back around the side of the house, water dripping from her body, her clothes now soaking wet.

Diana was sitting on a large, uneven stone that served as the front stoop. Her long, curly red hair was streaked with white. She wore an old blue T-shirt that hung loosely over her body, and sat with her elbows on her knees and her hands folded under her chin. Ruth felt herself become smaller again, looking at Diana's knees. They reminded her so much of her mother's—sprinkled with forgotten hairs, freckled, and lined with wrinkles. The kind of wrinkles that looked like a ripple in a calm pool once you throw a stone into it, the small waves echoing away from the source.

Diana shaded her gray eyes from the sun, looking up at Ruth, and pointed to the grass next to the stoop. Ruth crossed her legs and sat down, still soaking wet. Diana handed her a tuna sandwich and a kitchen cloth patterned with faded yellow ducks.

"Thank you," Ruth said, but she just stared at it until Diana shrugged.

"Eat it," she said. And Ruth took a bite. The bread was soft behind the thick crust, and the tuna was cold and salty. She ate while Diana looked her over, not realizing how hungry she had been. A few minutes of silence passed while Diana swirled some pollen that coated the surface of a small puddle in the stone next to her, and Ruth started wondering whether Diana had known she was coming.

"My dad said you needed help for the summer," Ruth said in between bites.

Diana looked at her, her eyebrows crumpled together, exposing a long divot that ran down the center of her forehead.

"Did he . . . forget to call and say I was coming?" Ruth asked.

Had Diana just forgotten? Or had Joel never called to confirm? Ruth realized she was breathing fast, worried about going back home, until a look of recognition swept over Diana's face.

"Yes! An assistant!" she said. "Sorry. Things always start to fly out of my brain when I get busy . . . I'm working on the edits for this photo book and I've always hated the writing part of these things. Yes, of course, I knew you were coming today."

Ruth nodded and continued eating, feeling uncertain. Neither of them spoke. Ruth started to sense an awkwardness in the silence, and the thought that she was alone crept in on her, even as she sat next to Diana.

"How long has it been since Maggie died?" Diana suddenly asked. Her voice was quiet, like she didn't want to disturb Ruth.

"Three months," Ruth said. She was staring at the ground, feeling tears build within her.

"Not very long," Diana replied, her voice quieter than before.

Ruth shook her head, looking at the grass as she let out a sob.

"Oh no, no." Diana scooted closer to Ruth. "It's okay." She took Ruth's head in her hands rather abruptly and laid it against her thigh, stroking her wet hair. Ruth let herself be comforted by this stranger, the softness of Diana's touch making Ruth's throat thick. Joel's attempts to console her never seemed to carry the same comfort. She cried for another minute and then sat up, wiping her eyes.

"Sending you off like that— Oh, Joel," Diana said, "what an asshole."

Ruth nodded. Diana was staring at her again, and Ruth got the sense that she was experiencing an intense emotion. Her face fell for only a second before lifting into a serene smile. "But I get it. He was probably right. It could be good for you—a change." Diana grabbed Ruth's empty plate, stood up, and opened the screen door. "Come on, I'll show you your room," she said before the door squealed shut behind her. Ruth stood, unfolding her legs, sore from biking. Wiping the rest of the tears away with the back of her hand, she peered through the screen door, the sunlit hallway visible behind it. Diana continued to talk to her from inside the house, and Ruth picked up only bits and pieces of what she was saying about photography, copyediting, and archives.

Diana paused, then shouted out toward the yard: "Oh! My nephew Charlie comes to stay for a week in August. It'll be a squeeze in here, but you'll like him."

The heat had already partially dried Ruth's wet clothes, and the sensation of the sun, warm against her back, comforted her like a hug. Music began playing inside the house. Diana did seem scatterbrained. Maybe she really had just forgotten. Another low breeze ran through the yard, and the leaves on the beech tree shook. Ruth smiled, and it felt good, like coming up for air.

"You coming?" Diana called over the music.

Opening the screen door, Ruth walked into the light of the hallway.

PART 1

June 2023

1

Ruth stared at her truck smoking in the sandy garage lot. The clouds were high and gray, and the wind coming off the ocean was unseasonably cold, rustling the branches of the privet bushes and the mulberry trees, all low and warped into odd angles from a life of trying to grow amid strong salt wind.

Wrapping her large flannel shirt around her chest, Ruth held herself close. The mechanic, her dad's friend Bill, approached her from inside the open shop door. A seagull circled and landed on the lip of the flat roof, seeming to look down at the barren scene, its eyes blank, its left foot broken, dangling midair.

It didn't feel like June—the gray sky, the thin air, the strong cold wind. Next door a construction crew was digging in a foundation, the ground ripped open, wet mud stuck to the claw of the excavator, the team nowhere around, everyone on break. The smell of the exposed earth hit Ruth, and she was brought back to her mother's cold face unrecognizable in the coffin that Ruth helped to pick out. For the past ten years, the smell of defrosting earth and mud had reminded her of the smell that emanated from the grave as they lowered that wooden box into the newly opened ground, fresh grass starting to sprout around the head of the new tombstone and red-winged blackbirds trilling in the trees above.

"She's dead, right?" Ruth asked, shaking the memory and pointing at the truck.

Bill sighed and stuffed his hands into the back pockets of his worn jeans. His look of pity made Ruth drop her hand from her eyes and wrap herself more tightly into her own arms.

"Sorry, Ruth—totaled."

"Can I sell it to you for any parts?" she asked.

"I can give you two hundred for it," Bill said, and Ruth knew he was being generous, that it was worth nothing. There was a moment when her pride told her to call him on his bluff, but she paused when she thought about what little was left in her bank account. The flood of shame that followed made Ruth's eyes drop to the ground.

"You don't have to do that," she said, still hoping that he wouldn't rescind the offer.

"Don't be silly," Bill replied, walking into the shop toward the old cash register on the counter. "The tires are still good. Those will go for fifty each," he said, approaching her with his arm outstretched and putting two hundred-dollar bills in her hand.

Ruth looked at the bald tires. She imagined them collecting rainwater behind the building, added to the pyramid of rubber that had no use.

"Did you see Joel before you came out?" Bill asked, and Ruth's gaze dropped to the ground again. She knew that her father had always asked him to keep an eye on her while she was out on the island.

"I didn't," she said. "It was a pretty abrupt move this year."

Bill's look of pity returned, and she knew he was going to ask her about Diana, about what happened, and how she was holding up. All of Block Island would know by now, Ruth thought. Already, *The New York Times* had run a short death announcement noting Diana's sudden passing, and her contributions to the fashion and photography world. Ruth had stopped reading after the first few words, unable to think about Diana in the past tense.

She had missed the calls the night before. It had been a busy shift at the bar in Maine where Ruth worked in the off-season, which she was glad about. She was leaving for the island at the end of the week and needed all the tips she could get, so she kept the bar open a little longer than usual, extending last call, hoping that the cash would fall more freely out of everyone's wallets as they finally settled their tabs. It was one in the morning when she finally looked at her phone and saw all the missed calls, voicemails, and texts from Charlie, Diana's nephew. Ruth closed the bar without cleaning, locked the door behind her, and listened to Charlie's messages huddled next to the dark building, the wind making it hard to hear.

"We're at Rhode Island Hospital in Providence. Diana's . . . Diana's dying, Ruth. She had lung cancer . . . for a long time and it got bad and . . . They don't know if she's going to make it through the night, and you need to come. You need to come now."

Ruth ran the short distance from the bar to her apartment, threw her clothes into trash bags, tossed them into the bed of her truck, and started driving south in the darkness without telling her roommate she was leaving. Watching the sun come up over the highway, she stopped only for gas and large cups of coffee that made her breath and stomach sour.

While she drove, she tried to understand what Charlie's messages meant and tried to focus on the road through her panic. Diana had been sick—lung cancer. She had known for a long time. Ruth ran through the past year in her mind, trying to catalogue the moments when she should have known, whether it had been obvious and she had missed it.

The first time Ruth had noticed Diana's wheezing cough was this past Christmas, when Diana had called to wish her a happy holiday. They'd ended up fighting, and the anger had driven any concern from Ruth's mind. But the last time they'd spoken, only a month ago, Diana had still been coughing, though she brushed it off as a cold, said she was taking care of herself.

Ruth was replaying the phone call, her foot weighing heavy on the gas pedal, the truck groaning to accelerate the last hour to the hospital, when Charlie called again to tell her that Diana had passed.

He was crying and Ruth held the phone in her lap, listening to the sound of him sob close to the receiver. Ruth hadn't made it in time. She let him cry, focused on the beeping of the monitors in the background, and said nothing. A feeling was growing in her, one that made her clench the steering wheel so that even in the darkness she could see the whites of her knuckles.

When Charlie hung up, Ruth kept driving. The walls of the cab seemed to tighten around her, the guardrail to her left feeling so close that her wheel would clip it at any second.

She hated herself in that moment for ever forgetting that she was alone. Then she hated herself for the self-pity. She hated herself most for not being there.

She kept driving, headed to Galilee.

When she arrived to catch the first ferry to Block Island, she ignored the familiar harbor, the faded and stained fishing boats that sandwiched the ferry, the circling birds, the abandoned Lighthouse Inn across the street, splattered in seagull shit.

Once Ruth backed the truck up the ramp and into the hull of the *Carol Jean* ferryboat, she turned off the engine, smelling exhaust, and listened to the reverberating din of cars and people echoing off the heavy metal hull. Ruth was loosely aware of the numbing haze she was in, could feel somewhere in the back of her mind how she was dissociating, pulling the knowledge of Diana's death away from herself, until she was left with only a thrumming tightness in her chest, one she was familiar with, one that she could handle.

A couple backed their vintage Land Rover up in front of Ruth's truck, their golden retriever sitting between them in the narrow cab. As they got out, Ruth admired their clean woolen sweaters, their pressed pants, their stylish eyeglasses. It was an easy affluence she should be used to by now, a quieter wealth that came from generations of security, of beautiful homes in coveted places, of grandmothers passing on tasteful furniture, solid gold earrings, property in Europe. There were many people on the island who looked like this, coming and going for weekends and holidays, trekking out to houses on the far west of the island, secluded from town. She had catered their parties over the years, passed trays at Fourth of July and Memorial Day celebrations, while friends of hers plucked the standup bass or shucked oysters on the pristine deck. These were the only times that Ruth felt unwelcome on the island, shooed off the properties as soon as she got paid, her bike rattling as she cruised back toward the noise of town, back toward the boarding houses for the summer employees, toward the raucous bars and boats.

Ruth was still staring as the couple led their dog toward the stairs and up onto the deck. After the ferry horn blared and she felt the boat jolt away from the dock, she let herself drift into a light sleep, the early morning highway lanes she'd sped through still burned into her mind's eye.

When she arrived on the island, she drove up the hill from the ferry ramp. The National Hotel stood large, white, and empty in the late spring morning. She made it the half mile out of town and onto the dirt driveway of her usual summer housing, a small, uninsulated cottage that was still boarded up for the winter, before the truck started to smoke. At first Ruth wondered if she was seeing things, but the gray fumes eked out the edges of the white hood as if it were a candle whose flame had just been extinguished, growing thicker and twisting in the wind. The smell of spent engine oil was sharp against the cool spring air.

The smoking truck provoked nothing in Ruth. She had pulled out the few trash bags filled with her things and placed them on the porch of the cottage, then called Bill and sat waiting for his tow truck to arrive.

Now, Ruth came back to Bill's face and the pity money in her hands.

"Thanks, Bill," she said.

Fear ran through her, looking at the truck. It had been the only thing she really owned, the most expensive object to her name, and now she put the two hundred dollars in her pocket, knowing it hadn't even been worth that.

Opening the driver's side door, she reached past the shells and dried flowers she kept in the cupholder to grab the journal Diana had given her out of the glove compartment. She started walking toward town, waving to Bill over her shoulder. She needed to keep moving.

There had once been a time when Ruth considered herself a writer. The school psychologist she was ordered to see after her mother died required her to journal, and Ruth continued doing it after the sessions ended. It never helped lessen her grief, as they suggested it might, but rather acted as a distraction, a filtering of her thoughts and observations onto the page.

She felt a sense of relief when she wrote things down—the way dirty snow looked on the side of the road, a man's shoe untied in the grocery line, the smell of the harbor when she walked home from school. Life felt more real when she could categorize it, put careful words to it, and read about it on the page. It was still something she found herself doing, mentally listing her surroundings, picking out the smallest detail and holding it in her mind, even if those thoughts didn't make it to paper anymore.

Diana had encouraged her, left books in her room that Ruth consumed, authors like Annie Dillard, Toni Morrison, Joan Didion, and Patti Smith. Whenever Diana introduced Ruth to someone new in town, she told them Ruth was a writer. Diana made sure Ruth always had a fresh journal and time set aside from their workdays for Ruth to spend on her own pursuits.

Now, Ruth looked down at the journal in her hand. Diana had gotten it for her as a birthday gift last year, and since then Ruth had barely opened it. She hadn't written anything worthwhile in years. Walking back toward town along empty streets, she tried to distract herself by thinking about where all her friends might be—the Costa Rica crowd, the St. John people, all traveling to other islands once the restaurants they worked at on Block Island closed for the season. October through April the island shrank down to a skeleton crew of only a thousand. Through the winter, those few remained to run things—the school, the health clinic, the library—as the sea brush stood ragged, flattened by snow and ice, and the winter wind ran over the once green hills, and the ocean's frozen waves broke against the shore. But it was June. People should be here by now.

Five years ago, after Ruth had graduated college, she spent the summer with Diana, just as she had for the four summers before that. But in the fall, without a plan to use her degree, she had to return to Joel's house. After she spent a bleak winter at home working shifts at the diner again and trying to save up money for a car, Ruth considered following those friends to the Caribbean, chasing the warmth. She had never traveled more than a few states over, and she didn't really have the desire to be so far from home, but she didn't know what else to do, where else to go. And when she had suggested trying to live on Block Island over the winter, Diana shot her down.

"What're you going to do?" Diana had asked. "Hang out with me here all winter? No, you'll get sick of me. You should move somewhere cold, somewhere where you can hibernate and focus on your writing, free from distractions—like Maine or something."

Ruth didn't feel pulled in either direction, but one day she found herself telling one of her regulars at the diner about maybe moving to Maine, and he said he had a friend who ran a bar in a small navy town. He could get her a job if she wanted.

So Ruth went. She liked the crowd at the navy bar. They reminded her of the fishermen on Block Island—the same red, chapped faces, the same gruff New England grit. It suited her. There was always short-term housing in a month-to-month rental place near the naval shipyard, which she took, usually with a random roommate.

Thinking about it now, Ruth was shocked that she had spent five winters there. She had never meant to, but it was as if inertia took over, and then when Covid happened, and restaurant jobs became scarce, it felt as if she were stuck in the routine. Those years all felt like a blur to her, leaving Block Island and driving up to Maine where her other job was waiting for her, the seasons switching over, Ruth swapping one life for another. She had thought it was all temporary. And that was the point—that she could always change her plans if something better came along.

The wind blew down the road and Ruth shielded her eyes from the sand it kicked up. She became uneasy thinking about what was temporary and what was starting to feel permanent, what cycles she could and couldn't break.

Ruth quickened her pace past the Catholic church, stark and lonely on its lawn, past sun-bleached flyers for multimillion-dollar homes in the windows of the real estate offices. She was heading to the rental place, hoping she could buy an old bike. A fleet of scuffed mopeds and bikes was pushed together so their handlebars looked tangled, the gears and the metal clumping together in a singular mass. The kid who worked there was huddled inside a small wooden hut out front.

"Anybody renting today?" Ruth asked.

"Nah," the kid replied, watching the soccer game playing on his phone, which was propped against the cash box. "It's too early."

For sixty dollars she purchased a rusted used bike with a wire basket they had in the back. It looked like it had been left outside all winter. She watched the kid's hands shake as he took the cash and handed her the change. The sun was growing weaker, and Ruth was surprised that it was so late in the day already.

As she pedaled past the statue of Rebecca standing tall in the traffic circle, Ruth almost stopped, her heart pounding. Looking up at the woman cast in white, Ruth heard Diana's voice echo in her ear over the grumble of her old truck as they cruised down into town.

"Tip your hat to our lady of sobriety," Diana said, nodding her head in reverence to Rebecca.

The statue had originally been a fountain, put in during the 1800s to curb alcohol consumption on the island, a fact Diana had always repeated to visitors. She would tell them about volunteering with the Historical Society to restore the statue, how they had found grapes and leaves in Rebecca's hair. They decided that the woman in the statue might also be a Greek cupbearer of wine to the gods, mixing the message of sobriety and consumption.

"She's lived many lives," Diana would say. "A complex woman, like me." Diana had been sober for as long as Ruth knew her.

Ruth pedaled out of town. The wind was blowing back against her face, and her exposed fingers grew red and stiff as she huffed up the hill, the gears on the bike cracking in rusty complaint. It had been a long time since Ruth had ridden a bike up to Diana's house, and she felt the cigarettes she had been smoking all winter in her shortness of breath. By the time she crested the hill across from the island airport, she was sweating. Small Cessnas lined the thin tarmac, and a bright yellow plane taxied in the distance, preparing to take off. Ruth wobbled off to the side of the road to catch her breath and watched as the propellers gained speed and the plane moved forward, rolling toward her until its wheels lifted off the ground and it teetered loudly into the sky. A deer's head popped up from the freshly green bramble in the woods beside her, and both the deer and Ruth looked up and listened to the loud buzz the plane made as it arched overhead. It was shrinking into the blue before she continued biking.

When Ruth reached the familiar turnoff for the driveway, the tires whispered as they rolled over the packed-dirt road. The privet bushes came into view, and Ruth stopped just outside of the tall archway they produced, a small gap in the bushes showing Diana's front stoop. Getting off her bike, Ruth stepped over a few fallen leaves, still there from winter, and into Diana's hidden yard.

Blowing hot air into her hands, she grabbed her journal from the basket of her bike, rested the bike on the ground, and walked up the grassy slope in front of her. The leaves on the large beech tree were new, still glossy, the red buds strewn across the base of the tree like a rash. The short, revived grass that covered the small yard was soft and green. Sitting, Ruth felt the damp earth underneath her and smelled the cool soil.

Looking at the empty house, Ruth's emptiness echoed back to it, the gaps in between the new leaves and the long branches of the beech tree showing the light of the already fading sky, her too-thin flannel letting the sweat she had worked up on the bike ride catch the cold air. She blew more hot breath into her hands, and she thought of all of the summers she spent living with Diana—the dinners they ate under the tree, the afternoons spent working in the garden, and the long hours in the office.

Ruth had considered Diana to be her closest living family.

Her phone buzzed in her pocket, and pulling it out she saw a message from her best friend, Lucy, pop up on the screen.

Call me

Ignoring the text, Ruth opened her journal to where a pen was lodged inside, acting as a bookmark.

She couldn't look at the empty page without thinking of their fight, of Diana's words, of the snow on the windowsill, of her coughing on the phone, and she wanted to throw the journal into the woods, wanted to roll over and scream into the grass.

She picked up the pen, her red knuckles hovering over the blank page, and realized how empty her brain was, a startling hollow sensation ringing throughout her body. She felt like she might cry. Diana's searing words played in her head again, and she was filled with an itching shame—a feeling she didn't know what to do with. What had she been doing all this time?

The feeling mounted, about to take Ruth over, but then her phone buzzed against the ground. Looking down at the cracked screen, she saw an incoming call from Charlie.

She watched the phone for a moment before picking it up.

“Hi,” she said.

“How are you?” Charlie asked. His voice was rough and familiar. It sounded like he had been crying all night.

How was she? For the first time since she had stopped driving, Ruth tried to take stock of herself. She thought about the smoking truck in the parking lot. She thought about the shots of bourbon she had been taking at work each night over the winter—one at eight-thirty, one at close, one while counting her tips behind the bar. She thought about the cigarettes she often smoked out back in the kitchen doorway, under the stairs—snow falling outside. She thought about shivering on the walk home to her dumpy winter rental. She thought about sitting in the hot shower, watching her skin turn red so she didn’t have to turn up the expensive electric heat.

Winters were lost time, Ruth always felt. Usually, she just needed to make it to June—make it back to the island, and her life would start up again as the days grew longer and the leaves unfurled from the branches green and ready for sun. But she was here, and it was June, and it still felt like lost time.

Despite her numbing haze, the realization that Diana wouldn’t be on the island, that she wasn’t here or anywhere, sank into Ruth’s chest. When she thought of Diana sick in the hospital, of her dying without saying goodbye, of their fight, Ruth’s anger at herself overtook everything. She stared at the empty house, the dissonance of her thoughts and the landscape disorienting her.

“Ruth?” Charlie asked again.

“I wasn’t there,” Ruth said instead of answering his question. As she spoke, the truth of it overwhelmed her. She felt robbed. There would be no goodbye, and there could have been. Diana had known she was dying. What she didn’t want to consider, what she wasn’t allowing herself to think of, was that maybe Diana didn’t tell her sooner because she was still angry with Ruth—that maybe they hadn’t been as close as she had thought.

“I know,” Charlie said. “I’m sorry.”

Ruth didn’t respond. She was trying and failing to imagine

Diana under the fluorescent lights of a hospital, wearing a papery patient gown. The last time she had seen her, the early October island sun had illuminated her face as she waved goodbye to Ruth from the ferry dock, her big straw hat looking more and more like a halo the farther the boat got from land.

"Why didn't she tell anyone?"

"I don't know," Charlie said.

The question hung between them.

"Where are you?" Charlie asked.

Ruth didn't want to tell Charlie she was at the house, that she was alone. She couldn't remember the last time she saw him on the island, and in that moment she missed him deeply. He was the only one who understood everything, who knew Ruth, who had known Diana. She imagined he was sitting next to her in the grass, that she could put her head on his shoulder.

Staring at the closed-up house, the hollow feeling consumed her again, and suddenly the past ten years felt blown apart and paved over, as if there had been nothing there, and she was once again seventeen, on the island for the first time after her mother had just died, and she was rotten with grief, waiting for someone to help pull her out of it.

Listening to Charlie's breath on the other line, hearing the concern for her in his voice as he asked her where she was, images she hadn't thought of in years came to Ruth—the two of them running like children through the forest trails, seagrass stirring as their legs passed by. Rolling in the hot sand, their young skin sunburned along the edges of their bathing suits. She could still feel the cold smack of the ocean as they jumped over waves together, their bodies nearly touching in the briny water, could see the sun hitting Charlie's dark hair.

She had a deep, intense yearning for that feeling, for that lightness. She wanted to feel that way again.

When Charlie had come to the island that first summer, in August, she was surprised by how well they fit together, their conversation so light and so easy. They spent whole days by each other's side, time passing without thought so that when the sun began to set, Ruth was always caught off guard at another day gone. As she lay in her bed, Charlie down the hall, her heart felt swollen and heavy as the nights ticked down until he would be back on the ferry, back to his life. Ruth thought it was impossible that he was interested in her as more than a friend—he was older, in college—but she still wanted him, still wondered. He paid attention to her in ways that made her feel seen for the first time in her life, looked at her in a way she had never been looked at before. And the first time he kissed her, Ruth knew that he had felt it all too. She realized after he left that first summer that she loved him, wrote it in her journal, felt it like a pleasurable ache in her stomach.

Sitting in the grass now, listening to his breath on the line, Ruth understood more deeply something she had thought many times before—their relationship was a smattering of *almosts*. Things said that almost meant more but were never fully discussed—momentum gained and lost each time he visited, each time one of them overcame the time spent apart and made a bid for connection over the years. Moments that Ruth felt on a deep level, but didn't have the confidence or the words to know what to do with, to pursue further. The lurking end of the summer always stood between them, the different lives they returned to in the fall keeping them from doing anything about it, asking for anything more. They had been so young, Ruth thought now. One of them always fumbled it as Charlie's departure date arrived—pulled away or said the wrong thing.

They came close, they told each other snippets of thoughts that contained the sense that there was something more there, but never the whole truth. The fourth summer he visited, he took her out to dinner, a real date, on the island, and Ruth crumbled under the pressure of it. She was quiet and uncomfortable in the restaurant, the way he was looking to her to be her normal self stuck in her mind. She didn't know what to do or how to act in this new setting, and kept thinking about how much the dinner would cost, worried about how much cash she had on her. She wanted it to go well but every time she thought about what would happen, what it meant, she thought of her life in the winter, so different from his, and she shut down more and more. She still thought about that date and shivered from embarrassment.

He started working at a big accounting firm that winter and stopped coming out to the island for a full week after that, saying he needed to put in his time. He and Ruth didn't speak for nearly a year, until August, on the day he was normally to arrive on the island, when Ruth impulsively called him. She had been sitting in Diana's yard, looking up at the beech tree, and the need to hear his voice was so strong that she didn't think about how embarrassed she had been, how much she had screwed it up—she just dialed.

They started calling each other regularly after that, talking for hours on the phone, their relationship picking back up again and forming into something else—something different, but still undefined.

Ruth would listen to Charlie talk about everything: his accounting job, the recreational soccer league he played on, his dreams of buying a house up in the woods of New Hampshire someday. She would tell him about her co-workers at the restaurant, the hike she took with Diana, a book she was reading, and he would ask her to send it to him when she was done.

Their ease and familiarity returned to them—the conversations a salve to Ruth. She could immerse herself into Charlie's life through his words as he painted a picture in her mind's eye—him walking down a busy Boston street on the way home from work, the buildings close together, the traffic loud and close. She could hear his key turn in the lock when he got home, the echo of the stairway up to his one-bedroom apartment, and she imagined she could see the old wood that she heard creak under each step as if she were with him, walking upstairs after a long day. Whenever they hung up, Ruth was surprised to find herself in her room in Maine, or wherever she was—the walls, the sounds around her all seeming foreign.

"An emotional affair," Lucy had said once about it.

"It's not an affair if we're not in relationships," Ruth replied.

"You don't know he's not," Lucy answered.

It was true. For all the time they spent on the phone, as if it were an unspoken rule, Charlie would never ask Ruth if she was seeing someone, and Ruth would never ask Charlie. To Ruth, it didn't matter. She had lived such a bifurcated life for so long that sometimes she forgot it was not the same for other people. It made sense that Charlie could mean so much to her in her summer world, over the phone, in their conversations, and not in her day-to-day life. For a long time, what happened after they hung up didn't concern her. She had no illusions that she could keep him, told herself that nothing was really going on during those hours that they talked, and so jealousy, even curiosity, wasn't on her mind.

Now, as she held the phone to her ear, she tried to put a name to what they were. He was the person closest to her in the world now that Diana was gone, but what were they, really? He felt too important, too close to call only a friend.

A few years ago, Ruth had slipped on the ice walking home from work and broke her wrist. She had sent him a picture of her cast, asking him to sign it as a joke, and he drove up to Maine the next day to check in on her, to keep her company, showing up at her door with a Sharpie in hand.

Ruth remembered sitting next to him in bed at the hotel he'd booked, wrapped in a plush bathrobe, the painkillers kicking in, making her feel foggy-brained and dragging her toward unconsciousness. She remembered telling him she didn't want to sleep yet, reaching for his hand, falling asleep on his chest, listening to him breathe. In the morning, she felt embarrassed and overexposed and couldn't meet his eyes for long.

Growing up, Ruth had often felt like a sieve, her thoughts and feelings bleeding out of her so that they never seemed like just her own. Always, her mom seemed to know what she was feeling before she had even put it into words, sensing when Ruth was sad or angry before she had processed the emotion herself.

When Maggie got sick, Ruth became more aware of this, saw

how her pain was hurting her mother—concern littered across her face. So Ruth became conscious of keeping her emotions to herself, of trying to stop the bleeding as she sat in the doctors' offices with her mom, hiding behind her note-taking, shutting her own feelings down, keeping her presence steady for Maggie, making sure she was something solid to lean on.

She had wondered how Charlie didn't know what she felt that night. It was so obvious to her. But now, sitting here, she considered for the first time that maybe it was because she wasn't a sieve anymore, that she had gotten too good at hiding what she was thinking, that in protecting herself she stopped showing the truth.

Staring at the house now, she saw herself and Charlie everywhere—giggling on the rooftop after having climbed out the window to watch fireflies, trying to throw rope over the lowest tree branch to make a swing, laughing with Diana at the patio table over coffee.

Ruth was struck then by the thought that she might lose Charlie too, that she had been lying to herself all these years when she thought nothing was going on, had been shielding herself from the permanence of actually reaching for Charlie—fearful that if she did reach for him he would be gone for good. She had been content to live in the almost if it meant not losing him.

Ruth wondered what they had been doing all this time, if she had made a mistake, if it wasn't blindly obvious that Charlie had always been her home, what she wanted, where she was the most comfortable, the most herself. As the thought bloomed in her mind, she found herself unable to speak. She was overwhelmed by a strong sense that everything was slipping out of her life, that she needed to grasp everyone around her tightly. Living in the almost felt in that moment like it was suffocating her, like she was in a box she had put herself in, and more than anything she wanted to get out. She needed to get out.

She realized that the last time she had called Charlie, months before Diana died, he hadn't answered, and the feeling of being trapped became frantic. The thought that she had suppressed her feelings for Charlie as the years passed, that she had never said out loud what he meant to her, had never told him she loved him, was crushing. She couldn't remember the last time she had said it to Diana either. What a waste of time.

"When will I see you?" was all she could muster, the words breathless as they left her lips, her mind full and racing.

"I'll be out for Diana's funeral," he said. "I think it will be the last week in June—on her birthday."

"Okay."

"I'll call you, okay?"

"Okay."

Hanging up, Ruth looked around at the bare trees, the outline of spring birds flying against the fading red of the sunset.

In the reverberating silence, Ruth focused on the sensation she wanted, the image of resting her head on his shoulder. Her feelings for Charlie filled her with a force that shocked her, taking the space of the numbness that had held her all day. She thought again of them laughing in their hotel robes that night, how after he left everyone had felt like a stranger, how often she had looked at his signature on her cast until they sawed it off, the message splitting in two—Watch your step, you maniac, love Charlie

Ruth would tell him she loved him when she saw him.

As soon as she made up her mind, she was filled with a startling sense of urgency, and she wondered if she could handle what would happen after, then stopped. She just needed to tell him. She wanted him to know.

Ruth had thought that being on the island would make her calmer—the familiar landscape soothing, the way she felt hidden here, like she could duck around a corner into the woods and disappear for however long she wanted, and she'd come out the same age, time standing still, like a character in a book. Lying down, Ruth felt like she was blending into the ground as she watched plane after plane fly over her, the sky darkening and the cold returning to her fingertips, to the ends of her toes, the dampness of the earth seeping into her clothes, and she had the sense that her edges were receding, the outline of her figure growing smaller, like a discarded Russian doll. A few times she thought she should leave but couldn't bring herself to move. She stayed until she saw her breath condense above her, until she saw stars.

2

Ruth shook her head at the rolled-up dollar.

"She doesn't do coke anymore!" Lucy called out over the music to the busser from the restaurant Ruth worked at. She reached over Ruth and smiled at him as he handed her the dollar, then leaned over, her stomach folding softly over the waistband of her tiny jean shorts. Ruth watched how the group looked Lucy over in awe, her necklace touching the table as she snorted the line. Lust, Ruth thought, was a visible phenomenon. She lingered a moment around the periphery to make sure Lucy was okay before wandering out to the kitchen, where it was quieter.

Opening the fridge, she pulled out a beer, popped the cap off the side of the counter, and lifted herself up onto it so she was perched there with her back against the few cabinets. From her post she could survey the other rooms that made up the small cottage she shared with Lucy. They had moved in a few years ago, after two summers at the restaurant's boarding house. A group was playing guitar in the side yard, and she could see some friends poking at the fire outside, the flames illuminating their faces. Ruth watched their figures move, imagining what they were whispering about as they leaned into one another. In the living room a group of people Ruth didn't recognize were passing around a joint on the couch, and Ruth thought about how the fabric would smell like weed and salt tomorrow during her pre-work nap. Then she remembered she wasn't working tomorrow—she remembered the funeral.

Ruth's mind wandered to Charlie. In the weeks since she last spoke to him, she had come close to calling him a few times, even dialing and hanging up quickly, unsure of what she would say once she had him on the line.

She hated living in the unknown—was embarrassed by her own wanting. It made her itch, as if her skin didn't fit—restless. Looking down, she noticed the label scratched off her beer bottle, unaware she had been doing it. Since that day on Diana's lawn when she decided to tell Charlie that she wanted to be with him, she felt more vulnerable than she could ever remember, laid bare as if the sun would burn her more easily, as if she had to hide from the wind. Loud sounds made her jump, and she was always moving—leg jumping under the table, fingers tapping against her water glass. Everyone assumed she was grieving, but truthfully she hadn't allowed herself to consider Diana, hadn't been back to the house since that first day she was on the island.

Her grief for Diana felt like it was always on her heels, constantly chasing her. If she wasn't vigilant, if she wasn't pushing it aside every moment, the void would consume her, would swallow her up, and leave her in a place she understood, remembered, a place she wasn't willing to go again.

Ruth took another sip of her beer. She watched through the window as a couple kissed in front of the bonfire in the backyard, their outlines visible in shadow form as their faces came together, and Ruth remembered the first time Charlie kissed her, ten years ago.

It had been the last night of his stay with Diana. They had spent the day not talking about him leaving in the morning, the anticipation of goodbye tingling throughout Ruth in a low ripple of bittersweet sadness. She wondered how she would feel when he was gone, and there was a piece of her that understood it would be new—no one had filled this space for her before, this space of wanting, lightness, and anticipation, so there was no way for her to know what the absence of those things might feel like, after having had it. Each time their fingers almost touched a shiver ran through her body, and she wondered if he could see it.

They were walking home from the beach, having ventured too far on foot by accident, and the sky was darkening slowly from blue to black. Ruth could see the two of them now in her mind's eye—their bodies bent forward to take the steep hill. The moon was full above them, the green frogs were croaking in the reeds next to them, and the crickets buzzed in the night, a low thrumming that matched the vibrations running throughout Ruth, a feeling that was almost more powerful than thought, her physical sensations taking over so that she felt permeable, like the island night was running through her—the thrumming crickets a part of the tingle she felt in the tips of her fingers as they hovered near Charlie's.

And although Ruth could still feel the phantom excitement that filled her seventeen-year-old self, she was aware that it was only a faint shadow warped by time. She watched in her memory as the two figures approached the green archway of Diana's house and stopped outside of it, tried to recall how Charlie had reached for her hand in the darkness, how they could hear a plane taking off in the distance, drowning out all other sound, as he stepped toward her. Their bodies, which had been nearly touching all week, pressed against each other, young and eager. It was a slow kiss, and adrenaline had stung in her chest. She had to stand on her toes to reach his face, so that she was leaning on him, reaching for him. Now, ten years later, as she sat among spent limes and bottle caps, the phantom sting of that kiss sizzled throughout her body, burning away the hollow feeling that came whenever she remembered Diana's funeral.

Her eyes glazed over into the middle distance as her breath quickened. She didn't even notice Louis entering the room.

"We find ourselves at another one of Lucy's summer solstice

celebrations," he said as he approached the fridge, then leaned against it. "I haven't seen you since you got back on island." He took a sip from his mug. "It's weird I haven't seen you. How have you been?"

Ruth looked at him, breaking herself out of her thoughts, and ignored the tone of concern in his voice. The nose ring he got a few years ago was snug against his red and peeling nostril. His arm hair was already bleached blond from the sun. The skin around his collarbone had a sheen, and she wondered if it tasted more like ocean or more like sweat. She took a sip from the cold bottle in her hands and lied.

"I've been good," Ruth said, nodding and trying to make it sound enthusiastic. She thought of the bleakness that had filled June so far, the unseasonable cold, the rain, how she had biked around alone every morning before work, unable to sit still, how at night, unable to sleep, she stared into the darkness of the cottage while Lucy slept on the other side of the room, the quiet that usually comforted her now stifling.

"You okay?" Louis asked, leaning back and examining her face. Ruth nodded and drank her beer, trying to breathe through the feeling in her chest. Charlie's face flashed back to her. It was like relentless waves forcing her under water, the vulnerable, exposed tension she had been sitting with all month—the idea that Charlie might say no. She needed to push it all away, replace it with something physical, something immediate.

"What're you drinking?" Ruth asked, leaning over to peer in his cup, aware of her low-cut shirt. For a second, she felt her past selves conflate. She was no longer twenty-seven or seventeen, but twenty-two or twenty-four, aware of her body and how to use it. She was trying to snap back into a version of her old self, one who had flirted with Louis a million times before, gone home with him every so often, back when choices mattered less, and when she didn't feel vulnerable at all.

"Rum," he replied. "You want something?" The corners of his lips lifted into a smile as he cocked his head to the side.

Ruth nodded, breathing deep, working to let go of that pulsing knot under her sternum. Turning, Louis hoisted a sandy canvas bag up onto the kitchen table. He pulled half-empty bottles out and reached into the cabinet next to her head for the cups, taking out her favorite mug and winking at her. Ruth laughed.

"Where's your boat?" she asked.

Louis lived on his boat in the summer and worked for a fishing company on the island, going out early mornings and bringing back what they were able to pull up from the ocean.

"It's docked by Ballard's for now. I move it out to New Harbor next week. Been waiting on some dinghy repairs and Chris is doing me a favor letting me stay there. Why?" Louis asked, his eyebrows raised.

Ruth shrugged.

The last time Louis and Ruth had had sex was four years ago now. At the time, he'd been working odd jobs on top of fishing while saving up for his own boat, so he was living in the bird shack above the clay bluffs out on the west side of the island, doing a research project for the Nature Conservancy on piping plover migration. One afternoon in July, he had invited her out to see the cabin. Now, as Louis placed the mug in her hands, she remembered the thin walls, the small camp bed, and how the sun baked their sweaty bodies through the window while he ran his hands over her. She remembered the freedom of knowing there was no one around, of hearing the ocean roaring somewhere outside below them.

There had always been something about Louis that drew Ruth in—his lithe body, his sharp blue eyes, their gaze clear and steady behind thick blond lashes. He was rippling with life, taut and energetic, yet grounded and sturdy. It was something she felt like she could absorb when she was around him, could lick off his skin. Looking at him now, she imagined tracing the lines of his self-given tattoos with the tip of her tongue.

"To the solstice," he said, and they clinked the thick ceramic mugs, making a hollow sound. Louis held eye contact with Ruth while they drank, until Lucy skidded into the kitchen. She stopped and cocked her head at them before laying herself across Ruth's thighs with a cartoonish flourish. Ruth lifted Lucy's thick curls off of her friend's neck and placed the sweating beer bottle on the place at the top of her spine where she had a tattoo of an eyeball. Lucy shivered.

"Don't be so sexy, Ruth," she said. Lucy straightened and took a sip of someone's discarded beer on the counter. "You made it. Happy solstice," she said to Louis, although she took Ruth's free hand and began to pull her gently off the counter. "Will you come with me, please?"

Ruth landed on the worn wooden floor and began to follow Lucy, then turned back to Louis, who was now standing alone in the kitchen.

"Are you sticking around?" she asked.

"I'll find you," he said.

Ruth nodded and weaved through the crowd after Lucy's tanned back. Once they turned a corner into the hallway, Lucy stopped short and turned. Her eyes were swimming in red and almost unfocused.

"Louis? Why?" Lucy whispered in Ruth's ear. Her lips were wet, and her breath was hot and smelled of tequila.

"Maybe," Ruth responded, shrugging. She took another long drink of the rum in her mug and felt it burn through her chest, warming her cheeks. Lucy frowned and stuck her tongue out, mock displeased.

"Come meet my new friends instead." She grabbed Ruth's hand again and pulled her over to their old and faded couch. On the coffee table there was a shriveled joint stamped out in the clamshell they used for an ashtray.

"This is Ben, Cayce, and Willard," Lucy said, motioning to each.

"Hey, hi," Ruth said.

"Ruth has worked on Block Island for ten years!" Lucy said, grabbing Ruth by both shoulders and shaking her before sitting down. They were all stoned and only nodded vaguely in her direction. Each of them looked very young to Ruth, and Ruth couldn't place where she'd seen them before. Must be their first season, she thought.

Everyone at the party worked seasonally on Block Island—restaurants, housekeeping, landscaping, charter boats. They had the sunburned cheeks of people who labored outside, the scraped knees and shins of those whose jobs used their bodies. There was a pile of kitchen clogs by the front door from people who came straight from their shifts, and Ruth had already passed conversations about people tipping poorly, arguments with management, and a fight over who was sleeping with the bartender at Captain Nick's.

"That's a long time," the girl, Cayce, responded after Ruth had already looked away. "Do you, like . . . own a business here?"

Turning back to the girl, Ruth shook her head. She thought about the last ten years, and they didn't feel like a long time at all to Ruth. The hollow sensation returned. She felt too insulated, too claustrophobic.

Lucy was now in deep discussion with the guy, Ben, her hands on his knees, drawing small circles with her finger. Standing, Ruth slipped out of the room before Lucy could notice she was gone. She wanted to find Louis. She needed air. She needed to be submerged. She needed a distraction from the oscillating numbness and exposure that gripped her. Ruth stepped onto the porch and saw a string of people smoking and leaning against the railings. Down farthest, she could see a woman leaning against a post and holding Louis's hand out in front of her, under the light.

Ruth approached, her steps creaking the old wooden deck—the woman was reading his palm, turning it over in her hands, caressing lines across it with her fingers.

"Truth is very important to you," she said, "and so is love."

Ruth smiled to herself as she walked toward them. Louis looked at Ruth and gently pulled his hand away from the woman's grasp. Ruth had to stop herself from chuckling. As if she had any right to be jealous, she thought. She looked the woman up and down. She was definitely Louis's type, and she imagined seeing them together at another party later in the season, imagined their bodies intertwined on his boat, and felt nothing but restlessness. She turned to Louis.

"Do you want to swim?" she asked.

"Yes," he replied, and Ruth turned, pulled her towel off the railing, and hopped down the steps to the yard to wait for him.

"I'll see you next time," Louis said to the woman.

"It's a small island," she replied.

"It sure is," Louis shouted over his shoulder, disappearing into the house.

Ruth waited in the darkness of the front lawn and observed the party. The group in the side yard saw her standing, watching, and whispered to one another. Ruth realized she must have looked like an interloper instead of one of the people who lived in the house.

In a few moments Louis emerged, stepping under the moths careening around the exposed porch lightbulb. Somewhere inside, Ruth had the vague understanding that she was using Louis to distract herself, that she wanted his body underneath her, the smell of the ocean around them while they fucked just to keep her away from the grief, to help her forget the threat of the funeral tomorrow, the possibility of Charlie's rejection—as a way to keep moving.

Louis bounded down to meet her in the grass.

"What?" he said, examining her face.

"Nothing," Ruth said, ignoring her thoughts.

He threw his canvas bag over his shoulder, and the two of them started off barefoot over the thick grass, his flip-flops dangling from his fingers. They ducked under the hedges and out into the street. Their feet led them the fastest way to the water by memory. They passed two of the island bars, Tigerfish and Yellow Kittens, still open, and both quickened to get past without being seen by anyone.

Louis and Ruth reached the first dune, under the last streetlight of town, and climbed up the path to the beach, the sound of the small waves growing more crisp. Ruth's feet sunk into the dark sand, and it was cool against her hot skin. They jogged to the left, away from the light and the mouth of the path, and dropped their towels, both starting to remove their clothes without speaking.

Ruth pulled her tank top up over her head and felt the open air against her exposed breasts. Pulling off her shorts too, she hooked her thumb over the underwear and took them down to the sand. Louis was already naked, waiting for her. They started walking down to the black water, picking their way over rocks until the waves reached their feet. Ruth looked up at the stars smattered across the sky. She could see the distant lights of the mainland on the horizon. She could feel Louis's eyes on her body. The ocean splashed against their legs and hips as they waded farther in. Louis dove in first, disappearing into the darkness. She stopped, listening to the water, feeling its cool touch enveloping her skin. She waited to see his figure break out of the blackness, slick and shining, before she dove under too.

The darkness enveloped her, and the water moved below, around, and above her. She pulled against the ocean floor blindly, her hand grasping sand and letting it go as she crawled along the bottom. Ruth stayed under the water until her lungs burned—only then did she emerge back into the night, where she sucked in the air, water dripping down her face, pooling in the corners of her lips. She felt the tension in her chest release. She was submerged in the island—under the stars, in the water moving around her. Then she felt Louis next to her, and she escaped into his arms—their limbs together, their wet mouths slick with kissing and ocean water.

They emerged, dripping.

3

The next morning Ruth woke up on Louis's boat. The small bed in the cabin had forced them to sleep close together, and her skin was sweating where they'd touched. His cat, Perry, was curled up on the floor, next to the empty condom wrapper. She reached down and stroked Perry's soft back. Louis's palm rested against her lower belly, which suddenly felt too intimate. Most of her wanted to shrug out of bed and leave without having to talk to him, but a small part wanted to relax into it, shut her eyes. She realized she hadn't been held like that in a long time. The boat continued to bob gently against the dock. The room had a pleasant smell of ocean must, rum, and sunscreen. Ruth fell back asleep, her hand still and limp on Perry's small, purring body.

The ferry horn woke her with a jolt, causing Perry to squeal and claw at her hand.

"Ow!" Ruth yelled, throwing her legs over the side of the bed and jumping up.

"Jesus," Louis said as Perry jumped up and took her spot, curling up on the pillow next to Louis. "What happened?"

"My dad is on that ferry," she replied. Standing, she looked at him. The things she'd always romanticized about him now looked different to her in the sober light of morning. She was surprised she wasn't more bothered by the relapse, by using Louis to distract her from her thoughts, but Louis was comfortable in his predictability. They wouldn't have to talk about this, Ruth knew. It would just be another one of their scattered encounters from over the years. Predictability and comfort were what she had been searching for all June—her skin begging to be washed in salt water, her lips yearning to be chapped red from the sun, her feet asking to walk barefoot over familiar paths.

Ruth closed the wooden door to the small bathroom adjoining the bedroom. The mirror was half clouded over. Leaning in, she saw her bottom lip was split, dried blood lining the crack in the middle. Her hair was salt-encrusted from the night swim. She touched it, and the strands were crisp and hard.

Ruth thought back to the night before—the way Louis went down on her, the boat swaying around them until she came hard, grabbing his salty hair, his hands on the crease of her hips.

She always thought that she looked best after sex. The light in her eyes was brighter, the color in her cheeks revived, even the dried blood on her lip made her feel beautiful. She licked it off and ran the faucet, splashing her face with what water sputtered out. When she emerged, Louis was gone. The ferry horn blasted again. Rummaging through the mess in the room, Ruth picked a faded T-shirt off the top of Louis's clothes pile and threw it over her body, tucking the long ends into her shorts. She took the ladder up, remembering to duck before she emerged on deck. The morning light was bright and hot, and as her eyes adjusted she saw Louis reclining with Perry in his lap, a cigarette in hand.

"I'm taking this," Ruth said, motioning to the shirt. Taking two strides, she threw her legs over the side of the boat and leaped the short distance to the dock.

"I want that shirt back, Ruth!" he called after her. "It's lucky!"

"You'll get it," she said, trying to be careful of her bare feet against the wooden boards as she ran. She wished she had brought shoes. Turning the corner, she fought the onslaught of people filtering over to Ballard's beach bar just off the ferry. Some people seemed drunk already, swaying and red. Ruth jumped to get a look at the other people getting off the boat. The crowd was thinning out now, and Ruth saw her father standing along the fence, waiting for her. His gray T-shirt was tucked into his jeans, and his toes poked out from overworn Birkenstocks. Ruth noticed his beard was uneven in both color and shape. The gray had taken over more territory since the last time she had seen him, and it was longer on the right. Joel looked her up and down and laughed, his hand slapping against his firm, round belly. He threw his arm around Ruth and pulled her in roughly, in a way that always suffocated her, his arm putting pressure on her neck.

"You look like shit," he said, and laughed. Ruth knew he was joking, but she couldn't help it—she pushed him away.

"Yeah, well," Ruth said. They started walking into town in an uncomfortable silence.

"Sarah and Bill are making dinner later," Joel said eventually, then paused. "Will you come after the service? They would love to see you."

Remembering the funeral made Ruth's hangover pulse in her head and her stomach roll.

"Maybe," she said, feeling guilty. She sounded like a teenager.

"Okay," Joel responded. They were quiet for a minute. Ruth noticed the difficult way he took the hill, his legs looking like extra luggage that he struggled to bring along with him. A wave of concern passed over her, and she felt the tension in her chest return.

"We can get breakfast together, though," she offered.

"Will they let you in the diner with a bloody lip and no shoes?"

Ruth ran the back of her hand across her mouth and looked down at her feet. Her big toe was also starting to bleed.

"No," she said, a tired smile breaking across her face. He laughed and pulled her in again for another hug.

. . .

At the diner, Ruth chugged ice water and tried to be pleasant for her father. She hadn't seen Joel in months. Normally, she stopped at the house on her way back from Maine, and they had dinner before she got on the ferry. With everything that happened with Diana, she had forgotten to tell her father she was on the island until he had heard the news and called her. Looking at him, she felt guilty for how much time had passed since they had seen each other.

She had been surprised when Joel told her he intended to come to Diana's funeral. He was never very open about discussing Ruth and Diana's relationship, even if he had been the one who sent Ruth to her.

"Your eyelid is doing that droopy thing it does when you're tired," he said. "Big night last night?" Joel leaned back in the cherry-red booth. Ruth pulled ice into her mouth and began to chew.

"Lucy's summer solstice party," she replied through the ice, her voice garbled.

"Ah."

"How's Hank?" Ruth asked. Joel's dog, Hank, was a safe subject—that and her truck, but with the truck dead, Hank was all that remained in their well-worn conversation territory.

"Oh, he's good."

They sat in silence for a few moments, Ruth trying not to feel uncomfortable, knowing it would make her act cold, and wishing that wasn't the case. She and her father had never been very communicative, and at a certain point he had stopped asking questions about her life, and eventually she stopped asking him questions about his.

"You *are* going to the service, right?" Joel asked finally, trying to open the sugar packet for his coffee, the visible arthritis in his swollen knuckles making the action difficult. Ruth leaned over and softly pulled the sugar packet from his hand, tearing it open and pouring it in his mug for him.

"Thanks, kid," he said.

Ruth stared into her now empty water glass and focused

again on her breathing, her mind drifting to the service and to Charlie, to what she'd decided she was going to tell him. He had called her a few times over the past weeks, but Ruth found herself unable to answer, afraid that he would be able to tell from her voice that something was different. She wanted to wait until she saw him to tell him what she had been thinking—to make sure the feeling was real and not just another figment of her imagination.

As Ruth wondered, she saw her phone light up on the diner seat. It was a message from Charlie.

I'll see you later, right? I have something to tell you!

Ruth's chest flooded with adrenaline.

"Of course I'm going," she said. Joel only nodded. He reached out and put his hand over hers for a moment before pulling it away, seeming to have thought better of it.

4

A few hours later, Ruth pushed her bike down the grassy hill from the porch. She had showered and put on a dark blue dress, unable to fully commit to wearing black. Her scuffed, strappy event shoes hung from the handlebars. She had turned down Joel's offer of a ride to the service in Sarah and Bill's borrowed car, and Lucy was going to meet her there. Ruth wanted to bike herself in case she needed an immediate getaway, and she needed to plan what she would say to Charlie, run it over again in her mind.

"I'll see you soon!" Lucy called out from the porch.

Five years ago, the first summer Ruth had moved out of Diana's house, she lived in restaurant housing with a roommate assigned at random: Lucy. It had been Diana's idea, encouraging her to stretch her independence, spend more time with people her age. Lucy had arrived with an antique duster bag full of colorful sundresses and tiny jean shorts. Ruth had been intimidated by the way Lucy took up space, her sleeve of tattoos, the delicate line of rose-gold hoops that hugged her small, tan ears. She was beginning to wish for the solitude of Diana's house when Lucy turned, sat on her thin bed, and pointed to Ruth's copy of *Housekeeping* by Marilynne Robinson.

"I love that book," she said. "So, should we go to the beach?"

Now, Ruth waved back, grateful for her friend. She headed out across the lawn. Once the dewy morning grass gave way to sand on the side of the road, she slipped on her shoes, got on her rusted bike, and started pedaling out of town. Whenever she tried to think about what she would say to Charlie, her throat tightened and she had to pedal faster, her fingers squeezing the handlebars until her knuckles showed white. *I love you. I made a mistake. I want you.* They all sounded too simple. Maybe today wasn't the right day, but the idea of waiting any longer was almost as unbearable as the thought of Diana's funeral.

Before moving in with Lucy, Ruth had spent five summers living in Diana's house and working as her assistant. She fielded calls from magazines, helped Diana with captions and forewords for photo books and articles, and managed her schedule.

Diana had been a major photographer for *Vogue* in the late nineties and early aughts, shooting portraits for actors, models, writers, and once an ex-president. She shot so many covers that there was a stack of old magazines in her office that filled the shelf, all faded from the summer sun and warped from the damp ocean air that permeated the house.

When Diana quit fashion photography and left New York City to come back and live on Block Island full time, she continued taking portraits every now and then when someone requested her specifically. Otherwise, her work became more experimental, and as she faded from the world of fashion, she gained greater traction in the art world.

At first when Ruth had moved into the house, she felt uncertain about her role as Diana's assistant. Diana brewed coffee in the morning and left a mug out for her, along with a box of negatives and Polaroids with a handwritten note asking Ruth to digitize everything and put it on Diana's external hard drive. Ruth spent the first few days alone in Diana's "office"—a back room inside the house covered in stacks of swollen paperbacks where she kept her old, boxy desktop computer, scanning pictures and looking out at Diana's working shed. Every so often, she saw a figure move across the windows or a curtain flutter closed.

They hovered around each other, growing more uncomfortable, until one hot afternoon, when Ruth was absorbed in digitizing a photoshoot, Diana knocked on the door to the office, catching Ruth off guard. She hadn't noticed her leave the shed and walk across the lawn to the house, didn't even hear the front door open.

"Have you gotten in the ocean since you've been here?" Diana asked.

Ruth shook her head.

"Get your bathing suit on," Diana said.

When Ruth walked through the screen door onto the grass, Diana was already in her old Chevy truck, the windows down. Ruth got in and closed the truck door behind her, and Diana pulled out onto the road. They took a left and drove down a packed-dirt street lined with old maple trees. Eventually the road ended and they pulled out seemingly on the top of the island, the ocean so close and blue just over the edge of the cliffs. Diana kept driving until they pulled into a trail parking lot.

"We have to hike down to the beach," she said.

They walked along the green path not talking, eventually arriving at a rocky beach empty of people. The sky felt wider to Ruth here, the blue a deeper hue than she had seen before.

"So, Ruth, what do you like to do?" Diana asked as she stepped over the rocks.

Ruth was quiet. It was an uncomfortable question.

"Let me add that I am actually curious. I'm not just trying to fill the silence," Diana said. "People feel the need to fill silences a lot and they end up saying a lot of meaningless . . . nothing, ya know?"

Ruth didn't know how to respond. She wasn't sure someone had ever spoken that directly to her.

"I realized this morning that it's been a little quiet around the house. I'm working on this photo book and it's been on my mind a lot, and I forgot that it might be strange for you—me not being very chatty after you just moved in."

"It's okay," Ruth replied. "I'm not that chatty right now either."

Diana seemed to consider that for a minute before responding. "Okay. That's good to know. Thank you for understanding."

A moment passed where Ruth tried to think about the original question. "I like to read," she said eventually. "I like to ride my bike."

She felt like she sounded ten years old. The truth was she *did* feel young—she hadn't spent the last few years of her budding adolescence pulling away from her parents like the rest of her peers, but rather clinging closely to them, orbiting around her mother. Her few friends understood, but eventually Ruth felt like she couldn't relate to them anymore. She had never been on a date, hadn't been to any parties, and until recently had spent most of her time either at the doctor with her mom or working at the diner. She didn't understand their lives, and they didn't understand hers. At a certain point, the distance started to feel like a chasm between her and her peers, one she didn't have the energy to cross.

"Your life has looked . . . a lot different from what people your age are used to," Diana said, as if she understood exactly what Ruth was thinking. "People don't want to hear about hospitals and chemo and shit. They don't know how to deal with it. They hope they never have to."

Ruth nodded. It was true. She often felt like if she were to say what she was thinking or feeling out loud, she would drive people away. Slowly but surely.

"Reading and riding your bike though, that's good stuff—fortifying stuff. The kind of stuff that will carry you through the bad times," Diana said. "I know I told you I have some writing that I needed help with—for this book. Do you think you'd like to help me with it?"

"I don't know if I would be great at that," Ruth said, thinking about her journal.

"Well, if you read a lot, you're probably already better than me. Plus, don't worry. I have an editor who goes through all this stuff. It's actually pretty low stakes. It would be a big help to me."

"Okay," Ruth said. She wasn't entirely sure she had a choice in the matter. That's what she was here for—to help Diana.

When they got past the rocks, to the beach, Diana spread her towel out on the sand and headed down to the water, stopping at the edge and letting the small waves crash onto her legs.

Ruth dropped her towel and went to stand next to her.

"Did you always want to be a photographer?" Ruth asked. She had to raise her voice so that she could be heard over the crashing waves.

Diana was staring at the water, wiggling her toes in the sand.

"Yeah," she said. "My dad was a photographer for our local paper, so I grew up around all the equipment, would go with him on assignment and watch him shoot. He would stay up late into the night working on his own stuff though. I thought he was the coolest."

Ruth thought about what Diana's house must have looked like as a kid. She imagined walls full of photographs, all in glossy black frames. The walls in Ruth's house growing up had been bare, except for a few photos of Ruth as a child, some art she had done in kindergarten, and her parents' wedding photo. Besides that, the house was sparse, and it had seemed to Ruth like they might always be leaving, like her parents thought that the house was temporary, although this was never said.

"But you get that," Diana said.

"I get what?"

"Growing up in an artistic household."

"What do you mean?" Ruth asked. Diana didn't answer right away, and Ruth tried to think what she could be talking about.

"My dad paints houses. That probably doesn't count though," she said, trying not to make Diana feel like she was wrong.

"Not your mom?"

"My mom?" Ruth asked, trying to understand what Diana was referring to. "No, not even a little bit."

Maggie had worked as a kindergarten teacher during the school year and spent the summers as a housekeeper for beach rental properties in the Narragansett area. Ruth grew up going with her mom to help her during the turnovers, tagging behind her as she made beds and cleaned toilets, asking her questions or making up imaginary stories about the people who owned the houses they cleaned. Maggie followed Ruth's stories closely and listened, asking questions, wanting Ruth to tell her more as she was crouched over wiping down a bathtub or washing dishes that were left in the sink.

Diana looked at Ruth before dropping her eyes back to the sand. "Oh," she said. "Right, I guess I forgot. I thought I remembered your mom taking pictures on my camera sometimes. She seemed like a natural!"

Ruth thought of the photos her mom made her pose for over the years—kindergarten graduation, Easter, how she had framed her favorites and hung them in the kitchen. They all seemed normal to Ruth—nothing special.

"Do you have any pictures of her?" Ruth asked.

For a second, Ruth thought Diana hadn't heard her because she didn't say anything. Ruth was about to repeat herself when Diana spoke.

"I don't think so, honey. We weren't actually all that close, you know? Just fast friends during that one summer. We didn't keep in touch or anything."

"Oh," Ruth replied. She was surprised by how crestfallen she felt. It had been nice to think she was around someone Maggie had known well—a close friend.

"I'll look when we get home though. . . . It was a long time ago," Diana said. "There could be some pictures somewhere."

After that day, Ruth's life started to even out on Block Island. She would work for Diana in the morning and then often, at lunchtime, Diana and Ruth sat under the beech tree and ate sandwiches and strawberries or peaches when they were in season. Then, depending on how much work was left to do, Ruth would take off on her bike to the trails, hiking through the dense wooded paths until she came out on a beach that tourists couldn't easily find. She'd read while the waves crashed wild against the shore and listen to the dull rainmaker sound of the rocks being moved back and forth by the ocean. Sometimes, when she felt she was truly alone, she'd take off her bathing suit and lie in the sun naked next to debris washed up from the water and dissolve herself into the sounds and the smells, the light from the sun bright orange against her eyelids, melting into her surroundings.

Diana had paid her well, better than Ruth realized at the time, which helped Ruth in the fall when she started at the University of Rhode Island. Maggie had wanted her to apply when she was alive, so Ruth had, although she was unsure of what she wanted to do there and concerned about the price, even with scholarships and grants. Over the summer, she had been close to deferring, citing her uncertainty, but Diana had encouraged her to go, saying Ruth would regret it if she didn't start college now, that she had heard good things about the English department.

From the first day of classes, though, Ruth could tell college didn't suit her. She was still living at home with Joel, commuting to school, and working at the diner five days a week. Drifting on and off campus, Ruth observed the other students in her classes, listened to the girls in the row ahead of her whisper about parties from the night before and talk about plans for beach days over the weekend as they all funneled out the door after the lecture was over. They seemed to be lousy with time, and Ruth envied them for it from afar. It made her miss Block Island deeply.

Sometimes it felt impossible to make enough space for school. Her ability to focus had plummeted after her mother died, and it was difficult to remember how she had ever done well academically before. None of it seemed to matter. Her mind would wander during lectures, and her eyes would glaze over while she studied, thinking about Maggie, thinking what they had been doing this time last year, thinking about every last they had together—last beach day, last walk around the neighborhood, last birthday.

The only time Ruth truly cared about class, got to her seat early, finished the assignments long before they were due, was in the creative writing seminar that Diana encouraged her to take. She inhaled the reading lists, asked for more, and spent her free nights writing and editing her stories. It was the first time that she had written something longer than a few pages, and she was amazed by how good it felt to escape into her imagination. She started to believe all that Diana had told her—that maybe she was talented, that she could make a life of writing.

The work eased the pressure of her growing loneliness. She thought about the characters in her stories as she walked across campus, waited in a coffee line, and at the diner when a guy stiffed her on her tip. She wondered what her characters would do, how they would be different from her—storming out into the parking lot and throwing his two dollars in his face. She thought about trying it just to see how it would feel—to be able to write it more truthfully.

In her free time, she researched the authors she loved most and tried to understand what it took for one to become something like a Clarice Lispector, a Zadie Smith, or a Virginia Woolf.

When she graduated with her English degree, she told Joel and Diana that maybe she could work at a magazine or in publishing, but the truth was, when she thought about what she wanted to do with her life, her mind was filled only with Block Island—filled with those morning bike rides, lunch under the beech tree, lying naked on an empty beach, reading, writing, and talking about art. She almost took a job as a copywriter in Providence, but when she looked at the starting salary, she balked. She couldn't imagine scraping by at a desk in an office, driving down an hour in traffic from Joel's house, not having the freedom of her summers with Diana. It wasn't worth it to Ruth. She didn't understand how writing and Block Island would fit into that life. She told herself that writers needed to be out in the world, needed time to create, and she could make more money in a week waiting tables. She told herself that after a year or two she would revisit finding a writing job, that a few short years wouldn't matter.

What she told no one, except for Diana, was that she thought maybe if she wrote something good, something like one of her favorite authors, she could sell it and have the life she wanted, could buy a small house on the island and fill it with books and spend her time escaping into her stories, and Diana agreed, told her to go for it, to work hard, to bet on herself.

But Joel discouraged Ruth's dreaminess about the island whenever he could.

"Win the lottery," he said. "Then maybe you could live on Block Island. Though the insurance would still put you under. Diana is rich. We are not. Don't forget that."

She tried to ignore her father. She'd find a way to spend the rest of her days writing in a shed like Diana's, eating under a tree like Diana's, reading with a large sun hat on, a cat asleep at her feet. She would bet on herself. But as she got older, she began to see the truth in Joel's words, although she never admitted it to him.

As the years passed, Ruth's routine calcified. In Maine, whenever she had a bad night working at the bar and started looking for other jobs online, she realized that anything else she could get would be a pay cut at this point, and she couldn't afford that.

Ruth came to understand the difference between people like Diana and her father—how money could cushion you from stress, and how without it, that stress worked against you all your life. She learned how lucky one had to be to enjoy the simple, unattainable luxury of sitting under an old-growth tree in your wide yard, the ocean visible in the distance. Sometimes she looked up prices of homes out of curiosity, trying to fuel her motivation, but instead she felt nothing but shock at all the zeros.

Joel worked hard as a painter, and his body wore the aches and pains from reaching and crawling in other people's homes, from falling off ladders. There were moments when Ruth wondered what she had been thinking, that she could really have Diana's life too, if she just worked hard enough, if she did something great, if she wrote a novel and it sold a million copies, maybe. But something great started to slip out of the frame as time went on. She was working doubles five, six days a week, and was too tired on her days off to spend time writing.

Trying to write something worthwhile began to feel like carving against the inertia of her life, like walking upstream in waist-deep water. She couldn't keep up against the mounting restaurant shifts, against her bank balance that got knocked down every time she thought she was more secure. Whenever she thought she could cut back on work, the truck needed new brakes, her seedy landlord hiked the rent up or held on to her security deposit, or she got sick and missed out on a week of income and had to pay the bills from the walk-in clinic.

Ruth wondered sometimes if being so close to Diana's world for all those years had done something to her, had made her think she was a part of it too, made her believe in the impossible fairy tale, made her think she had the same safety net they had, that everything would work out.

The life of an artist started to seem like something she could never have, something only people with time on their hands could accomplish—and in Ruth's mind people who had time were people who already had money. So she began to resent writing, to distance herself from it on purpose. She stopped waking up early to write, allowed herself to sleep, and didn't feel guilty about it. She told Diana to stop calling her a writer—she wasn't one.

She was living month to month in run-down apartments with random roommates to get through the winters, only so she could make it to June and move back out to Block Island. In her dark moments she wondered if it was worth it.

Now, as Ruth pedaled hard up the familiar hill toward Diana's house, the sun was strong and beating against her dark dress. As she sweat, her heart began to pound, and echoes of Ruth and

Diana's last fight started to press into Ruth's memory: *It's not enough. . . . It's just a cold.*

She pedaled harder, the burn in her legs a distraction. She wasn't ready to think about that. Instead, she thought of Charlie, of his text: *I have something to tell you.*

She had tried not to think about what he might mean, wouldn't allow herself to hope, to consider it might be the same as what she wanted to say. Cresting the hill, she saw the ocean on the horizon, clear and blue, and nerves ran through her. She realized with a sinking feeling that she had allowed herself to hope all along anyway.

5

Ruth stepped through the green archway of privet, and muscle memory led her to the right, where she propped her bike up against the rock wall. Looking out at the lawn, she saw the rows of chairs lined up with an aisle down the center. At the front of the aisle was a small side table with a black stone urn sitting in the middle, and next to the table was a large poster. The poster was a blown-up photo Ruth had taken of Diana at her fiftieth birthday party. She had been playing around with Diana's camera when she made Diana pose for the portrait. Diana had almost said no. She hated to have her picture taken, but she wanted to encourage Ruth, so she offered reminders before looking into the lens. Ruth flinched seeing it. In the photo, Diana's face was perfectly illuminated by the summer six o'clock sun. Her gray eyes shone from tears, although she was smiling. She had cried a lot that night, Ruth remembered.

"I never thought I'd make it to fifty," she had said to Ruth after people started going home. The two of them were sitting on the stoop side by side, the lights hanging from the trees making the yard look like an oasis of fireflies.

Today would've been Diana's fifty-ninth birthday.

The thought made Ruth stop, tears stinging her eyes. By avoiding her grief all month, she hadn't prepared herself for this. Joel saw her from his seat, and Ruth winced at the heavy way he leaned on the chair as he got up and headed toward her. His shirt was wrinkled. Sarah and Bill turned to wave to Ruth from their seats.

"How are you doing?" her dad asked.

"I'm okay," Ruth said. It was only at that moment that she realized she was clenching her fists. Looking at her dad, she remembered the last funeral they were at together—Maggie's. He had worn the same shirt then too. Ruth was supposed to give the eulogy for her mom, but when it came down to it, she couldn't do it. She had felt guilty for months afterward. She still felt guilty when she thought about it. Joel turned and waited for Ruth to join him.

"I just need a minute, I think," Ruth said. Joel nodded, looking relieved as he headed back to Sarah and Bill. Ruth knew her father wasn't great at comforting her, even if he wanted to be.

It was a large gathering, and Ruth didn't recognize half the people there.

Diana had traveled often during the winters, staying at her apartment in New York or with friends in Miami, Italy, and Los Angeles—sometimes for months at a time. Ruth had met some of those people over the years as they came through New England and had heard stories about others, but there were still many people in Diana's life that remained a mystery to her. Diana was good at keeping secrets.

She scanned the crowd, looking toward the house for Charlie, until she felt someone approach next to her. She felt a hand on her shoulder, and the pressure made her inhale sharply. Turning, she saw him. His beard was stubbled, and Ruth imagined the scraping feeling it might leave across her cheek if she were to kiss him now. Over the last few weeks, her dreams had been filled with glimpses of Charlie. Always, he was in the distance where Ruth couldn't reach him, or turning a corner, ducking out of a room as she was entering, leaving her with a lost feeling. Having him in front of her was disorienting. She felt herself wanting to reach out and hold on to him so that he would stay put.

The thrumming tension of what he might say returned stronger than before, and in a flash she remembered Louis's body curled against hers that morning. She didn't feel guilty. She only wished it had worked better to calm her.

Charlie's suit was rumpled and rolled at the sleeves, and his brown hair was cut short, the waves that Ruth was so used to erased. It looked like Charlie had been crying, and the sight of his watery brown eyes made tears float to the edges of Ruth's eyelids, although they did not fall. He pulled her into a hug. Charlie was tall enough that Ruth's face was buried in his chest, his soft linen shirt pressed against her cheek. He smelled like laundry dried in the sun and faintly of nervous sweat. He rubbed her back, still holding on, and she felt small, encircled in his arms.

Ruth knew she had missed him, but seeing him now confirmed the thoughts and feelings that had taken her over since the night she'd laid in the grass at Diana's. She knew her love for him was real—felt it in her body so strongly, like she had found the moon after searching a dark and empty sky.

The idea of waiting until after the ceremony seemed impossible. For some reason, there was an urgency that she couldn't shake, that she had to tell him as soon as she could.

They held each other without saying anything, and when they pulled away he wiped his cheek and smiled.

"You've been hard to reach," he said.

Ruth nodded, feeling bad about dodging his calls, and took a deep breath.

Feeling his arms around her still, she was sure that he knew what she wanted to say, that he wanted to tell her the same thing. Looking over Charlie's shoulder, she saw Diana's attic window—their secret place. They would meet there most nights when he was staying with Diana to climb out on the roof and lie in the thick of the night to watch stars, sneaking cigarettes and whispering so as not to be heard. Ruth decided she would ask Charlie to meet her there so they could talk in private.

"Could I talk to you later?" Ruth asked.

"Yeah, of course. I want to talk to you too," he said.

It was about to come pouring out of her now, and she knew she needed to wait. She had opened her mouth to tell him to meet her at the attic, where she knew she'd finally have the courage to tell him how she felt, when Charlie looked over her shoulder and nodded to someone behind her.

"It's about to start," he said, distracted. As he walked toward the seats, Ruth felt deflated, her nerves buzzing, until Charlie stopped and turned to wait for her to follow. It was what she had wanted—for him to stop leaving so quickly, to wait for her. Stepping toward him, Ruth felt stronger in her resolve to tell him how she felt, and more capable to face the day. She spotted Lucy waving from the seat she had been saving for Ruth, then turned back to Charlie, but he was gone. He had slipped away from her without saying anything else and headed for the first row.

Lucy and Ruth's seats were near Diana's garden, and Ruth couldn't help but glance over at it. Normally, at this point in the summer, the plants would be calf-high, bees buzzing around the pollinators and over the thick bushels of basil, thyme, and rosemary. Nothing had been planted this year—only low weeds lined the dirt, and some wildflowers grew intertwined with the fence. The crowd settled into their seats, and Ruth kept looking at the garden until the sound of someone clearing their throat pulled her out of her head and back into the moment.

The crowd settled and conversation died. Diana's sister, Lynn, took her place in front of everyone with her hands clasped at her waist. Her mouth was heavy, her thin lips turned downward like a basset hound's. Her nose was lightly dusted with the same freckles that Diana had. A biplane flew overhead, and she waited until the droning noise faded, looking frustrated. Ruth shifted in her seat. Lynn's hair was a duller red than her sister's, and it was clear that while Diana and Lynn had shared the same wild curls, Lynn had attempted to fight them with a straightener. The humidity had pulled out curling frizz from her tight bun, making her look frazzled and unkempt.

Ruth knew Lynn well.

Lynn was Charlie's mother, and every summer that Ruth lived with Diana, Lynn would come the very last weekend of Charlie's visit to escort him home. Ruth had to give up her room and sleep on the couch in the living room. She always thought the timing of the trip was intentional so that Lynn could make sure Charlie returned to his real world and that he wouldn't get sucked into the "abyss of Block Island," as she called it, worried he would never want to leave and would "throw his life away" to live here all summer.

"Charlie is studying really hard," Lynn would say, and then later, "Charlie has a really busy job. He doesn't have time to spend months doing whatever he wants."

Diana always had the same reply. She'd roll her eyes and sneak a wink to Ruth, then say, "I think doing what you want is a noble effort actually. Most people are incapable of it."

But still, every day, Lynn complained that the little island was driving her crazy, then pat Diana on the head and say things like, "You should really come visit us more, get off this tiny rock. I don't know how you don't go insane here. When was the last time you used your apartment in New York?"

To which Diana would wave her off.

That first summer Ruth lived with Diana, she overheard Lynn in the kitchen one morning. It was early, and they must've thought she was still asleep or couldn't hear them, or maybe Lynn knew Ruth could hear them and she didn't care.

"It's kind of like freeloading, isn't it? How much can she be helping you, really? You don't need anything," Lynn said.

"She does help me," Diana had answered. "I do need help. I work a lot, actually." She laughed, but Ruth could hear the gentle annoyance in her voice. "Plus, I love Ruth."

"How do you even know her again? I mean, who are her parents? Where are they?" Lynn asked.

Ruth was confused by Lynn's question—and angry at the tone

she used. Diana had been quiet for a second, the faucet running, until she replied.

"Maggie."

There was a muffled response.

"Diana," Lynn said, her voice firm as if she was scolding her.

Diana shushed her sister, and then Ruth could no longer hear what they were saying. Later, the words replayed in Ruth's mind as she laid on the couch staring at the living room wall while the sun slowly came in. What was behind Lynn's tone? The two sisters didn't speak for the rest of that trip.

"I know Lynn can be tough," Diana said to Ruth after that first visit. "But she does *mean* well. She used to love it here too actually."

"What?" Ruth asked, not believing Diana, who sometimes, Ruth thought, could be too forgiving.

"Oh yeah, she was obsessed."

Ruth stopped herself from saying how much she doubted that, not wanting to upset Diana. Clearly Diana and Lynn were close despite their differences, and Ruth didn't fully understand their relationship.

In the years that followed, Ruth got the sense that Lynn never stopped trying to convince Diana that she was freeloading, that she wanted something from her.

Looking out past the garden now, Ruth remembered the night that she and Charlie had slept under the stars, staying out till sunrise. It was the first time she had gone to an island party, and she kept saying she was too drunk to be inside, so Charlie laid out a beach blanket and brought their pillows outside. She remembered nestling into his body, the ground uneven and solid beneath her, still warm from the hot day, his fingers brushing the hair out of her face, how he kept asking if she was okay, if she needed more water.

At the thought of Charlie back then, Ruth's head twitched. She wanted to look for him again—to find his face in the crowd. But Lynn started to speak, and Ruth stopped herself.

"Thank you all for coming to celebrate the life of my sister,

Diana. It warms my heart to look out at all of you and know how much she was loved," Lynn said, stopping and scanning the crowd in a practiced way. Ruth and Lynn locked eyes, and Ruth saw her eyebrow raise for a split second before she continued.

"Diana was truly a one-of-a-kind woman. Many of you know her from her work as a photographer, some as neighbors, and some from her devoted love of this community."

Here, Lynn took a long pause.

"Diana could be a hermit. She loved this place, sometimes too much. I was always trying to get her to move home, to spend more time with family, but . . . this island came first."

Ruth felt the strain in Lynn's voice, the underlying anger at her sister, who didn't tell anyone about her diagnosis until she had only a short time left. For a moment, Ruth felt more connected to Lynn than she ever had before. She was angry with Diana for dying too.

"She loved many people in her lifetime," Lynn continued. "So many people knew her in so many different ways, and I'm no public speaker, so I've invited others to share what they loved about our Diana. If you'll join me in welcoming them," Lynn said, gesturing.

Lucy turned to look at Ruth, but Ruth kept her face stony and looking straight ahead. The town manager got up, and then Diana's agent, then a woman Diana had dated in New York for a few years, then a cousin Ruth had never heard mention of, and, eventually, Ruth tuned it all out. She focused on her breathing and looked out past the portrait of Diana at the leaves gently shaking on the beech tree.

She wasn't surprised that she hadn't been asked to speak. She knew that Lynn had never considered Ruth to be close to Diana in any real way. But what was growing inside of her, what she hadn't expected, was how she already felt like an outsider. Watching each person stand and talk about Diana, Ruth felt more and more like a visitor. Diana was her family, but sitting in the back row, the people getting up to speak more and more loosely connected to Diana, she started to feel like a stranger, a funeral crasher.

She remembered a morning when Diana had been out working in the studio all night. She was sitting at the table under the beech tree, her legs up on the table, her body curled like a caterpillar that's been poked, smoking a cigarette, a pot of coffee next to her. As Ruth came over, she stubbed the cigarette out in a clamshell, waving away the smoke like she was a teenager who had just been caught.

"I thought you quit," Ruth said, sitting down.

"One of my many demons," Diana said. "I was up all night battling them."

Ruth glared at her, and eventually Diana handed the pack over.

"I'm sorry," she said. "I know."

The memory put a pit of sadness in Ruth's stomach. She tried to distract herself by letting her mind drift to Charlie again: his soft touch, how her cheeks burned every time he was in the room. They both seemed so young and innocent in her memories, so much more full of life. She itched to tell him how she felt, to get him alone after this and ask him if he loved her too, ask him if it was crazy, ask him if it was too late to try.

"Lastly, the one closest to Diana, my son, Charlie," Lynn said. Lucy squeezed Ruth's arm, and she was brought back to the present as Charlie stood from the front row, buttoning his dark blue suit jacket. He stood next to his mother, who put her hand on his shoulder before she sat down.

"Thanks, Mom," Charlie said, clearing his throat and looking at the urn next to the portrait. It only struck Ruth then that he seemed different than she remembered him. Although she tried, she couldn't identify what it was that had changed. Charlie cleared his throat.

"I did love Diana, although I don't think I was closest with her," he said. "I always thought that was Ruth, actually. I was a little jealous about that, Ruth. Sometimes it seemed like you guys had your own language." He looked in her direction. She was amazed how easily he found her in the crowd. Ruth felt people shift in their seats to look at her, some chuckling and nodding in agreement. All of the blood in her body seemed to be caught in her throat. Looking back at Charlie, Ruth felt her heart swell, but Charlie moved on quickly and gracefully, already looking away.

"Diana had a way of making everyone around her feel special. She listened, not as if she was waiting to reply but as if she was really curious about what you were going to say next, as if she could learn something from everyone she talked to. She asked questions. She wanted to know more about this life, wanted to go after what she found interesting, never apologizing for it. She looked at people and saw more than the average person did, I think. She pulled out the best in them. She pulled out the best in me." Charlie stopped here and cleared his throat. Ruth could see his eyes watering. He glanced at the portrait of Diana, smiled, took a deep breath, and turned back out to the crowd.

"She saw people. A lot of this she did through her work, but it was also just the way she lived. I know we all think of Diana as the life of any party, but I wanted to talk about Diana in her many quiet moments because she was, most often, a recluse. Some days, it was hard to get her to leave her studio—even for food.

"When I spent summers here, it sometimes seemed like she was in a trance, standing in the middle of the yard with a cup of coffee, shuffling barefoot to her studio past midnight to keep working. I never really understood what she was doing until she showed me—until she described what she saw in each photograph, pointing out the details and letting me in on her secret game. It was rare that she let anyone into her studio, but once, when I was nine, she invited me in. Even as a kid, I could see in her photos what she was looking at out in the world, what she was asking about her surroundings. I was always jealous of her ability to do that, to ask what felt like the real questions, to create something.

"Well into my teenage years, I would spend my winters waiting for the time when I could come visit Aunt Di. She'd pick me up at the ferry. Only then did I feel the summer truly begin.

"I'm going to miss having coffee with her under that tree. The world was a special place to her. It was a more special place with her in it."

Charlie choked on the last word and quickly returned to his seat. Ruth realized she had been holding her breath. The ache to be next to him, to hold his hand, was so strong that Ruth felt herself almost stand to move toward him, but she stopped herself. She looked over at Lucy, whose face was coated in tears. Lynn stood back up.

"We're happy that the home will remain in the family and that we will continue to be a part of this community. Charlie will be marrying his wonderful fiancée, Nadia, here, on Labor Day weekend, which is such a blessing. I know Diana would have loved her," she said, smiling at a woman in the front row and clapping.

Ruth wasn't sure she'd heard Lynn correctly. But the applause grew and Ruth saw the woman in the front row lean her head on Charlie's shoulder.

Charlie was getting married—*married.* She felt like the air had been sucked out of her lungs.

"Now, please join us for refreshments inside as we toast to Diana and to the future." Lynn's voice broke into Ruth's shock.

People stood and started talking in hushed tones, but Ruth stayed put. She couldn't move. She looked at the attic window and felt the hope that had been blooming burst within her. As she peered through the crowd, she saw a thin woman with her hand on Charlie's chest. Her hair was thick and blond, pulled back into a crisp, low bun. When had he started seeing someone? How had Ruth not noticed her earlier?

Lucy leaned in and whispered, "Hey—come on. Let's go."

Ruth blinked and wiped her eyes. Her whole body was rigid as they left their seats, the last to do so. Lucy and Ruth walked over the grass at the back of the crowd to the shade of the large twisting beech tree.

"What do you want to do?" Lucy asked, looking up at the house, her forehead furrowed in concern. Ruth followed her gaze to see Charlie and his fiancée standing on the patio, talking to the town manager, Laura, and her husband. She stared at them, at the way the woman next to him touched the small of his back—so familiar. They looked like they fit together. Ruth realized then that she had never actually seen Charlie with another woman. Once, when she visited him at Columbia, she noticed how girls lingered around him and flirted. It was easy then to separate College Charlie from the Charlie she knew. She had watched him laugh with those women, confident, before he drifted back over to Ruth with the smirk she was used to, whispering in her ear, asking if she was having fun.

It had made Ruth passively curious about who felt they knew Charlie best—about what he was like in that world. But she had never seen him hold someone else so easily. She hadn't assumed he had been single all this time, but she figured he would tell her if it was serious, if he was thinking of proposing.

Ruth tried to picture herself standing next to Charlie, how it would look from someone else's perspective. It was an image she had seen in her mind many times before, but suddenly, she couldn't.

"I don't know what to do," Ruth said.

"Maybe we should leave," Lucy replied.

Ruth hadn't told Lucy about what she'd been feeling recently, but Lucy knew her history with Charlie, and Ruth was sure her friend could sense that she was unraveling.

"Yeah, that's a good idea," she said. Instead, Ruth started walking to the house. Lucy caught up and looped her arm into hers, like she was trying to restrain Ruth.

Charlie and his fiancée dipped into the door just before Ruth and Lucy approached. Looking back, he caught Ruth's eye but turned away and continued inside. She felt a gap open between them that she hadn't been expecting. The comfort she usually gained from him seemed inappropriate now, and the conversation she had been planning seemed comical, and all at once she was embarrassed. Imagining the words "I love you" falling from her mouth made her wince, tingling shame running through to her fingertips. What had she been thinking?

The screen door was being held open by a round stone the size of a small soccer ball. Ruth recognized it from a hike she and Diana took down to Black Rock Beach on the south side of the island a few years ago. Diana had deemed that it was perfect, picked it up, and hauled it all the way back up the trail, to the car, then dropped it on the stoop—Ruth recalled how strong she had been. For a second, she was almost glad she had never seen her sick, thin, and drowning in her hospital gown. It would have been too much.

Once again, muscle memory took over, and Ruth stepped through the doorway into the small kitchen. Most of the guests were already settled in the sunny, wide living room, their black clothing contrasting against the bright yellow walls. Ruth looked at the kitchen and was struck by how much had already been cleared out. The tiny jars of dried flowers, the mismatched bowls, the worn-out runner rug—all of it was gone. Only a few things remained: the art on the walls, the tea towel with small ducks on it folded near the sink.

"Damn," Lucy said under her breath, noticing all of the change. Ruth felt overcome with rage and forgot for a minute about Charlie. Her body seemed to divert from grief to anger as a welcome distraction, and she strode through the living room, making her way to the bar. They had missed the formal toast already, and people were milling about, talking in low voices to one another. Someone was playing music from a small speaker, Diana's well-loved record player sitting in the corner, going unused. For someone who loved to plan parties, Diana had given no instructions on her funeral, or even indicated that she wanted one. Ruth remembered a conversation they had once had about death.

"Just throw me in the ocean," Diana had said. "But make sure you weigh me down properly, and take a picture of my body in the sand first."

"That's dark," Ruth replied.

"I know," Diana answered.

At the bar in the corner of the living room, Ruth reached for a bottle of wine and poured two full glasses, emptying the bottle and putting it back on the table. She was heading back to Lucy when she overheard the conversation next to her and stopped to eavesdrop.

"I would be shocked if they didn't sell it within the year—you know, after the wedding," Laura said to Bonnie, the librarian.

"Really? She said it was going to stay in the family," Bonnie replied.

"Well, yeah, but Lynn hates it out here . . . and Charlie. I don't know. I think they wanted something out on Nantucket. That's what his fiancée told me earlier. She said her family has a set of homes there."

"What's her name?"

"I forget."

"I thought the will wasn't all sorted out yet," Bonnie said. "Diana's agent said there were some problems with it."

"Oh, interesting."

"Why would they get married here then?" Bonnie asked.

"Charlie was telling me earlier that they were having a hard time deciding, but after Diana died, it felt like the right thing," Laura replied.

"That's sweet," Bonnie said.

Ruth's face burned.

"How much do you think they could get for it?" Bonnie asked after a minute.

"Well, that tiny house on Corn Neck sold for over a million last month, so I think they'll do okay."

Ruth considered someone moving into Diana's house, tearing down her studio, painting the walls a bland gray, listing it on Airbnb. The thought was infuriating.

"Ruth. Hi." Beth, Diana's agent, approached Ruth, leaning over to give her a hug around the neck. Over Beth's shoulder, Ruth watched as Charlie and his fiancée showed the ring off to someone Ruth didn't know. It caught the sun coming in from the window and refracted small rainbows against the yellow walls.

Beth pulled away. "How are you doing, sweetie?" she asked.

Ruth's mind was blank, her eyes still catching the rays of the glittering ring each time Charlie's fiancée spoke with a flourish, her hand waving as if she couldn't stop.

"I'm . . . okay," she said, thinking it was the answer least likely to continue the conversation.

Beth nodded her head in a sympathetic way and said some more words that Ruth didn't register, then patted Ruth on the shoulder and walked away.

Ruth brought the wine back over to Lucy, who was looking at her with worry in her eyes, and Ruth wondered what she must look like. Her skin was tingling now, and she realized the wine in her glass was already gone, although she didn't remember drinking any of it. She turned and noticed more things missing from the house—the books, the whittled driftwood figurines, the piles of folded quilts, the sea glass collection. Her eye caught a box of photographs sticking out from the back hallway closet. Joel was in the corner with Sarah and Bill. His eyes widened as he took a step in her direction, probably trying to stop her before she walked over to Lynn, who was standing against the window. Ruth moved past him before he could intercept her.

Looking her up and down, Lynn smiled, the corners of her heavy mouth lifting for only a moment.

"Good of you to come, Ruth," Lynn said.

"Redecorating already, Lynn?" Ruth felt emboldened, like the last drop of herself was being overcome with a wave of another person—someone who would make a scene at a funeral.

Lynn's expression showed nothing, but her stare was cold

and steady. She looked Ruth over slowly, her eyes landing on her mostly empty wineglass, at the small pool of backwash in the bottom.

"There's a lot to get done before the wedding. This place will probably look quite different by then, I imagine. Nadia has very different taste than Diana did. They make a beautiful couple, don't they?" Lynn said, continuing before Ruth could respond. "I know you two had some kind of a fling over the years, but you never struck me as the type to want something serious."

Ruth had always known that Lynn suspected something was going on between her and Charlie, always felt her disapproval, but in this moment she could understand what Lynn was hinting at—*It was never going to be you, because you were never good enough.*

"And you've got to get the place ready to sell, right?" Ruth asked, her anger pulsing through her, the words falling out of her mouth. "Clear out any sign that she ever even lived here? What're you going to do with her things, sell them on eBay, make some money off your sister's untimely death?"

Lynn looked for a brief second as if she had been stung, and through her anger Ruth felt her stomach drop. She knew she had stepped over the line, had been cruel.

"You've always been too familiar," Lynn said, nodding to herself. "I hope you'll understand how inappropriate that is now. But to be frank with you"—Lynn took a step toward Ruth, crowding her, Lynn's voice an even whisper—"whatever happens here now is really none of your concern. And actually, I think it's probably time for you to leave. This will be family and close friends only quite soon. You don't want to overstay your welcome."

She smiled and put her hand on Ruth's shoulder before gliding away back into the crowd. Ruth could feel people looking at her. Her dad came to her side.

"Time to get out of here?"

Ruth turned toward Joel. His face was grave, and she felt his concern for her, his pity. She let the rage return, focusing on it as she walked straight back the way she came, put the glass in the empty sink, and brushed past Charlie, alone now, on her way out. He said something to her, but Ruth kept walking to her bike. She rode through the hedges and away from the house, her body trembling. She was an outsider. She was no longer welcome.

6

At work the next night, Ruth couldn't shake the manic, nervous feeling that had gripped her since she left the funeral. Luckily, the restaurant's manager, Whitney, had the night off. Otherwise, Ruth was sure she would've been sent home hours ago. She'd dropped two plates of food already, burning her hand on the soup as it spilled, and had been short with a table of tourists who kept ordering things that weren't on the menu. Every time she tried to refocus her attention, her mind filled with Lynn's face, she felt Lynn's hand on her arm as she dismissed her, and she saw the changes to Diana's house again. As for Charlie, every time she thought of the engagement, she felt so embarrassed she wanted to scream. She tried to block it out, focus on the tables in front of her, but she was only half paying attention, unable to get the image of the ring casting rainbows across the walls of Diana's house out of her head.

Blocking it out wasn't working. She was constantly looking over her shoulder, in the direction of the door, imagining Charlie would walk in at any moment, order a drink at the bar, and wait for her to get off her shift so they could talk. This made her even more frustrated, except this time at herself. It was like she was seventeen again, and she had just met him. All winter that year, on the mainland, she had looked for him in places he would never be. She had looked for his car coming down her street, in crowds at the diner she worked at even though he had never been there before. She had expected him to show up at her door.

As the night wound down and her tables trickled out, Ruth released a sigh. It was almost over. The streets were quiet, and she leaned on the service station in the back room by the kitchen, rubbing her eyes until she heard the door click open. The hostess went to greet the guests, and Ruth knew the last-minute table would be hers due to her poor performance.

"You just got a two-top," the hostess said, brushing past her, and Ruth nodded in defeat. Standing up tall, she took a deep breath, trying to release the tension in her shoulders, grabbed the water pitcher, and headed back out onto the floor, doing her best to turn her attitude around for one more table. As she rounded the corner she stopped short, and some of the water slopped out of the pitcher and onto the ground.

Charlie and his fiancée were holding hands over the table. They let go as she approached, Nadia smiling at Charlie as if they had been caught. Ruth ignored the spilled water and reached for Charlie's glass, not looking him in the eye.

"Ruth!" Charlie shouted, leaning back in his chair as she reached over him. Ruth put the full water glass down and stepped back, bumping her hip out and leaning the water pitcher against it. She needed to fill Nadia's glass, but she could tell her hand was shaking now, so she stopped herself, trying to buy some time.

"Charlie," she said, looking into his eyes. They were warm and brown, like always. His stubble had grown since yesterday into a shadowy beard.

"I didn't know if you still worked here or not. Sorry for coming in so late. I wanted to show Nadia this place."

Ruth forced a smile as he motioned to the woman sitting across from him, thinking of all the times he had waited for Ruth after work here.

"Ruth, this is my fiancée, Nadia."

Ruth looked over at the woman, shifting her body to face her, so as not to be rude. Nadia was petite, her face narrow and angular with prominent cheekbones and pink bowed lips. Her tight bun was gone, and her hair fell loose and wavy around her shoulders. Her highlights looked expensive or maybe they were natural—either option was hard for Ruth to stomach. Nadia's mouth lifted into a bright smile, and she held out her hand. Ruth struggled awkwardly to shake it, the water pitcher sloshing again.

"Hi," Ruth said.

"Nadia, this is Ruth. She's the one I was telling you about. She was really close with Diana," Charlie said as Ruth and Nadia dropped hands.

"Ohhh, wow, yes, of course. Sorry, I've been meeting so many people this weekend," she said. "Diana had so many friends."

Ruth nodded, unsure of what else to do. She tried to ignore how she was getting recast as a friend of Diana's, tried to stop herself from thinking about Nadia staying in Diana's house. Looking at her colorful sundress and the gold bracelets that hung from her dainty wrists, Ruth felt simple in her clogs and became acutely aware of the soup stains on her jeans.

"It's so nice to meet you. I'm sorry for your loss," Nadia said, cocking her head to the side in sympathy.

As Ruth looked at her, she noticed that Nadia's face was clear—pale and untouched by the sun. She thought of her own uneven complexion—the freckles and small sun spots that had already begun to form from all her time spent outside. Ruth managed to smile.

"Nice to meet you too." There was a long pause, and Ruth squirmed. "So, drinks, you two?" she asked as she recovered, putting her waitress voice back on to mask her feelings.

"Oh, you know? I think we just wanted some dessert. Do you guys still do that chocolate cake?" Charlie asked. Ruth nodded and started to walk away.

"Ruth?" Nadia called.

Ruth turned.

"Could I have some water, please?"

Ruth brought the cake over and placed it between them, before setting two spoons down. Fumbling them, she flinched as they clattered against the table.

"So you two must've spent a lot of time together then?" Nadia asked, picking up her spoon and pointing between Ruth and Charlie with it. She looked at ease, but Ruth was thrown off by the direct question and wondered if Charlie had ever mentioned her to Nadia before. Then again, what would he have said? What were they to each other? He would've told Nadia they were friends, Ruth thought. Ruth looked at Charlie and thought of the last time they had spoken to each other, as she sat in Diana's yard. He had probably already been engaged then. She thought of how she hadn't heard from him for months before he called her from the hospital, her few calls going unanswered. She tried not to think of him seeing her name pop up on his phone while he was with Nadia, tried not to think of him silencing it and then forgetting altogether that she had called.

Charlie didn't answer Nadia's question right away.

"I lived with Diana every summer up until a few years ago," Ruth heard herself saying, sounding uncertain, like it wasn't true.

"Yeah," Charlie jumped in, "so Ruth was there whenever I visited—for the most part."

Ruth furrowed her eyebrows at him, but he was looking down, taking another bite of cake. She lingered, and the moment seemed to stretch.

"Oh, right," Nadia replied, picking up the spoon and pushing it down into the whipped cream and chocolate.

"So, are you guys in town just for the week?" Ruth asked.

"Well, the wedding is coming up pretty quick, and Mom is super overwhelmed with the house and the planning, so we're going to stay out here until then," Charlie said, looking at Nadia.

"Yeah, we were crazy to think we could plan a wedding this quickly! But we couldn't imagine waiting," Nadia said.

"I'm going to work remotely and stuff," Charlie added.

"Right," Ruth replied. She always forgot that some people could pick up work and take it with them wherever they wanted to go. Ruth wondered what Nadia did for work. She was about to ask her when Nadia nodded and leaned back in her chair, her face breaking into a sudden smile, a practiced smile.

"Thanks for the cake," Nadia said, and Ruth, feeling dismissed, turned and left the table. She tried not to watch from behind the bar as they fed spoonfuls to each other and giggled in the dim lighting. It was hard not to imagine Nadia in white, shoving wedding cake into Charlie's mouth while well-dressed people cheered and lifted glasses of expensive champagne. She felt the gap between Charlie and her widen again. Here she was, their waitress, not at all a part of his world. It had been mere circumstance that ever brought them near each other, an illusion of closeness. And here Charlie and Nadia were—gorgeous and in love. What had she thought would happen? That Charlie would have waited for her? That if she had just told him sooner, it would be her across the table from him? That he also thought of her as the one that got away?

The other servers had been done for a while and were all out back with their shift drinks, smoking and counting out their tips from the night. Ruth stayed behind the bar, polishing and repolishing the same glasses to avoid going over to Charlie and Nadia's table. The door opened, and Ruth instinctively checked her watch—past nine. She was about to call out that they were closed when Louis walked around the corner and up to the bar. Seeing him, Ruth had a physical memory of the other night, could feel his arm draped over her body in sleep.

He looked at his watch as he leaned over the back of the bar seat.

"You're closed—shoot," he said. "I'll head out. I just wanted to see how you were doing."

Ruth looked at him, not registering what he was saying.

"What do you mean?" she asked.

"The funeral. I tried calling you, but you didn't answer."

Ruth had kept her phone on silent since the funeral and had been ignoring it.

"Oh, sorry." She still wasn't sure why Louis felt the need to check on her. "Sit, it's not too late," Ruth said, waving her hand, the rag she was using to polish flopping in the direction of the seat.

"Okay, thanks." Louis pulled out a chair.

"What can I get you?" Ruth asked, not looking him in the eye.

"Rum, please," he said, a smirk breaking out on his face.

Ruth turned and pulled down a bottle of rum and a short glass from the back bar, pouring the brown liquid into it. She placed the glass in front of Louis, floating a cocktail napkin down onto the wooden bar first.

"Something for you?" Louis asked. "To cheers with?"

Ruth shoveled out some ice left in the well into another glass and poured the same brown rum on top of it. Ruth held her glass up and met Louis's.

"To Diana," he said.

Ruth only nodded, and as she drank her eyes went to Charlie and Nadia again. The cake was gone from their plate, and they were back to holding hands over the table, leaning in toward each other. Louis looked behind him in the direction of Ruth's gaze. Putting her glass down, she cleared her throat, the liquor burning a little on the way down.

Charlie and Nadia stood then, their chairs scraping against the wood floor. Nadia walked to the front door and bounced out onto the sidewalk, closing the door behind her without a word while Charlie put money down on the table, looked around for Ruth, and waved, his eyes landing on Louis. Louis raised his glass in greeting, and Charlie gave a small nod. He took a few steps toward the bar, looking like he was unsure what he should do.

"Thanks, Ruth," Charlie said.

"Yeah, no problem." Ruth's voice sounded like she was talking to a stranger.

Charlie nodded at Louis. “Hey, man.”

“Hey,” Louis said. His eyes were flitting between Ruth and Charlie.

“I’ll see ya,” Ruth said, dismissing him. She could feel Nadia’s eyes on them from the sidewalk.

“Yeah, okay,” Charlie said, his voice uncertain. He stood there for another second. “Bye.”

The door closed behind him, and Ruth watched Charlie put his arm around Nadia’s shoulders as they walked away, disappearing from sight.

Louis looked at Ruth.

“That’s Diana’s nephew, right?” he asked.

“Yeah, Charlie,” she said.

“You guys used to be a thing, right? You were his island girl?”

Ruth was getting annoyed now.

“Drink your drink so I can close,” she said.

Louis nodded and took a deep sip. “Is that his new girlfriend?”

“Fiancée,” Ruth said, wiping the bar down.

“Oooh.”

They didn’t talk for a moment.

“So, are you doing okay, though?” Louis asked. “I’m sure yesterday was hard. I was a drunken, blubbering mess after my uncle’s funeral.”

Ruth looked up at Louis. Two years ago, Louis’s uncle, who had raised him, and who worked with him every day at the same fishing business, took his own life over the winter. He left Louis his boat, *Pearl*. Ruth was in Maine when it happened, and her car was in the shop at the time, or she would’ve come down for the funeral. The memory softened Ruth toward Louis. His concern seemed genuine, and while it was a surprise to Ruth that he cared, she decided to stop scrutinizing his motives. He was just being kind.

“It was awful,” Ruth said. “They’re already changing the house.”

Thinking about it, Ruth poured herself more rum and held the bottle up to refill Louis, but he shook his head.

"I'm sorry. That sounds like a really shitty time," he said.

Ruth shrugged. She didn't want to talk about it anymore.

Again, she remembered his body against hers only a few nights ago and she wondered if it was some kind of cosmic retribution that Charlie was engaged, that if she hadn't slept with Louis, none of this would be happening.

Walking around the bar, she cleared Charlie and Nadia's table, wiping the crumbs of chocolate cake and putting the cash in her book. After she did her tip out, she started wiping down tables and putting the chairs up. Louis got up and helped her.

"You don't have to do that," Ruth said.

"Yeah, well," was all Louis said. "How're things at the restaurant?" he asked amid the clanging of the chairs.

"My tolerance for people has hit an all-time low," she said, thinking of how awful her shift had been.

Ruth had always liked the fast-paced environment of waitressing, the impermanence, and the way that issues were resolved quickly—if you broke a glass, you swept it up. She liked being busy, liked always having something to do with her hands. It helped her turn her brain off, and the money was good—could be really good, not that she ever got to save any of it. She wasn't great at budgeting, and while everything was getting more expensive, people's tips remained the same.

Ever since Diana had died, each shift felt like it might break her, and even when she was slammed, her mind wouldn't quiet down. Every time she put a plate in front of someone without getting a "thank you," she felt anger stir within her. Things that used to be just part of the job were now wearing on her.

The chairs were all up. Louis reached into his pocket for his wallet, but Ruth waved him off.

"Don't worry about it," she said, walking back behind the bar. Then, after a second, she added, "Thanks for checking on me, I guess."

"You're welcome, I guess," Louis said, turning toward the door, before twisting around to face Ruth again.

"Hey, that was . . . nice the other night," he said. "I mean, it was fun."

Ruth stopped, surprised he would bring it up. "Yeah." She nodded. "It was."

"Like old times." He leaned against the doorframe, one hand on the handle, looking perfectly at ease. That was something she'd always liked about Louis—he wasn't uncomfortable with himself. "All right, I'll see ya," he said. "You can stop blushing now."

Waving, he closed the door behind him.

Ruth stared at the empty restaurant for a full minute, her feet aching in her clogs.

7

Later that night, at home, Ruth lay awake while the white noise of the fan pulsed through her ears. She had just turned off her phone, and the absence of its light in the darkness left her eyes blinded and blinking. She was filled with the slight shame that always accompanied a social media deep dive on someone. Charlie didn't have an Instagram, but finding Nadia had been easy. Her profile was private but linked to a public account called @Nadia_artful with over three thousand followers, which Ruth had clicked on and scoured for the last indeterminable amount of time. It turned out that Nadia was an art teacher at an elementary school in Boston and a jewelry maker on the side. She made earrings, rings, and necklaces and sold them at trade shows, at fairs, and on Etsy. The videos on her page were mainly of her soldering something, or polishing a finished gold piece, but a few videos showed clips of her dancing in her studio, holding a steaming cup of matcha in a handmade mug, while the sun poured in onto her fresh face. Some of the videos showed student work, talked about how arts programs were underfunded in the city, showed images of her at city council meetings, speaking into a microphone, her face passionate and serious.

The artist and activist Ruth was looking at wasn't the image she had pasted onto Nadia, of the put-together rich girl, and she felt a combination of surprise, shame, curiosity, and rancor. Nadia was a good person. She taught children. She made a difference in her community.

Scrolling back to the videos of Nadia making jewelry, Ruth found herself burning as she looked at the high ceilings and the fogged-over windowpanes of the studio space—she was jealous. She thought of her old dream of writing in a tiny cottage like Diana's studio and felt guilty about the empty journal sitting on her desk. If Nadia could teach kids full time and have a dream business on the side, what was her excuse? Ruth couldn't imagine what space in Boston would cost, but thinking of how her parents had lived on Maggie's teacher salary and Joel's painting income, and what Laura had said about family houses on Nantucket, she doubted Nadia was paying for it all on her own.

There were photos of what must be Nantucket on the profile—swaying dunes, a well-dressed family with white teeth, blond hair, and energetic smiles, all sitting around a colorfully set table out in a field—casual yet curated, both idyllic and unattainable.

Ruth wanted to sleep, but she kept thinking about Lynn's face, Charlie's hand on Nadia's hip, the images of the field on Nantucket, Diana's house changed. Finally, she sat up in bed and grabbed clothes off the floor, pulling them on in the dark, slinking out into the hallway, and shutting the door softly so as not to wake Lucy. Ruth yanked up the hallway window and climbed out onto the roof. A breeze went by, ruffling the overgrown hedges. From her perch a few buildings away she could see Captain Nick's Bar lit up, could hear the music coming from the dance floor. People spilled out of the building and into the rim of light around the bar, shouting. Fireflies drifted over the darkened yard, blinking every so often. Ruth watched one of them move higher than the rest, up over the hedges, over the houses.

At once, everything felt wrong. She couldn't tell Charlie she wanted him. Charlie was getting married. Diana was gone, and Ruth was . . . what? Aimless. She realized she had never felt this sense of dread before—that before now there hadn't been anything wrong with feeling aimless. She thought about the last ten years and the rhythm she relied on. Her English degree had offered her nothing but student loans. Every winter was the same, pouring drinks and waiting for June. All of a sudden, she felt older now than she had ever expected to, and everything felt like it had been a waste of time.

She had spent her childhood building her world around her, each day working hard to lay the bricks—paying attention at school, learning how to make friends, imagining what her life would be like when she was ten, fifteen, twenty. But after Maggie died, it was as if she came back to the house she had been building and the whole thing had been blown up, and there was nowhere she could go that the broken pieces of her life weren't scattered, getting in her way.

Even when she tried to move on, to focus on something new, it felt like if she looked down, she would see herself carrying that heavy load of bricks around with her and there was no place to put them down, no matter how tired she was. It no longer seemed like a safe bet to start building again. If her world could explode again at any time, then what was the point?

It was only on Block Island that the weight felt lighter, that she could sometimes forget that it was there long enough to let people into her life, past her defenses. But as fall came around and the days got shorter, Ruth would remember the way things were, and it seemed best to keep living moment to moment—better to keep working nights and taking the cash home with her, maybe count it, maybe not. Best to leave the next five years, the next ten years, off the table. Nothing was a sure bet.

Feeling the weight in her chest, Ruth couldn't hold back the memory of her fight with Diana anymore. Couldn't avoid Diana's words, couldn't ignore that maybe it was the real reason that Diana didn't tell her about the cancer, that in the end Ruth had failed her.

. . .

Diana had called her that past Christmas. Ruth was asleep after working late at the Navy bar on Christmas Eve, pouring gin and tonics and whiskey for people who were either lonely or drunk, each one growing sadder and the crowd growing louder until two in the morning. All the while, the Santa hat Ruth was asked to wear itched and burned the skin on her forehead. Each year, Joel asked her to come home for Christmas, and Ruth always said she had to work, that she couldn't afford to pass up the holiday time-and-a-half pay. It was true, but what Ruth didn't say was that the idea of being home for Christmas made her feel like the room had lost all air, like she was drowning.

"Were you still sleeping?" Diana asked.

"It was a long shift," Ruth said, trying to defend herself. She wasn't sure what time it was. "It was Christmas. It sucked."

"What are you going to do today? Are you hungover?" Diana asked.

"I'm not sure," Ruth replied, ignoring the second part of the question. "How's Miami?" she asked, wanting to change the subject.

The line was quiet until Diana coughed. Then, after a moment, she said, "Listen. I sent you an email."

Ruth pulled her phone away from her ear and opened her email app on her phone. It was filled with ads and subscription reminders, but Diana's message was at the top.

"What're these?" Ruth asked, opening the email and scrolling through the links. She clicked on one and a job listing opened for a publishing assistant in New York City. She clicked on the next one—grad school, an MFA.

"I'm worried about you," Diana said.

"Why?" Ruth asked.

"I feel like it's time."

"Time for what?"

"Time for you to move on from this phase of grieving."

Ruth realized she was holding her breath. She wanted to tell

Diana to stop, wanted to hang up, but couldn't bring herself to. "What did you say?"

"I feel like you are intentionally stalling out your life, and I'm worried. You're not always going to have Block Island to come back to."

"Why not?" Ruth asked. She couldn't imagine a world where she didn't have Block Island to return to. It seemed like an overly dramatic thing for Diana to say. It was out of character.

"Do you want to be bartending a Christmas shift when you're sixty?" Diana asked.

Ruth thought about the night before, the way her feet ached, the way the crowd got more drunk and more sad, how *It's a Wonderful Life* played silently on the TV and how disorienting it was to watch George Bailey fight for his life as someone knocked their drink across the bar, the beer spilling onto her shoes.

"I made good money last night. You're being . . . really snobby," Ruth said.

"Weren't you going to Maine so you would write? So you could dedicate time to that? You have to really grasp at whatever time you have to make something, you know. It's so much easier not to. It won't happen unless you're dedicated to it, unless you fight for it."

Ruth became angry then. She wondered if Diana understood how exhausted she was at the end of each day, how when she woke up in the morning her brain buzzed as if plagued by tinnitus from all the mindless conversations she couldn't help but absorb from the night before, how when she went to sleep each night she was still wired, still pictured herself behind the bar, drink tickets pouring in, people shouting at her for another cocktail. What was she supposed to write about? How to make a martini?

"I'm just saying . . . don't you want more for yourself?" Diana pushed.

"More what?"

"Fulfillment. Are you fulfilled right now? Have you ever asked yourself that?" Diana was picking up steam. "I mean, making money is one thing. I get that, but what do you do the rest of the time? What are you working toward? What do you want from your *life*, Ruth?"

Ruth was quiet. What did she want from her life? It was something she hadn't thought about in a long time. Looking at the blank wall of her temporary room, no art hanging, few personal touches because she would be gone in a few months anyway, she had the gut feeling that this wasn't it, and she did not know what to do with that information.

"I'm not working on anything," Ruth said. "I am not an artist. I don't have any hidden talents. This is it."

"Well, that's just not true, but okay, fine. You're not an artist. You could volunteer? You could teach? You could . . ."

"And what if I love my life?"

Diana sighed. Ruth felt her defenses come up, the lines she told herself whenever she doubted her course. It was unrealistic, this vision Diana had of her. Maybe at one time she had wanted it, had pictured it, what it might be like to spend her time writing, dedicating herself to the characters in her stories, but Diana was sheltered, didn't know how much it cost now just to get by. She had been removed from the pressures of life, secluded on her artist compound long enough that she was out of touch. Diana had stepped out of the river a long time ago, but Ruth was still there, still trying to stand in one place without getting swept away.

"I have connections I can help you with, Ruth. I've offered them so many times. People *dream* of access like this, of any kind of leg up. You're behaving like a child. You need to think of your future."

Ruth didn't know what to say. Diana had never spoken to her like this before, with what sounded like anger and disdain.

"I'm just worried that you're going to . . . end up with regrets," she said. "I know you're afraid, but I'm worried. I want to make sure I push you to try."

"This is me trying," Ruth whispered, growing tired. She didn't want to fight with Diana.

"Well, I have to tell you. It's not enough. I want more from you. Your mom would've wanted more from you."

Ruth felt her defenses fall. She was left among her rubble, alone—Diana's words cutting and cruel.

She wanted to hide. Ruth watched snowflakes build thin walls against the windowsill's edge and felt the familiar burn of shame in her chest.

"Well, I'm sorry, but this is who I am and what I have. I understand if you don't like it," Ruth said, speaking slowly, thinking of Diana's crowd of artist friends—their openings in big cities, their book signings, their new restaurants, their residencies in French cottages. She wasn't surprised Diana felt this way. Ruth had known all along that she didn't belong in their world. Maybe Lynn had been right. Maybe Ruth had been Diana's charity case all along, and now she was disappointing her. Her investment wasn't paying off.

"Ruth," Diana said.

The line was quiet. Ruth couldn't tell how she felt. It wasn't the first time Diana had suggested that Ruth could be doing more with her life—wasn't the first job posting she'd sent, or apartment listing she'd shared from real estate agent friends. But it was the first time she indicated that she wasn't proud of Ruth, that she was actually unimpressed. As the silence continued, the burning within Ruth's chest faded away, settling into a heaviness. She wasn't proud of herself either, and she definitely wasn't impressed. It wasn't a stretch then that Diana would feel the same way.

"Do you want to come down and visit soon?" Diana asked, her voice softened.

"I thought you were in Miami," Ruth said.

"I'm back next week."

"I'll see if I can get work off."

But she didn't. She didn't come down. The next week Diana called and apologized, and they talked, although carefully. As months passed, Ruth felt silly for making such a big deal about the argument. She had gotten a stretch of days off in March, but when she called to say she was coming down, Diana said she was traveling again, that she would see her in June, and then it had been too late. Ruth never asked Charlie how Diana had looked in the hospital. She didn't want to know, but history gave her an idea. The image was hard to forget.

Thinking about her mom made Ruth's heart ache and the tightness in her chest return. Maggie had been only forty-two when she died, passing a few months before her forty-third birthday. Now that Ruth was twenty-seven, almost twenty-eight, that fact felt heavier than ever—it felt like no time at all to be here, to live.

Her parents had told her about the cancer in a family meeting—Joel, Maggie, and Ruth sitting together at the kitchen table. Ruth had been scared that she was in trouble. It was rare that the three of them were ever in the same room together on purpose. She knew her mom had been called back for more imaging, that they had taken a biopsy, but at the time, she had said it was probably nothing and Ruth didn't know enough to be worried.

Her mother was the one to say it: breast cancer—stage four—metastatic. Ruth didn't fully understand but listened as her mother explained that the cancer had spread into the lymph nodes and popped up elsewhere in the body, making it harder to get rid of.

That was in March, and Ruth remembered that nothing green had yet sprouted. There was a cold rain falling, and dirty remnants of icy snow lined their driveway. Ruth stared out the window and listened to the rain plunking off the gutters above. She imagined the snow melting. She wanted it to melt. She wanted to break something.

It was those metastasized tumors that kept Ruth up at night. The tumor in the breast was removed in surgery, but the part that kept resounding in her mind as she tried to sleep was the word *incurable*. They could use treatments, chemo, radiation, the doctors said, but there was no cure for metastatic breast cancer. Some people could live twenty years, and some people might live only one. Ruth began to look at her mother—her earlobe, the back of her neck—and imagine small tumors everywhere underneath the skin, until she had to close her eyes and try to burn the image away in order to see her clearly again, to not think of her in parts being overtaken by disease. She stopped hanging out with her friends after school, stopped doing her homework, and only went to her job at the restaurant because her parents told her she must.

Even there, she spoke to no one if she could help it, and, once home, she would sit on the couch next to her mom while she read, Ruth reading over her shoulder, wanting to be as close as possible. She decided to keep her tears to herself, and how scared she was too, talking about it with no one—there was no one to talk about it with anyway.

Ruth held her mother's hand during the infusions and covered her hands and feet in the heavy ice packs meant to protect the fingers and toes from neuropathy. She took diligent notes on the chemical names of all the drugs they were giving her, on the side effects, on when to take them and with what. She noticed the faraway look on Maggie's face as the chemo dripped from the bags, the way she couldn't look at the red chemicals, how the smell of the place made her nauseous.

Everyone told her to give her mom space, but Ruth ignored them. She had been in the room, was always in the room, to write down what the nurses told Maggie about the nausea she might experience, about how food might start tasting different. Ruth watched later at home as her mom pushed plates away and excused herself, walking swiftly to the bathroom and closing the door, the click of the lock behind her, the flush of the toilet.

On Maggie's second infusion, something went wrong. The nurse left the room for a minute, and Maggie's face bloomed a fast and angry red—a color that Ruth had never seen before. Ruth watched as the blue of Maggie's eyes grew stark against her red cheeks and her searching panic became focused on Ruth. Maggie grabbed at her chest and opened her mouth, gasping.

"I can't breathe," she said, her fingers searching, clawing against her chest as if for air, her eyes on Ruth.

Ruth leapt up from her chair. "Help!" she screamed, her own voice inaudible to her as Maggie's monitor started beeping loud and persistent. A crowd of confused nurses swarmed Maggie as she looked up at them. Maggie's terror was burned into Ruth's memory—tears falling down her red face, her blue eyes darting back and forth, looking to the nurses for help, her pupils dilated. Ruth got out of the way so the nurses could get to Maggie as her mother's body began to convulse.

The nurses gave her Benadryl and steroids for the allergic reaction to the chemo, standing over Maggie for another half an hour as her body continued to shake, as her color slowly returned to normal, as Ruth wrung her hands in the background to stop from crying. They had said it was normal, that it happened sometimes, but for weeks afterward, at the diner, while the cook shouted where to take the food, Ruth would again see her mother's searching eyes, her scared and disoriented face, and she would start tearing up. She'd drop the plate in her hands onto the pass and run to the walk-in freezer, her ragged breath condensing in front of her while she tried to smear the tears away so she could get back to work. Even now, Ruth still had flashbacks to that moment.

Ruth had brushed her mother's soft hair until it had fallen out, until she was afraid to pull at the lingering strands, until Maggie asked Ruth to shave it for her. They spent an afternoon in a thrift store looking for colorful, soft scarves that she could wear on her head, but every time Ruth showed her one, Maggie would find something wrong with it, say it wasn't her color, or she didn't like the pattern. She would adjust her baseball cap and ask if she could meet Ruth in the car, claiming that she suddenly felt tired. She began to feel tired all the time.

It had been a winter day the following year when Maggie told Ruth she was going to her next appointment alone. Ruth had been upset. Her mother scheduled the appointment while Ruth had to be in school, which was unusual, and during chemistry class Ruth stared at the tan linoleum floor and listened to the buzz of the fluorescent lights, ignoring the lesson. She skipped last period and hid in the library, crouched in the back corner, until she thought she could leave the building undetected. Her family lived close enough to the high school that Ruth could walk home.

The walk along the main road took her about an hour. She listened to the whooshing drones of each car as they sped past her, heard the occasional obscenity shouted from a window, and wondered what was happening at the doctor's office.

Maggie was waiting at home when Ruth arrived. It had started raining halfway through her walk, and she was soaked and shivering. Maggie ran to the bathroom to get a towel, then wrapped Ruth in it and hugged her close, her body frail and her hug weak. Sitting together on the couch, Maggie told Ruth that she wanted to stop with the treatment, that the doctors had done all they could do. She was tired, and they had found a metastatic tumor in her brain. Ruth sobbed, angry, broken sobs in her mother's arms until she fell asleep from exhaustion.

Her mother had insisted on a Catholic funeral, and Ruth remembered feeling uncomfortable in the thin black dress she bought at Saver's for the occasion. She stared at the sculpture of Jesus on the cross and felt nothing. People hugged her and tried to look into her eyes. She remembered none of the ceremony, the house inside of her blown apart, the numbness stepping through the rubble to find her, taking over.

Maggie, Diana, and now Charlie—the weight had never felt heavier to Ruth, and as she felt it sink within her, she realized that it might never leave her, that this was her life, and she was scared.

8

Over the next few days, Ruth found safety in work. She needed to distract herself, so she signed up for extra shifts, pulling doubles until finally no one wanted to be covered anymore, and she found herself with a day off and no plans. She woke up to her phone ringing, and as she leaned over to answer it, a small note fell off her exposed stomach.

RELAX—PLEASE.

Ruth looked over to Lucy's empty bed and answered the phone.

"I'm getting on the ferry in one hour. Are you working again, or can I stop by?" It was Joel. Ruth could hear the crowds around him. She imagined him standing on the sidewalk, forlorn, and she felt a deep sadness move through her. He had been out on the island with Sarah and Bill since the funeral, but she hadn't seen him since then. Suddenly, she remembered this had been his one summer vacation.

"No. I'll be here," Ruth replied. After she hung up, she saw the date on her phone screen, although she already knew what it was, had been anticipating it for the past few days—June twenty-seventh. Maggie's birthday. She would have been fifty-three this year. Sighing, Ruth looked down at the note now on the floor—*Relax*. She wanted to, but all she felt was guilt for ignoring her father draped over her like a heavy blanket in the heat.

Ruth was sitting in the shade on the porch when Joel walked up the short hill to the house. He put his bag down and lowered himself to sit next to her, leaning on her shoulder for support. She had poured him a cup of coffee, and without saying anything he picked it up and took a sip. He smelled faintly of cigars. The two of them didn't speak for a few minutes.

"I'm sorry I wasn't around more this week," Ruth said, staring down at her toes. She hadn't answered his many calls since the funeral and replied to his texts with just—*I'm working*.

Joel nodded.

"It would've been nice to spend some time with you," he said after a while.

Ruth put her head in her hands and felt Joel's rough palm land on her shoulder in a loving way, but still, the weight of it made her want to shrug out from underneath it. Her dad pulled it away.

"Don't feel bad. I just don't get to see you a lot, that's all."

Ruth looked up at her father. After her mother died, she'd had a moment of accepting that Joel would die too. At the funeral, she had watched him cry over her mother's casket as it was lowered into the ground, and she acknowledged in a logical part of her brain that one day she would be alone in the world, and maybe soon. Ever since that moment, she found herself holding her father at more of a distance, even though they hadn't been very close before.

Diana had embraced Ruth with her warmth and sought her out with closeness, and had quickly taken the place of parent in Ruth's mind. Joel's remoteness seemed to Ruth like a choice, like he was happy with the arrangement, that it didn't bother him to be someone Ruth wouldn't rely on.

Joel was never the healthiest guy. He had been a smoker since he was fifteen, only quitting last year after a big fight between him and Ruth, and he drank three or four Red Stripes every night with dinner. These things worried Ruth, and she told him that, but she wasn't around enough to know if his habits had gotten any better.

"How're you doing, Dad?" Ruth asked, watching him now. She had scrolled through some old photos on her phone after she saw him get off the boat, and they confirmed what she suspected: He looked a lot older than he had just a year ago.

"Oh, I'm fine," Joel answered. "Just getting sore a lot more than before, you know."

"Are you going to the doctor regularly? Do you stretch? Walk the dog?"

"Of course I walk Hank," her dad replied, his eyebrows wrinkling, offended, not answering the other questions. She knew she had ruined the moment and that he would close now, like a clam. It was frustrating to her how touchy he could be, how closed off. It only highlighted how much more difficult it was to connect with him than it had been with her mother or Diana.

He cleared his throat.

"Listen, there's something I need to talk to you about," he said. Ruth turned and faced him. It was unlike Joel to introduce a conversation this way.

He held his hands, wringing them in a way that was familiar to Ruth, his elbows resting on the worn knees of his jeans. He looked out into the yard, away from her.

"What's going on?" Ruth asked.

"I think I'm going to sell the house," he said, then paused. "Actually, I am selling the house."

"What're you talking about?" Ruth asked.

"Well, it's big for just me, and you don't really come home that often. Somebody asked if I was interested in selling it, they made an offer, so I started considering it, and it made a lot of sense. They want to pay way more than we bought it for, and I've been wanting to travel a little, with Hank, go to some national parks before I'm too old to really enjoy them."

Joel was rambling now, and Ruth could tell he was nervous. She wondered if he remembered it was Maggie's birthday.

"When?" Ruth asked. It felt like what he was saying was coming through water.

"I'll be moving out in September," Joel said. "I was going to tell you when you stopped at the house on your way here this year, but . . . and I never thought that this would happen, with Diana."

"What're you going to do with her things?" She could hear the anger in her voice.

"Give them to you," Joel said. "Of course."

Ruth tried to think about taking her mother's things with her between Maine and Block Island. She thought about them sitting in a storage unit. It all felt wrong.

It was predictable for her father to keep running. He had been running from Maggie's death since it happened, not wanting to talk about it, shipping Ruth off to someone else, outsourcing the emotional parenting to a complete stranger. Ruth shook her head.

"Were you even going to ask me how I felt?"

"Ruth. I'm old. Selling the house for this much money is a big deal. I don't expect you to understand, but . . . maybe you can try."

As they walked in silence to the ferry, Ruth pushed her bike alongside her, the clicking of the wheel picking at her and making her anxious. After they hugged goodbye, Ruth watched Joel get on the boat alone, melding in among the couples and families. His walking was slow and labored. It made her stomach tighten to watch, and she didn't know what she was angry about now—at herself for wasting time with him while he was here or for not checking in with him more, or at him for selling the house or for his ever-present distance—but when he disappeared up the stairs, she let out a breath of relief. She wandered to the closest bench, ignoring the day-trippers and the sounds from cars rushing by, sitting in the shade. Her childhood home had been her last real anchor to stability, a place she could land if everything else in her life went south, but now that was gone. She stayed there as the ferry horn blared and the boat pulled away from the island, exiting the harbor and turning up white water until it was a speck on the way to the mainland. She wanted to cry but nothing came, only the familiar heaviness in her chest.

A family holding ice cream cones sat down next to her and pulled her out of her head. Standing, she walked back into the sun, the light blurring her vision before she spotted Charlie in the distance, alone on the sidewalk among the crowd of people dispersing from the ferry landing. Adrenaline rushed through her and she instinctively turned away from him. Her phone buzzed in her pocket. Pulling it out, she saw Charlie's name. She considered ignoring it for a second, and then, answering it, she turned around. He was walking toward her with his phone to his ear, weaving in between day-trippers to catch her.

"Hello?" Ruth said.

"I was going to come find you today. Do you have a minute? Can I talk to you?" He was walking quickly toward her like she was about to bolt away. Part of her wanted to say no, she was busy, but she didn't move, and as he got closer she put the phone down.

"Sure," she said. He was now standing in front of her.

"Okay. Thanks." He looked almost shy as they began walking together. Ruth wondered where they were going, but Charlie said nothing right away. The sun was at full strength, and people were ducking under covered porches, headed for shade. Ruth looked at the time—noon.

"How's your dad?" Charlie asked, breaking the silence. Ruth realized her face must still be wearing a heavy expression.

"I'm not really sure," she said. "The same, I guess."

Charlie nodded, his eyes on her, their concern deep and unsettling. For a second, Ruth had forgotten how much Charlie knew about her family. She remembered that she had been hesitant to talk about Maggie that first summer on Block Island. There were moments when she felt distracted by her grief—the island sparkling new in front of her, all the people she was meeting, and sometimes she felt like a new version of herself, one that hadn't lost a mother.

And Ruth sometimes forgot how much she knew about his family. Charlie's dad left them when he was twelve, had gone to San Diego for a business trip and never returned. He didn't bring any of his things with him, but called and told Charlie he could come visit him in a couple of years, though Charlie never did. If Lynn brought him up, Charlie would leave the room, and Ruth knew that he was as good as dead to Charlie.

Walking next to him now, she wondered what that would feel like, knowing your father was out there somewhere, how it would feel to be a kid anticipating a call on your birthday that wouldn't come. She imagined the secret hope that must have been suffocating. She wondered if Charlie thought about him at all, if he ever asked himself whether his father was the same person in his new life, if he wore similar clothes or made the same jokes as he had when he knew him.

"Fuck. It's hot," Charlie said, breaking Ruth out of her thoughts. "I need a swim. Can we swim first? I mean—do you want to?"

Ruth shrugged, still trying to understand what he was thinking. After the last few days and all of the changes, it felt like they shouldn't be alone with each other, like it was wrong now.

"Yeah—all right," she said. She always wore her bathing suit under her clothes on her days off.

They turned off the road onto the dunes that led down to Baby Beach. It was the same route that she and Louis had taken a week before. Ruth thought of Louis's body in the water. It was odd—that night already felt like it happened months ago. The two of them dug their toes into the hot sand, picking through groups of families until they found a clear spot. Charlie pulled off his T-shirt and dropped it to the ground while Ruth pulled her sundress up and over her head. Charlie was looking at her, she could feel it, as they headed down to the water. It was high tide, and both of them dove under a wave as it came toward them. The water was cold, and as Ruth rose, she felt her head clear and the tension in her chest dissolve. Everything smelled like salt as she took a deep breath, and the sun shone on the ripples in the water—Ruth laughed, relieved at the moment of lightness.

"What?" Charlie asked, although he was smiling too. He was still pale from the time in the city, and the sun reflected off his lightly freckled skin. Ruth admired his body—the wide shoulders, the curving muscles of his long arms. She wanted to trace the line of his pelvis with her fingers—feel the thin layer of skin against the bone.

"Okay. What did you want to talk about?" Ruth asked, trying to focus. "Where's Nadia?"

Charlie's eyes darted away and then back to her, almost too quickly to catch, although Ruth did.

"She and my mom went up to Providence for dress shopping," he said. Ruth fell back into the ocean, feeling it sway around her, thinking about the fact that they were alone on the island, that he had come to find her.

Neither of them spoke until Charlie splashed her.

"I just felt weird after the service and the restaurant, and Mom said something happened between you two. I wanted to know that you were okay," he said, the words coming out in a blurred rush.

The thought that Charlie felt pity for Ruth made everything inside her snap shut. Standing in the water, she started to make her way back to shore, her legs dragging against the current.

"I'm great," she replied, annoyed at the petulant tone in her voice as she stepped around rocks. She thought again of serving Charlie and Nadia cake the other night, and her pace quickened. Of course it was just pity. Charlie followed her out of the water onto the shore.

"Okay . . . good," he said as they walked up the beach. They didn't have towels, so they wiped their faces on their clothing, which had grown hotter sitting in the sand. She was on edge after his question. Standing next to him, she noticed how the water found paths down his body, falling in rivulets down the hair of his chest to his stomach. Beads of saltwater dotted his eyelashes like dew until he wiped his face with his shirt.

"I also need to give you some things. Things that Diana left you," he said, looking at her straight on. "I wanted to do it while they were gone . . . to give you some time in the house."

"Your mom made it pretty clear I wasn't welcome there anymore," Ruth said.

"Well, she's not there," Charlie replied.

Ruth thought of the house, the studio, the yard. It was all she wanted to be there again, to sit on the grass, to listen to the birds and the small planes drone over the ocean, to feel like Diana might still be there.

"All right, let's go," she said, picking up her things. She started to walk without waiting for him, thrilled at the thought of him trying to catch up to her.

9

They walked to where Charlie had parked Diana's truck in town. Ruth put her bike in the back and got into the passenger seat, the old gray cloth bench sagging in the places where they both sat. Dried flowers hung from the rearview mirror, and film canisters rolled around the floor. Leaning her head back, she relaxed against the soft headrest and closed her eyes, allowing her body to feel the jolting rhythm of the truck heading up the big, familiar hill toward the house.

"Do you remember the time we went to that bonfire?" Charlie said, pulling Ruth out of her head. She looked at him, the sun coming in through the windshield, his arm resting out the window, a familiar look on his face.

"When?" Ruth asked, although she remembered clearly what he was talking about. It was the same night she had been thinking about at the funeral.

"The one down on the bluffs," he said. "You know, the one where you almost fell in!" He threw his arm out and jabbed her in the side so that she squealed and recoiled from the playful touch.

"No, that never happened," Ruth said, her voice sarcastic.

She remembered that night well. She had just turned twenty, and he had just graduated college.

"You demanded that we sleep outside," Charlie replied, laughing.

Ruth recalled it again—how she fit into the crook of Charlie's arm and fell asleep smelling salt in his beard. She didn't say anything, just looked at Charlie's profile, wondering what made him bring up that moment now.

"There were so many stars," he said.

She tried to evaluate his tone. Should she tell him her feelings anyway? Tell him that he was making a mistake? That they were right together? That they understood each other? But Diana's house came into view, and Charlie coasted into the driveway.

"That was a good night," was all Ruth could think to say as he turned the car off.

Getting out of the truck, they were quiet. Ruth wanted to stay in this moment, stay playful with Charlie and ask him what he was thinking, but she felt uneasy. They walked under the green arch, not saying anything. Ruth stood in the yard—still now, and without all the chairs from the funeral, it was almost back to the way she remembered it—and soaked it in. The gold light on the green leaves, the wildflowers growing by the tree line, Diana's studio with the door standing open.

"It's almost like she could be in there," Ruth said, staring. She felt Charlie come up next to her—close but not touching.

"I know, like she's going to walk out any second. It's . . . so weird being here without her."

Ruth walked over to the studio door, looking in. Diana normally didn't like people in the studio, even to visit her, so Ruth's time inside had been limited. She usually just caught glances of Diana standing over her desk, or spotted the hem of her cuffed linen pants as she shut the door behind her for darkroom time. The one-room studio was natural wood, and the floors were splattered with chemicals that left patterns of holes in the clear varnish.

"It's . . . untouched," she said.

She walked over to the desk—a giant wooden slab. Diana had been working on a new show, but no one had known what it was, not even Ruth. There were photos on the desk that Ruth recognized from Diana's earlier collections—children running through a sprinkler, a woman smoking on a stoop, her face half in shadow. Ruth touched the photos gently, pushing them across the table and then sliding them back to their original places, wondering what Diana had been thinking about the last time she stood like this, wondering why she had pulled out these specific photos.

She wondered about how much her death had been on Diana's mind in those months leading up to June. To think of her here, alone, keeping this secret, made Ruth's heart seize as if it were breaking.

"What're you going to do with it all?" Ruth asked, turning to Charlie. "Throw it out?"

Charlie stood in the doorway, his face shadowed, the sun behind him forcing him into an outline.

"What? No. Of course not. I mean, I don't know the exact plan, but . . ." He trailed off. "I loved her too, you know. She was my family."

"She was my family too," Ruth snapped, feeling anger pour through her. She imagined Joel already packing up their house, what he must be throwing away without a thought. They stood there—tension running between them until Ruth sighed, realizing she was taking it out on Charlie.

"Sorry. Yeah. I know. It's just . . ." And she couldn't finish the sentence. She couldn't say what she was thinking because she was thinking that Diana was dead, Charlie was getting married, and she couldn't tell him he was important to her—really important. Now there was no more room for any of that. He wasn't going to be in her life anymore, not the way she wanted. She'd waited too long.

"Sorry," she said again, taking a deep breath.

Charlie leaned against the doorjamb. "It's okay."

"What else did you want to show me?" she asked, trying to bring the moment back to life.

Charlie stepped out onto the lawn and walked to the house, now illuminated by sun. Ruth stood for a moment within the frame of the doorway, watching his figure grow smaller, before she followed at a slow jog. Cicadas bleated in the trees—their cries dying out overhead. It was getting hotter as midafternoon approached. Sweat ran down Ruth's face and in between her breasts. She stuffed her hair up under her ball cap to get it off her neck. Opening the screen door, she walked into the kitchen. The room felt more welcoming than it had the other day, even though it was just as changed. The windows were open, and with a light breeze, the sun came through onto the furniture and floor. If Ruth could forget what was gone, then she could imagine she was in the house alone or that Diana was taking a nap upstairs after a long night in the studio, and her body would feel more at ease.

"Up here!" Charlie called.

Ruth turned the corner into the dining room and went up the steep, narrow staircase. She loved the smell of old wood that permeated the house, the faint must that clung to the wallpaper from all the ocean air and open windows. She rounded the landing and stopped in the hallway. Diana's room was to her right, door closed. On the left was the first guestroom. She couldn't stop herself from peeking in as she walked past. Charlie and Nadia had pushed together the twin beds. They were unmade, the sheets and comforter pulled back. Ruth noticed the pillows so close together, the underwear on the floor, the expensive luggage overflowing with beautifully colored clothing. She snapped back before Charlie might catch her staring and stepped up to the last bedroom that used to be hers, leaning against the doorframe.

Although Ruth hadn't lived in the house for five years, Diana had kept some of her touches there even as it was turned into a guest room. There were photos Diana had taken of Ruth on the walls. She had always thought it was strange that Diana wanted

Ruth's room to have photos of her in it, but Diana insisted that she liked them, that in the winter when Ruth was gone, she would come and sit, and it was nice for her to see Ruth there. Looking at the photos, trying not to cry, she was surprised that Lynn hadn't already taken them down. Ruth's blanket was still folded at the foot of the bed, and an earring tree Diana had given her stood empty on the dresser. Charlie was on his knees, bent over to retrieve something from under the bed frame.

"Is this a secret?" Ruth asked, worried, even though no one was home.

"Well, no—but also yes," Charlie said from the ground. Ruth waited for him to continue. "At the hospital, I was with Diana, and she told me some things to take care of—to do. She had a will, but she wanted to add some last things. The will has been taking a long time—it's stressing Mom out."

Ruth had never expected Diana to have a will. She was disorganized and hated paperwork more than anything, always calling Ruth in a frustrated rage when it was time for her to renew her license or apply for permits with the town.

Ruth ignored the mention of Lynn and looked at the box. She lowered herself down to the floor and sat, staring at it.

"I just didn't want you to wait for some pieces of her that she wanted you to have," he said, and Ruth's adrenaline raced.

"I'll be downstairs when you're done—or—well, just call if you need me."

Charlie left the room, and Ruth listened as the floorboards creaked on his way downstairs. She stared at the box for a minute longer and then pulled it up onto the bed. It was heavy. The mattress sank in a familiar way around her. Ruth thought about all the nights she spent there sleeping soundly after working all day and playing in the sun—innocent. She thought of touching herself alone in the dark when Charlie was in the other room.

She held the box in her lap for a full five minutes, looking at the lid. She reached to take it off a few times, but kept stopping herself for reasons she didn't understand. Each time she nearly opened it, she thought of Charlie downstairs, of the conversation left hanging. The void of grief was pulling at her. If she opened it, she knew that she would be sucked down, that whatever was inside would make her face a truth she wasn't ready for—some finality to Diana's life that she was not willing to accept. Diana—reduced to a box. No, she wasn't going to do it. Later, she decided.

Before heading back downstairs, Ruth stopped in the upstairs bathroom and closed the door. The half curtain on the open window fluttered as a breeze came through. Ruth glanced around the room while she peed, picking up Nadia's makeup bag and looking inside. There were a few tubes of nice concealer that Ruth opened and patted on the back of her hand, a Chanel lipstick, and a pot of expensive-looking face sunscreen. Ruth thought of the giant tub of cheap sunblock that she and Lucy shared, which smelled like plastic but was only five bucks at the department store. Ruth put the makeup bag back and looked down at the inside of her bikini bottoms. There was something beige there and Ruth picked it up in alarm, holding the piece of latex covered in discharge between her fingers. For a second her mind was blank, not registering what she held, before recognition flooded her and her other hand went to her mouth. She stared at the curved piece of broken condom that had fallen out of her sometime during the morning.

Ruth thought of the darkness of the boat, the wrapper on the floor, and couldn't remember the condom breaking. She continued to stare at the piece of rubber without seeing it, blind fear pulsing within her. She counted back the days, trying to multiply them into hours since she and Louis had sex, but already knew it was too late to get emergency contraception, not that there was a pharmacy on the island anyways. Ruth ripped toilet paper from the roller and wrapped the piece of condom up several times, throwing it in the trash. Standing and flushing, she stared in the bathroom mirror, listening to the sound of the old toilet, and washing her hands robotically.

"It's fine," she said aloud to herself. Then, looking at the box sitting on the ground, Ruth thought of Charlie downstairs. She realized her hands were shaking.

Box in her arms, Ruth sped down the stairs. Charlie was sitting on the couch, his glasses on, reading a John Steinbeck novel. Ruth felt a strong desire in that moment to walk up behind him and tousle his hair, even though it was so short now—to trace the shape of his ears, feel the soft space where his neck met his skull. She watched him at ease for a second before coming around the couch.

Charlie looked at her, and for a split second Ruth thought he knew what she had just found.

"What was in it?" he asked.

"I haven't opened it yet," she said, her heart still racing. "Wait, didn't you put this together?"

"No. It was like that already. She only told me to find the teal box and to make sure you got it."

Whatever was in the box, Diana had assembled it, had made it ready for her. Looking at it, however, she didn't feel curiosity, only a painful drag of awareness that Diana was gone.

"So when are Lynn and Nadia getting back?" she asked, stalling.

Charlie looked at his watch. It looked expensive, Ruth thought. She couldn't remember him wearing something like that before.

"The eight P.M. ferry, I think."

"Let's go back to the beach," she said. "We can go to Rodman's Hollow, hike down to Black Rock, and swim again. It's too hot to do anything else."

Charlie took a deep breath and looked at Ruth with tired eyes, although she couldn't read his expression.

"Don't you want to know what's in there?" he asked.

"Not right now," she said. His gaze was steady, taking her in, and she couldn't help but feel like he was trying to read her mind. The attention made her uneasy, like it always had.

"I don't know . . ." Charlie trailed off.

Ruth only shrugged, as if it didn't really matter to her.

"Beautiful day to spend inside," she said. The box was heavy, and holding it filled her with a high-strung feeling, like Charlie had to say yes or she would be alone with the box and her thoughts, which would cause her to snap.

Charlie looked out the window, and she could tell he was thinking it through.

"What's the harm?" she asked.

He seemed to consider that, and Ruth wondered what he was thinking. Was he wondering whether he wanted to spend time with her, or whether Nadia would be angry if he did?

"All right," he said.

Ruth felt her shoulders drop, relief washing through her. She left the box on the countertop. Charlie ran off and returned shortly with a backpack, two towels rolled up and stuffed out the top. They filled their waters and left through the side door, the screen door slamming, making them both jump.

"God, I love that sound," Ruth said, the lightness from earlier returning.

Charlie laughed. "I forgot how sentimental you are," he said, shaking his head and grabbing his bike from the side of the house.

"How can you not love that?" Ruth asked, motioning back to the door.

"It's loud and broken. It doesn't have to be like that," he replied.

"You're missing its charm."

"Everything has charm to you." He jumped up onto the truck, lowering Ruth's bike down to her.

He looked at her sideways and pushed off, pedaling away, shaking his head with a smirk. Ruth pushed off too, and pedaled hard to catch up with him.

10

As they hiked down to the beach through the green unmarked trails that she knew by heart, Ruth was overwhelmed with the sensation that time had stopped—that it was circular or that, somehow, this moment was not real at all. The honeysuckle nearly fell out over them from the brush—the fragrant, vaginal flowers luring them in with buttery tongues of petals. Charlie insisted on leading the way, although he had admittedly forgotten where to go, and at each fork in the path he'd turn back to Ruth to await her direction.

"How do you forget this?" she asked, pointing to the path on the left. "You've been coming here since you were a kid."

"I know. I haven't been out in a while though . . ." Charlie trailed off. She wondered if he was feeling guilty for visiting Diana less in the past few years.

"You've been busy," Ruth said, thinking of Nadia, trying to mask any emotion. Nevertheless, Charlie looked back at her.

"I've been busy," he repeated, turning away.

They approached another unmarked fork in the trail. The hedges ran so high they couldn't see beyond them, like in a maze. The left trail grew dusty as it went downhill. The other remained green—wildflowers swaying in the occasional breeze.

"Wait, let me guess," Charlie said, stopping short. She nearly slammed into his back, but Ruth couldn't help but smile as he rotated, the smirk returning to his face. Then he pointed to the left.

She laughed and nodded. They walked on in silence.

Ruth thought again how it felt like it used to, when they would hike for hours across secret trails on the island, ending up on an empty beach and pretending that they were marooned, that they were searching for treasure, coming away with driftwood and fishbones bleached white from the sun. She was embarrassed thinking of how those trinkets had followed her between apartments, how they were sitting on her windowsill back at the cottage right now.

"So—you're getting married." Ruth could hear her voice layered in fake excitement. "That's . . . wild," she said, trying to correct her tone.

Charlie chuckled. "Is it?" he asked.

"Honestly?" Ruth responded. "Yes, it seems crazy to me anytime anyone gets married. Especially when I know them."

"You don't believe in marriage?" Charlie's tone was casual, unaffected. He didn't break stride or look back at her. The absence of his gaze allowed Ruth to answer almost as if she were daydreaming.

"No. I do believe in it—I want it in theory—but when I see other people doing it . . . it always seems like a mistake to me. It doesn't make much sense. They just seem so young."

"A lot of people get married way younger than thirty," he said.

She thought about her parents, her few friends from the island who had gotten married, but mostly she could only think of the countless engagement announcements she saw online from people she went to high school or college with—the ring, the dress, how for months afterward they seemed consumed with that one single day. The people in those photos all still looked like the teenagers they were when she knew them, and Ruth always thought that it was like children playing "wedding." She knew the thought was judgmental. She had only shared it with Lucy, who didn't believe in marriage anyway.

Ruth remembered sitting once with her mother on their front stoop, where the last of the sun would land. She couldn't remember now what had prompted Maggie's words, whether Ruth was upset about a boy at school, but she remembered the faraway look her mother got in her eye as she spoke.

"One day, you'll have a first love and it will end and it will hurt. You'll see them move on, get married, become a stranger, and you'll be sad, but it will be okay. You will be okay."

Ruth thought about it now—about Charlie getting married and becoming a stranger. It didn't feel okay.

Charlie paused in front of another fork, and Ruth pointed left. They continued walking.

"Maybe you're just not in that place in your life then," he said.

Ruth considered that. She thought about marrying someone, but the image of the other person was blank in her mind. She looked at Charlie and was reminded of a time when she used to imagine marrying him. Even as she loved Charlie now, she didn't fantasize about marrying him like she used to. She used to hang on his words when they would talk about his future and wonder how she would fit into it. She was young then, and the thought of that kind of surrender to someone made her feel conflicted now. She had her own life on the island. She had her rhythm. The idea of someone new fitting into it at this point seemed less and less likely. Charlie seemed like the only person who might.

"We're not so far apart, you and I," she said, trying not to sound defensive.

Charlie exhaled. "In age no—but . . . don't get mad."

"What?" she asked.

"I mean, we're not far apart in age, but maybe we're just at different points in our lives," Charlie answered. "Maybe we want different things."

"How do you mean?" Ruth asked, trying to understand what

Charlie might think she wanted when she didn't even know herself. She had always felt that aside from when he was on the island, Charlie moved in realms she only partially understood. Sometimes he talked about stocks in a way that made Ruth think he was joking, or he'd tell her about his home renovation projects in the city, showing her everything he was doing over video calls. Ruth would picture painting a room with Charlie, music playing in the background, paint getting on their hands and clothes. She didn't hate the thought—she yearned for it even—but then she would look at the battered walls of whatever month-to-month rental she was in and come back to reality.

"Well, for example, I've been at this job for a while now. I've gotten promoted. I have a community in the city. . . . I'm pretty settled," he said.

Ruth wrinkled her nose at the word—*settled.* It sounded like he didn't even fully understand what he was trying to explain. To Ruth, it wasn't that they were at different points in their lives, but that they had different circumstances altogether. He had money and she didn't.

"So you can only get married if you're an accountant with a mortgage?" Ruth asked. She felt like Charlie was putting her into a box, relegating her to a life she hadn't agreed to.

"No, that's not what I mean," he said. "You know—I want a family. I want to be married. I want to have kids. I'm just . . . ready to start moving toward that life."

Ruth almost stopped walking. She thought she knew Charlie well, but she had never heard him talk about a family before, about kids. To her the two of them still seemed like they were seventeen.

They walked on in silence for a moment before Charlie looked back at Ruth.

"Do you want kids?" he asked.

The image of the broken piece of condom flashed in her mind. "I don't know," she said, her heart rate quickening. It wasn't something that Ruth often thought about. A few of her friends were parents, and although she was almost thirty, it was something that still felt like it might happen in another life—maybe to another person.

"You would be a good mom," Charlie said.

"Thanks." She yanked a tall blade of canary grass from the trail and started wrapping it around her fingers, fidgeting. When she thought of caring for someone, mothering someone, she was brought back to the months Maggie declined rapidly, how Ruth was there with a hand on her forehead, hoping she didn't have a fever, how she cleaned her mother's clothes. She knew that it wasn't the same—someone at the end of their life and a baby just at the beginning—but it tainted the thought of parenting with a sadness she was worried she couldn't erase.

There was a part of Ruth, too, that felt resentful whenever she observed mothers with their babies. When she waited on families at the restaurant, the mother always seemed locked in on the child, her face hovering over the stroller, her own food mostly untouched, while her husband was absorbed in his meal, absolved from the concern. Watching them, it seemed like the parents were in different worlds, and Ruth always wondered whether she had what it took to be in a mother's world, and whether she even wanted to be there.

But now she started imagining Charlie as a father, walking with a toddler sitting on his shoulders. It was easy to picture. She tried to think of herself pregnant, her body round with her hand on her belly. She felt her palms start to sweat.

"Anyways, sorry to get heavy," Charlie said.

"It's not heavy," Ruth said, although she heard the uneasiness in her voice.

"Have you been writing?" Charlie asked. The question surprised her.

Ruth thought about her journal and the words she put down on the page, only to abandon it. She thought about how hopeful she had been at seventeen, and all of Diana's encouragement. She hadn't told Charlie or anyone else about the fight last Christmas. For a second, she considered telling him now, but thought better of it.

"Not at the moment," Ruth replied.

"You should be writing, Ruth!" Charlie shouted, stopping fully and turning around to look at her.

"Why?"

"Because it's your passion. I loved how happy you sounded when you were working on something. I'm still mad you never sent me a story. You said you would. Plus, you should be moving toward something—whatever it is. You know, taking steps."

"You sound like a self-help podcast." Ruth tried to ignore the memory of Diana saying the same thing, even as she thought about how stuck she'd been feeling—how everything had seemed stale. After a moment, feeling prickly, she countered, "Accounting is your passion?"

"No, but . . . I don't know that I have a work passion. I like doing a good job. I like coming home, living my life, you know. I feel like it's different for you."

Ruth's eyebrows furrowed. "What do you mean? I work at the same restaurant I have for the past five years. I live like a seasonal nomad. How can you call that a passionate lifestyle?"

"You're going to do something out there." He gestured out with his arms. "I feel it. You just need to start taking steps."

"Now you sound like a fortune cookie," Ruth said, although she had softened toward him. Why when people believed in her, did she have to shut them down? Her throat grew thick at the thought of all of Diana's belief in her, how it had gone nowhere—wasted energy.

Charlie laughed.

They approached another fork, and Ruth pointed left. Her eyebrows were still furrowed. Charlie looked at her.

"You're mad," he said.

"I'm not," she replied.

"Liar."

"I just disagree," she admitted.

Charlie shrugged. "You and Diana were so similar. . . . I don't know."

Ruth considered this. Had they been similar? Was she nearly

as passionate? Ruth had always looked at Diana as someone who she aspired to be, someone whose life she admired but was ultimately unattainable.

"What's your theory then? What's next for you?" Charlie asked, breaking her reverie.

"Are you asking me what my five-year plan is, Charlie?" Ruth asked, a smile breaking on her lips.

"Yeah, maybe I am, Ruth," he replied, his tone matching hers.

Ruth thought about the question and her feeling of restlessness returned. She was too old to quit the service industry and get an entry-level job somewhere else, and she could make more money busing tables or tending bar than she could with anything from her English degree at this point. It was what she had been telling herself for years. And yet, the idea of going to the restaurant tomorrow without any kind of a greater plan suddenly flooded her with dread, a feeling she now realized had been building for some time. Writing? She hadn't written anything longer than a journal entry in years. She wasn't a writer.

"I've got nothing for you there," she said to Charlie, feeling depleted.

"You'll figure it out," he said. "I'm confident about this. We're not so different. I was joking, really."

Ruth suddenly saw it clearly, the vast difference between the lives they led. The gulf she had been watching expand between her and Charlie since the funeral had reopened. She wanted to fight her way back to the closeness they used to have, the spark she felt, the comfort that existed in Charlie's orbit, without thinking about the future.

They walked along until Charlie stopped, swinging his backpack around and pulling out his water bottle. Ruth watched his hands. She imagined a wedding ring on his finger.

"Isn't it odd that women have the whole engagement ring thing, and men have nothing? I guess in the traditional way, at least," she said.

"You just said *traditional* like it was a dirty word." Charlie laughed, then took another sip from his water bottle. "I don't think it's weird."

"Would you have been upset if Nadia proposed to you? With an engagement ring and everything?" Ruth tried to imagine Nadia doing that. The image didn't get too far.

"You're trying to make me sound like a . . . misogynist."

Ruth laughed. "Would you have been?" she asked again.

"Pleading the fifth," he said.

Ruth nodded. "So, how'd you two meet?"

Charlie didn't answer right away, and Ruth worried she had crossed a line somehow.

"We met in the city—through a friend."

"Like a setup?"

"Kind of, yeah—we were invited to dinner, then it became a double date, you know?" Charlie replied, walking again. While Ruth understood, she had never experienced anything like that before. Her dating history was thin and short. In Maine, men and women flirted with her from across the bar, came back a few nights in a row, and eventually slid their numbers back to her on their receipts. Sometimes she ended up in their beds, unable to sleep, flannel sheets scratching against her bare skin. She would look around their houses while they slept, slink off to the bathroom trying not to make a sound as she filed away the details of their lives in her mind—a Carl Jung book on the nightstand, a taxidermy fox by a fireplace, a collection of antique pots hanging from the kitchen ceiling, an old lab who watched her pass without raising his head. She usually left before they woke up, would sometimes return a few times over a winter, but when she moved away in the summer, she always stopped responding to their messages, and when she saw them the next winter, they were icy. She didn't blame them, although she also didn't feel bad. She never made any promises, and she could never justify spending much time with someone unless she was infatuated with them. She didn't get the point of mediocre encounters.

Summer hookups were easier. No one expected anything to last. It was what she appreciated so much about Louis.

Watching Charlie walk in front of her, his head tilted toward the ground, it seemed like he didn't want to continue the conversation, and Ruth realized that this was the first time in ten years they had ever talked about romantic partners.

"When was that?" Ruth asked. "The setup."

"We met in September," Charlie said.

Ruth counted back in her head—ten months. Charlie had been in a serious relationship for the past ten months and she'd had no idea.

"When did you propose?" she asked. She sounded robotic.

"Right after Diana, I guess . . . early June."

Somehow the fact that all this time Charlie had been in a relationship—a serious relationship—that Ruth knew nothing about made her feel more unmoored and confused. She couldn't shrug it off as nothing, as an obvious mistake. They'd had nearly a year of experiences together, and the thought that she'd spent the last weeks planning how she was going to tell him what she felt, while he was planning a wedding, made Ruth infuriated at herself.

There was no real reason why he should've called to tell her he was thinking about proposing. She understood that on some level, but somehow she still felt like it was a betrayal.

"A whirlwind romance," she said, counting the months again.

"I mean, it's been almost a year. Not that much of a whirlwind. . . . And when you know, you know, I guess," Charlie replied.

Ruth raised an invisible eyebrow at the platitude, but she had nothing to say in response. There were very few things in her life that she felt like she *knew*—everything else felt elastic, ebbing and flowing. She knew Block Island was the place for her, and she also knew that it was probably impossible for her to ever really live there. She knew that life ended quickly and all at once, and people were gone before you wanted them to be.

"You think it's too fast," Charlie said, interrupting her thought. "It's why I didn't tell you sooner."

Stunned, Ruth considered what to say. She wondered if that was the real reason. But before she could respond, the path veered left and the open ocean appeared in front of them—wide and blue. They watched from their vantage point as waves broke against the rocky shore in a white glaze before retreating back to the ocean. The Southeast Lighthouse stood atop the bluffs of clay in the distance, looking precariously close to the edge from this angle. Time had eroded the large lawn that used to be between the lighthouse and the bluffs. The island was shrinking, Ruth thought.

"Wow," Charlie said, looking at the view. She only nodded, the lost thought still perched on the edge of her tongue. They maneuvered over rocks to a gap in the bushes where a thin rope attached to an old wooden post dangled down the steep path. Charlie grabbed onto it and climbed down the short, sloping cliff to the beach below. Ruth followed behind him, dexterous in her movements. At the last step, Charlie jumped off a small boulder to reach flat ground before turning to hold out his hand for Ruth. Grabbing it, she stepped off the rock, landing close to him. He lingered there for a beat, long enough to make her step back. She was reeling between which version of them they were right now. There had never been a time, apart from when they weren't speaking, that they were ever just friends—friends without any sort of romantic tension. There had never been a time when the line had been firmly drawn. So now it felt like every word was still flirtatious, but how could it be? They walked over the rocks, toward the sand. The water was much rougher here than in town, and the bluffs rose up behind them like a wall, the ocean wild in front of them. Ruth looked up and down the beach. There was no one else there.

Pulling her dress off to reveal her bathing suit, she dropped it on the sand, making her way to the water, which rose up and crashed at her feet, scrambling the rocks beneath her. She waded through the calmer tide pools, through the white water to the wave break, diving under just as a wave curved and arched before its crash. Beneath the water, she could feel the breaking wave roll over the top of her head, the momentum pushing her back. The current was strong. She emerged and turned, bobbing for a moment. Looking back at Charlie, she tried to wave him in, but he shook his head from the shore.

"It's too rough for me!" he shouted, and another wave came that she had to duck under. Ruth was a strong swimmer. She normally enjoyed the push and pull of the ocean—taking relief in a force that was larger than her—but now Ruth felt the intensity of the undertow, and for a second she stopped pushing against it, and a creeping thought came to her mind as she felt the tug of the ocean bringing her farther out to sea. She considered giving in to that feeling, allowing herself to be swept away. She imagined how small the island would look from the distance, how untethered she would feel from it all—like a balloon let go of by a distracted child, their small grip relaxing for only a second. She wondered what it would feel like to drift away—to disappear.

The ocean sparkled, choppy waves moving toward her, so that she had to duck underwater every other breath. She felt her heart beating in her ears and her breath quicken. Ships throughout history had wrecked off this point, the strong currents and rocky bottom breaking the hull, filling it with water. In the winter, the unlucky sailors washed up on the shore frozen solid, ice coating their skin.

Another set of waves was coming in, larger than before. Looking back, she saw Charlie stand and walk down to the water's edge, his hand shielding his eyes from the sun. He seemed concerned. For a long second, she questioned whether she had the will to get herself back to shore, felt the exhaustion of fighting before she even tried, and was taken aback at her own passivity. Looking at Charlie, she pressed the dark apathy to the corner of her mind and began to swim.

Pushing against the water, she caught the next few waves

and rode them in, so she was once again in the calm shallows, her stomach touching the sand, her face only a few inches above the tidepool's surface. Trying to slow her breathing, she could feel Charlie's eyes on her and her cheeks burned, the image of the tiny island still echoing in her mind. She had scared herself, how quickly her mind went to giving up.

"Are you okay?" Charlie asked.

Ruth nodded, still staring down into the tidepool.

This close to the water, she saw tiny fragments of seaweed pass under her eyes, noticed their translucence in the light. Sand particles glittered and a hermit crab scuttled past Ruth's hand. She watched the trail it made, the glinting sunlight on the sand shifting as the surface of the water trembled. She stared for a while to calm herself down and watched the liminal space of the tidepool, the thin lip of water that contained so much life so that Ruth wondered about the barriers between her world and its world, about the gulfs that could not be crossed no matter how much she wished, about all the impossible distances. A rippling wave moved through the tidepool, picked the creatures up and moved them slightly closer to the shore. Ruth watched them keep swimming as if nothing had happened.

Feeling Charlie above her, Ruth pushed herself up, water cascading from her body. They walked back up the beach together, hopping from rock to rock until all became gritty sand, where Charlie had laid out the towels. He was looking at her again.

Ruth's body had changed in the past few years—away from her old effortless and trim figure and toward hips and thighs, a stomach that folded in on itself when she crouched and breasts that moved when she walked. She felt older, fuller—she took up more space than she had even a few years ago. The expanse from that twenty-four-year-old body to now seemed impossible to recross. She was changed. In some moments this fullness made her feel strong and alive, and in others she felt the quickening fear of time, of permanent change, sweep over her. She felt the heavier way her body landed as it ran, remembering clearly still how it felt to be sixteen and run for hours without getting tired, the springy way she used to move. Charlie pulled off his shirt and sat on the towel. He began tracing lines in the sand with a small stick. Ruth sat down next to him, her body dripping wet.

"Do you feel older?" Ruth asked, leaning back. She was aware of the sunlight glinting off the water droplets on her body.

"Well . . . sure, but how do you mean?" Charlie asked.

"When you think about yourself at twenty-one, does that person feel familiar to you? Do you think you're that same person?"

Charlie kept drawing circles in the sand, and Ruth watched him, wondering what he was thinking.

"I don't like to think of myself then," Charlie said after a minute.

"Why not?" Ruth asked, sitting up, not expecting this response. A crowd of seagulls barked nearby. Their moaning was loud and persistent.

"I don't know . . . dumb choices . . . wasted time," he said, trailing off, flicking sand away with his stick.

Ruth's body began to pulse with adrenaline. "Wasted time?"

Charlie looked up from his sand circles into Ruth's face, and for a second she was sure he was talking about them—how they wasted time with each other. But Charlie leaned back, opening his body to the sun, his arms supporting him, his elbow in the sand.

"Just stupid decisions, I guess," he said.

Ruth felt like he was deflecting. "I don't think you were that bad," she said.

She tried hard to remember Charlie as he was then. There was a sweetness, an openness that emanated from him in the way he cared for people. She wondered if Nadia saw that same openness or if it was a version of him that only Ruth would get to know, one that had faded or maybe just shifted as he had gotten older. Even now, Ruth could tell she was making him uncomfortable with her questions, although it was what they always used to do, and she remembered the look on his face from back then—eager to examine his own mind with Ruth, as if it were a game. His past openness had felt so . . . loving. It was the only word Ruth could think of for it. She had felt loved even though that was never something spoken between them.

"You've always been too lenient with me," Charlie replied.

"So be it," Ruth said, but she wondered if it was true.

Looking at Charlie, Ruth tried to really see him as he was now, without thinking of the past. She realized then that for all she knew about his life outside of Block Island, it existed only in her head. For all he had told her about during their phone calls, of his house, his friends, it was all imagined. But Nadia had been there for all of it. Nadia knew what his friends were like at a dinner party. She knew how late he slept on a Sunday morning, she knew the particular mess of his room, because she was there.

And suddenly Ruth wondered why she had spent so much time holding on to something that was so fragmentary and never asking for more. Why did she love that she never had to commit to Charlie, that they never had to call it real—to call it anything? Now, as whatever they had was slipping away, she thought of Nadia somewhere shopping for bridal gowns, imagined her twirling in front of a mirror, asking herself how she wanted to look on her wedding day.

"What about you? Do you feel old?" Charlie asked. "How do you feel about your former selves?" His tone felt slightly mocking.

"Do you not like my questions?" Ruth asked, trying to ground herself back into the moment. Now she was the one trying to deflect. Charlie raised an eyebrow at her, indicating that he knew what she was doing. She sighed.

Ever since Diana died, Ruth had been thinking often of herself at seventeen. There had been other meaningful summers, but that one still rang out as the start of everything, the time when she felt the most vulnerable, cracked open by grief and life—the most open. It sparkled in her memory, and it felt a hundred years in the past. She considered the girl she was the year after her mother died, when she first met Charlie, the way the island had been the perfect landing ground, how she had immersed herself into it, letting it swallow her whole. Thinking about that girl felt like thinking about a child, although not much had really changed since then.

"You can do it," Charlie coaxed, and for a second Ruth felt like she didn't want to tell him her inner thoughts. She felt like he might not understand them.

"I really want to know," Charlie added, and Ruth felt him tugging on a line to bring her nearer to him.

"I like her," Ruth said. "I like that person, but no, she feels like someone else."

"What do you mean?"

"She was so fragile. I guess I feel old in that I don't feel fragile anymore. I don't feel much. I don't believe in the things that I used to."

"You don't believe in things? Who are you? Nietzsche?" Charlie laughed, his eyebrows raised. Ruth laughed at herself too. She felt like she had said too much.

"No, it's just that life could be anything. How do you completely believe in any one choice? When it could have gone a million other ways had you done something different? And then it doesn't matter because something dumb can happen and you get hit by a car, or get in a ski accident, or you get cancer and die."

Once Ruth started talking she couldn't stop, like this feeling had been expanding, unnoticed, within her for a long time, slowly taking up space. Charlie looked like he wanted to comfort Ruth, so she kept speaking to avoid his words.

"You're going along, and then suddenly those core memories have passed, and you're talking about golden days? It scares the shit out of me," she said.

"Do you feel like things have passed you by?" Charlie asked.

Ruth turned to Charlie. She thought of what it would look like, really look like, to be with him, to hold his hand walking down the street, to come home after work and see him reading a John Steinbeck novel on the couch. She had never stayed with anyone long enough to talk to them about her anxieties, or to learn to rely on them—to expect them to show up for her when she needed them, to allow them to. Charlie was the closest she ever had to that. And she didn't have him at all.

"Yeah, maybe," Ruth said.

"But we're talking about golden days right now," Charlie replied, breaking Ruth's daydream.

Ruth fell back onto her towel. She felt the sun hot on her skin, the bright light orange behind her closed eyelids. The depleted feeling returned. She wished the sun would burn it away.

"I like your questions," Charlie said. "I was just kidding."

"Nadia doesn't grill you about your thoughts on life?" Ruth asked. She felt like she should whisper Nadia's name.

"Not like this," Charlie said. "It's more a conversation than an interrogation."

"Sorry."

"I'm just kidding."

She thought about reaching across the expanse between their towels in the sand and pressing her body against his, hers wet and cold and his hot and dry. She thought how the kiss would taste of the ocean water still dripping down her face, and imagined them peeling off their bathing suits and having sex right there on the beach. How afterward they would lie on the sand naked and fall asleep, waking up only when the tide rose high enough to lick their toes.

There had been times when they had come close before, their bodies pressed together in the cold sand by the dunes until she was breathless, his hands all over her, or once when Diana was away at the farmer's market, Ruth in his bed, the smell of him everywhere—sunscreen, Irish Spring soap, the floral shampoo he used whose scent she could never put her finger on.

Something always stopped them from going further—a late-night walker on the beach, the sound of Diana's truck coming up the driveway—and they'd quickly pull apart and rejoin the group by the fire or go to their separate rooms in the house. Ruth remembered those moments after they separated, her heart still racing, her body alive, left confused and wanting. It was hard to look at him afterward. And his week on the island was always over too soon for them to have another chance to talk about it. As time went on, she had the sense those memories were becoming warped and slipping away from reality, that she couldn't hold on to them. She told herself she had romanticized the way his hand felt holding her head, or the feeling of his lips on hers, that it wasn't as good as she remembered.

The last time they had been to Black Rock together, six years ago now, had been the closest call. It was the day after their bad date, and Ruth remembered the feeling of Charlie pulling the tie of her bikini top off on this same spot of beach, of her skin exposed to the sun. She recalled his mouth on her, his finger curled over the lip of her bikini bottoms, about to tug them down, when they heard rocks falling overhead and looked up to see a group of hikers scrambling their way down the treacherous path, holding on to the rope. It had been Charlie's last day on the island. He left on the eight o'clock ferry that night, and they grew more distant after that, and the next summer was when he stopped coming out for the full week. But even the years following, when they'd only have a couple of days together, she and Charlie would sit at the table under the beech tree long after Diana went to bed, a bottle of wine between them, talking, the night stretching out before them, as she wondered if one of them was going to cross the line.

"What're you thinking about?" Charlie asked, and Ruth somehow felt like he knew the answer.

She wondered whether Charlie even remembered the last time they were here, whether it had crossed his mind as they climbed down the bluff, or if it was forgotten—just another almost. And Ruth was suddenly overcome and frustrated by all of the almosts, of the late nights wanting to say what was on her mind, what she felt like she knew he was thinking too. Maybe it was because it was too late. He was engaged. It didn't matter now.

"The last time we were here," she said.

"Oh," Charlie replied, looking at the sand.

The moment hung in the air between them, and Ruth watched as Charlie put the stick down and leaned over his knees, staring at the ocean.

"I think about that day . . . sometimes," Ruth said, surprising herself. It was almost as if the words slipped out on their own. "What might have happened."

The waves were crashing louder now, high tide creeping in closer to where they sat. Ruth smelled the ocean spray in the air, felt the forceful beat of her heart, the blood rushing through her.

"Me too," Charlie said.

She squinted into the sun toward him.

He shielded his eyes, looking at her.

Ruth laid back and stretched out on the towel, her hands above her, fingers dipping into the sand, and although everything was different now, she lied to herself and decided it was that day, that no time had passed, that they could pick up where they left off.

She took a deep breath.

"Come here," she said, exhaling.

She waited. Everything inside her was still. Her eyes closed again. The sun was hot against her cheeks, and she started to feel nervous, until she felt his shadow fall over her. Taking a breath, she opened her eyes and Charlie was above her, blocking out the sun. His expression was difficult to read, intense, his eyes scanning her face. Looking at him, Ruth could feel the erasure of the last ten years, could ignore the changes in her body, their bodies, could forget the woman shopping for wedding dresses, because in front of her was Charlie and he was the anchor to Ruth's past.

She pushed herself up onto her elbow, and now their faces were inches apart. Looking down at his lips, then up into his eyes, she was about to close the distance, but then, stunned, she felt herself hold back. Her certainty wavered, and she didn't know what she was asking for anymore—to be together now? To go back in time and do things the way she wished they went? What would it mean?

"Ruth?" Charlie asked. His face was uncertain, although he didn't move away.

There was a moment when Ruth didn't breathe, and Charlie said nothing. She was about to pull away and apologize, the tension too much.

"Wait," Charlie said, and his hand lifted, his fingers slid through the wet hair behind Ruth's ear.

He looked at her lips but didn't move.

Ruth felt Charlie's breath against her mouth. She was sure he was going to close the gap and kiss her. If either of them twitched, their lips would touch, but then, quickly, he leaned away, letting his hand drop gently from behind her head.

He sat back and looked at her. Ruth couldn't tell what he was thinking. Her blood was pulsing in her ears. He seemed torn, angry.

She should just tell him, she thought. Tell him that he was making a mistake. Tell him that they should be together.

"Charlie?"

"Yeah?"

Ruth paused.

Charlie's phone started to ring.

11

Charlie let his phone ring for a second before turning from Ruth and reaching across the sand. A photo of Nadia in a rose garden filled his screen—her smile wide and beautiful, the picture caught mid-laugh. Charlie answered the call.

"Hey, babe, how's it going?"

Charlie leaned away, and Ruth watched the curve of his spine become more pronounced as he curled over his legs. A wave crashed loudly. She felt cold.

"What's that? Yeah, I'm at the beach."

Ruth wondered what he was going to say. Adrenaline was running through her chest. She didn't move.

"Yeah, I'm by myself. Just reading." Ruth looked away, embarrassed. The image of the Steinbeck book flashed before her eyes, left on the couch armrest. "Okay, so what time? Okay, yeah, love you too."

As the words *love you* left Charlie's mouth, Ruth felt her stomach flip. She stared at the ground, her eyes out of focus.

Charlie put the phone down onto the towel, and neither of them said anything for a moment, Ruth still looking at the same spot—a tiny sand spider crawling across the surface of the beach, scuttling up a trail, and hopping underneath the closest rock.

"They're on the boat right now coming back. I guess the dresses were bad. . . . We have to go." He pushed himself up, sprinkling Ruth with flecks of sand. "Sorry," he said.

She stood slowly. Her body was still wet.

Back on the trail, Charlie let Ruth lead, no longer wasting any time. Neither of them spoke. Their footsteps were the only sound between them, and Ruth was glad she was in front so she could hide her face. She felt anxious in the silence but didn't know what to say. Replaying it in her head, she kept thinking of the way he looked at her, his hand behind her head, his lips inches away.

They emerged at the mouth of the trail where the bikes were. Pulling them out of the rack, they walked to the top of the dirt road to where the trail pulled off into the street. A Jeep drove past them, blasting loud electronic music. The sound grated against Ruth, ripping her out of her head. They mounted their bikes, and Ruth looked at Charlie. He was staring at the ground.

"Charlie—" Ruth said, but he interrupted her.

"Will you come get the box and take it home? I don't know when I could get it to you next."

His voice was not unkind, but he seemed distant, and Ruth knew she had broken something—some mutual understanding. The image of him pulling away from her on the sand replayed again in her mind, and she became self-conscious. She had forgotten about the box. Nodding, she turned her bike, and they pedaled off in the direction of Diana's house. The sun had moved up and over the island in the late afternoon and was falling down on the other side. It was approaching magic hour, and the oppressive heat of the day had been exchanged for a warm breeze. Everything looked dipped in gold. It might have been the most beautiful night of the summer so far, but Ruth saw none of it.

Eventually they approached the driveway, and Ruth slid to a stop.

"I'll wait here," she said.

"Okay," Charlie replied and biked on. He reappeared out of the green archway a few minutes later, holding the teal box in his hands. He handed it to Ruth, who deposited it into her basket.

"Listen," she said, wanting to apologize.

Charlie's phone started buzzing.

"I've gotta go, Ruth," he said, looking down at his feet.

She stared at his downturned face, a frantic feeling returning to her. Again, she had the urge to hold on to him, not let him leave this moment. Instead, she turned away from him then without saying anything more, her wheels picking up speed. The last thing she saw was Charlie holding the phone up to his ear, looking confused in her direction—looking lost. Ruth pedaled until she began to cruise down the hill. She focused on the feeling of the wind over her face and the thrill of going a touch too fast. She tried not to think about what might have happened—what almost happened.

Ruth pressed on her brakes and slowed as she approached an intersection, stopping just as Lynn's Range Rover pulled to a stop directly across from her. Nadia and Lynn were in the front seat. Their expressions were both stony as they noticed Ruth. There was no question where she'd been: There wasn't anything up this way except the house, and the dirt roads were too rough for casual biking. The car accelerated, and Ruth stood waiting. Before they passed completely, Nadia waved and her glare disappeared, replaced with a sudden smile that seemed forced. Ruth raised her hand uncertainly in return. She was sure she'd seen Lynn's eyes on the teal box. The car continued, and Ruth took off again toward town.

When Ruth turned onto the dirt driveway of the cottage, she dismounted her bike, grabbed the box, and sank to the grass, her knees hitting the ground with a soft thud. Lying on her back, Ruth stretched out her arms and legs like a starfish and held her breath. In her silence she could hear birds moving in the nearby bushes, could hear the cooing of a mourning dove on the phone line that crossed the street. A small cloud of gnats thrummed a foot above her head, and she watched their bodies orbit one another and bounce like the particles of an atom. Rolling over, she allowed herself to breathe and rested her chin on her forearms, staring into the blades of grass, trying to pick out the smallest thing she could see. As a ladybug traversed a dandelion in front of her, Ruth's body remembered the almost kiss, and she thought about almosts: They almost loved, they almost kissed, they maybe almost meant more to each other than they did.

In the stillness, she couldn't ignore the broken condom anymore. She tried to trace back every detail of the night she and Louis had sex, but her memory was already blurry at the edges. Her period had become irregular in the last few months, which she attributed to stress and coming off her IUD after it got displaced. It had nearly perforated her uterus, requiring a trip to the emergency room that left her laden with unpaid hospital bills. There was no way of knowing where she was in her cycle. This both comforted Ruth and scared her more deeply. It was too early to take a test. She would just have to wait.

Ruth had always had a fear of getting pregnant, even when she was so young that the closest she'd ever come to boys was looking at the back of their crew cuts in the line at school. When Ruth was a child, Maggie had brought her to Catholic mass every week. Ruth wore a white dress on her first communion, sat in the confessionals and tried to come up with sins she needed to tell the priest, although she often made things up to sound worse than she really thought them to be. She didn't know now whether it was for the thrill of the lie or to more quickly get out of the small wooden box that reminded her of a coffin.

She remembered how her mind drifted in the hour during church, how she'd look at the stained-glass windows depicting an emaciated Jesus, drops of red blood falling down from the cut in his side. She had been afraid of God, worried that she wasn't doing it all right, the kneeling and the crossing, that something was going to happen to her because she didn't bow her head low enough while she prayed, didn't sing loud enough, that whatever happened, it would be her fault.

Ruth was eleven when the boys were taken out of the Sunday School classroom by a male teacher so the mom in charge of Ruth's class could tell the girls in the room all about the sins of women, about how sex without marriage made you unclean, and how the worst thing of all was abortion. She handed out a book with drawings of a fetus in a womb wearing a halo and God's palm on the mother's belly. Looking around the room, Ruth saw some girls nodding their heads in fervent agreement, as if this was something they already knew about, something that was talked about in their house.

One of the girls who looked worried, like Ruth, raised her hand.

"What happens if you get an abortion?" she asked.

"Abortion is murder," the woman said, her voice calm but stern. "Murderers go to hell."

After that, Ruth would have dreams of burning—of monsters and fire, and always she was being chased, running, trying to hide. When she woke, she was sweating and her breath was fast and shallow. One night she woke herself up screaming. Maggie came running into her room, turned the light on, and got into bed with Ruth, stroking her hair, the comforting scent of her lavender soap filling the room.

"I was in hell," Ruth sobbed. "Because I got an abortion. In my dream."

Maggie had been silent for a very long time. Ruth worried that Maggie would be angry with her for dreaming about it, even thinking about it.

"Where did you learn that?" she asked finally.

Ruth had told her mom about the book. Maggie continued to stroke her hair until she had finished speaking.

"Do you want me to stay in here?" Maggie asked when Ruth was done.

Ruth had nodded.

The next Sunday, Ruth dressed for church, expecting their

normal routine, but when she came out of the bathroom she saw her mom still in her bathrobe, drinking a cup of coffee and reading the paper.

"Aren't we going to church?" Ruth asked.

"No," Maggie said. "Not today."

They never went back.

The memory made Ruth feel like she was a child again, sitting in the pew, clacking her black shoes together and trying to read the sermons out of order in the Bible. She had rarely paid attention, her gaze and mind wandering, making up stories in her head about people a few pews away.

She believed that women had the right to choose, voted for people who thought that too, but whenever she wondered what she would do if *she* got pregnant and didn't want to be, she didn't know. She wondered if the old fear would return, the cartoon from the book more seared into her being than she'd realized. She worried she wouldn't be able to bring herself to get an abortion, even if she wanted one, for fear of a hell that she didn't believe in anymore.

Ruth turned over in the grass and put her hand under the waistband of her shorts, pressing on her lower abdomen to see if she could feel anything different. Pushing herself to her feet, she walked up the small yard to the cottage, heading for her bed. She would just have to wait, she told herself again, feeling exhausted.

In her room, Ruth pulled her phone out of her bag. There was a list of messages and missed calls from Lucy and Joel. She was about to put the cracked phone away when it started to ring in her hand. Beth's name flashed on her screen. Diana's agent. Ruth almost ignored the call but then she thought of Beth's warm hug at the funeral and picked up.

"How're you holding up?" Beth asked, the sound of the city on her end making it almost impossible for Ruth to hear her. For a second, Ruth thought she was referring to Charlie, then she realized that was impossible. She tried to focus.

"I'm good, ya know, fine," Ruth said, wondering why Beth was calling.

"So listen, do you remember Ethel? One of Diana's editor friends from *Vogue*?"

Ruth tried to picture her but couldn't. Diana had many friends visit the house over the years.

"Not really," Ruth said. She was distracted. The image of Charlie's mouth so close to hers was still in her mind. She lifted her fingers to her lips before snapping back to the moment. "Why?"

"Well, she wanted me to reach out and let you know to expect her call. I'm not exactly sure what it's about," Beth replied.

Another call started beeping in. Ruth pulled the phone away and saw a New York number. "I think this is her," Ruth told Beth.

"All right, sweetie," Beth said. "We'll talk soon."

Beth hung up, and Ruth stared at the phone for another second before answering it.

"Hello?"

"Hi, Ruth? This is Ethel Bishop. How are you?" The woman on the other end of the phone sounded like a news anchor to Ruth—loud and formal.

"I'm okay, Ethel."

"As you probably know, I was one of Diana's colleagues at *Vogue*. We did a lot of work together during her time here, and I came out and stayed at the island house a few summers ago," Ethel said.

Ruth remembered now. Ethel had drunk too much rosé with lunch and fell asleep before dinner.

"I'm sorry I couldn't make the service," Ethel continued.

Ruth nodded, not saying anything. She was starting to wonder if this was just a sympathy call when Ethel cleared her throat.

"So Diana knew she was dying soon," Ethel said, "and she knew we were going to do a large article on her, her work in the fashion world, and her new show coming up. It was morbid, but she had a lot of opinions about the whole memoriam thing."

Ruth's mind went blank. "Wait . . . you knew about the cancer?" she asked.

"I did, yes." Ethel cleared her throat again. Ruth could tell her tone was making Ethel uncomfortable.

"Oh," Ruth said.

"Yes. So, she wanted you to write the piece. She made me promise to give you a shot, be your editor," Ethel said. "She said you used to do a lot of writing for her and about her work—that you were the only one worth my time."

"I'm sorry," Ruth said, still thinking of Diana confiding in Ethel. Who else had known? "I'm not sure I'm understanding you."

"Listen, I'm sorry I'm just getting to you now. I meant to give you more time with this, but it's been a crazy month. This is very . . . unorthodox, okay? It's not really something that happens at *Vogue* every day, just so you know, but Diana meant a great deal to me, and this was something she asked of me before she died. I'd like to offer you a shot at the article. We want to run it in December, after Diana's exhibition opens," she said, then paused. "I mean, I can't promise anything. Diana sent me the pieces you did for her, and they were definitely promising, but this is a really big article in print and all."

Ruth was silent. She was thinking back to their argument, to the connections Diana had offered her in the past, how she had turned them down.

"Are you there?" Ethel asked. Ruth could hear a pen tapping against a desk in the background.

"Yeah, I'm here," she said.

"Do you think you're up for it? I mean, I'm sure it will be emotional. I get it if you think you're not interested," Ethel said, and Ruth could hear her working to be sympathetic, although the doubt was palpable in her voice.

"No one here knows I'm doing this. I have a backup writer on file in case it falls through, but . . . I hope it doesn't. Diana wanted it to be you, after all," Ethel said.

Ruth didn't know what to say.

She thought about her shift at the restaurant the night before, how bored she had been even as the night got busier and busier, how she couldn't stop thinking about Nadia's studio in Boston, about how quiet it must be, how much work she must get done. Ruth thought about her old dreams, of how long she had wanted her life to transform. She didn't know if it was Charlie getting married, her dad selling the house, or Diana being gone, but it felt like she was getting forcefully pushed to move from every direction. Something about Charlie's words earlier, so similar to Diana's, made her consider what would happen if she finally tried. It had been so long since she had put any effort toward a real change, and the idea of pulling herself out of her same cycle began to feel possible.

"I'll do it," Ruth heard herself say, but the second it was out of her mouth a sharp worry settled in, making her wish she could take it back. What was she thinking? She hadn't written anything in years.

"Okay, great, well—I'm going to send you an email with some of our correspondence about it. It will be a profile of her life and work, but feel free to take an angle that feels authentic to you, you know? You knew her well. Get me a draft by August seventh. But not a shitty first draft, okay? Really, it should be a second or a third draft."

"August seventh?" Ruth looked to the calendar Lucy had staked to the back of their bedroom door.

"Yeah, if it's not working by then, I'll have to go with someone else so that it's ready in time. Does that sound fair to you?"

"Okay," Ruth said, then cursing how uncertain she sounded, "Yes."

"Oh, and Diana wanted you to use her studio."

"What?"

"Yeah, I have it in one of our emails here. She wanted you to write in there. She sent me that email fairly recently. I think she was in the hospital."

Ruth stopped. "I don't think that'll happen," she said finally.

"What do you mean?"

Ruth explained how Lynn had essentially banned her from the property.

"I see," said Ethel. "Well, let me contact Beth, and we'll get back to you. I have it here in writing that those were her desires, so maybe that will change things. Don't worry about it. We'll handle it," she said and hung up.

Ruth sat on her bed, staring at the fan circling, the worry she felt at saying yes growing now into a dull panic. She was close to calling Ethel back and telling her she'd changed her mind until she heard Lucy's steps on the porch. After a second, the scent of a joint wafted in through the open window. Walking downstairs and opening the screen door, Ruth saw Lucy's feet stuck out over the ledge of the porch railing.

Lucy had been busier than any summer before that Ruth could remember. She was working at Eli's four nights a week and in the mornings alternated between interning at an art gallery in town and volunteering at the Block Island Historical Society. Lucy had been invited to assist in coordinating an upcoming exhibition of Manissean art, planning collaborations with the Historical Society and promoting upcoming events with the archaeologists, historians, and the Manissean people both on the island and back on the mainland. She fell asleep hard each night and woke up early, buzzing about the gallery and upcoming restoration projects and exhibitions.

Lucy was reclining in her bikini, smoking, her curly hair pushed up and over the back of the chair, creating the effect of someone floating.

She looked over at Ruth, patting the seat of the chair next to her. Ruth sat down, and Lucy passed over the joint. Taking it between her fingers, Ruth inhaled, sputtering a cough as she exhaled and handed it back.

"How was volunteering?" Ruth asked.

"It's great, but I am so fried. . . . I should've been doing this for years though. You know, I feel like I used to forget about all the history here. Now I can't look anywhere without thinking about it—all the layers and layers of people who lived here, who loved this place."

Ruth nodded. She was reminded of the summer she met

Lucy, how enthusiastic she was about everything on the island. Ruth kept expecting her to get swept up in the Block Island social scene and leave her behind, but she never did, always taking Ruth along wherever she went.

That first summer they lived together, Ruth showed Lucy the spots she had found over the years and they would swim, then lie like starfish on giant boulders, roasting in the sun. Ruth listened to Lucy describe over and over the kind of life she wanted, how she wanted to be a sponge, accumulating life experiences wherever she floated. "Joy is not meant to be a crumb," she said, quoting Mary Oliver, whose books Ruth kept on the shelf in their room. It was the first time in a long time that Ruth had a female friend, someone her age, who wanted to hang out with her, and being around Lucy was exhilarating. The confidence she carried was infectious, and Ruth admired and envied the ease Lucy carried through life.

Lucy exhaled again and passed the joint to Ruth, breaking her out of her thoughts. She knew the only reason Lucy was here this summer was to check on her, that she was having a hard time getting a job at a gallery and would've stayed closer to the city to keep looking for work if Diana hadn't died.

There had been a few times since Lucy had arrived that she had tried to talk to Ruth about Diana, wanting to gauge her grief, to help her along. While Ruth was grateful for her friend, she never wanted to discuss Diana with Lucy.

Lucy couldn't understand, Ruth thought—she hadn't really lost anyone before. Diana's had been the first funeral she had attended as an adult. Her family was alive and healthy. Her parents called often, and Ruth listened while Lucy spoke to them in the kitchen on speakerphone, or as she folded clothes on her bed. She heard the engaged questions they asked her, the laughter at her answers. Ruth could envy Lucy's lightness all she wanted, could try and soak it up by being around her, but she knew the truth. It wouldn't change anything. Their lives had been too different.

"What's that?" Lucy asked now, pointing to the teal box.

Ruth realized she was still holding the box, then explained everything to Lucy, how she hadn't opened it. Lucy's eyes grew wide as she told her about the almost-kiss with Charlie, about the call from Ethel.

"Wow," Lucy said, sitting up and leaning over her knees. She took another drag from the joint then stubbed it out in the clamshell ashtray on the small table between them. "Wow," she said again, turning to Ruth. "That's amazing!"

"What do you mean?" Ruth asked. None of it seemed to be touching her.

"The article! You have like an *in* at a huge magazine. That would be . . . insane to be published there, you know? To be in print? To have a byline?"

"Yeah," Ruth said. Something about it still felt wrong. She tried to imagine it, the path it could set her on, something to add to her abandoned résumé. She thought about being able to honor Diana, to write something deep and meaningful, something that could explain how much she meant to her. It seemed momentous and terrifying, and she felt her throat grow tight, tears building at the idea of it.

"And the box!" Lucy exclaimed. "Open it now!" Lucy didn't notice Ruth's reddened eyes or the quick tears she wiped away.

Ruth felt instinctively protective. Lucy's tone implied this was a fun game, and she was confused by her lack of response to what she just told her about Charlie. She looked into her friend's eyes, which were growing red around the edges from the joint, and decided to forget it.

And yet, she was tempted to open it with Lucy there, to not have to handle it alone. Her hands hovered over the lid, then stopped.

"I feel like . . . I just—I need a break from this or something. For a minute," Ruth said. She wanted to crawl into her bed and close the door behind her until people forgot she was there. Lucy sat up and slapped her thigh.

"Good! Because we haven't been able to hang at all. I mean, I get it, but still. Let's go for a sunset swim. I'll call some people!"

Standing, she held out her heavily ringed fingers, and Ruth allowed herself to be pulled up. Grabbing the teal box, she ascended the stairs behind Lucy, who wondered aloud what they had at home to make margaritas. Ruth pushed the box under her bed.

Later, she thought.

The next day Ruth pulled out her laptop. It crunched from sand as she opened it, and she became annoyed with herself, thinking about how long this computer would live. She tried so hard to keep her things nice so that they would last, but she couldn't get the sand out of anything she owned, and it was difficult with all of her moving—something always got lost or damaged. Lucy made her a pot of coffee before she left for the gallery and put it in front of her at their desk.

"For the writer," she said with a flourish, backing out of the room and closing the door behind her. The quiet click of the door made Ruth flinch as she looked at the blank document open in front of her, at the blinking bar against the white page. The box fan whirred at the foot of the bed and Ruth heard the front door slam as Lucy left the cottage. Ruth stared at the empty page for what felt like a long time before pulling her phone out and looking at the calendar. She had six weeks to finish.

Sitting down to write about Diana made the memories and images Ruth had been avoiding stream through her mind. She was gripped by the thought of what might have happened if she had made it to the hospital in time, had seen Diana, been able to hold her hand one last time and say goodbye. It was impossible to consider without thinking of how she had done the same thing with Maggie ten years before, how empty her mind had been of what words to use to say how much she loved her mother, how angry she was at Maggie leaving, how much she wanted her to stay. Ruth felt tears on her face at the thought, the feeling in her chest the same as it had been on that day, the feeling of Maggie's hand clear in her mind, her body too smart to ever truly forget what it felt like.

She wanted to do right by Diana, to somehow tell her all she had meant to Ruth, to write something deserving of her—to paint her in all her complexity, to accurately describe the solitude that she worked so hard to carve out for herself, her dedication to art, her curiosity about life, her generous spirit, how much she cared, but Ruth didn't know where to start.

Reaching for her journal, she tried to find something she could use, but it was full of only lists and descriptions of things she could barely remember now. It read like gibberish, and she shut the journal in frustrated dismay.

Closing her eyes, she saw the inside of Diana's studio in her mind's eye, the light coming in, the dried flowers hanging on the backside of the studio door. Suddenly Ruth remembered how Diana left a sunflower at Ruth's door every year on Maggie's birthday. Her throat dried, and she felt the grief envelop her like she was sinking into it, until her phone began to ring on the desk next to her laptop. Ruth's heart jolted. It was Beth calling again. She wiped her eyes and cleared her throat.

"Ethel and I talked to Lynn and the lawyer," Beth said.

Ruth's breath felt loud. "Right."

"Okay, so here's the deal. It turns out that Diana sent the lawyer a letter about this, expecting Lynn's . . . 'reservations,' let's say. I guess it was really important to her that you be there. So, although the ins and the outs of the will still aren't sorted . . . Well, anyways, she called Lynn herself."

"So, it's all cleared?" Ruth asked.

"She had some . . . stipulations," Beth said.

"Oh?"

"As long as it's only you and you adhere to a certain schedule, then you are allowed in Diana's studio. She'll also give you her computer and any files you need."

"Wow," Ruth said.

"Yeah, that last part was shocking to us too. Okay, so I've gotta go. I'll email you the schedule. But, Ruth?"

"Yeah?"

"Are you sure you're okay to dive into all this? I think the article might be a pretty big deal, you know, with the upcoming exhibition and all—the first posthumous show. It would be better to tell Ethel now if you think you're not up to it. She'll understand."

In a flash, her body felt coated in cold sweat, the remaining tears still wet on her face.

"I'll be okay," Ruth said, not believing it. "Diana wanted me to do it."

"Okay. I'm going to be checking in. August seventh is pretty close."

"Okay," Ruth said. She hung up the phone. She realized her hands were shaking.

PART 2

July

1

On the first day of July, Ruth awoke before the sun. It had taken her a few days to gather the courage to think about going into Diana's studio. Beth had sent her the schedule Lynn was insisting on: Ruth was allowed to be in the studio from five-thirty until nine in the mornings between Monday and Friday. She wondered if the early hours were an attempt to limit her contact with Charlie.

Although Ruth had gotten home from work past midnight, her eyes opened at the first sound of the alarm she'd set for five A.M. She rushed to quiet her phone so that it wouldn't wake Lucy, who rolled over in her bed, groaning in annoyance. Crouching in the early dark, Ruth groped around under her bed for the teal box. Feeling the corner against her fingertips, she slid it out. Ten minutes later, she left the house in bike shorts and a tank top, the teal box under her arm, stuffing a piece of peanut butter toast in her mouth. The sun was catching the morning fog, and the pink hue over the green grass made Ruth stop and watch.

The bike ride to the house was invigorating. It had been a long time since Ruth had been awake this early on the island,

and she admonished herself for the late nights and the late mornings. It felt healthy to watch the sun rise, to watch the landscape change from fog to sunlight, to hear which birds woke up and when. It felt like things were moving.

It wasn't until she turned onto the road and passed the sign for the house that she started to feel a sense of trepidation spread within her. What would happen if she saw Charlie? She hadn't told him she was coming, and they still hadn't talked about the almost-kiss. Then, for a second, Ruth had the terrifying thought that Charlie had already told Nadia about what had happened, that she would confront Ruth. It was difficult to get her body to move forward then, the anxiety in her chest tightly wound. Ruth tried to distract herself by worrying about Lynn. Would she play supervisor and insist on standing over Ruth's shoulder? Would she kick Ruth out when time was up?

Getting off her bike, she began pushing it beside her to make less noise, approaching the green archway and crossing into the yard. She remembered just a few days ago, driving through it with Charlie. It felt like it was five years ago. Now she was alone. Was he inside? She imagined him and Nadia in the twin beds they'd pushed together. Did they spoon? Were their legs intertwined? Did she snore? Ruth bet she wore matching pointelle pajamas to bed instead of the giant ripped T-shirt that Ruth wore most nights.

The ocean glittered in the distance, a sliver of blue on the horizon. Dew kicked up onto the backs of her calves as she stepped through the grass. Diana had often let it grow long enough that Ruth worried about ticks, but Diana had said that the birds preferred it long and luscious. Now the yard was mowed short, and the decimation of the garden was complete, with sod laid over it, the clunky material mismatched against the natural grass. For the wedding, Ruth thought.

Looking toward the house, Ruth examined the windows for an outline of Lynn standing with her arms crossed, watching her, but she saw no one.

She left her bike against the rock wall behind some bushes,

scooped the box out of her bicycle basket, and approached the studio. Ruth recognized the key in the doorknob—the blue, worn ribbon swaying gently in the breeze. Turning it, she pushed the door open and stepped into Diana's studio. The air was heavy, the room dim.

Ruth put the box down and looked around. It was a small, square room, with a low but vaulted ceiling and a loft for storage. Diana had put in new blackout curtains in the past few years, which were folded up at the top of each window like an accordion. Below them were the familiar old kitchen towel curtains, drawn over the small windows. As Ruth pulled the thin fabric back, she saw the sun color the wood of the ceiling and illuminate spiderwebs in the corners along the beams. There were dangling ornaments of cracked seashells and long strands of dried seaweed laid across the windowsill. On the other side of the room was the large porcelain bathtub, which Diana had fitted with an overlaying tray that held the shallow pans for the photo developing chemicals. Canopied over the tub, there was a drawstring with clothespins meant for drying the photos out. Behind the tub was a small wash closet with a curtain for a door. Along the far wall, under the loft, was the hulking enlarger machine for developing film, and squeezed next to it there were two gray filing cabinets that held negatives and photos that didn't make it into past exhibitions, organized and archived. In the corner was a heap of camera equipment and sealed boxes of photo paper that had accrued a layer of dust. The room was quiet and warm, and the smell of old wood and faint chemicals was strong and comforting.

She approached Diana's wooden desk. The photos had been rearranged since she and Charlie had been in there last, and Ruth was unsettled by what else might have been disturbed and by whom. For a second the communion she was having with Diana faded at the thought of Lynn in the studio. But when she noticed the film canisters arranged just so on the corner of the desk, the pens and scrap paper with little notes tucked underneath them, the feeling was restored. She stared at the film canisters for a long moment and imagined Diana placing them there without a thought, moving on to her next task. Ruth remembered feeling this way after her mother died, how preciously she'd prized the notes her mom had left herself on the fridge, how they'd transport Ruth back to watching Maggie write them while she was on the phone with the internet company or paying the cable bill, how she had doodled, the pen tracing over and over the same lines as she discussed overdue payments. The notes on the fridge made the hand real again, made the handwriting haunted.

When Joel wasn't home, Ruth regularly opened the drawers of her mother's wardrobe. She'd look at the sweaters folded in a haphazard way, the stains she remembered on some, the threads loose on others. She'd run her hands gently over the fabric, feeling it brush her open palms, her fingertips. She'd lean down and smell the familiar laundry detergent, the wood of the wardrobe, and feel a passing sense of comfort.

It was in these moments that her heart, so young, felt the most betrayed by time and by the world. It was then when she felt most alone in her grief. Joel allowed this behavior for a little while, until the day he cleared the notes from the fridge and Ruth had broken, snapping at him.

After that, Joel became less tolerant about Maggie's things and more wary of Ruth. He didn't throw out Maggie's belongings, but it was clear that the reverence that was once shown to them would not continue. They moved the wardrobe into Ruth's already cluttered room, and he called the high school and arranged for Ruth to meet with the school psychologist once a week.

The psychologist was a woman in her forties named Celine, who Ruth had served at the diner before. She would come in with her family, and Ruth remembered pouring water for them, the kids laughing at something their dad said, how nice it all seemed. In their meetings, Ruth never told her that she had waited on them, and the woman didn't seem to remember either.

The sessions lasted for forty minutes in a small, windowless room in the school building. The table between Ruth and Celine was littered with stress balls that had smiley faces on them, packets of condoms, and boxes of tissues, along with pamphlets featuring teenagers sitting, their heads in their hands, the word *Depression* superimposed over the picture.

Ruth knew the psychologist earnestly wanted to help her. She could see the restrained empathy on her face, and she sometimes wondered if it came from her training or if her mother had also died. It wasn't the well-meaning pity she was used to seeing. While it helped Ruth to sit in a quiet place with someone, whenever Celine tried to push Ruth, she shut it down.

"What do you plan to do with all your mother's things?" Celine asked her in response to the incident with the notes.

"Leave them where they are," Ruth replied, indignant.

"Do you think that's realistic? Life is going to move on. You're going to go to college. Things will change," the psychologist said. Ruth remembered how the word *change* hadn't meant anything to her. The idea that life could be any different than it was in that moment seemed like a sweet idea—seemed unlikely.

School had ended soon after, and with it the sessions with the psychologist. She became resigned, didn't make a sound, came in from her shifts at work, and got into bed. It didn't matter. Joel still sent her away, Ruth's new phase of grief more frightening to him than the last.

Now Ruth felt the ghost of that same obsessive urge to not disturb anything, to preserve it and call back Diana by doing so, but the feeling passed with some effort. She touched the film canisters lightly with her fingertips, then pulled out the canvas chair and sat at Diana's desk as she had never done before. She opened her computer and her journal and stared at them uninterrupted for an unknown length of time. After that, she poked the screen on her phone, watching it light up—no messages. She opened it and scrolled through Instagram, her eyes glazing over at videos of summer parties, boat trips, concerts, baby announcements, beach fires. They all blurred together in an unsettling collage before she realized she was procrastinating and dropped the phone into her bag, frustrated at her lack of discipline.

Ethel had forwarded Ruth her communication with Diana about the article, along with some notes about it: bullet points about Diana's career, Block Island—things that Ruth already knew. But she froze when she scrolled to the email Diana had sent Ethel. She read it a few times over.

> Dear Ethel,
> You remember Ruth from when you came to visit? She and I worked together for many years and she was a major piece in writing my photo books. She's an excellent writer, very close to me, and really the only woman for the job of this post-death article (even though, as I've said, it seems to me there is no need for this article at all. Just let me pass into the ether of the world without mention, I say). Regardless, I'd like for her to write it. I know she doesn't have many publications under her belt, but you can coach her. I'm asking for this.
> Love,
> Diana

Ruth couldn't identify how she was feeling.

Now that she was sitting in Diana's studio, as she had imagined doing so many times before, with a blank page in front of her, Diana's words in her mind, a disorienting realization began to bloom within Ruth. Maybe she had only considered writing as part of her identity because Diana had fed this narrative to her. Why had Ruth never thought of this before? Diana was the one who put the books by her door, who introduced her to friends as a writer, who gave her journals as presents and offered her time to write during the day. When Ruth was thinking about her major, Diana had asked why she was even considering anything other than English. And the minute Ruth left Diana's orbit, she had let it all drop, like a child who didn't want to do her homework.

Ruth had felt for so long like she had let Diana down by wasting her talents. But now she wondered if she was ever any good, or if this was just something Diana wanted her to be, an idea planted within Ruth enough times to make her think it was her own. The thought took over. Now Diana had pushed too far, had given her something that meant too much.

She read and reread Diana's email to Ethel, and instead of feeling grateful or sad she just felt frustrated. An article for *Vogue*? What was Diana thinking?

She was going to mess this up. Standing, she looked around the studio again, noticing all the small trinkets, but instead of nostalgia or grief she felt anger building within her. Why didn't Diana tell her she was dying? She had to know Ruth would be crushed. Why did she tell Ethel? Who else had known?

Finally, Ruth's eyes landed on the teal box, and her anger churned within her. Why go through the trouble of putting together a box instead of just talking to her?

She lifted the lid and looked inside.

2

At first the contents seemed unremarkable. A small camera case took up almost half the box, but then Ruth recognized it. Opening the case, she pulled out Diana's first camera, her Pentax K1000—the one Ruth used to take her portrait on her birthday. She turned it over in her hands, feeling the sturdy weight, and went to wind the lever back, expecting that the camera was empty of film. Instead, she felt the familiar tug as she clicked to a new frame. Looking down, she saw that three photos on the roll of film had already been taken.

Setting the camera aside, Ruth assessed the rest of the box's contents. She picked up a thick envelope—it was full of photos. As she pulled the stack out, she noticed some folded papers and negatives wrapped in a loose rubber band, some shells and old San Pellegrino bottle caps scattered across the bottom of the box.

After pulling the photos out of the envelope, Ruth brought the first one close to her eyes, the familiarity of the faces in the picture shocking her. She recognized her mom, although she looked like a teenager. Her head was turned, her mouth open in a laugh as she glanced back at the photographer. Next to Maggie was a young Diana. There was a lighthouse in the background, which Ruth recognized as North Light, and both women were looking up at the camera, laughing, their arms touching. The photo was black and white—Diana's preferred medium—and the tones in the photo were deeply contrasted from the brightness of the sun against the shade created by their bodies. Their teeth were a vivid white, and Diana's large sunglasses were dark, like the shadow over Maggie's eyes from shielding her face.

Ruth flipped the photo over. At the bottom right, in Diana's familiar handwriting, it said—

Maggie and I at North Light, taken by Lynnie.

Ruth stared at the name, *Lynnie,* before flipping the photo over again. It was a perfectly framed shot. The women were in the front, the lighthouse off to the right. She wondered if Diana had directed her sister or if Lynn had taken the camera in her own hands, acknowledging the beauty of the two women, wanting to capture the moment for them. Ruth stared off into space, trying to imagine Lynn as a younger woman, laughing with Diana and Maggie, drinking cheap wine at the beach. She couldn't.

Just then, Ruth heard a car engine start. Looking out the window, she saw Lynn's Range Rover backing out of the driveway. She watched it disappear through the archway of privet.

Diana and Ruth had talked about her mom often that first summer. She would come up while Ruth weeded the garden or while she was archiving Diana's old photo collections.

"How long were you friends?" she remembered asking.

"We were pretty close for the one summer she lived here," Diana replied, sitting at her desk.

"How old was she?"

"Twenty-three, I think? I was thirty."

"Why was she only here for one summer?" Ruth asked. At

that point, Ruth was already sucked into the island, obsessed with every part of her days there. She couldn't imagine anyone wanting to leave. Diana laughed, acknowledging her thought without it being said out loud.

"She met your dad over the winter . . . and, well, we just fell out of touch." Ruth looked up at Diana. "We were never that close to begin with."

Now Ruth pulled out each photo from the envelope and laid them out in front of her, one by one, on Diana's desk.

Every photo was of her mother—her mother and Diana.

Standing now, Ruth looked over the collage, some pictures overlapping one another on the wooden surface. It was an exhibition of the two women most important to her, each in their radiant youth. Seeing them together, as she never had when they were alive, was dizzying. The smiles she saw were so familiar that when she closed her eyes they remained in front of her multiple times over.

It was odd to see so many photos of them. In Ruth's memory, Maggie hated having her picture taken as much as Diana did. She would duck out of the frame, sometimes even going to the extreme of cutting herself out of prints in the time before they had a digital camera. There hadn't been any images of Maggie around the house aside from the wedding photo that hung on the mostly bare wall.

Ruth stared, mesmerized by the different glimpses into her mother. And Maggie stared back at her in each frame—holding a book in her lap, biking and smiling behind her at the camera, her naked body jumping out of a wave, skinny-dipping.

Ruth realized it was jarring to see evidence of her mother's body so intact after all the surgeries, chemo, and pain she had gone through. Without knowing it, those images of Maggie had been the ones most present in her memory, pasted over any other image—stuck.

The last picture she pulled from the envelope was of a young Diana, her face scrunched up in laughter with the precursors to her familiar wrinkles visible around her eyes. Flipping over the photo, she found Diana's notation.

Me by Maggie. Late August.

A heart was drawn next to the words. Ruth put the photo down. Dazed, she pulled the teal box over. There was another, thin envelope with her name on it. She slid a typed letter out of the envelope and began reading.

> Ruth,
> Cancer is maybe the worst thing that's ever happened to me. I generally haven't minded getting older. People start to believe you after a while that you like to be alone. They stop trying to set you up with people you would never get along with just to fill a space. I like to be alone—as you know. But these days my body hurts, and my heart is often weighed down. I cry a lot. I hide this from you. It's Christmas and we just had an argument, maybe our worst. I shouldn't have called. I had just talked to my doctor and . . . well. My plan is to give this to you as soon as I can. I hope you won't be too mad at me. Although I understand if you are. I hope we can talk about it.
>
> The first summer I worked here, I was lifeguarding at the town beach. I had been working as a photographer for the *Providence Journal* when I applied to the Guggenheim fellowship and got rejected. I took it pretty hard, quit my job, and moved out to the island for the summer to be a lifeguard. They usually didn't hire women, even in the nineties, but people who could swim well were scarce that year, so they took me anyway. Maggie was working at the snack counter, and we became friends. We would bike around the island, exploring the trails and taking pictures. Some shots from my first show were from that summer—the shot at the bluffs. You like that one.

You already know all this by now because of the photos, but I lied when I told you I didn't have any pictures of your mom from then. I thought if you saw them, it would be obvious. When I look at them, it's obvious to me how in love with her I was. I decided the day you showed up at my door that I wasn't going to tell you that, so I lied and said we weren't really all that close.

I thought your mom might not have wanted you to know. You didn't seem to know why you were at my house, and it didn't seem right to tell you. It's something that I'm regretting now. I could have been more honest. I could have been braver. You could have known me better.

Maggie was my first love, my only real love if I'm being honest with myself and being honest with you—which is what I'm trying to do now. God, I loved her. I loved her so much.

But your mom felt confused about us—about what to do. Whenever I talked about a future together, she would shut down. I was planning to move to New York in the fall and I wanted her to come with me. She was such a talented artist. I had dreams of us making it together, me in photography and your mother as a painter.

My parents knew I was gay since I was fifteen. They never blinked an eye. Your mother's parents . . . well, I heard at one point that your mom left the church after you were born, but when we were together she was still practicing, and her parents were . . . very staunch Catholics. I think she was scared. When she left for the mainland at the end of August, she told me not to contact her. She said she needed time to think. It was a hard fall.

It was Thanksgiving and I was in New York already when I heard from her next. It was a letter saying she was coming to me, that she missed me—that she loved me. I spent the next weeks preparing for her in my apartment. Those moments were some of the happiest of my life, I think—imagining our life together. But she didn't show up the day we had planned. I waited at Penn Station all day. When I got home that night, there was a message on my machine. She said she wasn't coming. She said she couldn't speak to me anymore.

The next summer I returned to the island to work as a housekeeper for the woman who used to live in this house, and started working at the Frank Segel Gallery on Spring Street. The one that closed down a few years before you got here. I was still heartbroken. I expected to see your mom around every corner. Then one day I did—outside of the bakery. She was very pregnant and had a ring on her finger. I wanted to talk, but she wouldn't look me in the eye. Joel came around the corner then, and she introduced him as her husband. I was confused and hurt. I tried calling, I tried writing letters, but they had moved already. All the letters got returned. All the phone calls reached disconnected lines. I just wanted to understand.

Eventually I gave up. I saw them sporadically over the years on the island. They would come out for day trips to see Sarah and Bill. I remember you as a toddler, covered in sand, smiling up at me. I was spending my winters in New York at that point, absorbed into the photography world. I got my job at *Vogue*. Things got busy. I buried myself in work, and life went on. Then your mother passed away, and although I hadn't seen her in years, it felt like I was thirty again. I wished I could have seen her. I should've tried. I wish I had known she was sick. I guess that's kind of ironic. I haven't told you that I'm sick. I'm sorry.

And then, one day, you showed up at my door. It was the biggest surprise. You looked so much like Maggie. I was stunned by how much my heart broke all over again, how much it was like no time had passed at all. I couldn't believe that Joel had sent you to me, that he knew anything about me and your mother. I had convinced myself that she never thought of me, that I had meant nothing to her. Seeing you, I wasn't so sure.

I called him that first night, after I knew you were asleep. He said you weren't doing well. He said you needed help. He said Maggie would have wanted it. I'm not sure how much your father knew about us, but it felt wrong to ask.

It was so easy to accept you as a daughter in my life—and that's how I've always thought of you since I've met you, Ruth. You're my family.

I couldn't bring myself to tell you I was sick and probably going to die, Ruth. I couldn't tell you that someone else you loved was going to die. I am so worried about you, and I know I've been cowardly in not telling you until now, but I couldn't.

I hope you can forgive me for keeping all of this from you. I guess I was still protecting my little broken heart and trying, in my flawed way, to protect you.

Love,
Diana

Ruth kept rereading the letter and looking at the two women's faces. Their beauty was being transmuted the more she looked. They were supposed to be the two people she knew best in her life, but in that moment they felt like strangers. Diana had been meaning to tell her, but she never did. She had photos of her mother all along. Ruth wanted to yell at Diana, to ask what she had been thinking, why she had hidden all of this. The feeling built until Ruth was sweating, and she realized she was clutching the letter, the paper wrinkling under her touch. The painful frustration of knowing there were no answers other than whatever Diana had written that day, that there was no one she could ask, made her fold, exhausted. What else had Diana been keeping from her?

She put the letter down. Then something else fell out of the envelope onto the table. It was a small piece of journal paper with Diana's rushed scrawl on it.

Go to the studio and up to the loft. Look in the black bin. Back right corner. Your mom's art from that first summer. She left them for me when she went home.

Love,

Diana

Ruth looked from her seat up to the loft. She stood, the sound of the chair legs scraping the floor startling her. Her whole body felt charged—electric. Approaching the ladder, she pulled on it to make sure it was secure before stepping up into the loft. Crawling into the hot space, she was aware of the thick layer of dust on the floor and the cobwebs around her. There were piles of things that looked forgotten, and she dug through them until she saw a black storage bin duct-taped shut at the handles. Ruth pulled it toward her. There was enough space in the loft for her to squat above the bin and peel off the duct tape that had become loose, the glue melting from the heat. Cracking open the lid, Ruth looked inside and saw several canvases and some sketchbooks.

On the back of the top canvas, Ruth recognized her mother's handwriting, although she hadn't seen it in years, and her face became hot. She stared at the words—*Happy birthday, June Baby! Your favorite dunes and where we met—Town Beach, 1994.* Flipping the canvas over, Ruth looked at the painting. It depicted the dunes she was so familiar with on Corn Neck Road, their sloping pyramidal shapes and the sun hitting them at six o'clock. The colors were intense, and the brushstrokes were active, swaths of color working together, so that the shades felt alive. The sun struck the canvas through the window, and the colors were even more vibrant. Not knowing what to do with the relic in her hand, she put it down next to her and picked up the next one. The handwriting on the back was in charcoal. *Diana nude, North Light, Morning, 1994.* Turning the canvas over, Ruth saw a figure painted loosely, curved over in the water, reeds behind her.

Ruth had never seen her mother paint, or even heard her mother express a desire to do so, although the notes she made for grocery lists and reminders often had sketches on them—rough outlines of the window in their kitchen or of Ruth's face. Ruth had saved a stack of these after Joel had thrown them out that day, pulling the salvageable notes from the trash. They were pressed into the back of her journal from that year. Ruth looked back to the paintings. She was struck by their confidence. The brash brushstrokes finding their form, the bold colors blending together in a way that made Ruth feel the energy put into them. Why had Maggie never painted like this during Ruth's life?

The heat of the loft hit her in a rush, and she felt faint. Putting the canvases back in the bin, she closed the lid and lowered herself down the ladder. When she got there, she sank onto the cool, shaded wooden floor. Her breathing became erratic. She thought of her mother during her life, how devoted she had been to Ruth, how hard she had worked. There was a creeping feeling now that maybe it wasn't what she had wanted, what she had planned, that she could have had something more but had been stuck in a life she didn't want—all because of Ruth. She tried to imagine her mom in the city, living as a painter with Diana, working to make ends meet. To Ruth's knowledge she had never even been to New York, but Ruth also hadn't known she had been a painter.

A bang somewhere in the direction of the house interrupted her thoughts and made her head snap up. Scared, she stopped breathing and listened. If she hadn't heard Lynn's car leave earlier, she would've thought it was her coming to interrogate her on her progress.

"I just feel like things are moving really fast!"

Ruth heard Charlie's voice from the porch. Her hand shot up to her mouth. She felt like she was somewhere she shouldn't be, but she crawled to the door, peeking through the low window to see Charlie and Nadia's figures in the distance.

"So what are you saying? You want to postpone the wedding?" Nadia shouted.

"No. I don't know," Charlie said, then paused. "It was just a suggestion."

"A suggestion? We've already spent so much money on this wedding. I told you I didn't want a long engagement."

"I know, it's just—"

"You proposed to *me*, Charlie!" Nadia yelled.

"I know."

"You said 'when you know, you know.'"

"I know."

"So are you saying you don't know anymore?"

"No, that's not it."

"Did something happen?"

Ruth's hand was still over her open mouth.

"Is it Ruth?" Nadia asked.

Ruth felt the silence that followed stretch, her heart beating in her ears.

"I'm just worried we're rushing it," Charlie replied, finally.

"Right. That's not a no." Nadia walked back into the house. Charlie threw his hands up in the air and followed her inside.

Ruth didn't know what to do. Her time in the cottage was running out, but she couldn't leave now in case they saw her. Charlie's words hung in her mind. Was he reconsidering the wedding because of her?

"I'm going for a run. Don't follow me," Nadia said over her shoulder as she slammed the door. Charlie followed her into the driveway. Ruth heard Nadia's shoes hit the dirt road, their scuffing growing quiet until there was silence.

She waited, her breath caught in her throat. Then the alarm she'd set on her phone started buzzing in her bag, and she scrambled over to it, digging through the loose papers, old receipts, the apple she brought, her journal, cursing how disorganized she was until she found her phone and turned it off. She sat on the floor, trying to be quiet. But her breath was loud and she could hear her heart beating, the sound of rushing blood making her dizzy. It seemed as if anyone nearby could hear it too. She heard the steps approaching in the grass and the knock on the door.

"Ruth?" Charlie said.

She didn't reply.

"I just saw your bike, Ruth," Charlie added. He sounded exhausted.

"Hey," she called.

Charlie opened the door, and the sun poured in, illuminating Ruth on the floor, under the desk, the sun hitting the photos.

3

Ruth stood up, the dust from the floor sticking to her sweaty legs. Charlie looked defeated, awkward, hurt. He ran his hand over his face, and it was the first time Ruth thought that he genuinely looked older—not just different, but older. She could see the time that had passed marked on his face, and she was struck again after reading Diana's letter, after the photos, by how much she might not know about his life too, by how hard it was to *know* anyone deeply. The thought made her hungry to know, made her want to make up for any time she'd lost while hiding her feelings. She wanted to ask him every question she could think of—about the quiet stressors, the moments that made him feel real in the world, the moments that made him feel light, feel sad. Diana was a sadness they shared, but what about all the others? Ruth had been reminded, again, of how little time she had with anyone, and she felt the strongest desire yet to tell him her feelings. She opened her mouth, but Charlie spoke first, oblivious to the storm moving through Ruth's mind.

"So, you heard all that then," Charlie said. His voice was full of apology, although after the other day, Ruth expected him to be angry about the intrusion.

Ruth felt self-conscious, trying to decide what to do with the force of her feelings. “I’m going to be around sometimes,” she said, changing the subject. Charlie was overwhelmed. It wasn’t the time. She explained about the article, and Lynn’s rules. “I should probably leave. My time slot is up.”

“She won’t be back until the afternoon,” Charlie replied. They stood in silence for another moment.

Ruth thought about what happened at the beach. She didn’t know what to say about it. Should she apologize? For a second, looking at Charlie, it felt like that moment hadn’t happened at all. And she wondered if she didn’t mention it, whether it would become just another thing left unsaid between them, a moment that would warp in her mind away from what really happened, her brain cracking it and melting it down as time went on, into a mere etching of a memory rather than the memory itself.

“Are you okay?” Ruth asked.

“I’m just . . . thinking about some things,” Charlie said.

The statement hung in the air between them. Charlie looked at her for a beat before glancing over her shoulder into the middle distance. Ruth’s adrenaline pulsed inside her. His eyes landed on the desk, and her mind returned to the collage of Maggie and Diana that she had almost forgotten about. Charlie’s eyes narrowed at the pictures.

“What are those?” he asked. “Can I look?”

For a second Ruth wanted to keep the photos to herself, to hold them in her hands and look at them undisturbed. But another part of her wanted to share the secret with Charlie, who might understand—who she wanted to understand. Ruth folded up the letter from Diana that was still in her hand, slid it into her pocket, and walked over to the desk.

“That’s your mom?” Charlie asked, pointing to the photo of them laughing on the beach. He picked it up and brought it close to his eyes, examining it and looking up at Ruth. “She looks just like you. She’s gorgeous.” His eyes lingered on her face before he put the photo back. “So they were together?”

Ruth realized she had been holding her breath. His compliment had stunned her. She looked at a picture of her mother blowing a kiss toward the camera. Her eyes were sparkling, and she seemed lit up from the inside. It was a look she hadn't seen often from her mother, certainly not directed toward Joel. It was strange how her mother looked exactly how Ruth remembered, but so much younger than she ever knew her—twenty-three. There was another photo of Maggie in the concession stand window, her chin resting on her hand, her elbow folded against the counter, bright in the light, staring off in the distance. Diana's portraits always revealed an intimacy with their subjects—made it seem like they had whispered secrets to each other before the shot was taken. But these held a deeper emotional weight, and Ruth wasn't sure whether it was because of her own connection to the women, or if Diana's love was still living somehow, pouring out in the photos.

"What are you thinking?" he asked.

"Look at that." Ruth pointed to the photo where her mother was blowing a kiss. She thought of Diana's words: *God, I loved her*. She couldn't ignore her love for Charlie, but she didn't know what he felt about her anymore. She wondered what it looked like to the outside world, how it would look if it were caught in a photograph, how it might look to Nadia.

"It looks like love," Ruth replied.

"Yeah, it does," Charlie said.

They hovered over the photos, nearly touching, and Ruth felt the gap disappear between them in their shared silence—felt how close they were in the quiet sound of their breath. Just then Charlie's phone began to buzz, and Ruth remembered Nadia. She flinched at the sound.

"It's my mom," Charlie said, and Ruth thought he sensed what she was thinking about. Answering it, he stepped outside into the sun, and Ruth began to gather the photos, stacking them back together and putting everything in the box. She stuffed the rest of her things in her backpack, except for the camera. Ruth looked up toward the loft, toward her mother's paintings, and felt a pang of indecision. It felt wrong to leave them.

Hanging up, Charlie sighed again as Ruth stepped into the sun and shut the door to the studio.

"How often will you be here?" he asked.

"Every day, I think."

Charlie nodded. "You're going to do a great job," he said. "With the article."

Ruth felt an impulse to touch him, but the softness left his face, and she saw worry creep in as he looked between Ruth and the green archway. He smiled, but it looked like a grimace—a failed attempt.

"Well, I've gotta go," Ruth said, feeling anxious. Charlie nodded.

"I'll see you," she said. They waved, he headed off to the house, and she off to her bike. Then something stopped Ruth. She felt the camera in her hands, the shutter button under her fingertip, thought of how Charlie's face looked above her at the beach, and she wanted to capture it.

"Charlie!" she called.

He turned around.

"Yeah?"

"Can I take your picture?"

Then she saw him smile for real, easy, and he looked like his old self, like the Charlie she had first met ten years ago, any sign of change disappearing at this distance. Quickly, she picked up the camera, focused the shot, and pressed the shutter button.

As Ruth biked home, she thought about the contents of the teal box as it bounced gently in her bicycle basket. Her mind's eye filled with the images of her mother and Diana, with the paintings, and she became agitated with questions. She tried to imagine the women as she had known them, together in the same room.

Ruth considered what had kept Diana from telling her as the years went on. Maybe that first summer it made sense, but what about every year after that? What about all the times Ruth told Diana she wished she could know her mom now, wished she could talk to her. The realization that Diana had lied to Ruth for years settled into her mind and made her jaw clench, coloring each inhale as her breath grew faster.

The more she tried to understand it, the angrier she grew at all of the secrets. She had been grieving these women, but now it seemed to Ruth that she didn't even know them, and that they hadn't wanted her to.

4

Upon arriving home, Ruth paced the bedroom. Lucy was out again, the faint smell of a cigarette indicating her recent departure. She pulled out her journal and tried to write how she felt, looking at the letter, at the photos stacked in the box, but she couldn't understand it all. Sitting on the floor, she pulled her knees up to her chest. She decided to call her dad.

Joel answered on the second ring.

"Hey, kid," he said. Ruth could hear Hank barking in the background. "Getting ready for work?"

Ruth had forgotten about work.

"Hey." In the bedroom mirror she could see her face, crumpled and distorted. She looked away.

"What's going on?" Joel asked.

"I got a letter from Diana," Ruth said.

Her dad stopped fidgeting on the other end of the phone and cleared his throat. "What do you mean you got a letter?"

"She left me a letter and a box of photographs she took of Mom. She also had paintings that Mom did, and she said that they were in love and that she was surprised when you sent me to her." She realized she wasn't making sense, but the words were falling out of her.

"What did the letter say?" Joel asked. He sounded calm, which infuriated Ruth.

"Why does that matter, Dad? Can you just tell me the truth?"

The frustration she had felt earlier at not being able to ask Diana any questions was building again. She recognized anger in her voice, and realized that Joel had lied to her too.

Joel let out a deep sigh, and Ruth heard him open the door to let the dog outside, the barking dissipating in the background.

He didn't say anything for a while, and Ruth listened to his breathing.

"Your mom was never really . . . in *love* with me," Joel said. "I'm sure you could probably tell that growing up."

Ruth lapsed into silence. She tried to remember her parents as they were when she was a kid. It was rare that they ever went out on a date, or were very affectionate in front of her. She couldn't really remember them ever kissing each other goodbye, leaning on each other after a long day, or holding hands. Ruth hadn't thought anything of it at the time. She didn't know anything different. They were always kind to each other, but thinking about it now, Ruth could maybe sense Joel longing for Maggie in a way that she hadn't understood before, a longing that was never reciprocated.

"What do you mean?"

"You know we met at a church event, right?" he asked. "It was a food drive, and I was there doing construction on the place, not really at the event, but your mom was—she was there with your grandparents."

Ruth could hear the choked emotion from her father. For a second, she felt guilty for asking anything of him.

"We went out on a couple dates," Joel said, clearing his throat—the sound loud in Ruth's ear. "We . . . spent the night together. . . . I thought things were going well, but then she told me she was sorry, that she was still in love with someone else. She said she was moving away."

Ruth wasn't sure if she was making any sound. She heard the ferry horn blow in town, the familiar sound startling her out of her concentration.

"But then she called me a month later and asked if we could meet. She told me she was pregnant."

Ruth tried to imagine the meeting. Her mind built it in the diner she used to work at, the sounds of coffee being made, the ring of the door as it opened, the nervous look on Maggie's face.

"So, I proposed," Joel said. "I thought your mom was . . . perfect. And you! I was so happy about you."

"Oh," Ruth said.

She tried to imagine her mother packing secretly for New York, planning to leave her parents' stifling house, the many hanging crucifixes looking down at her. She tried to imagine Maggie and Diana together, walking down a city street holding hands, the freedom she'd been so close to having.

Then Ruth's mind was filled with the image of a pregnancy test, of Maggie's face fallen into fear and sadness . . . because of her.

When Ruth had asked as a child about how her parents met and how she came to be, her mom looked at her for a long time and told her that she was a miracle, that Maggie never thought she would get to have a child, and she would hold her close and say that Joel and she were so lucky. Ruth stopped asking as she got older since the response was always so vague and seemed to make everyone uncomfortable.

She was putting the pieces together now. Her mom had decided she was going to New York to be with Diana. She had a plan, and then she found out she was pregnant. She tried to imagine what that would feel like, and she was overcome with a tunneling sadness so deep and mounting that she felt her hand grow weak around the phone. Was she the reason her mom gave up her dream, gave up her life?

Joel kept speaking, trying to console her, but Ruth wasn't listening.

"Your mother loved you most in this world," she heard him say now. "You know that."

"Why didn't you tell me?" Ruth asked.

"Why would I ever tell you that? It didn't matter. We wanted you."

Ruth wasn't listening to any of the consolations. If anything, they were making her angrier. "So you knew about Diana?" she asked.

"Over time, your mother felt like she could tell me."

"Tell you what?" Ruth pushed.

"Diana was the one that got away, I guess."

"What about the painting? Why did she stop painting?"

There was a beat of silence on the other end of the line.

"I don't know what you're talking about," Joel said.

After hanging up with Joel, Ruth sat on the floor. She watched dust particles float into the sun spot and catch the light, watched how they moved, trying to numb her mind. It felt like her body was pulsing, existing as a separate entity from her brain. She let the pain roil within her for another moment before she grabbed her phone again and texted Charlie.

I need you to do me a favor.

5

After sending the message, Ruth felt the dead space of waiting hang in the air. She grew more frantic as she thought of how much Lynn had already cleared out of Diana's house, how it was only a matter of time before Lynn directed her attention to the studio. In her mind's eye, she could clearly see Lynn opening the bin of paintings and discarding them without a second thought.

Eventually she realized she was going to be late for work, and Ruth scrambled to get ready, shoving her notepad in her back pocket, slinging her hair up into a messy bun, and grabbing her wine key from her desk. Walking, the sun was still strong, and it burned against her black T-shirt. The restaurant was five minutes from the cottage into town, and as Ruth headed toward it she saw Nadia, Charlie, and Lynn step out of the bakery. Nadia had her hand on Charlie's shoulder and was talking to Lynn. Ruth crossed the road to avoid being seen, but Charlie spotted her. Feeling frenzied, she picked up her phone and pointed at it. She kept walking without looking back to see if Nadia and Lynn had seen her.

All night at work, Ruth kept pulling her phone out when she thought no one was looking, waiting for a text back from Charlie. It was almost Fourth of July weekend, and the restaurant was slammed with tourists, all the locals who usually dined there hiding or cooking at home. Ruth's section was full of tired families and sunburned couples, already tipsy, their voices growing louder and louder as the night wore on, their laughs looser, all of it grating on her.

Finally, at seven-thirty, Ruth felt her phone buzz in her pocket. Looking at her tables, she saw at least five things she needed to do, but she turned on her clogged heel and fast walked past a guest to the bathroom, locking the door behind her and reading the message from Charlie—

What's happening?

Ruth called Charlie, not thinking about what he could be doing, whether he was with Nadia or Lynn. The phone rang for a while, and Ruth thought she was going to have to go back out onto the floor without talking to him.

"Hello?" Charlie answered. His voice was almost a whisper.

"Charlie, I need you to do something for me," Ruth said. "It's urgent."

Ruth described the paintings upstairs in the studio. "I need to get them," she said, explaining her fears about Lynn.

"Okay, I'm sure we can do it sometime soon. She's not going to clear out the studio, don't worry—"

"No, I need them tonight," she said. Her voice sounded foreign to herself.

There was silence on the other end of the line. Someone banged on the bathroom door. Ruth could hear people talking while waiting for the bathroom outside.

"Ruth—" Charlie started, but Ruth cut him off.

"Charlie, please. I need this."

There was silence for another minute.

"Okay. Text me when you're done with work," he said. "I have to go."

"Thank you."

Ruth turned the faucet on and ran the water cold, sticking her face under it. Lifting her head up, she looked at herself in the mirror. Her features seemed blurry, like they were melting away, like they had been changing for some time and she was only noticing it now. Dabbing her face with a paper towel, she threw open the bathroom door and walked past the line of five women that had formed. Someone yelled something at her back, but she didn't hear it. Taking a deep breath, she went back to work, picking up a plate of gnocchi from the window pass.

At the end of the night, Ruth was racing to get all of her side work done. The clank of the polished silverware as it hit the pile of forks made her nerves feel more and more frayed. Her last table was still sitting, although their drinks had been empty for half an hour. They had already closed out, but Ruth saw them looking around to order another drink. She checked her watch. The restaurant had closed forty-five minutes ago. Anytime one of the servers was about to walk out into the dining room, Ruth grabbed them by the arm and begged them not to. She didn't want the table to have any reason to stay. Finally, they got up slowly, still talking while standing, and after five more minutes they left the building. Ruth ran out to the table then to start clearing. She could see one of the people from the table point through the window in her direction, but she kept moving.

"What's your deal?" her co-worker asked as she helped pick up the empty glasses and spent napkins.

"I just have to get out of here," Ruth said.

She was polishing the last of the glasses behind the bar when Lucy approached the front door. Looking in at Ruth, she knocked and waved. Ruth ran around the bar and opened the door, letting Lucy in before locking it again behind her.

"Wow," Lucy said. "I thought there would still be people in here. Town is crazy." She sat down at the bar, and Ruth continued polishing. "Hey, so I know you have to wake up super early to get to the studio, but I wanted to ask you if you wanted to get breakfast tomorrow, after you're done," she said. "Or, you know, we could go out for a quick drink somewhere now."

Ruth felt her phone buzz again in her pocket. Pulling it out, she read the text from Charlie on the screen.

Are you done yet?

"Who's that?" Lucy asked.

"It's Charlie. I can't get a drink tonight, but yeah, let's do breakfast tomorrow," Ruth said. "I might not go to the studio anyways."

Lucy didn't say anything, and when Ruth looked up at her, she was staring at Ruth with an intense gaze.

"What?" Ruth asked.

Lucy shook her head and smiled, seeming to have snapped out of it. "Okay, you almost done? I can give you a ride home."

"I'm not going home," Ruth replied.

"Okay . . ."

"I'll tell you about it tomorrow." Ruth realized she was being distant and forced herself to smile. She shoved the empty glass rack back in its spot under the bar and took off her apron.

"Okay," Lucy said, and Ruth could tell she was annoyed. Lucy got up from the barstool and started to walk out without saying anything more. The door closed behind her, and Ruth flinched at the rattle it made.

Ruth called Charlie as soon as she left the back door of the restaurant, but he didn't answer. Walking along the dark sidewalk, she heard the waves breaking just beyond the dunes. There was a squall coming, and the wind had grown heavier in the nine hours that Ruth had been working. She called again, standing in the wind, but again he didn't answer. People walked past her on the sidewalk trying to get to the bars, and Ruth listened to a band getting back on stage somewhere a few buildings away. She texted Charlie.

I'm done. Call me.

For a minute she stared at her phone, waiting for the three little dots to indicate that Charlie was typing, but they didn't come. She watched the clock change in the corner of her screen, put the phone away, and stood motionless in the darkness again. The propulsion to get her mother's paintings out of the studio and away from Lynn had gotten her through the night. She had known it would be difficult, that Nadia would want to know why Charlie was leaving so late, where he could possibly be going. She realized she was testing him. She wanted him to show up for her, even if it was hard, even if it meant lying to his fiancée. She wanted him to prioritize her. Recognizing this, her body deflated with embarrassment. She thought back to the fight she had overheard between Nadia and Charlie that morning. Although Ruth hadn't formed the thought fully at the time, it was clear to her now that she'd assumed Charlie having second thoughts about the wedding came from their moment at the beach. Now she wasn't so sure. Did it matter?

As the adrenaline from the night crashed within her, Ruth sat on the edge of the sidewalk and felt the distraction of the paintings, of Nadia and Charlie, fade away, laying bare the real fear that was gripping her.

Again, she tried to imagine the sense of freedom that Maggie must have felt at the idea of choosing Diana, choosing New York, of the possibilities she must have hoped for, only to lose that whole life without even getting to taste it, the hopes turning hollow and empty. She wondered how Maggie had lived with those husks of dreams, whether they had eaten away at her in the dead of night or pulsed through her like a call to leave when she couldn't get baby Ruth to stop crying, whether they had turned inside her and fed the cancer, causing it to spread, to multiply. That, actually, Ruth had been the reason, the source of everything that turned Maggie's life upside down—that *she* was a cancer.

The thought scared Ruth so much that she stood up and

started walking to the beach, moving quickly, trying to trick her mind into dropping the thought.

Ruth had always felt that Maggie put her first, had never questioned that she was loved, and from the outside Maggie had seemed content, often joyful, as a mother. But considering it now, at twenty-seven, learning about what Maggie gave up, Ruth felt a sense of guilt she didn't know what to do with. What would Maggie's life have been like if she hadn't gotten pregnant? If she had decided not to keep the baby?

The feelings that she had been trying to ignore all night, all day since she read the letter, the similarities that had been growing sharper and sharper in her mind, ran through Ruth. As she walked onto the dark beach, the fact that she might be pregnant at that moment struck her with such force that she had to sit in the sand, her body limp and tired.

Ruth tried to scan her body, to see if she could sense any difference, even though she knew it was too soon to tell, but all she felt was her heart's sharp and fast beating. She tried to breathe, but she felt like a weight was pressing on her sternum.

Diana and Maggie had lost each other in life. They had been *so* close to having what they wanted, having each other, only for it to crumble as Ruth came into the world. She thought of Charlie, of all the times they had missed each other, how she always felt like she was on the cusp of something with him. She was terrified by the idea that they would miss each other again, that she could lose what little hope she had in the same way her mother had, like it was a cycle she was destined to be a part of.

Since Diana's death, Ruth had been feeling like everything was slipping out of her grasp, like sand through her fingers, no matter how hard she tried to keep everything in place. Now she sat on the cold beach alone, staring out at the water. The ocean, usually her source of calm, felt to her then like a black hole, unable to soothe, empty of meaning. Wind blew over the dunes, scattering sand up toward her face. She felt exposed, uncovered—alone.

6

When Ruth woke the next morning, Lucy wasn't in her bed. The light was muted, and Ruth could see clouds moving quickly across the sky through the window. Going to the mirror, Ruth looked at her puffy eyes. She could have slept for longer, but a text from Lucy had woken her up—

I'm at the bagel shop

Ruth wondered why Lucy would've gone without her. Usually the walk into town in the morning was part of their routine, part of their time to catch up. Throwing on a sundress, she looked down at her phone just as a text from Charlie popped up. She opened the message.

I'm sorry. I couldn't get away.

Clicking the screen closed, she stood in the middle of the room and heard the ferry horn blow in town. Country music grew louder and then soft again as a car drove by. She felt nothing. Looking in the mirror, she again had the sense that she was unrecognizable to herself. The dress was something she had worn for years, but somehow all of a sudden it looked wrong. Her hair had grown—not in a way that was unusual for Ruth, but now it seemed ragged. She had a faraway look, the sharp edges smudged, the whites of her eyes dulled. Grabbing an old pair of sunglasses, she left the room and headed into town on her bike, feeling uneasy.

Ruth coasted up to the bagel shop, catching sight of Lucy's curls as she turned the corner in the long line. Ruth propped her bike up in the rack, and people grumbled as she excused herself until she was next to Lucy.

"Oh, hey," Lucy said.

"Why didn't you wait for me?" Ruth asked.

"I was out of the house a lot earlier. I went swimming, and then I headed over to the gallery. I had a lot of calls to make. Plus, I didn't know if you were going to get any writing done today. I figured I would give you the room and just bring food back for you," she said. "*Did* you do any writing?" Lucy looked at her.

Ruth lifted her sunglasses and rubbed her eyes against the hot morning sun. She felt she was being observed.

"No. Not yet anyways," she said.

Lucy looked away, and Ruth felt a coldness bubble up between them as they shuffled forward in line, not speaking. It was an awkward silence that she didn't know how to fill. It confused her. She had never felt that way before with Lucy.

The line moved again, and Ruth was about to ask Lucy what was going on when her phone started to buzz in her pocket. Pulling it out, she saw that it was Ethel's New York number.

"I'll be right back," Ruth said. "It's about the article."

"Okay," Lucy replied, shrugging.

Ruth walked out and onto the sidewalk, sitting on an empty bench that faced the road.

"Hello?" she answered. Her voice sounded shaky.

"Ruth? It's Ethel."

"Hey, Ethel," Ruth replied, trying to steady her voice.

"I just wanted to check in and see how you were doing. If you had any questions about the material I sent over—if I could help with anything. I realized I didn't exactly tell you that you could bounce ideas off me."

Ruth had wanted to use the article to say goodbye to Diana, to write something worthy of what she meant to her, but her mind was so muddied now with the banal unfairness of death, of people reduced to items left in boxes, to letters instead of conversations, to questions, secrets, and lies, that whatever confidence she'd convinced herself she had was gone now.

She wondered if Ethel already had someone else writing the article, someone who had been working hard for this shot that Ruth had been essentially throwing away. She dug her fingernails into her palm out of anger at herself until they left crescent-shaped dents along the creases. She thought of the restaurant last night, how much Ruth had to mentally fight with herself to get through the shift.

Ethel said something about sending any pages Ruth had over and Ruth pulled herself out of her head.

"Oh, yes," Ruth said, staring at the indents left in her hand. "I have a strong start. I just wanted to get the pages in better shape before sending anything over to you. It's going well though," she lied.

"Oh! That's great news. I was worried for a minute. I know how much Diana wanted this," she said, and a swelling shame expanded to consume Ruth. "All right then. Well, feel free to email me with pages or questions."

"Thanks, Ethel," Ruth replied.

As Ruth hung up the phone, she stared into the middle of the road, at the different-colored bikes swerving in and out of her line of sight. Ruth shut her eyes to slits so everything melded like a kaleidoscope held up to the sun. She tried to lose focus on her stress, wanted to keep dissociating, until she felt someone approach, breaking her reverie. Startled, she saw Louis standing next to her.

"Hey, man, yeah, we know each other," Louis said, nodding at Charlie.

Just then Lucy emerged with a paper bag of food. She handed Ruth a coffee.

"You disappeared," she said to Ruth, sounding annoyed. Then she nodded in Charlie and Nadia's direction. "Look at these lovebirds. Getting ready for the big day?" Her enthusiasm gnawed at Ruth.

"Yeah—it's stressful though. A lot of work," Nadia said, turning to Charlie, who nodded in agreement after a second.

Lucy pulled out a giant bagel half, covered in cream cheese.

"And we're having this big Fourth of July party, which was stupid," Nadia said. Then, as if she had let something slip, she stopped.

Charlie looked up from the ground at Nadia, who was avoiding his eyes.

"That sounds fun," Lucy said, seemingly unaware of Nadia's sudden awkwardness.

Charlie was looking over their heads and Ruth could feel him torn between doing the polite thing and inviting them or letting it slide to save Nadia.

"You should all come!" he said, politeness clearly winning out. Then, as if committing to the idea, he repeated, "All of you must come after the parade."

Nadia silently nodded in agreement, although Ruth thought she saw a flashing glance toward Charlie before she put her sunglasses down to cover her eyes.

"Absolutely, yes. It's going to be a lot of our friends from Boston. . . . It'll be fun!" she said.

"At Diana's house?" Louis asked.

Nadia nodded again. "At the house, yes."

Ruth prickled at Nadia's distinction—*the* house, not *Diana's* house.

"Will your mom be there?" Lucy asked Charlie with a mouth full of bagel. Ruth felt her chest tighten. Even if she wanted to go, she wouldn't be able to with Lynn there.

"So when are you going to get that lucky shirt back to m
he asked, sitting down on the bench next to Ruth.

"Huh?" she asked, raising an eyebrow and shielding her e
from the sun. A headache began to pulse through her. Her m
was still on the phone call.

"What're you doing tomorrow night?" Louis asked.

"What?" She felt like her brain was working through m
trying to catch up to the moment. Louis ran his hand thro
his hair, and Ruth wondered then if he was nervous.

"I was thinking, if you were free . . ."

Louis paused and a couple walking hand-in-hand passe
them on the sidewalk. It was Nadia and Charlie. Nadia
laughing so hard that she stopped and folded herself into C
lie's shoulder, wiping her eyes. As she uncurled herself, N
noticed Ruth and came to a stop in front of the bench, Ch
lurching like he had been planning to walk straight by.

"Hi!" Nadia said energetically. Her face broke into an ex
grin, another giggle escaping her, which made Ruth ur
Charlie and Nadia's hands were intertwined, and Ruth
dered how they had made up from the fight she'd heard c
porch—wondered what promises had been made. C
glanced at Ruth, looking sheepish for a second, until
caught his eye.

"Hey," Ruth said. She was unsure what her tone sounde
Louis looked at each of them, seeming to appraise the situ

"Is this your boyfriend?" Nadia asked, her face gr
brighter, pointing to Louis and holding out her hand.
shook it and smiled.

"No, ma'am," Louis said, shaking his head. "Just a frie

"This is Louis. He lives here," Ruth said in explanatio
dering if Nadia had been pleased at the idea of Ruth h
boyfriend.

"Oh, hi! I'm Nadia, and this is my fiancé, Charlie," s
motioning behind her to Charlie, where he stood, looking
didn't know what to do with himself.

Charlie's eyes met Ruth's before replying. "No, she's visiting her cousin in Montauk for the weekend."

Nadia looked between them, then added in a rush, "Please say you'll come. I won't take no for an answer." Ruth wondered if her enthusiasm was really to avoid seeming impolite. She watched Nadia glance back at Charlie, his expression unchanged.

The group was silent for a minute before Louis broke in. "Well, I'll definitely be there," he said.

"Okay, great. I'll have Charlie send you all the details," Nadia said, looking at Lucy. "See you soon!" She waved and kept walking toward the bagel shop, Charlie trailing behind her. The group was quiet for a second. Louis got up from the bench.

"Well, I guess I'll see you two at the party," he said. Ruth watched him walk away. He stepped easily through the crowds toward his beat-up green truck, and she felt an impulse to run after him and get in.

Lucy handed Ruth her bagel. "That'll be interesting," she said.

The next day Ruth woke up to her alarm at four-thirty in the morning. It was dark out and there was a cool mist hovering over the ground as she got on her bike and pedaled to Diana's house, the sound of the bike chain protesting against the hill. When she got there, she didn't look toward the house but jogged to the studio, eager to be inside. She still hadn't responded to Charlie's message, even though he had called three times yesterday after the run-in. His words from the morning before made her shiver in embarrassment—*I couldn't get away*.

Closing the door to the studio behind her, the silence seemed to thrum in her ears. It was hot in the dark room, but Ruth resisted the urge to open the window. The feeling of insulation was comforting to her. As she stood there among Diana's things, a sense of calm enveloped her, a feeling that she allowed to percolate for another moment before moving and unsettling the spell. Sitting at Diana's desk, she opened her laptop, the still-blank document popping up white and bright on the screen.

Ruth tried to focus. The call from Ethel had made her aware of how close the deadline really was.

Ruth decided to try ignoring the letter from Diana, ignoring their relationship altogether, and focusing on her career. Ethel had sent Ruth a folder of all of Diana's previous work at *Vogue*, and Ruth scrolled through the many photos of models in slightly outdated hemlines and makeup, finding it difficult to see anything of Diana within them. If she hunted for it, the contrast or the framing of the photographs started to look familiar, but once she looked at the photographs all together there was nothing there that she could respond to.

She had asked Diana about her time at *Vogue* once, after Diana had returned from a photoshoot in the city. By that time it was rare that she stepped back into the world of fashion photography, but sometimes a creative director would call her and woo her back to New York for another project.

"Did you ever like working there?" Ruth asked after listening to Diana vent about the experience from where she lay, prostrate on the couch—whenever Diana returned to the island from the mainland, she promised she would never leave again if she could help it, swearing under her breath about four-lane highways, how everyone was welded to their cellphones, and dogs that took shits in the middle of the sidewalk.

"Oh, yeah. I mean, of course," she said. "It was the job that pulled me out of relative poverty. I learned so much." She looked at the ceiling, her red hair falling over the side of the couch and dusting the wooden floorboards.

"How broke were you?" Ruth had asked. It was hard for her to imagine Diana any different from how she was when she met her. Diana had sat up and laughed.

"Just starving artist stuff. If I had needed to, I could have gone home to my parents, but I never wanted to. I wanted to try," she said. "I think sometimes that kind of desperation is the thing you need to push you into what you really want. I was working at an all-night diner making shit tips and hating my life, going to magazine and theater parties, and trying to meet people who would give me a job somewhere in the art world. Things were pretty bleak for a while. But little by little it worked."

"But did you like it?" Ruth asked, sitting on the floor near where Diana's head rested on the couch. She was trying to imagine what that kind of faith in yourself would feel like—that it would all work out, that you were on the right path.

"Of course," Diana said. "It was thrilling."

Now Ruth looked up past articles that had been written on Diana—about her multiple photography books, reviews of past shows, the *Vogue* covers, and her eventual Guggenheim fellowship, but they all talked about her like a stranger, and Ruth couldn't see the person she knew within the words. Even the photos of her looked like someone else, glossy, the wrinkles and sunspots that Ruth knew erased from her face. After a while she clicked out of every open tab with an alienated feeling. She tried starting with a memory, writing down the conversation on the couch, but the words felt wooden and forced.

She deleted them, watching as the cursor blinked until she was left with the same blank page. Closing the lid of the computer, Ruth's eyes went to the loft. The sun had risen and morning brightness was catching dust motes floating up by the clutter of boxes. Standing, she climbed up and brought the bin of Maggie's paintings over to her again.

She pulled out the painting on top and looked at the lighthouse, the ocean, and Diana's vague figure. Ruth ran her fingers over the textured paint of the choppy water, examining the way the colors collected along the sides of the canvas and where they stopped, the brush becoming more visible in the wispy lines of color.

Ruth thought about what Charlie had said on their walk—about her being a good mother. She tried to imagine a child in her arms, but the vague image only filled her with a lost and broken feeling. Picking up another painting, Ruth remembered the time spent following her mother around other people's houses, the way Maggie made her feel sheltered by love, how the world felt too wide after she was gone, and how Ruth had needed to hide from it.

She couldn't see herself within any of those motherly actions, couldn't imagine how it would feel to have someone small look at her with eyes that looked like hers, with tiny arms outstretched, searching for comfort. Thinking about it made her heart race. Waiting for her period was making her more nervous with each passing day. She still had time, but she was beginning to worry.

The broken feeling returned like a smoke sitting low within her lungs. She wished that the paintings made her feel closer to her mother, that they felt more like the gift she was sure Diana intended, but the more Ruth stared at them, the more she felt that her mother was farther away than ever before.

Joel had been calling her every day since they last spoke, even asking if he could come out to the island again to check on her. Ruth had not answered any of the calls but sent a message telling him not to come. She knew she wouldn't have to convince him, that he would be too fearful of pushing her farther away to do something so drastic.

Thinking of what Joel told her about Maggie, she wondered how alone her mother must have felt in a marriage without passion, without real connection, and with no room for change. If Maggie had lived longer, would she have left them, gone looking for Diana or for the version of her life that she gave up when Ruth was born?

Ruth put the paintings back, feeling more unnerved than she had the first time she saw them. The sinking feeling in her chest remained as she climbed down into the studio, and she stood in the center of the room, paralyzed. She wanted someone to orient her, move her in the direction that would make most sense, bend her elbows as if she were a paper doll. Glancing back at the paintings, she packed her bag even though she still had an hour left to be in the studio. Closing the door behind her, and looking up toward the house, she saw Nadia walking toward her on the grass. Ruth froze. She thought of running to her bike and fleeing, but she knew she couldn't.

"Hey," Ruth said, unsure of how her voice sounded.

"Morning," Nadia said, and Ruth couldn't help scanning the house over Nadia's shoulder to see if there was evidence of Charlie or Lynn. "No one else is awake," Nadia said, noticing.

Caught, Ruth just nodded. They stared at each other for a second, and Ruth realized she had never looked Nadia square in the face. Doing so now was almost painful. Her cheekbones were prominent, and her skin had a tawny glow that illuminated her blue eyes.

"I really want you to come to the party," Nadia said.

Ruth felt trapped.

"I feel like you're important to Charlie and we're getting married, so I should get to know you better."

"What do you mean?" Ruth asked. The sun had risen over the trees and was shining in Ruth's eyes. Holding up a hand so she could see, she felt herself begin to sweat.

"You're Charlie's friend, and Charlie's friends matter to me," Nadia replied.

"Oh, yeah, of course," Ruth said, the image of his lips inches away from her face clear in her mind.

She sounded sincere, but something about the invitation still made Ruth wary. Maybe Nadia wanted to observe her with Charlie, to see if she had anything to worry about, or maybe she really did just want to make more of an effort with Charlie's friends. For a second, Nadia's intense stare made it clear to Ruth that going to the party would be a mistake. Whatever her secret motive might be, Ruth didn't want to be a part of it.

But then she thought of Nadia and Charlie's fight on the porch, the lost look in Charlie's eyes as Ruth pedaled away from him after the beach day, the love she still felt for Charlie seeping out of every pore. Ruth wanted to see the two of them together, to understand what it was about Nadia that made Charlie say, *When you know you know*. Maybe it would help Ruth let him go, or maybe she would see that their relationship was fragile—that there were more cracks in it than were already visible.

"Yeah," Ruth replied. "I can't wait."

7

The next morning Ruth watched as the sun brightened the trees out her window as it rose. She laid in bed as the sun got higher, but she could not make herself move toward the door, toward the studio. The feeling of being frozen that had consumed her yesterday was still there, indecision coloring everything around her.

Eventually Ruth made her way to the small desk that she and Lucy shared. She wrote for an hour, each sentence slow to emerge and looking wrong on the page. She had just over a month to send Ethel a draft of the article. But instead of the pressure moving her forward, it seemed to float around her, unable to touch her. Ruth brought out the box of photographs and flipped through a few, the shots now familiar to her, like a slideshow of memories that could almost be hers.

Ruth read Diana's letter again, Joel's story now in the back of her mind too. Whenever Ruth tried to imagine Diana and her mother together, there was a rightness to the image. It sprang up in her mind easily, and Ruth found herself smiling while thinking of them walking down a city street together, hand-in-hand. But at some point she would realize that in this imagined world there was no place for her.

The feeling that she had stood in the way of their happiness became all-consuming. It caused her to stare in the mirror, wondering about the features that resembled Maggie and looking for features that reminded her of Diana, although there were none—of course there were none. She was overcome with the angry need to ask questions. The information she received was so incomplete, and the fact she couldn't ask her mother about Diana seemed like the cruelest reminder that they were both gone.

She sat at the desk as the air in the small room grew hotter. The weather forecast said the high that day was going to be one hundred and one degrees. She was sweating through her shirt and drops were falling down her neck. The heat made it impossible for Ruth to focus. Lifting the camera out of the box, she stared at the top, at the four photos that were already taken on this roll of film, and wondered what the first three could be.

When she heard her phone ring, she was worried it was Ethel again, somehow knowing that what she had written that day was worthless. But it was Charlie. Ruth stared at the name on the screen. She was still angry that he had stood her up the other night. She thought about not answering but picked up the phone just before it went to voicemail.

"Hello?" she said.

"You didn't come to the studio today," Charlie replied.

"No," Ruth said, staring at the Word document in front of her, trying not to read what she had written.

Charlie didn't say anything else. Ruth heard a small scuffling in the background and imagined him sitting on the back deck, tracing the boards with a found twig.

"Hello?" Ruth said again.

"Listen, I'm sorry about the other night."

"It's okay, you're married. I don't know why I thought I could sneak you out in the middle of the night with me." Saying the word *married* made Ruth want to shrivel up. She wiped sweat off her forehead.

"I'm not married," Charlie replied.

"Basically married," Ruth said.

The line was quiet for a minute and Ruth listened to Charlie breathe, wondering what he was thinking.

"I can get you the paintings now," he said, breaking the silence. "If you want."

Ruth thought of holding her mother's artwork yesterday, how disoriented they made her feel. When she had called Charlie the other night, it had seemed like keeping them with her, away from Lynn, would be the only thing that could fix her. Now the idea of seeing the paintings felt too potent, a reminder that maybe she didn't know her mother as well as she thought she did, a reminder that they were just items, a discarded memory compared to what she really wanted.

"Where's Nadia?" Ruth asked instead of answering.

Charlie sighed. "She's getting ready for the party."

"Aren't all these people coming back for your wedding that's in like two months?" It was the first time she had said the timeline out loud. Two months, Ruth thought. That was nothing.

"They're mostly people from Boston who wanted somewhere to go for the Fourth," Charlie said. "The Fourth is a big holiday for Nadia."

The restaurant Ruth worked at had decided to close for the Fourth of July this year. The air conditioner in the kitchen was broken and the fry guy, Joe, almost passed out the night before from the heat. Ruth had to bring him cold, wet towels out on the loading dock and hold them against his neck before his color returned to normal. This would be the first Fourth of July in a long time that she wasn't working; in fact, Ruth couldn't remember the last Christmas, Thanksgiving, or Fourth of July that she hadn't spent standing at a table, waiting on people in some capacity. She thought about the traditions that other people had, that Nadia must have, that Charlie must have, that they would build together. She was jealous.

"Do you not want me to come?" Ruth asked. "I know you were just being polite . . ." She thought about telling Charlie about yesterday morning, how Nadia had invited her again, but she didn't want to talk about her any longer.

Charlie didn't answer for a minute.

"No, you should come," he said. "I want you to come."

"Are you okay, Charlie?" she asked, sensing something in his voice. "Do you want to talk about something?"

Ruth had a flash of his face hovering above hers, saltwater dripping down her temples, how she could have sworn they were just about to kiss. It already felt like a long time had passed between then and now.

He was silent for a long minute.

"Do you think I'm rushing things?" he finally asked. "With the wedding?"

"What?" Ruth asked, stunned.

"It's okay, you can tell me what you think." He was speaking quickly, like the words had been building up and were falling out of him.

"Do *you* feel like you're rushing things?"

"I've just been . . . I don't know," he said. "Ruth?"

"Yeah?" She didn't know if she was breathing.

"Have you ever thought . . ." Charlie started and then stopped.

"Have I ever thought what?"

Again, there was silence on the line. Ruth listened as Charlie took a deep breath.

"I've been having these dreams of you lately," he said. "Well, *more* dreams of you lately."

A droplet of sweat dropped off the tip of Ruth's nose and onto the open journal page in front of her. Staring at the paper as it wrinkled from the moisture, she tried to focus on her breathing. "What happens?" she asked.

"You're there but you're across the room and you look at me like . . . like you don't know me. I wave, I try to get your attention, but you never see me."

The similarity of their dreams startled Ruth. She was about

to tell him how she understood, how she always woke up feeling like she was leaving something important behind. Just then she heard car tires over gravel on the other end of the line and even before Charlie spoke, she knew it was Nadia getting home.

"I've gotta go," Charlie said. "I'll see you at the party."

The line went dead. Ruth sat at her desk and continued to stare at the blinking cursor.

Later that evening, Lucy and Ruth approached Diana's house on foot, walking up the steep hill.

"Jesus. How many people are here?" Lucy asked, dragging her finger along the side of a black Mercedes-Benz SUV and leaving a trail in the dust from the dirt road. The license plates were all from New York and Connecticut, and while that wasn't an uncommon thing on the island, it gave Ruth a sense of foreboding to add to her already racing thoughts.

"Did you write today?" Lucy asked, hiking her colorful tie-dyed shawl up so that it was draped across her back, framing her tanned shoulders.

Ruth thought again of the blinking cursor and the document filled with useless sentences. She knew the deadline was approaching, but it seemed to her like if she made no progress and didn't call Ethel, then the whole thing would evaporate back into the imaginary world that it belonged to and the rhythm of her life could continue the way it had been.

"A little," Ruth said.

"How's it coming?"

"I don't know. I might call Ethel and just give the whole thing up."

She still hadn't told Lucy about the paintings or her conversation with Joel. Every time she thought about explaining what was happening, how she felt, she stopped herself. She felt like Lucy wouldn't understand, would push her to keep writing without thinking about how Ruth might be feeling because she had no experience with the things you find after a death—all the sad, small treasures.

They walked on in silence. Looking at Lucy, Ruth could tell she was angry. She stopped in the middle of the dirt road.

"Are you mad about something? What's going on?" Ruth asked.

Lucy turned and glared at Ruth for a beat before throwing her hands up into the air.

"You know what? Yeah, I am kind of pissed, Ruth," she said.

"About what?!"

A car drove by, kicking up dirt and pushing them to the edge of the road. Ruth almost backed into the BMW parked behind her. The dust settled and they were alone in the street again. Lucy shook her head and stared at the ground between them.

"What?" Ruth asked again.

Lucy looked up. "You have this big shot—this amazing shot—that Diana *gave* to you, literally put it in your lap . . . and you're not even trying."

"I am trying," Ruth said. But then she thought of all the false starts, how she deleted everything she wrote at the end of the day.

"Come on, Ruth."

"Listen, there's been . . . a lot going on and maybe this was a nice offer but it's just not going to work out right now," she said. The words felt slimy with exhaustion. She knew she was being cowardly, was hiding, but any alternative made Ruth feel like she was folding up from pressure, like a gum wrapper rolled between two palms, growing smaller and tighter.

"Do you know how . . . how much I would kill for the *huge* leg up that you have right now? How lucky you are?"

Ruth didn't say anything. She understood that someone else might have made more of Diana's connections all these years, the way she moved in circles where opportunities were like party favors, handed out with ease. Ruth had reached for none of it. She knew she was lucky, she just had never felt worth any of it.

"So, yeah, watching you throw that away makes me kind of mad at you," Lucy said. "I thought you were smart."

"Excuse me?"

"I said I thought you were smart."

Ruth knew her mouth was hanging open. She didn't know what to say.

Lucy continued. "And what about all this stuff with Charlie?"

"What do you mean?" She could hear herself being defensive.

"You're, like, getting sucked in, and he's getting married, Ruth! He's just . . . so besides the point. I don't get it."

"What do you mean, 'besides the point'? What does that even mean?"

"When I first met you, you wanted to do something with your life. I know you're sad, but you have to *do* something to help yourself. You have to get out of this fucking rut. Off this fucking island," Lucy said. "And you have this chance. It could spark something for you. It could be big and you're not even trying. You're just . . . letting life happen to you."

"I can't have a meaningful life here?" Ruth asked. She knew she was being obstinate, that she wasn't addressing the main point.

"Of course, Ruth. If you wanted to make your life here, you could do it so easily. You've had the chance so many times, but you don't . . . every time you don't. It's like you can't commit to a life. It's like you don't know what you want or you don't think you can have it so you keep doing the same thing you've been doing since you were seventeen!"

It was true that Ruth had been offered opportunities over the years—people asking her to partner in a small business, an oyster or flower farm, or opening a new restaurant. Ruth always said no. She thought about it, considered it, but in the end she never got back to the people or said no altogether. Choosing one thing always felt too permanent.

"What about you?" Ruth asked. "What's your big plan?"

She instantly felt bad for the question. She knew what Lucy's plan was. She thought of all the hard work Lucy had been putting in this summer, of what she was giving up to be here with Ruth.

Ruth wanted to say thank you, had thought about what a gift it was that Lucy was here for her, but each time she tried she felt something stop her, a shadow of resentment growing within her. She didn't want to thank Lucy for not moving on without her. She didn't want her to move on at all.

And Ruth suddenly felt like an immense burden at the thought. Even thinking about Diana and all she had done for Ruth—it all seemed coated in obligation. Lynn was right. Lucy was right. She did nothing to help herself. She was a drain on the people around her.

"You're right, Ruth, my big plan isn't really working out," Lucy said. "I'm working really fucking hard at it and it's not working out."

At that moment, Louis's green truck revved up the hill, kicking up dust as he pulled over behind the BMW. Ruth and Lucy fell silent as the engine cut and Louis jumped out and onto the dirt road. He was wearing faded jeans with the shadow of a rip growing on the front knee and a blue button-down that Ruth had never seen on him before. His hair was still wet and Ruth guessed he had jumped in the ocean before coming here. He approached the two of them and stopped a few feet away, reading their faces.

"Everything okay?" Louis asked. "What happened?" He looked concerned, and Ruth recognized the anxious jump toward expecting the worst-case scenario. Suddenly Ruth thought of Louis's uncle—about loss, about someone calling and telling you bad news. Jumping to the worst conclusion was something she did too.

"Yeah, we're fine," Lucy said.

They stood in the road for another second until the sound of a taxi coming up the hill made them keep moving toward the house.

Stepping through the green archway, they walked onto the yard. Ruth surveyed the party, her heart still loud in her ears, beating fast from her fight with Lucy. She didn't want to be there. People were sprinkled across the lawn, and Ruth watched as they brought wineglasses to their lips and shielded their eyes from the setting sun, nodding and laughing. Diana's old faded croquet set was out, sitting untouched in the middle of the field. A couple, the man in khaki shorts and the woman in a long gingham dress, walked out of the back door and onto the porch, calling back to someone inside the house.

"We're underdressed," Ruth said, noting the slip dresses and the pressed linen shirts.

It was strange to see so many people Ruth didn't know on Diana's lawn, going in and out of her house as if they belonged there. But as she watched Charlie open the screen door for Nadia, Ruth realized that she was the one who didn't belong anymore. She watched the door swing shut as Nadia stepped out of the house and noticed its usual echoing slam was absent. Looking closer, she realized it was a different door altogether. Scanning the yard, she saw the deck had been power washed, and the furniture on it was something she had never seen before, a dark gray that she could imagine being pulled from an issue of *Architectural Digest*. A lot had been done since the last time she was inside the house.

Lucy shrugged at Ruth's comment and started walking toward the party. Louis and Ruth followed. There were red, white, and blue streamers hanging from the beech tree and Louis Prima was playing from a small speaker on the porch. Ruth observed Nadia as they got closer. She was wearing a cornflower-blue cotton dress. It was short, tight, and fit her well. She was barefoot and her hair was in two low braids with strands falling out the edges. Ruth inwardly seethed at the effortless beauty she exuded and tried not to look down at her own old sundress, tried to forget about the sun-bleached shoulders and the cotton that was threadbare in places from overuse. She never thought to buy more summer clothes, preferring what she had been wearing for years, but now she felt shabby.

Lucy got to Nadia first and hugged her, her shawl swallowing

Nadia up so that she was engulfed in color and fringe. Charlie stepped down from the porch, wearing tan khaki pants rolled up at the ankles. In one hand he held a Miller High Life by the neck and in the other was a glass of white wine. The top three buttons of his loose linen shirt were open, and the collar fluttered in the breeze. He stopped when he saw Ruth, his smile fading for a second before Nadia turned and reached for him. Ruth realized she had been standing, staring, and not moving. She was frozen, not wanting to move forward, yet not wanting to turn back.

Louis put his hand on Ruth's shoulder and gently guided her toward the group. She couldn't imagine what her face looked like. The gesture felt too intimate, but she felt the comforting hand working too, felt the knot in her chest release. Charlie looked at the hand on Ruth's shoulder, then at Louis. The only one in the group who was beaming was Nadia.

"Ruth! I didn't know you two were together!" Nadia leapt toward Louis's neck and embraced him in a hug, then did the same to Ruth.

"No, no no," Ruth said, confused. There was no way that Nadia didn't remember their exchange from the other day. Ruth wondered whether she had brought it up to insinuate that there seemed like something more there, or to encourage Ruth to go for it; maybe Nadia wanted Ruth not to be single.

"Oh," Nadia said, still smiling. "My bad."

Louis's hands were now back in his pockets. Ruth tried to catch Charlie's eye. He seemed serene in a way that infuriated her.

"Wow," Louis said, looking around. "This place looks brand-new." He gave a sideways glance to Ruth.

"I like it," Lucy said.

"Come! Yeah. I'd love to give you a tour. We're in the process of getting things ready for the wedding here. A lot of work needed to be done," Nadia said. She started walking toward the house. The clouds were getting closer and thicker, causing an eerie gloom over the sun that still shone on the grass.

"Just a few things that were broken, really," Charlie said. His voice was defensive.

Nadia laughed.

"A lot was broken," she said, her hand going to his cheek. He smiled as she ran her fingers over the curve of his ear as if to move a strand of hair before bouncing at a quick pace toward the front door, the ice in her white wine jingling against the clouded glass.

It was such an adoring gesture—Ruth's stomach dropped.

"We needed a new front door. If I heard this thing slam one more time, I was going to lose my mind," Nadia said.

As Nadia led the way into the house, Ruth kept her eyes on the back of Charlie's head. He didn't look behind him as he held the door open for her. Ruth grabbed the shining gold handle. The old door had been thin wood, with chipped blue paint and a thick mesh screen that mosquitos bumped up against in the night. The bottom had been scuffed from years of being held open by shoes, or propped open by rocks brought back from the beach. Ruth wondered if Charlie had known when they'd talked about its charm that it was about to be replaced. She wondered if he had decided not to tell her, to spare her feelings. It felt like he'd lied to her.

As they walked into the kitchen, Ruth realized that the light that used to hit the pale yellow walls now fell flat. The room had been painted light gray. Ruth felt betrayed—angry that Charlie would let this happen, that maybe he preferred it this way; angry that she was alone in wanting to preserve any sign of Diana. She wondered when this had all occurred. She hadn't heard of anyone on the island working on the house. Did they bring a team over from the mainland?

"We wanted to update the color to something more universal," Nadia said, gesturing to the walls as she kept moving into the living room.

Lucy walked ahead next to Nadia, commenting on all the changes in a high, appreciative voice. None of it was Lucy's taste and Ruth knew Lucy was still mad at her, was saying these things knowing how they would hurt Ruth. The fact that she was in a serious fight with Lucy, the worst they ever had, almost made Ruth nauseous.

Through the window, Ruth saw the color of the garden change. The viridian green of the leaves darkened as the sun waned. Thick clouds were rolling in and the air coming through the open windows was heavy.

"When's the wedding again?" Lucy asked.

"Labor Day weekend," Nadia said, her eyes growing wide.

Ruth looked at Charlie. What was he thinking? They kept walking through the house but now Ruth wasn't even paying attention to the changes that Nadia and Lynn made, although she could feel Louis's eyes on her, concerned. Her own eyes were glazed over in concentration, replaying Nadia's hand on Charlie's cheek. It suddenly seemed clear to her how irrelevant she was. What was she doing here?

8

Ruth realized she hadn't seen a sunset at Diana's house in a long time. The reds bloomed under the low wall of clouds across the sky, mirroring how hot it was. The air had only grown heavier and more humid as the evening went on. Everyone was sweating and holding cold drinks against their damp necks.

She felt she was living in an alternate universe. Why was she in Diana's house, the house she used to live in, as a party guest? She felt the pull of the studio and thought about closing herself within it and ignoring the sounds of revelry outside. Walking to the cooler, Ruth passed Charlie and Nadia talking to a tall guy wearing a tight button-down. He looked familiar, and Ruth realized he was Charlie's housemate in college, and the blond woman standing next to him was his girlfriend. Their names came back to her: Peter and Ellen.

In all their time knowing each other, Ruth had only visited Charlie once off the island, the winter after they first met, when he was a junior at Columbia. It was the only time she had been to New York, and she had watched from the train window as the buildings grew taller and closer together, until she was in a world that looked foreign enough to Block Island that it could be a different country.

When Ruth got off the train, she walked with the flow of people out into Penn Station, observing the way they sped by with such fast intention. The crowd seemed to swarm around her as she stepped into the main terminal. She was trying to decide which way to go when Charlie found her, scaring her as he touched her on the shoulder.

They took a cab back to his apartment and Ruth remembered feeling awkward seeing him in this new space, so different from the island. She remembered feeling suddenly like she had nothing to say that he would find interesting, and she was insecure in all her winter clothes, realizing how old they were, although she had never cared about her appearance around him before. They had spent most of their time together in bathing suits, her wearing no makeup with hair knotted from the salt.

Things loosened up once they were outside. He gave her a tour of the campus and she asked him about his classes, concerts, and what it was like to live in the city. He took her to his favorite college bar, sneakily ordering two beers and handing one to Ruth under the table. It became exhilarating to Ruth, seeing Charlie in this different world, so far from Block Island. She even tried to picture herself living there, carrying textbooks with her to her next class.

That night, they sat around his kitchen table drinking with Peter and Ellen, who declared they were all going to a party.

"Are you sure you want to go?" Charlie had whispered to her. Ruth was excited at the idea of leaning more into college, into his world.

"Yeah, of course," she said.

"Let's get ready together," Ellen said to Ruth, grabbing her hand and leading her toward the door. "My apartment is down a floor."

"We all love Charlie," Ellen said in the elevator. "All my sorority sisters have crushes on him."

Ruth didn't know what to say. She couldn't identify Ellen's tone, what she was really trying to communicate.

In the apartment, Ellen sat Ruth down in front of a lit mirror, offering her clothes and shoes to wear. Ruth started to feel uncomfortable. They were things she would never buy, and she tried to say no, but Ellen insisted.

"I like what you're wearing, but I think you'll feel underdressed," she said. Ruth looked down at her shirt, jeans, and Converse, suddenly feeling self-conscious, and agreed.

Later, Ellen's roommates arrived, and they fed Ruth raspberry vodka shots as they straightened her hair. She remembered the steam rising off her head from the straightener as Ellen went over and over her dark brown waves to the point where Ruth was scared they would burn. Her split ends were more noticeable after the girl was done, and the hair fell unnaturally flat against her head and shoulders.

When they were done working on Ruth, the girls looked at her with detached approval, and Ruth had felt all at once like a toy—a doll they were having fun dressing up, making over.

At the party, Ruth had felt out of place, and the shots of raspberry vodka had caught up to her, making the room sway. Every time she caught a glimpse of her reflection in a mirror, she didn't recognize herself. The borrowed shoes cut into the back of her heels so sharply that they began to bleed. In the bathroom, Ruth pulled them off, looked at the bloody mess, and saw the brand stamped on the bottom.

A cold panic rose up and pierced through the haze in her brain. She didn't know a lot about fashion, but she could tell she could not afford to replace them. Panic swam through her, clashing with the vodka. She threw up in the dirty toilet while girls banged on the door and yelled at her to hurry up.

She left the apartment and walked out into the dark night by herself. She hadn't brought a coat to the party, and she took off the shoes so she could run down the street to Charlie's building. When she got there, her feet were numb. She pretended to fall asleep on the couch, and in the morning she wrote him a note saying she was fine and left before he woke up. She stuffed her torn-up feet into her thin Converse sneakers, taking the ruined shoes with her and throwing them in a trash can outside of the train station.

By the time she got home, blood had seeped through the canvas of her sneakers, and she had three voicemails from Charlie wondering where she went and if she was okay. Ruth was so embarrassed that she couldn't talk to Charlie for months and only apologized when he finally told her how worried he had been.

Now Ellen approached the cooler and Ruth didn't know what to say, wondering whether Ellen would remember her. It had been years ago, but Ruth felt another drip of shame as she realized that even now, almost ten years later, she still couldn't afford to pay the woman back.

Ellen picked up a beer can and looked at Ruth.

"Hi, I'm Ellen," she said.

"I'm Ruth." She waited for recognition and anger to cross the woman's face, but she only nodded.

"How do you know Charlie and Nadia?"

Ruth let out a breath of relief.

"I'm an old friend of Charlie's," Ruth said, looking at him. "And you?"

"Oh, I introduced them," Ellen said. "Yeah, Nadia is a family friend and I knew Charlie in college. I've been trying to get them together for years but Nadia finally moved to Boston and I got to play matchmaker."

Ruth didn't know what to say.

"Aren't they fucking perfect together?" Ellen said. "It's disgusting."

"Yeah," Ruth replied. "Perfect."

And as she looked at them standing together at their party, at their house on the island, at the streamers waving on the beech tree, she believed it.

Heat lightning flashed in the distance. After Ellen excused herself, Ruth felt someone tap her on the shoulder. She turned to see Louis, but said nothing. He said nothing in return. Looking at him, she saw a vulnerability that scared her, that confronted her with her own resistance to vulnerability. It seemed like he was trying to tell her something.

"Are you having fun?" Louis asked.

Ruth surveyed the party. People were laughing louder and dancing now, having relaxed over the hours. There was a beer pong table going somewhere inside. She nodded, her eyes on Charlie and Nadia, who were talking in low voices, Nadia standing on tiptoes to whisper something in his ear, Charlie's hand on her lower back to support her.

"Yes," she said.

"It looks like it," Louis replied.

Ruth turned back to Louis.

"You seem very . . . attentive," Ruth said, although the word sounded wrong and made her feel like she had let something slip.

"Oh?"

"No, I just . . . Why are you so concerned about me?"

Louis shrugged and took a sip of his beer. It was dark where they were standing and Ruth tried to make out his blurring edges, tried to search for the hallmarks of him—the nose ring, the arm tattoo sticking out of his shirt sleeve. It was a game she used to like to play as a kid.

"What're you doing?" Louis asked, leaning in toward her.

"I'm smudging your edges," Ruth said.

Louis closed his eyes halfway so he was matching Ruth. "Tell me."

"When I was little, I used to sit outside as the night got darker and things grew blurrier around me."

"Why?"

"I liked to watch how things changed—how leaves faded from green sharp sharp edges into a . . . rustling blur, until you couldn't even tell what they were anymore except when the wind blew through or a car drove by, lighting everything back up."

Ruth didn't know why she was telling him all of this, but it was comforting to step away from the party, to talk with Louis, who was never uncomfortable, who didn't need her to explain all the connective tissue of her thoughts to understand them, who took everything in stride.

"So what're my edges now?" Louis asked.

"Nose ring, shoulders, knees, tattoo," she said. "What're mine?"

Louis studied Ruth, his eyes still half-closed. He was quiet for a minute.

"Sunburned lips, elbows, moonlight, hair."

Ruth nodded. She felt seen.

"Just being a good friend by the way," Louis said. "Not being extra attentive."

"Oh," Ruth replied. "Thanks." She had forgotten what she had asked him.

Ruth hadn't seen Lucy in a while, but she could hear her squealing laughter down at the beer pong table. A raindrop hit the top of her head, and looking down, Ruth saw the splatter marks of the rain begin to polka-dot the deck. The storm came through as a downpour, shredding the streamers in the trees, making them seem more like Halloween decorations within a matter of seconds.

"No!" Nadia cried.

The partygoers ran inside, tracking dirt and grass across the floor. The lights glowed on everyone's wet hair. Then, in a flash, the power cut out. People fumbled for their phones, and soon the room was partially illuminated in the cold glare of their lights.

"Charlie! Do we have any candles?" Nadia cried out.

And Ruth thought then of the attic, of her secret place with Charlie, the box of candles she knew was up there. As people shouted, Ruth noticed that Charlie was looking at her from across the room. For what felt like a long time, she held his gaze.

"I'll get them," Ruth said. No one heard her except for Louis and Charlie, whose eyes followed her out of the room.

Turning the corner, Ruth left the noise and walked up the stairs. Feeling her way into the second-floor hallway, Ruth absorbed the comfort of the quiet and familiar space. She was buzzing, thinking about Charlie's eyes on her. The electricity between them was so clear that he must have felt it too, Ruth thought.

Stopping below the pull-down door to the attic, she jumped to grab the string above her but could not reach. After trying again, she was about to give up when she heard footsteps coming up the stairs behind her. She waited, her breath caught in her throat, not allowing herself to hope, expecting to hear Nadia's voice asking if she had found anything yet. But the footsteps were heavier and as Charlie's phone light preceded him, she recognized his outlined figure walking toward her.

Charlie didn't say anything, and as he approached Ruth leaned against the wall to make space for him in the narrow hallway. She felt his body close to hers as he lifted his arm to pull down the door. The ladder dropped and made a soft thud as it hit the floor. Charlie still didn't say anything as he stepped back so that Ruth could climb up. She couldn't read his expression in the darkness, his face still hidden behind the phone light. As Ruth climbed up the ladder and into the darkness of the attic, the voices from the party below grew more muffled.

Charlie followed behind her.

9

The heat was even more oppressive in the attic, coming off the wood like a sauna, the smell of old furniture and boxes carrying through the thick air and sticking to Ruth's skin. Charlie stepped up behind her, the floorboards creaking under him. The light from his phone glanced across the floor toward Ruth and the bin of storm provisions in the far corner, before it went dark. Ruth could hear herself taking a deep breath, although she could barely feel it. She tried to ignore the tension building in the room and pulled out her phone. After a second, its light shone back into the corner of the room.

"Will you help me with this?" Ruth asked, pointing at the bin.

"Turn off your light," he said.

Ruth paused, then put her phone in her pocket. Her pulse quickened in the hot darkness. The floorboards groaned as Charlie stepped in her direction. She stood still, her breathing stopped until she felt his body against hers, felt his hand in her hair.

Inhaling, his scent mixed with the attic in a swallowing wave of nostalgia. Charlie kissed her neck just below the ear and Ruth felt her skin tingle.

It was dark enough that she couldn't see his face, but she could feel it like on the beach the other day, right there in front of her.

Ruth stretched so that her arms were wrapped around his tall frame and her body pressed to his as his arm encircled her waist. She thought about asking him what he was doing, if he was sure, but her mind went blank as she felt his hands move across her hips, holding her to him.

His face hovered next to hers, his breath hot, until Ruth stood taller on her toes and found his mouth in the dark.

The kiss surprised Ruth. It didn't feel the way she had thought it would—different than she remembered, something new. It was firm and insistent. Her thoughts blurred into the background. She wasn't thinking about their past, wasn't thinking about what this meant; she was only feeling, wanting to get Charlie to the floor, crawl on top of him, and ignore the party downstairs.

Ruth ran her hands under Charlie's shirt, feeling his skin, pulling on the inside of his belt. She was lightheaded.

They didn't hear the footsteps below until Nadia's voice echoed from the hallway.

"Do you guys need a hand?" Nadia called up from the bottom of the ladder.

They sprung away from each other.

"We've got it," Charlie called, and his even voice caught her off guard.

"Why are you in the dark?" she asked.

"My phone just died," Charlie said. "Ruth left hers downstairs."

Ruth felt strange about how easily the lie came to him, guilt dawning on her now that they were apart.

"Oh, well here, use mine," Nadia said, and Ruth heard her steps on the ladder as the light from her phone filled the attic. Ruth turned her body so the light wouldn't hit her. She was sure if Nadia saw Ruth's face, red from where Charlie's beard scratched against her skin, her hair mussed from his hands in it, she would know what happened. Ruth's body felt so touched, so alive and buzzing, that it seemed impossible that someone looking at her wouldn't notice.

Charlie walked across the attic and Ruth thought that Nadia would know from looking at him too, but she didn't say anything as she handed Charlie the phone.

"Hurry up, please," Nadia said from the bottom of the ladder before returning downstairs. Ruth stood in the attic, unsure of what to do as Charlie took two steps across the room, shone the light on the bin, and cracked it open, pulling out candles and handing them to Ruth.

Ruth stood there, her arms full. Her skin was still tingling where he had touched her, and she could feel the blood moving in her body. Sweat was dripping down her back. There was no hesitation when she spoke.

"Do you really want to marry Nadia?"

Charlie looked at her and his forehead was crumpled, his lips red. "I don't know."

"Oh." Ruth didn't know how she felt.

"I'm sorry," Charlie said, and he climbed down the ladder, leaving Ruth alone in the darkness.

When they returned to the living room with the candles, everyone applauded, their faces throwing strange shadows against the wall in the cold glare of the phones they held up toward Ruth and Charlie. Ruth stopped in the harsh light. She felt trapped, that everyone knew what just happened. She had to force herself to keep moving across the room, toward the party. Charlie put the candles down around the table, lighting them, and the room took on a warmer glow. Stepping toward Ruth, he held his hand out for the candles in her arms without meeting her eyes. She tried to keep her face blank as she handed them over. Ruth caught Lucy looking between her and Charlie, her face grim.

"It says it's supposed to pass soon," Nadia said, looking at her phone. Charlie sat next to her and put his arm around her, resting it on the back of the couch. Louis patted the spot next to him and Ruth sat, ignoring the way he concentrated on her face. Ruth could still taste Charlie's mouth on her lips. There was a bottle of tequila on the coffee table, next to the newly lighted candles, and Ruth grabbed it, taking a long swig, trying to wash out his taste. The alcohol burned on the way down.

"All right!" someone shouted and the rest of the room erupted in cheers.

She passed the bottle to her left without looking, staring at the flickering candles and leaning back.

"Let's play a game," Lucy said as the bottle made its way around the room. The guy she had been flirting with all night was playing with her hair on the couch. "Never Have I Ever," she said.

Ruth's head snapped in Lucy's direction.

"Nooo, I hate that game. It makes me feel old and slutty. I always lose. I've done it all," Ellen said, lifting her drink as a toast to herself before taking a sip.

"Even better," one of the guys replied.

The room laughed. Ruth thought about leaving without telling anyone. She imagined the night air walking home. She wanted to be alone.

"Great," Lucy said.

She stood in the center of the room, the candles illuminating her eerily. Lightning cracked outside, close, and as the room shouted, Ruth remembered with a sinking feeling that she and Lucy had walked to the party, that her escape routes were cut off.

"Five fingers. You have to put one down if you've done it and you have to drink," she said. Everyone lifted their hands up except for Ruth and Charlie.

"Are you playing?" Nadia asked, looking at Charlie, who was looking into the middle distance, not paying attention.

"Sorry," he said, lifting his hand and smiling at Nadia, making Ruth's stomach constrict and the tequila pulse through her head. She felt dizzy.

"Ruth?" Lucy asked. Ruth felt everyone's eyes on her.

"I'm just going to watch," she said, glaring at her friend. "I've lived a boring life."

Louis looked at her, his eyebrows raised.

"Be that way," Lucy replied and pointed to Ellen. "You go first."

"Okay . . . Never have I ever . . . had a threesome," Ellen said, looking around the room. Five or six people groaned and put a finger down, drinking.

"Please," one of them said before taking a sip from their cup. The room laughed and Ruth felt it move through her like a piercing—too sharp.

Two other people went and the room grew loud, the group laughing and asking questions about who and where, about the details they didn't know about one another, about sex in public places and nights spent in jail. Ruth didn't see any of it. Her eyes were now on Lucy. She was trying to keep herself from looking at Charlie, who was half-obscured by Nadia. Finally, Lucy stood up and made a thinking face.

"I don't know," she said. "What's left?"

There wasn't any doubt in Ruth's mind that Lucy had her question ready before they started playing.

"Never have I ever . . . been in love with someone in this room," Lucy said, looking around.

Ruth had to fight to keep her eyes on the table. She began to sweat.

The couples in the room complained, putting their fingers down and kissing their partners before they drank. Out of the corner of Ruth's eye, she saw Louis put a finger down, to which Lucy pointed and squealed, everyone looking at Ruth. Ruth's head snapped in Louis's direction, her eyes narrowed. What was he doing? He must have been joking, playing it up for the room. He smiled and shrugged, and Ruth turned away, annoyed. Not meaning to, her eyes went to Charlie, who was staring at the floor. He hadn't put a finger down yet.

"Charlie?" Lucy asked.

"Babe, what're you doing?" Nadia asked, laughing.

"What?" Charlie asked, looking up, like he was ready to defend himself.

"Haven't you . . . been in love with someone here?" Lucy asked. She turned and looked straight at Ruth, raising her eyebrows, and Ruth felt her nails digging into her palm. Most people in the room followed Lucy's gaze toward Ruth, uncertain. Ruth was ready to say something, but Nadia threw out her arms dramatically, clearly not having noticed anything.

"Hello!" she called. "What about your fiancée?"

Everyone turned away from Ruth, to Nadia and Charlie.

"Oh! Right! Wow," Charlie said, turning toward Nadia, putting a finger down and taking a long, deep drink from his beer until it was gone.

Nadia looked at him and her eyebrows furrowed, then her head snapped in Ruth's direction just as the lights came back on. The crowd cheered again, relieved, as the fan above them began to struggle in a circle. Ruth met Nadia's eyes for a brief second, her expression sharp. Then Nadia stood and went with the flow of the party, out onto the porch, leaving Charlie on the couch.

"It stopped raining!" she cried from outside. "The fireworks are back on."

"Thank God," Ellen said, standing. "That was getting awkward."

As the room emptied, Lucy trailed behind.

Ruth grabbed Lucy by the arm. "Hey."

"What?" she said, turning.

"What was that?" Ruth seethed.

"Ruth, they're getting married," she said. "Let it go." For a moment she looked sincere, cutting through the angry, drunk facade. "What is this about anyway? Have you thought about that at all, that maybe you're distracting yourself? Do you feel *anything* being here in this house? The walls are all painted gray! You haven't said a word about Diana all summer, Ruth. You need to deal with this."

Lucy looked at Ruth as if she were about to hug her until she thought better of it. Ruth saw her eyes move to Charlie, who was still on the couch, then back to Ruth.

"He's not worth it," Lucy said and walked away.

Turning, Ruth saw Charlie looking at the floor. She waited for him to say something to her, to do something, but he stayed there, unmoving.

Ruth walked out of the kitchen, past the door that didn't slam anymore, and out into the yard. She dipped toward the edge of the lawn, out under the green archway, so she was on the dirt road in the darkness, the sounds of the party erupting behind her. Pulling out her phone, she saw another missed call from her dad. She clicked on his name and put the phone to her ear, listening to the faint drone of the dial tone.

"Hey, kiddo," Joel said, answering the phone on the third ring. Ruth didn't reply. She could hear party sounds in the background on his end of the line. She realized she didn't know what her dad normally did on the Fourth of July. "Ruth?" he asked. "Are you there?"

"Hi," she said. "Is this a good time? What're you doing?"

She was pacing around in the dark road, her skin hot.

"I'm just watching the fireworks from the porch," he said. She imagined him alone on the small deck, the house filled with packing boxes already.

"Is it busy over there?"

"Oh yeah. The neighbors are going after it. But Hank needs me on fireworks nights, otherwise he loses his mind and tries to escape." There was a beat of silence. Ruth didn't really know what to say, why she had called him back. She felt herself gearing up for a fight.

"Are you okay? You haven't been calling me back," he said. Ruth still didn't reply. "Shouldn't you be out doing something fun?"

"I feel like maybe I've had enough fun," Ruth replied. She thought back to all that he had said on the phone the other day, thought back to how fragile Joel had seemed the last time she had seen him. "You don't know a lot about my life, do you?" she asked, suddenly overcome with rage as she thought about how her father had retreated even more from Ruth after Maggie died, how he never asked her what she was feeling or thinking, how he often forgot that Ruth had needed him—needed him to go grocery shopping, to show up to the parent-teacher conference, needed him to be curious about her life.

All at once she felt so alone and so childlike as she looked around in the darkness, her heart rate quickening, the familiar feeling of things growing smaller and heavier within her, all of it pressing on her chest.

Joel was silent.

"Like what I want out of life, what I do with my days, who I hang out with?" she pushed.

"You don't tell me much," he said after a long time.

"Why wouldn't you ask? Why wouldn't you be more curious about your daughter's life? I'm your only kid and my mom is dead. It's up to you to be curious—to care."

"I call you," he said. "I don't want to bother you."

Ruth thought about her dad's phone calls—how he only asked her about logistical things, tripping over questions about car insurance, her job, before talking about fishing and Hank until the conversation dried up and one of them made an excuse to get off the phone. She thought about him selling the house, how he sent her away, how none of this might've happened if he hadn't sent her away, if he had tried just a little bit harder.

"You didn't even try," she said. "She had been dead only three months before you gave up and sent me to Diana."

Ruth had never said anything like this to Joel before, hadn't let him see this side of her since he pulled Maggie's notes from the fridge. The day Joel put Ruth on the ferry to Diana, she had made a promise to herself that if he didn't want her, then he would never get the real her ever again. Now that she was starting to say what she meant, it felt like years' worth of anger was funneling through her—at Joel for sending her away, for selling the house, at Maggie and Diana for dying and leaving her here with so many questions, at Charlie for not making up his mind.

Joel didn't say anything. The sound of fireworks crackled over the line while she waited.

"I thought I was doing the right thing," he said. "I thought she could help you more than I could."

"It makes me sad. I don't want to be that kind of parent," she said. Saying the word *parent* made her think only of the broken condom, of Louis's hand on her stomach, of not knowing what was happening right then in her body. "I don't want to be a parent who can't handle emotions. Who doesn't know how to talk to their own kid." She was rambling, saying the things she had kept to herself for years because she knew they would hurt his feelings, things that she knew would stick with him—and yet she kept going.

"You're right. It makes me sad too," he said after a long minute of silence.

Neither of them spoke for a moment.

"Listen, Hank's crying in there and . . . well, I gotta go," Joel said, his voice stern, different.

"Okay," Ruth said, feeling empty and broken.

"All right."

He waited a moment, then hung up the phone when Ruth didn't say anything more. She could see the tail ends of the fireworks bursting above the bushes, could hear them going off in the distance. She sat on the edge of the road, where the dirt met the wet grass. Pulling her knees up to her chest, Ruth remembered being a teenager, hormones coursing through her, and how when she was feeling extra combative she would fight with her mom and not know why. Thinking about Maggie, Ruth crumpled. She missed her mom's body, how her heartbeat felt through her thin chest when she hugged her—the most familiar sound in the world.

She wished she had someone to unleash her sadness on now, someone who would still love her after she came back to herself. She was tired of feeling disposable, tired of feeling like the thin tether between her and everyone else was going to snap, leaving her adrift. She laid her head against the grass and tears fell down her temples, catching and pooling in her outer ears.

Once, five years ago, when Ruth visited Joel between returning from Maine and heading out to Block Island for the summer, she had heard faint squawking upon entering the house. Hank greeted her and then trotted into the other room.

"What's that sound?" she asked.

"I was mowing the lawn and found him," Joel called from the back room. Ruth paused, concerned, before heading to find her father, who was standing over a shoebox with a tiny dropper in his hand. Approaching it, Ruth felt wary. Inside the box was a small baby bird, its skin pink and exposed, the beginnings of feathers protruding from its tiny wings like armor too thin to do any good. The bird was leaning up against a small hand towel, its legs crossed unnaturally underneath it. Mucusy brown blobs, which Ruth realized were bird shit, were dispersed throughout the box. The creature extended its neck as Joel dropped a gooey wet substance down from the dropper. The bird missed it and the glob hit the cardboard. It was only then that Ruth noticed a half-eaten banana next to the box.

"I don't think birds can eat banana, Dad," she said. "Where did it come from?"

Joel took her out to the tree and pointed up to the bird's nest. A mother robin swooped and tweeted at them, disturbed.

"We should try to put it back," Ruth said. But when Joel got his tallest stepladder and placed it beneath the nest, it still couldn't reach, and Ruth was worried about him falling. She was annoyed they were in this position at all, but when she looked down at the bird peeping, so small and fragile, a feeling of protectiveness washed over her. She didn't trust her dad to do it correctly, so she volunteered to climb up the ladder and put the bird home. But when it came time to pick the small, pathetic creature up, she didn't want it to touch her hands—she was disgusted by its newness, its fragility, the trembling throat outstretched for food. She didn't want to feel its tender heartbeat against her palm, didn't want to accidentally break its toothpick legs. At the last second, she used the towel to scoop up the baby bird, thinking it would be better, and climbed up the ladder, but as she got higher the robin parents started to swoop in more closely, defending their nest. Ruth wobbled, worried. She could feel the small life quiver in her palm through the towel, and its vulnerability in her hands made her scared instead of strong. She needed to stand on the very highest rung in order to reach, but she was unstable. As she reached for the nest, the bird's spiky, developing wings got stuck on the fabric of the towel and it tumbled out of Ruth's outstretched hand, falling again from the height of its nest toward the ground. Ruth watched its poor little body tumble through the air in slow motion, shame filling her chest as she watched it hit the ground.

"No!" Joel called out, and Hank barked from inside. Within a second, Joel scooped the baby bird up in his bare hand as Ruth came down the ladder, apologizing. Deftly, Joel scaled the ladder and put the bird in the nest, secure. Below, watching him, Ruth was nothing but angry at herself, at whatever was so broken in her that she couldn't bear to touch the baby bird. Later that night, Ruth had looked up whether they'd done the right thing. She read in the glow of the computer light—*if the nestling is injured beyond repair, the parents will kick it out of the nest.*

Now Ruth wondered if she'd been unfair to Joel.

"You and your father are so similar," Maggie had said once when Ruth was younger.

"What?" Ruth had asked, bewildered by the statement.

"Oh yeah," Maggie laughed. "Quiet, emotional, and stubborn. You have whole worlds in there that you keep to yourselves," she had said, pointing to Ruth's forehead. "I feel like I'm a miner around you two, trying to dig up what you're really thinking."

Ruth realized that she was so hard on him because she understood more than she wanted to how he felt, how hard it was to say what you meant. It was half the reason she used to write things down. It was the reason she was so hard on herself too.

In the darkness, Ruth sat up and listened to the party until she heard footsteps approaching. She wanted it to be Charlie so he could explain what had just happened in the attic, but Louis's thin figure rounded the corner instead.

"Hey," he said. "Are you okay?"

Ruth thought about whether or not she was okay. Her mind was blank.

"Could we leave?" Ruth asked.

Louis looked at her and she saw his familiar frame illuminated by a faraway streetlight, the edges glowing orange.

"Yeah, let's go."

10

In the truck, Ruth and Louis were both silent, and the sound of the tires rolling over the dirt road filled the car. When the road turned from dirt to pavement, the silence became more pronounced. Ruth was oscillating between replaying her fight with Lucy and thinking about Charlie's body in the darkness, about how scared she was of the intensity of wanting him, about his "*I don't know*."

"So, you still have a thing for Charlie, huh?" Louis asked. His tone was casual, like he was talking with a friend, but the question caught Ruth off guard.

"What are you talking about?" she asked, worried that it had been more obvious than she thought.

"It just seems like you two still have some . . . unfinished business or something."

"Why did you say you had been in love with someone there?" Ruth asked, ignoring his comment and turning to him in the dark truck, trying to make out his expression. Louis was quiet for a beat as they turned onto Spring Street, the ocean dark to their right.

"Oh, I was kind of joking," he said, laughing. "I thought I was in love with Lucy once—from afar."

"When she first came here?"

"Yup," Louis said. "I was helpless to her charms."

Ruth remembered the first summer Lucy arrived, how everyone had swooned over her, flocking to her. It still amazed Ruth sometimes that Lucy had managed to find Ruth through all her fans, that their friendship had stuck.

Thinking again of her fight with Lucy, Ruth's body became stiff.

"I never knew," Ruth said, talking to avoid her own thoughts. "You should've told her."

"Yeah?" Louis asked.

"Of course. I think people should know that kind of thing."

They were descending the hill and pulling up to town. From this distance, Ruth could see children dappled with the bobbing light of glow sticks, holding their mothers' hands or being carried home on their fathers' backs.

"Let's go to Nick's," Ruth said. She hadn't gone out to the bars in a long time.

"Are you sure?"

"Yeah, what do you mean?"

"You just seem . . . off, I guess." Louis was looking at her now with concern, all edge gone from his voice.

"I just want to have fun," Ruth said, her voice low, looking out at the people on the street.

"Okay, yeah, let's go to Nick's," Louis repeated. He parked his truck on the road by the dunes and they got out. Yellow Kittens was loud, and as they walked past a woman was yelling at her boyfriend, both of them holding plastic cups full of something blue. Louis and Ruth weaved through the groups of people occupying the sidewalk. They parted and came together, parted and came together, so that Ruth looked out for the shadow of a rip in his pants, the glint of his nose ring under a streetlight. As they walked up to Captain Nick's, the colors and music from inside poured out onto the street. Bartenders bounced on their tiptoes behind the bar, covered in glitter, cracking cans open and shaking drinks. It was a scene that made Ruth smile in remembrance. She wanted to forget everything that happened that night, that had been happening lately, and go back five years to when she was in the thick of things, going to disco nights every week, doing coke in the bathroom, dancing onstage until sweat made the glitter run off her skin in sparkling rivers.

Approaching the line at the door, Ruth's head buzzed from the tequila she drank at the party. Her friend from the restaurant was working the door and stamped their hands, waving them into the bar without paying a cover. Fireworks were still exploding in the distance, and for a brief second Ruth could see them erupting faintly off of the mainland. The crowd at Nick's was a mixture of tourists and locals, some in red-white-and-blue bikini tops and face paint. *Jaws* was playing on a big screen in the background and Ruth watched as the swarm of beachgoers ran to the shore, blood coloring the ocean. The DJ was playing the Bee Gees and Ruth followed the noise inside, not waiting to see if Louis was behind her. People she knew waved as they passed, and Ruth weaved through the dancers to the bar at the back of the room.

Louis appeared next to her and put his elbows on the bar, leaning forward. He ordered Ruth a drink and the bartender nodded, the glitter on her face accentuating a small scowl. At first Ruth didn't understand her reaction, but then she recognized her as the same girl who had been reading Louis's palm at the summer solstice party. It must seem like they were a couple to this girl, who had seen them leave Ruth's party together, and now here like this. Louis and Ruth touched cups, let them hit the bar, then raised them back up, making eye contact before drinking, Louis wiggling his eyebrows like a cartoon, making Ruth snort into her tequila soda. They didn't speak, just turned to the dance floor and watched the colorful spectacle in front of them. Ruth drank quickly, the buzzing in her head growing even louder. Watching the dancers, she felt the room begin to move in slow motion, the colors and the sound blurring together so that she needed to close her eyes to stay steady. She felt the night catching up, felt her breath get faster. Opening her eyes, she turned to Louis, who was looking at her, an unreadable expression on his face. She thought about what he'd said in the car—*unfinished business*—then pushed the thought from her mind. Watching the room move, Ruth was filled with the same detached feeling she had earlier standing in Diana's yard, looking at the partygoers drift across the lawn, where she used to belong.

A girl Ruth recognized who was a lifeguard at the town beach approached Louis, waving vaguely at Ruth before engaging him in conversation. Ruth saw her old self in her—the thin, tanned girl in ripped jean shorts, her tight tank top riding up to sit on the very top of her hips, glitter smeared across her cheek, her flip-flops old and worn-down so that Ruth imagined the small hole in the heel from overuse. She didn't realize she was staring until Louis waved goodbye to the girl, turned, and lifted his arms to both of Ruth's shoulders.

"You okay?" he asked, his eyes flitting between each of hers.

She knew she wasn't okay.

"Wanna dance?" she asked.

Louis dropped his arms and Ruth put her empty cup on the bar, moving past him and reaching for his hand as she walked by onto the dance floor. She could feel the callouses on the bases of his fingers from hauling lobster pots and gripping oar handles. Weaving into the pit of people, Ruth turned and watched the colors from the lights dance off his salt-crusted hair, the back of his sunburned neck, the loose button-down shirt that hung off his shoulders like a curtain. In the middle of the dance floor, he spun her around under his arched arm. Then they started dancing. Ruth moved her body hard, each movement energetic, and before long she was sweating. She and Louis twirled and threw their hands up, and he came in close, his hands falling on her hips. As they danced, a feeling of raw loneliness pulsed through Ruth. Everything suddenly seemed to be moving too quickly. She thought about Charlie's body enveloping hers in the attic.

The smell of the musty room, of the worn wood, of his skin—it all washed back over her with so much strength that she felt herself inhaling and searching for more. Louis was dancing, his eyes closed, and as the colors from the lights changed across his face, Ruth felt a wave of dizziness drop through her. She stopped moving so that Louis jolted against her and his eyes sprung open.

"Let's go to your boat!" Ruth shouted in his ear as the last piano chords of "Dancing Queen" played and groups of women shouted, throwing their arms around their friends. She needed to do something. She couldn't be alone with this feeling. Ruth thought Nick's would make her feel like her old self, but she couldn't get rid of the sensation that she was outside looking in, that she didn't belong here, at Diana's house, or anywhere anymore. Pulling back, Louis's face was blank, then brightened. He nodded.

In the truck, Ruth started to feel self-conscious about inviting herself over. They hadn't spoken much and the loud thrum of the truck filled the silence.

"Where are we going?" Ruth asked after a minute.

"The boat is out in New Harbor now," Louis said. "We have to take the dinghy out."

Ruth considered walking back to the cottage instead, but the thought of waking up and Lucy being there was unbearable. She could sleep on the beach, she thought, under the stars. She had done it many times before, but this time it didn't feel romantic. It felt sad. She nodded as they coasted down Ocean Avenue toward New Harbor.

At the dock, Ruth stumbled toward the dinghy and Louis helped her get over the side, the boat rocking as she sat.

"Careful there, sailor," he said. He stepped into the boat, untied it, and began pulling at the motor. Once it was up and thrumming, Louis directed the dinghy away from the dock, heading out into the night.

They maneuvered through the darkened moored boats, and soon the Great Salt Pond opened around them, the other boats few and far between. In the distance, the old Coast Guard station stood, outlined by the moon, and the ripples in the water were illuminated in its silver light. Ruth took a deep breath. She contemplated jumping into the black water, allowing herself to be engulfed by it, allowing it to clear her head.

As they coasted up to Louis's boat, he cut the engine. Faraway sounds echoed from around the island, traveling over the harbor. As the boat got closer, the sound of the water slapping against the hull grew louder, until it was right in front of them.

The boat ride had quelled Ruth's insecurity around inviting herself, and she felt comfortable in the shared silence—didn't feel the need to fill it. She climbed up the ladder and onto the deck before feeling her way down the short stairs to the cabin, remembering to duck her head. She had just been here only a few weeks ago, in the same kind of darkness, but that moment felt so long ago now that it was almost odd to see the cabin still there, looking the same as it had that night. Louis flipped the switch on the wall behind her and the room was filled with a warm light and a soft buzzing. She turned and reached for Louis, her palms against his chest as they kissed. Her heart began pounding again. It was a manic kiss. She was trying to erase herself into it, like she had the first night, but it wasn't working, her body confused by the difference in his touch, the thought of Charlie's hands still imprinted on her skin. Louis responded at first, his hands holding her face. She reached for the button of his jean shorts, but he stopped her and took a step back, falling on the bed.

"Let's just sleep," he said.

Ruth looked at him. A slow realization was dawning on her, through her thickly clouded mind.

"I'm just too drunk, I'm tired. I wouldn't be any good," Louis said quickly.

He didn't seem drunk, Ruth thought as he slipped his jeans off over his thin legs, stepping out of them so he was in only his cotton boxers. He went into the bathroom and started brushing his teeth while Ruth stood where she was. She felt awkward and stuck for a moment until he brought her a fresh toothbrush already coated in a layer of striped toothpaste.

"Do you have a stash of these for your many guests?" she asked, trying to keep the tone light, even as she began to feel like she had overstayed her welcome.

"A man needs to be prepared," he said, although he sounded subdued.

As Ruth brushed her teeth, she felt suddenly tired, so physically tired that she thought she might fall asleep standing up. Louis got into bed and Ruth spit the foamy toothpaste into the sink. In the mirror, her reflection was ragged and sunburned. Turning off the bathroom light, she found her way to the small bed in the dark. Again, Ruth felt Louis's body against her back, felt the arm drape over her side, the hand resting on her drooping stomach. She fell asleep to the rhythm of his breathing, the bobbing of the boat. Somewhere in the corner, Perry purred in his sleep.

When Ruth woke up, Louis wasn't next to her but Perry was staring at her, his tail swishing against the floor behind him. Her head throbbed and she sat up slowly, mad at herself for drinking so much, for being hungover. Once upright, she looked around the cabin in a haze. Louis's clothes were folded in neat piles on shelves that looked homemade and there was a big bottle of sunscreen on the counter—the same cheap brand that Ruth used. There were small piles of shells placed indiscriminately around that made Ruth smile. A stack of swollen paperbacks was constructed next to the window, and Ruth's headache pulsed as she tried to read the titles on the worn spines from across the room. The sheets were striped and soft, and the light came in through the open cabin door onto them.

Ruth turned to look out the porthole next to the bed. The sun was already high, and the water was sparkling over the blue.

The Coast Guard station was bright white in the sunshine. She wondered how late it was. Boats skated by on the water headed to the channel out of Great Salt Pond and into the ocean.

Looking at the island from this small round vantage point made her feel a level of peace she hadn't experienced in a while. From there, she had a sense of removal from all of it, a voyeuristic sensation that made her feel insulated within herself. It was different from the gnawing feeling that she had the night before, the feeling that she was on the outside. Seeing her clothes on the floor, Ruth felt a rush of embarrassment wash over her. She was about to gather her things and bolt off the boat when she heard a thump from above, the boat rocking, then Louis whistling and the crinkle of paper bags.

"Hello!" Louis poked his head over the top of the stairs and Ruth had to shield her eyes against the sun coming in behind him to look in his direction. He had an unlit cigarette behind his ear and an armful of brown paper bags, the head of a sunflower poking out of the top of one.

"What's all this?" Ruth asked.

"Provisions for one of my many guests," he said jokingly, and Ruth remembered her comment from the night before. She was surprised it seemed to stick to him so hard. Ruth thought Louis knew he had a reputation.

She went into the bathroom and closed the door behind her. Pulling out her phone, she opened the calendar app and counted the weeks since she thought her last period was. She counted them again. If she was right, she was now definitely late. Louis's feet were loud above her head. Standing, Ruth looked in the mirror and saw her face was flushed red. She hadn't told Louis about the broken condom. For a second she considered whether she should, whether she would feel lighter, but the idea of telling Louis would make it more real, and it wasn't yet. A little late was nothing—normal. Stress, she told herself. It was just stress.

Ascending the stairs to the deck, Ruth shielded her eyes from the sun. Louis had pulled out a folding table she didn't know he had and placed the bags on it. The sunflower's rough leaves fluttered in the wind. Louis was nowhere to be found.

"Hello?" Ruth called. Instead of an answer, there was a splash. Crossing the deck and looking over the edge, she saw Louis treading water next to the boat, his body floating and illuminated by sun in the Great Salt Pond. Ruth pulled her dress off so she was down to her bra and underwear, stepped up onto the lip of the side, and dove into the water too. It was cold and briny, and the depths felt soft and all-encompassing as her body was pulled downward. Coming up, she took a breath of morning air and tasted the saltwater traveling down her face into the corners of her lips. Her hangover subsided. Louis's eyes glinted along with the sea as they treaded water next to each other. Ruth felt a wave of shyness as he smiled at her, although she felt her face break into a smile too.

"Thought you might need the saltwater treatment," he said, splashing her face.

"I was sloppy," she said. "Sorry. I hope I didn't . . . I'm sorry if . . ." Ruth tried to think of the words to explain how embarrassed she felt.

"What? No, you were just a little buzzed is all. Don't think twice," he said, waving her off.

Ruth leaned back and floated in the water, feeling her body rise and fall as she breathed, the sun on her eyelids, the sound of bay slopping against the boat audible to her ears just under the surface. The water supported her, and her slow breathing relaxed the knots in her neck, ever-present from carrying plates and heavy glass racks at work. She didn't know how long she floated for, but when she lifted her head and started to tread water again, Louis was gone. Ruth looked around, until his dripping head poked over the side of the boat.

"There's the ladder around the other side," he said. Ruth nodded and started swimming around the bow, touching the barnacles slick with seaweed on the water line of the hull as she went. As she rounded the port side and grabbed on to the bottom rung of the ladder, Perry's orange head peeked out from over the edge. Pulling herself up the ladder, she felt the water run off her now cooled body. Standing on the deck, dripping, her thin bralette and her underwear clung to every curve of her breasts, her hips. She sat down on the hot boards of the deck, letting the sun hit her, and felt relaxed. She thought about Louis living out here, about the quiet nights he must have, the cool mornings, just him and Perry. She wondered if he ever got lonely.

"Do you have plans today?" Louis asked, handing her a thin worn towel. She could sense his eyes dropping to the deck next to her body, avoiding looking at her head on. Ruth thought of the article. The idea of sitting in the studio or in her house with Lucy both seemed impossible after last night.

"What day is it?" Ruth asked.

"Friday."

"I have to work but, you know, not until three," she said. When Ruth thought about the restaurant, her hangover returned worse than before.

"I thought we could have a morning." Louis leaned back in his folding chair. "You know, if you want." He started pulling out bagels from the paper bag. He handed her a coffee and arranged the sunflower in an old mason jar, filling it with water he kept in large gallon jugs by the cabin door.

"Wow," Ruth replied, looking at the display. "What do you want to do?"

"I was thinking we'd go out to North Light," Louis said, his mouth full of bagel. "We could bike there. Kill off some more of your hangover."

"Okay," Ruth replied, nodding. The last thing she wanted was to be alone with her thoughts.

Before they left town for the lighthouse, Ruth ran to the cottage to change. Lucy's minivan was gone but Ruth still felt the need to hurry, as if she wasn't supposed to be there. While in her room, searching for shorts, she thought about the peculiar morning she just had—the bagels, the swimming, the sunflower. There was a quiet voice inside her that recognized the signs of flirting, the care Louis took in getting her breakfast, the way he played her childhood game the night before, but Ruth shrugged these off. They had been friends for a long time. It wasn't so strange that they would hang out, that he would be kind.

As she was leaving, she remembered Diana's camera. Running back up the stairs, she grabbed it off her desk. Louis was waiting for her on his bike at the mouth of the driveway. Walking her bike down to meet him, Ruth slung her camera over her neck. Then she hopped on and they started pedaling out to Corn Neck Road, away from town. At first Ruth's body protested and she felt wobbly, but the more she pedaled, the better she felt. Sweat dripped off her face.

As they biked the long road out to the point, the distant lighthouse came closer and closer into view. They cruised around the bend up to the small, bustling parking lot and hopped off their bikes. Hiding them behind some beach rosebushes, they each kicked off their shoes and started walking the long expanse of beach to North Light, the very farthest point of the island in the distance. The crowds thinned out the farther they got from the parking lot, until they were alone. Ruth tugged at the camera over her shoulder, making sure it was secure.

They were quiet, the rocky terrain requiring their attention as they stepped from stone to stone until the beach gradually fell into deep sand. Someone had built a memorial for a dead seal on the shore, and stones encircled the openly rotting body while flies buzzed above it.

"I'm pretty close to buying Earl's fishing company," Louis said after they had been walking in silence for a few minutes. Ruth's head shot up.

"What?"

Again, she didn't understand why the concept of her friends growing up was so crazy to her. They had been on this island for ten years and Louis had been fishing under Earl's business for most of that time. It made sense that Earl would retire, that Louis would move up and eventually take over.

"That's incredible," she said. Louis fidgeted with his nose ring and looked away from Ruth out toward the ocean. She noticed a gentle pride emanating from him. In her mind, she realized she had been thinking of him as the unreliable guy she had known when she was younger. When had he grown up?

"Thanks," he said.

Seagulls cawed from the dune grasses as they walked through the path that split the birds' breeding grounds into two. They saw more than one dead bird bent at an awkward angle, sand overtaking their matted feathers. As the path veered right, they came upon the lighthouse. It looked so small up close. The peach-colored bricks contrasted against the sharp peaks of the copper roof, now tinted green from the ocean air. Five seagulls stood on the roof, and a few walked around on the brick patio before it gave way back to sand. Louis approached the front window and stood on his bare tiptoes, his tanned calves flexed under the ragged hem of his homemade jean shorts.

"Have you ever been in here?" he asked, turning to her and coming back down to his normal height. Ruth thought back.

"I went to that fundraiser here with Diana like seven years ago," Ruth said. "The one she did for the Historical Society."

"Yeah, they cleaned it up for all that," Louis said, standing on his tiptoes and peering inside. "I don't think anyone has been in there for a while." He turned back to her. "Let's go in." Immediately, she felt younger. She recognized more clearly the smirk that was on his face now. He ran his hand through his salted hair and bounced over to her.

"We're not going to break in," Ruth replied, chiding him.

"No, of course we aren't," Louis replied, sarcastically innocent, before he disappeared around the side of the building. Ruth stayed put and listened to the sound of the seagulls and the ocean breaking against the shore just over the dune's edge. She had come here often her first few summers. The hike out was arduous enough that it thinned out the people, often leaving her alone to write as the day sunk into golden hour. She liked to watch the bricks change color against the setting sun, watch the light on the water move, and notice how it highlighted the ripples differently. The mainland was clearest at this point on the island, and Ruth found solace in lying in the sand, looking at the wide expanse of water between her and the real world.

Ruth heard Louis's faint scuffling behind the building, a thud, and a curse before the front door of the lighthouse opened and he appeared. Standing aside, he held the door open for her.

"Nice work," she said.

"Tips are appreciated," he replied.

Ruth suddenly wondered what Louis would look like in twenty years—which features would change and shift, and which she would always be able to recognize in a crowd. She wondered whether they would still know each other or if they would have lost touch by then.

"Wait, stop there," Ruth said, overcome by the impulse to capture him as he was standing in front of her now. Swinging the camera around her shoulder and holding the viewfinder up to her eye, she snapped the photo.

Once inside, Ruth was transported back to the last time she'd been there, the night of Diana's event. She had brought in some big names from New York to help sponsor it and to attend, and had put up a small gallery show of the archival photos of the island and the lighthouse. That night, Ruth remembered, Diana had seemed like a beacon of everything good. Ruth had felt happy to be near her, to help her.

"Look at this," Louis said, holding out a stack of prints leaning up against the wall. He wiped the glass of the picture with his arm and a thin layer of dust spilled off. Ruth stood above the photo. Most businesses on the island had old photographs of the people who had lived and worked on Block Island throughout the years hanging in lobbies and bathrooms. There was always something about the pictures that pulled Ruth in, the familiar buildings and landscapes dotted with people she would never know, although it felt like she could, as if their connection to this place tied them together.

Louis and Ruth stood back, looking at the photo. In it, a couple reclined against a grassy hill. The woman wore a white dress with a high neckline, her face partially obscured under a wide-brim straw hat. Next to her, a man in a crumpled linen vest, his sleeves rolled up to his forearms, leaned toward her as if to kiss her on the cheek. Children were running at the top of the hill in the background, their figures blurred from movement. Ruth remembered this photo from the event. She had helped Diana go through and digitize all the pictures as well as enlarge them, frame them, and decide where they should be arranged. The small description in the corner was in Diana's handwriting but had been dictated by Ruth from the historical record on the photo, kept by the Historical Society.

"Annie and Leo Holmes met working on Block Island when they were both sixteen. They married in Charlestown, RI, at eighteen. Both worked at the Spring House, Annie as a housekeeper and Leo as a cook. Here, they recline after a day of work on the Spring House lawn. Their two children, Ida and Wesley, run in the background. 1901," Louis read aloud.

Ruth looked again at the faces of the young couple, who couldn't have been older than Ruth or Louis when the picture was taken. She thought back to the photos of Maggie and Diana. It seemed like they could be a part of this collection—a part of history. She wondered who had taken this photo, who had decided to capture this moment. The woman appeared to have just been laughing, and the man's eyes were intent on her face.

"That looks nice," Louis said, and Ruth nodded, feeling suddenly emotional.

"Seeing pictures of people who used to be kids, but are dead now, is always so weird," Louis said.

Ruth said nothing, looking more closely at the playful figures of the children running, the way their bodies were shadowed like ghosts.

"All the parents are so young in these old photos," Ruth said.

"I know, right? Imagine having, like, a four-year-old right now."

Ruth tried and couldn't. Her mom had her when she was

twenty-four, which sounded so young to Ruth. She couldn't even remember what she was doing when she was twenty-four.

"I can't," Ruth said, shifting her weight and trying to sense if she had bled at all yet, feeling her heart beat faster.

The room was quiet as they flipped through the pictures. After Louis's comment, Ruth couldn't help but think of each person in the photographs as dead and buried. When they flipped through to the last photo, Louis rested them all back against the wall.

"You were pretty young when your mom died," he said.

The statement startled Ruth, as if they were talking about someone else. "Seventeen," she said.

Louis didn't respond.

Ruth felt uncomfortable, visible. She looked around the room for something to shift the conversation. Seeing the mouth of the stairwell off to the right, Ruth walked toward it, peering up into the darkness. At the top of the stairs there was a door with a small window where the light came through, showing the sky. Ruth walked up the stairs and Louis followed, not far behind. The door was locked only by an inside latch, which Ruth unfastened before stepping out onto the ledge of the lighthouse, the large swirling glass bulb behind them and the dunes and the ocean spread out in front of them.

Thinking again of the photos downstairs, of the young couple with their children running behind them, and of all the photos of Diana and Maggie, Ruth suddenly felt suffocated by how colored her life was by grief. How it always sat on her chest and her mind, and how tired she was of it.

"I wonder if she ever regretted it," Ruth said, staring out at the ocean.

"What?" Louis asked.

Ruth explained Diana's letter, the conversation with her dad, Maggie's paintings—all of it. Louis listened, looking off into the ocean, leaning his elbows on the railing and nodding. Occasionally, he would look over at Ruth and seem like he was about to reach for her, but he stopped himself. Ruth realized she hadn't said it all out loud, that everything had been sitting within her, growing heavier. It was about to come tumbling out of her—the similarities between Maggie's pregnancy and Ruth's situation, her nerves about her late period—but looking at Louis, she stopped herself.

"She should've gone to New York," Ruth said, trying to ignore her last thought. "She would've been happier."

"You don't know that," Louis replied, turning toward her. "Maybe she really really wanted a kid."

"Maybe she never did."

"You know that's not true."

"There's no way to know that it isn't true," Ruth said, indignant. Her conversations with Joel and Louis were starting to feel similar. They didn't understand the piece that Ruth struggled with the most, that there was no way to ask, no way to know. They didn't understand how all the reassurances in the world didn't mean anything to her, that all she wanted was what she couldn't have—another conversation with her mother, another conversation with Diana. She wanted to know what had run through their minds, what they had *really* been thinking and how they viewed their choices as the years went on.

"There is no way to compare. She had me and that's all she knew. Sure, she could say she was happy but there is no way to know that she wouldn't have been happier. There's no way I can ask her," she said.

"You're going to go crazy thinking like that," Louis said. Ruth could tell he was worried about her.

"And then she died." Ruth ignored Louis's words. "She got cancer in her thirties and died. And what am I doing? I'm almost thirty and I've done nothing."

The seagulls groaned around them, circling and protesting their presence. The ocean moved in front of them, wide and green against the changing angle of the sun. She didn't know how long she had been talking; her mind was focused on the details, the way her mom looked in the infusion chair, the clumps of hair she hid from Ruth in the trash.

"She died and I had to watch," Ruth said.

"Ruth." Louis put his hand on her shoulder and Ruth didn't shake it off, the weight of his palm light and grounding. She knew that her mother loved her, and somewhere in her mind she could convince herself that her mother would have chosen her again, that nothing would have been different, but the image of Diana and her mother together, happy and young, wouldn't leave her mind.

She thought about the people closest to her and realized they were all gone or going. Diana was gone, Charlie was getting married, Lucy was angry with her and probably moving on to a job in some city soon, her father didn't know how to speak to her. She felt like she had been running a race and for the first time she looked around and realized she was running alone, that she had been running alone the whole time.

Ruth looked at Louis. She thought to the beginning of the summer, to his thin figure bounding down the steps to meet her, backlit from the porch, how his fingers had grazed her elbow as they went off to swim that night. For all she had thought about the people leaving her, she hadn't recognized his presence—sturdy and familiar, calm yet full of life. She felt a moment of warmth toward him, before it became clear to her. The flowers, the bagels, his checking in on her—it all came together in Ruth's mind and she took a step back.

"Why are you being so nice to me, Louis?"

"What are you talking about?"

"Come on."

Louis gripped the railing and leaned back, staring at the ground before turning to Ruth. "I think you're making a mistake going after Charlie."

Ruth felt cornered. The warmth she felt for him drained away. Lucy and Louis didn't understand what they were talking about. They had no idea about Charlie or about what Ruth felt.

"Charlie's getting married," she said, deflecting.

"Yeah, I know," Louis replied. "But that doesn't really change anything. I see how you look at him and . . . I think you're doing the wrong thing."

"Louis, you don't even really know Charlie," Ruth said, trying to brush him off. She didn't want to talk about it with him, didn't want to address the reality of her situation. How could Louis know what she was feeling? He had never been serious about anyone.

"He's not the right one," Louis said. "Maybe he was once, but he's not anymore. You're too . . . He's too . . ."

"Too what?" Ruth asked, ready to be angry. When he didn't respond, she said, "Let's just forget it," and took a step away. She watched Louis's face fall.

"Sorry. I'm sorry," he said, stepping back and stuffing his hands in his pockets. Ruth felt awkward all of a sudden. He started pacing, leaning against the railing and looking down at his feet.

"Fuck!" he whisper-shouted under his breath.

"What?" Ruth asked.

"What about me?" Louis asked, still staring at the ground.

"What?" She'd heard him but adrenaline was starting to flare up and her thoughts were muddled. She thought of him in the truck the night before, of him putting his finger down at the party. And Ruth realized he had been lying in the car about having a crush on Lucy, that he had been trying to tell her.

Louis stood up, took a deep breath, and looked back at Ruth. "I want to be with you."

The sun was bouncing off his skin and drenching his salt-bleached hair. It was all so familiar to Ruth. She saw herself in his sunburned cheeks, in his cutoff jeans. She had known him for so long. It was like he was a part of the landscape of the island to her, part of the landscape of her past. They were similar—too similar. Ruth thought then about what would happen if she let Charlie go, if she leaned into Louis right now and said yes. There was an intoxicating ease to the image. They would live on the island; Louis would buy the fishing business and Ruth would stay at the restaurant. They would see their friends every day and take long walks down Crescent Beach. There was a clear world in which they would make sense together, in which they would be right for each other.

"No," Ruth said, as much to Louis as to her own thoughts. Louis looked hurt. "You don't really want that."

"I do," he said.

Ruth felt a rising anxiety in her chest.

"I was young and dumb all those years, I know, but I'm not like that anymore. You said you should tell someone when you love them."

"You don't love me, Louis."

"Why would you say that?" Louis asked, his voice getting higher. "You have no idea how I feel, Ruth. I'm telling you. We're good for each other."

She wanted to leave. She wanted to be at home, at Diana's home, back in the bed she used to sleep in. She wanted no one to bother her anymore, she wanted to hear the faint noises of Diana making tea downstairs, hear her feet moving against the hardwood, hear the rush of a soft rain washing over the island. She wanted to feel her mother wrap her in a towel and pull her in, both of them smelling like saltwater. She just wanted to hide.

"I have to go to work," Ruth replied. "I have to go."

She turned and ran down the old dusty steps. When she got to the room below, she waited to hear footsteps following her but they didn't. As she burst out to the dunes, the sun assaulted Ruth's eyes. She walked away from the lighthouse and didn't look back. The seagulls wailed overhead. At the mouth of the trail, the body of the seal buzzed with flies.

11

At work that night there was a line at the door before the restaurant was even open. From the servers' station, Ruth observed with dread families cupping their hands to press their faces against the glass and trying to open the door. Pulling her phone out, she watched the time change from three fifty-nine to four. Whitney opened the restaurant and stepped back as, one by one, throngs of people stepped through the vestibule asking for a table, already upset that they were made to wait. Ruth knew from experience that she wouldn't be leaving until well after midnight. The feeling of unease that she had been trying almost violently to ignore was now crawling against her skin.

Her section was nearly filled within five minutes. Instead of starting the usual flurry of watering each table and going over the specials with them, she remained unmoved. She watched people pick up menus and look around at the other servers approaching their own tables. She watched the guests grow more impatient, and still she didn't move. Finally, she turned on her heel and made her way to the bathroom, her heart pulsing so that she could hear it in her ears. Ruth pulled down her jeans, then her underwear, and stared at the clean lining inside.

She stood, squatting in a hovering position, and reached her fingers down, finding the opening of her vagina. She pressed up inside of herself, feeling heat and pressure against her fingers, before pulling them out and holding them up to the light. Ruth looked for any reassuring sign of blood stained onto the pads of her fingertips or marked in the cracks of her cuticles, but there was none—just a shimmering glow of wetness. The pulsing in Ruth's ears grew louder.

"Ruth! Are you in there! Katie already had to water your tables and get drinks! Are you okay?" one of her co-workers called through the door.

"Shit," Ruth said to herself, standing, flushing, and shoving her T-shirt back into the waistband of her jeans. "Sorry!" she cried, washing her hands. She ran the water cold and splashed her face, not stopping to look in the mirror for fear of what expression of worry she'd see there.

She approached her first table with her water pitcher and leaned across it to fill a glass without recognizing Joel's friends, Sarah and Bill, sitting there.

"Hi, Ruth," Sarah said as she put down the glass on the table.

"Oh, you guys! Hi," Ruth said. She tried to avoid looking at them, making only brief eye contact before glancing away. "Are you ready to order?" She knew she was being curt, but she felt like if she slowed down to talk for even a second, she would break down in tears. Her fragility caught her off guard. She had been a waitress for twelve years, had swallowed her feelings and numbed herself to get through a shift more times than she could count. She didn't understand why she was cracking now.

Placing the water pitcher on the table, she pulled out her notepad from her back pocket and slid the pen out from the tight bun on top of her head.

"Oh, yeah, honey, sure," Sarah said, looking at the water pitcher crowding the table. "Go ahead, Bill."

Out of the corner of her eye, Ruth saw a new two-top sit in her section. As she left Sarah and Bill's table and walked toward the dish pit, Ruth watched the couple at the table look around them, seeming displeased. After dropping the dishes at the pit, Ruth turned the corner and grabbed the water pitcher from the servers' station before heading over to them, trying to get into the flow of the night, to breathe more deeply, get rid of the pulsing panic she was pushing down, just under the surface.

"Hey, folks, how we doin'?" Ruth asked.

The couple ignored her question. As she started to fill the first water glass, the man said, "Bring me a Tito's dirty martini with extra blue cheese olives and dirty ice," without looking at her.

"You would like a martini?" Ruth asked, staring at the man. She wanted him to look up, to look at the person in front of him, to *ask* for something, to say *please.* She wanted to make him care. She wanted him to be aware of his own rudeness. He raised his head, looked at her, and bugged his eyes out. It was a look Ruth was familiar with, one that meant *are you slow?* And she anticipated what would happen next.

"Uh, yeah?" he said, his tone making it clear that Ruth was wasting his time. Ruth could only push this so far. She had to nod and look away.

"And for you?" she said, talking to the woman, who also spoke without looking up, ordering the same drink as her husband, neither of them saying please.

She returned with the drinks, making sure they didn't wobble on the tray as she lowered the full martini glass down in front of the man.

"The ice?" the man asked without looking up to see Ruth holding the glass of ice midair.

"Yup." She put it down.

"We have a few more joining us," the man said, still not looking at Ruth as he took a sip of his martini.

Ruth looked at their table. There was no room for any more chairs.

"I don't think that will be possible, sir. The restaurant is full and we wouldn't have anywhere to put them," Ruth said, her voice robotic and firm. She was good at telling people no.

The man finally looked up at her.

"Can't you find some extra chairs?" he asked, looking around at the same cramped space that Ruth was and seeing something different, seeing what he wanted.

"Why don't I go ask for you," Ruth replied.

Ruth watched from next to the bar as Whitney approached the table and tried to squeeze two more chairs in, just as a man and a woman filed over from the front door, past the hostess, toward the couple. Ruth sighed and went over to take their order.

"We'll do a dozen oysters. You guys do oysters, right?" One of the men addressed the table. Ruth stood in front of them, holding her pad in front of her.

"Oysters look like fetuses to me—I morally object to eating them," his wife said, not looking up from her phone, reaching over to the other woman to show her something on it.

"Who gives a fuck, if you can pair them with wine," the man said, laughing. "Am I right?"

But the women were ignoring the men, the first woman scrolling through pictures of a baby that must be hers, flipping through the many shots of the little girl in different outfits while the friend cooed.

"So adorable," the friend said.

"That's all," the man said to Ruth, who had lingered too long, staring at the photos over the woman's shoulder, her mind spinning.

Ruth nodded to herself and left the group. As she walked away, she thought about the girl in the photo and wondered how she would grow up. She wondered what the odds were that she would be sweet, uncorrupted, or if she would ever work in a restaurant like this. Looking at her parents, she doubted it.

Ruth carried the oyster tray above the heads of the other diners, making her way to her table in the far corner. She lowered it and raised her voice to announce where each oyster was from, as she was required to do. The group largely ignored her, and as she studied the oysters, their flesh submerged in liquid, she too could not help but think of a fetus curled up and suspended in the womb. She quickly walked away from the table, not wanting to watch either of the men slurp one down.

"Ruth!" the chef yelled as Ruth walked past the kitchen. "What's up with all these substitutions on table nine?!"

"I know!" she said, putting her hands up. "I'm sorry!"

As she turned back into the dining room, she saw the hostess seating a new two-top in Ruth's section. She lingered by the computer for a second and tried to take deep breaths. Louis's searching eyes came back to her, making her flinch.

"Everything okay, Ruth?" Whitney asked, her eyebrows raised. Instead of answering, Ruth just kept moving. Her thoughts swirling through her mind—she wondered how many times she had filled a water glass in her life, how many times she had been stiffed on a tip, how many times someone had spoken to her rudely, how many times a man had reached out and touched her. She couldn't remember. It all blurred together.

Ruth's new two-top was seated in a nook behind a divider in the dining room, so it wasn't until she was reaching for the water glass that she recognized Nadia's blond hair. Across from her sat a petite older woman who had to be her mother. Ruth recognized her from the pictures on Nadia's Instagram. Her mother's hair was darker than Nadia's, but her features and bone structure matched the angles and curves of Nadia's face exactly. At first, Nadia didn't look up as Ruth filled her water glass, and Ruth could feel an anxious panic rising within her, meeting the rage she felt from the table before. She felt a nervous sweat prickle her underarms.

"Thank you," Nadia's mother said as Ruth turned to fill her glass. Only then did Nadia notice her.

"Oh! Ruth!"

"Hey, hi," she said, putting on her server voice, her server smile. It felt more difficult than ever before as she remembered Nadia's cold glance across the room at the party. She was amazed that Nadia was pleased to see her, and noting this, Ruth's stomach sank with guilt as she thought of the kiss.

"This is my mother. I was supposed to meet her on the mainland later, but she flew in this morning from Nantucket to surprise me and to help me with some of the wedding planning," Nadia said, gesturing toward her mother—beaming, prideful.

"A friend of mine's a pilot," Nadia's mother said in explanation, her hand waving it away as if she was embarrassed to discuss her private flight. "It's nice to meet you, Ruth. I've heard a lot about you."

Ruth couldn't imagine what she had heard or from whom. She looked kind, with a softly wrinkled face, probably in her early sixties. Like a slap, Ruth grew weak thinking about how she never knew her mom at this age. She stood, trying to think how Maggie's face might have changed, how the wrinkles in her knees might have grown deeper, or faded and dispersed as the skin grew soft.

"Ruth?" Nadia asked. "Are you okay?"

She nodded, trying not to think about what her face looked like, trying to keep it together.

"Listen, we're catching the ferry in an hour. Can we order with you now? We're kind of cutting it close," Nadia said.

Ruth nodded again and wrote down their order. She was walking back to the computer to put it in when the man from the oyster table waved her down.

"Excuse me!" he said across the room. The other servers' heads snapped in Ruth's direction, raising their eyebrows in pity before they returned to whatever they were doing.

Ruth took a deep breath and approached the table, but she couldn't make herself walk quickly.

"Yes?" she asked as she approached.

"This isn't a dry martini," he said, pushing it back in her direction, the remaining blue-cheese-filled olives bobbing in the cocktail that was already half consumed. Ruth flipped back in her notebook to his order and couldn't help herself.

"You didn't order a dry martini," she said. "You ordered a dirty martini."

But he was no longer looking at Ruth. He started talking to

the man sitting next to him, leaving Ruth standing there, the drink in between them.

"Okay, let me get this out of your way then," she said, reaching down for the martini glass and whisking it out of reach even as he turned and barked something about just taking it off the bill. Forgetting to yell "corner" as she headed into the dish pit, Ruth almost ran into her co-worker and nearly slipped on a puddle that was forming underneath the leaking air conditioner. Even though the restaurant was busier than it had been all summer, she couldn't find her footing in the night, couldn't access the numbing groove that had always worked for her.

As she walked back into the dining room, she grabbed the drinks for Nadia and her mother off the bar. Turning the corner, she saw Nadia's mom covering her face with her hands in laughter and Nadia leaning forward across the table like she had just shared a funny secret. As Ruth put the glasses down in front of the women, she felt another wave of jealousy toward them. She would never have a glass of wine with her mom at dinner, would never know what secrets to her life her mother might have shared with her as they both aged, as she saw more of herself in Ruth. For a brief second, she hated Nadia for all that she had, all that Ruth wanted.

Walking back to the computer, the room felt heavy. Ruth was about to make a detour to the walk-in cooler as she felt a sob growing in her chest, but a hand grabbed her arm and she was brought back to the present, to the man with the new martini in front of him. Ruth turned, yanking her arm back as a reflex. The man held his hands up like she was pointing a gun at him.

"Woah, relax," he said.

"What can I do for you?" Ruth replied, her tone robotic as she choked down her tears.

"A dry martini means there is no vermouth in it," the man said.

"I'm aware of that," Ruth replied.

"Not even a whisper of vermouth," the man said, ignoring her. "This is just wrong. Can I see your wine menu . . . and your manager too." He leaned back in his chair and reached for the martini. Ruth stared as he took a sip and put the glass back down. Normally, it would've been easy for Ruth to let this go. Moments like this, or worse than this, had happened countless times before.

But before she knew it she was leaning down, the wide edge of the glass meeting her fingertips as she tipped it over. She watched the full martini tumble into the man's lap, the liquid spread across his crotch, the olives bounce off his legs and onto the ground. He roared and stood up, but she couldn't hear him, couldn't see the other diners looking at her with their mouths agape. She turned on her clogged heel and walked toward the back of the restaurant, the chef yelling out from the line about a side of truffle pasta she had forgotten, unaware of what had just happened. Opening the back door, she stepped out into the hot night. The metal latch clicked shut behind her. The ringing in her ears faded and Ruth listened to the distant noises of town, so familiar to her. The ferry horn blasted, and Ruth looked down at her watch. The six P.M. departure. She and Charlie used to listen for the ferry horns. They would turn to each other whenever they heard one or saw it turning up water as it skated away from the island and say, "We're not on that boat," sharing the joy of staying on the island, of watching the day change into evening for one more night of summer. Ruth wondered how long she had been holding on to even one more night of summer. It suddenly seemed like too long.

She sensed something precious was slipping away, something she had always thought was the source of her happiness, of what made her special in this world. She got to be a part of this place, call it home. But she was so tired—so, so tired—and she started to wonder how it might feel to get on the next boat, drift away from everything as the night fell, the stars peeking through the clouds as she landed on the mainland without anything in front of her, with nothing but water behind her.

The back door swung open.

"What the fuck was that?" Whitney yelled. Her tone was almost as if she was scared Ruth might do something to her too. "Are you mental?"

"I can't do it, Whitney. I can't fucking do it anymore," Ruth said. She was tired of caring about rich customers who might have the power to make her life more difficult over an overcooked steak or a martini that wasn't what they thought they ordered. It used to feel like a game to Ruth—put on a nice face and make a lot of money. Now it just felt devastating and empty. She was tired.

"Ruth, I don't know."

"What, Whitney?" Ruth asked, turning to look at her.

"Things have been getting worse for a while," she said.

Ruth thought about that.

"You've had an . . . intense summer. Maybe you just need a break. Think about what you wanna do for a week. I'll call you," she said, looking at the concrete ground covered in stray cigarette butts, then closed the door behind her.

As the door clicked shut, Ruth laughed to herself. She had observed this move before. Whitney was too gentle to really fire anyone. She said she would call them and then she never would.

But Ruth knew she was fired.

She untied the apron at her waist and left it on an upside-down milk crate next to the overflowing ashtray where the line cooks smoked before and after their shift. Looking at her phone, she saw a missed call from Ethel and one from Louis. She turned it off and walked away from the restaurant. She had no idea where she was going. There was only so far she could go.

12

Ruth walked in the direction of the beach, away from town. She passed Yellow Kittens, Tigerfish, and the Beached. and soon the noise of the restaurants fell away and she was left with the crashing waves. It was still light out and people were on the beach below the road. The surf was larger than normal, crashing all the way up to touch the dunes where the sand was thinnest. Ruth eventually leaned down and pulled her clogs off her feet, unfurling her socks and stuffing them in her shoes to walk barefoot on the pavement.

What was she going to do? It wouldn't be long before the weekly rent for the cottage would suck dry the money she'd made so far this summer, and she didn't have any savings to dip into. Doing some quick math, she figured she could maybe last six more weeks before she would have to do something drastic. She tried to run through the list of other places she could work on the island, but it was midsummer and everywhere was staffed up, plus it seemed impossible she would be hired at a restaurant after that. The thought of leaving altogether filled her mind again but was now shrouded in impossibility. There was nothing for her anywhere else either.

Her phone buzzed in her pocket and Ruth pulled it out to see who it was. Ethel had been calling for the past few hours and Ruth had ignored every call. Thinking about what she had wanted the article to be, the tribute that Diana had deserved, and the pages of unusable writing on her computer at home made Ruth want to hurl her phone at the pavement. She suddenly felt like a waste—a desperate, sinking waste of a person.

She kept walking until she reached a path in the dunes far past the town beach. Walking over the hill, her feet digging into the sand, she looked out at the ocean. The waves were curling and crashing loudly, the white water foaming and rolling as it pulled back into the break. There were only a few families still there, spread out and standing in sweatshirts with drinks in their hands, throwing balls to their dogs down the beach and laughing, the sound of their conversation drowned out by the angry ocean.

Ruth walked to the water. Picking a spot in the sand, she laid down in her jeans and looked up at the sky changing color. She wondered what it must have felt like to be told that you were sick and it wasn't going to get better. Had Diana and Maggie felt alone? Had they ever felt as alone as Ruth felt right then?

The idea of either of them feeling this way made Ruth cry, tears falling down, dampening the hair at her temples. She had wanted to protect her mom, to do something to help, and she realized she still held within her the prevailing uselessness of it all, still ruminated over it, was still broken over it. What was the point if it could all end at any moment? If you could get hit by a car on your way to see your kids or get bitten by a mosquito and die of a disease you hadn't known about? Ruth knew that there were so many people for whom the threat of death and danger was more prominent, more tangible, but she had never been able to love the world the way she once did when her mother was well. She was scared—always.

Ruth was crying harder now, and she needed to sit up to breathe. She felt the last piece inside her finally snap, the one leg that she'd been standing on since Diana's death, the pain she had been hiding from, and the force of tears that had evaded her overtook her now with a strength she was unprepared for. Ruth didn't have the energy to fight it anymore, to ignore the loss.

The ocean had gotten rougher in the time since she arrived at the beach. Swimmers were pushing against the white water, stirred up with sand, fighting the undercurrent to get back to the shore. It seemed too dangerous to Ruth for all these people to be in the water, but even when someone looked like they were getting sucked out, a large wave would break, crashing into them and nudging them back to shore.

Ruth's tears dried on her face as her breathing slowed. She wiped her eyes.

Looking around her, Ruth noticed a woman and a toddler making their way down the beach to the water's edge. The toddler's small legs tried to keep pace with the woman, stepping over the rocks with care. Down at the end of the dry sand, they stopped. Ruth couldn't see the little girl's face but watched as her head tipped upward to look at her mother. The woman took off her dress so that she was down to her black bathing suit. Leaning down to her daughter, she said something before standing and bounding down to the waves, leaving the girl standing alone in the sand.

Lifting her knees above the water as it crashed around her, the woman dove into the waves. The ocean consumed her, lifting her and moving her to the side with speed.

Ruth focused on the little girl alone on the beach. Looking up toward the path, she expected to see another adult coming to meet the girl, thinking the woman's companion must not be far behind, but there was no one. Focusing again on the toddler, Ruth realized how distressing it was to see a child that small so untethered, no adult nearby. The girl couldn't be older than two, her tiny legs still pudgy with baby fat that Ruth could see at a distance. She wobbled, her hands out to her sides, the fingers curled in, and all at once Ruth was overcome by an intense sadness, and a sob from deep within broke through her. The little girl was too exposed, too alone in a dangerous place. The girl looked in the direction of the water, toward her mother, and Ruth thought then about how she had felt the first day her mother was gone, like she had been put somewhere she shouldn't be, in a world she didn't understand. She felt like she had been forgotten.

The waves were gaining more strength now, and Ruth could see the woman in the water was caught in the wave break, her head ducking under each curling wave at the last second before it crashed over her. Ruth sat up—alert. When the woman's head reemerged, she threw her arms toward shore, trying to catch a wave and get pushed in, the movement useless. Ruth realized she was holding her breath. Another wave came, breaking over the woman's head, and instead of moving her to shore, she popped up in the same place. A riptide had ballooned out behind her and Ruth could see the woman getting pulled out, although her arms were thrashing now, her strokes growing more desperate, trying and failing to get her back to land. Standing, Ruth looked around the beach. The few groups of families were still there, spread out, sitting in circles and talking while their children played in the sand nearby. No one else was looking in the direction of the woman.

Ruth's heart was pounding and the ringing in her ears returned. There were no lifeguards at this beach. Another wave broke and the woman's head disappeared under the ocean. Ruth then realized she was running, stripping off her clothes so she was down to her underwear. Hesitating at the water's edge, she looked to the right where a family was packing up for the day, a boogie board acting as a sled carrying their folded towels, a beach chair. Ruth lunged for the board. She could hear the family shouting, but turning, she said, "Watch her!" and pointed at the toddler before turning and sprinting into the ocean.

As soon as she was calf deep in the water, she felt the full strength of the current and the waves ram against her. It was difficult to get past the high white water that crashed toward the shore with such strong force. Attaching the Velcro strap to her wrist and carrying the board behind her, she dove under an oncoming wave and felt it thrust her back, away from the woman and toward the beach. She tried grabbing handfuls of sand along the bottom for as long as she could hold her breath, hoping to inch herself forward or at least hold her in place. When she emerged in the frothing ocean, she gasped for air and swam hard to get closer to the woman, who was looking toward the beach and screaming, the sound getting drowned out by the waves. Ruth looked back too and saw the toddler. She knew the mother's eyes were locked on her daughter. Another wave came, forcing Ruth down. She felt the line to the boogie board tighten, and suddenly she was afraid that it would snap and she would be stuck in the water too, neither of them left with anything to hold on to. She knew this wasn't what you were supposed to do—that you needed the right tools to rescue someone. But the boogie board was still there when she came up and she grabbed on to it. Ruth felt the riptide pulling her own body out in the woman's direction. Holding on to the float and catching her breath, she pushed it out in front of her toward the mother in the black bathing suit.

"Grab the board!" Ruth shouted.

Ruth was arrested by the woman's gaze. Her eyes were wide and crazed, her dilated pupils dark and visible. In a flash Ruth was brought back to her own mother's eyes—to Maggie in the chemo chair having an allergic reaction, searching for someone to help. Ruth's ears began to ring louder as she remembered her wringing hands, her feeling of uselessness, her inability to do anything for her mother as the nurses ran into the hospital room.

She hadn't been able to make a difference in the end. All her notetaking, all her worry and her care had done nothing to save her mom.

The woman lunged for the board, clasping it in her hands, pulling Ruth back into the moment. Ruth was careful to stay out of the woman's way as she held on to it. The pull was still strong and the boogie board barely supported their weight. A wave crashed over them. As Ruth came back up, she became acutely aware that they were in danger.

"It's okay," Ruth said to the woman, but also to herself. She was already growing tired from the swim. "It's okay, we're going to swim out of the riptide and we'll get back in."

The woman nodded and Ruth watched her breathing grow more even. Holding on to the front of the board lightly so that it wouldn't submerge further, Ruth started kicking to the side, parallel to the beach. She could see the spot in the distance where the water was more even and blue, and she tried to focus on it, but despite her kicking they weren't getting any closer. They were beyond the wave break by now and far away from land.

"I need you to kick with me," Ruth said to the woman.

"I can't. I need a rest," the woman called out, her voice ragged, her weight growing heavier against the board, making it harder for Ruth to swim.

Looking back at the island as she swam, Ruth was shocked by how far from it they were. It looked so small. Her breath was growing short from the effort, and she felt panic set in—it suddenly seemed impossible that they would make it back to land, and Ruth stopped kicking. She felt the tug of the ocean, felt how tired her body was.

Ruth thought back to the beach day with Charlie, to how she almost let the ocean take her away, how clearly she had seen it play out in her mind. She had never told anyone how often she thought about wanting to hide, to disappear, never explained how hard it was to keep her head above water all these years. In that moment it had been so easy to imagine letting all the weight she held within her sweep her out to sea, and without question she knew it—how strong the pull to give up had been that day.

But now the threat of drowning, of death, felt as real as it ever had to Ruth, and in her mind's eye she saw herself submerged, sinking, bubbles escaping her. She watched them slow one by one until they were extinguished and there was nothing but light shining through a blue and empty column of water—no other sign of her life, and almost as if her body was working on its own, rejecting the image in her mind, Ruth began to kick, slowly at first, then harder. She fought to get away from those thoughts, away from the load of bricks holding her down, and as she pushed, her breath strained and her adrenaline pulsing, she realized that Diana had been right, that Lucy had been right. That she had been hiding from it all, lying to herself about her grief even as she hid among the rubble of it, not taking any chances, not really living.

She was pulling up all the strength she had now, fighting for all of it—for the woman and the toddler on shore, for Diana and Maggie, and, for the first time in a long time, for herself.

The riptide's grip subsided as they swam out of it, Ruth's legs relaxing in relief. They were still far out, but the water was calmer. There was a crowd gathered on the beach watching them. Slower now, her body spent, Ruth continued to swim in.

On shore, Ruth saw someone holding the little girl's hand and she released a deep breath.

"She's okay," Ruth said, although the woman hadn't asked. "She's right there. Do you see her?"

"I see her," she said, her voice hoarse, her eyes fixated on her daughter.

When they reached the break, each wave pushed them closer to the shoreline until she felt the sand under her feet. Ruth held her hand out to help the woman stand and as soon as she could, she was running toward her toddler, who was wailing, her mouth wide open. The woman's steps were jagged and her legs almost gave out from underneath her as she fell to her knees and grabbed her daughter up into her arms. The woman was crying heavily now, sobbing and holding the small girl as people stood around them, eager to help.

Ruth sat on the sand, spent waves rushing over her legs.

"Someone get them some water!" a woman shouted.

A crowd formed around the mother and daughter and someone was on the phone with the island EMTs. Ruth watched from the outside until someone came over to her, draping a towel over her shoulders.

"Are you okay, sweetie?" the woman asked. "I think you just saved that woman's life."

Ruth nodded and stood. The woman reached out to try and help.

"You should really wait for the EMTs," she said.

"I'm okay," Ruth replied. She pulled the towel off and thanked the woman before walking up the beach to where her things were strewn in the sand. Ruth's throat was sore from the effort of the swim, her muscles complaining. The breeze was cold against her body and the skin on her arms was gooseflesh. Looking behind her as she approached the sandy path that led back out to the street, she saw the woman holding the child close in the sand, the girl's small arms wrapped around her mother's neck.

13

Ruth stood on the side of the road, wet and in her sports bra and underwear. The sun was beginning to set, the golden hour glow still sharp on the dunes, as she reached the base of the path that met the road. Looking across the street, she watched the way the reeds blew over in the gentle breeze, she smelled the sharp, herbal scent of the beach roses and the cooling sand, and she felt a surprising sense of calm. She wondered if things had been different, if Maggie had never gotten sick, whether her mother and Diana might have reconnected, whether Ruth would have ever met Diana—but there wasn't a sadness around the thought, only a curiosity, less weight attached to what could have been. Ruth looked back at the dune she had just crossed over. A Harrier hawk swooped down and disappeared into the brush. Crickets buzzed, making the brush pulse as if alive. Ruth thought of the painting, of her mother's looping handwriting on the back—*Happy birthday, June Baby!* She had always thought there was some kind of kismet in Diana and Maggie's close June birthdays, only days apart. Something about it tied the women together in her mind, even before she knew they had loved each other—they were summer children, like her.

She wished she could call her mother, could talk with her on her way up to Diana's house, could rinse her feet off under the hose and sit with Diana in the fading light reading and talking about books, could put her mother on the phone with Diana and watch their easy conversation, the way Diana might light up at her mother's voice. It was a dreamlike reconstruction, and she stood, holding it in her, cherishing the brief feeling of them all being together, of what that impossible configuration might feel like, might look like, before she let it go.

Once she was on the road, a Jeep drove past and honked, and the group of men catcalling from the windows reminded her of her current state. She was miles from home, still dripping wet, covered in sand, and in her underwear. Slinging her jeans over her shoulders and holding on to her clogs by the heels, she started walking back in the direction of the cottage, her summer-worn feet unfazed by the sandy pavement.

She walked slowly, feeling drained of the things that had been filling her. She could still feel the strength of the ocean trying to pull her and the woman under, the piercing adrenaline to act—to do something. The sun was half-submerged now behind the Great Salt Pond and the sky behind the dunes was growing purple like her mother had painted it. Ruth felt a wash of shame for avoiding the paintings, for avoiding the article. It was the fifth of July. There was still time. Maybe she could write something that Ethel could help her with. She could try.

Diana's old truck drove by her on the road. Watching it, Ruth was disoriented for a second. The imagined world she had been building felt so real that it seemed like her prayer had been answered, that Diana was going to hop out and bring her back to the house. The truck slowed and pulled over to the edge of the road in front of her. The car door opened, but instead of Diana, Charlie got out. He stood, watching her as she walked toward the car, his face somber.

"Can I give you a ride, miss?" he asked, a wan smile crossing his face.

Ruth didn't know how she felt. Looking at him, she remembered the kiss in the darkness, only last night, and remembered her anger at his ambivalence back in the room with his friends. But still, those things disappeared when she saw him, when the comfort of his gaze reminded her of all the years they had built with each other, not knowing it, not ever really choosing each other, yet becoming ingrained in each other's lives. All of that was impossible to erase now, even the lack of choice, especially the lack of choice. Looking at his face, the contours more familiar really than her own, she felt like the memories had physically changed her, and she could never know what he thought about it all, wasn't even sure that he thought about life like that. But she sensed that he felt similarly, that the same force she felt all summer was what put him in the truck and sent him out looking for her.

"Your friends are gone already?" Ruth asked, standing in front of him, bare and cold.

Charlie nodded.

"Did you just drop Nadia and her mom off at the ferry?" Ruth asked.

Charlie quickly looked at the ground before responding. "Yeah, she's on the mainland for the night."

"And Lynn is still away?"

Charlie nodded again. "I need to talk to you," he said.

Instead of replying, Ruth opened the passenger side of the truck and got in, not looking at Charlie as he closed his door behind him, started the vehicle, and pulled it back out onto the road. The last of the sun was gone from the sky now, and Ruth could see stars poking through the deepening purples and blues as the night took over. Her head lolled to the side and a great wave of peace and exhaustion swept through her. If she squinted her eyes, if everything became a little blurrier—the pond, the people, the stars—then maybe it could exist in another place and time, somewhere ethereal where she could stretch this second out to be as long as she needed, could ask the questions she wanted answers to, could fight the fights she should have fought, and linger longer in the moments that she still thought about as she fell asleep each night. Ruth reached across the short bench and, without looking, found Charlie's hand with hers. She weaved the tips of her fingers into the spaces at the base of his and felt the sand and salt that still encrusted her palm between their skin. His thumb ran over the base of her palm, where the bone still wasn't perfectly even from when she'd broken it years before, the same spot that he wrote *Love, Charlie* in Sharpie. He dug his fingers deeper into the hold, his large hand encircling her own, and Ruth fell asleep as the truck moved forward into the night. The streetlights flicked on as they drove underneath them.

The sound of the car door closing woke her up. In the darkness, Ruth could hear the crickets, see fireflies bouncing by the beech tree through the dirty windshield, and hear Charlie's footsteps over the dry grass around the car and toward her. Opening the door, he stood close as Ruth slipped out onto the ground.

"I was ready to carry you," Charlie said.

"I don't think I'm that helpless," Ruth replied.

Charlie seemed uncertain of where to stand. He hovered near Ruth as if to touch her, but didn't move or say anything, and after a moment Ruth brushed past him. She walked across the dark lawn, toward the outdoor shower on the side of the house that Diana had put in a few years ago at Ruth's suggestion. She fumbled in the dark for the faucet and turned the water on, and hot mist began to fall on her as she pulled off her damp, sandy underwear. Standing in the darkness naked, Ruth lifted her arms above her head. The air was more humid here than at the beach, and her skin felt touched by the buttery warmth of July. Trying to remember if she had ever been truly naked in front of Charlie, she began to feel exposed. She stepped fully into the water, ducking her head under the flow from the shower and reveling in the sensation of submerging herself within the water pressure, the breeze tickling the parts of her body that were still open to the air. The radiating sense of calm she felt earlier continued to fill the emptiness that had been burrowing through her for such a long time.

Turning around, she found Charlie standing where she left him, watching her, almost as if he was scared to come closer.

"You're like some kind of fairy," he said after a minute.

The water was catching whatever light from the moon it could grab and there were glints of it sparkling against the spraying water. Ruth threw her head back so she was submerged again, and when she looked back Charlie was still there.

He took a few steps toward her so he was in the puddles of the shower, the water splashing onto his bare feet and legs. Leaning over, Ruth found the edges of the bottom of his T-shirt and began to pull them up, looking up to his eyes to see how he would react. She considered the precipice she was on, whether it was worth the guilt she knew she would feel. All she wanted was to know what would happen.

"I really thought you didn't want me," Charlie said. "I tried so many times."

"I know," Ruth replied, and the sweeping relief at hearing those words was shocking to her. All of the moments when Ruth hadn't known whether they shared the same feelings, whether those feelings were even real, were now laid out in front of them for what they were—real, theirs.

Holding Ruth's eyes, Charlie lifted his arms and allowed her to pull his shirt off and throw it onto the lawn and into the darkness. Ruth reached his shorts, pushing the metal button through the hole and stepping back. Charlie pulled them off and took two steps into the shower, the water engulfing him as he wrapped his arms around Ruth, hot water running between their bodies as they fell together.

14

Later, Ruth sat on the couch with her hair wrapped up in a big towel, wearing Charlie's old Columbia sweatshirt. Pulling her legs up underneath her, she tugged at the hem of it so it covered her knees, keeping them warm. Although it was such a hot night that the air was still and humid within the house, she felt like she wanted to be held close by everything. She wrapped her arms around herself. Charlie emerged from the bottom of the stairs in fresh boxers and an old Ben & Jerry's T-shirt that Ruth remembered from summers past. He sat next to her, and Ruth felt like she was seeing a new person.

The memory of outside was still fresh on her skin, her lips red and her cheeks lit up with color. It was strange that something Ruth had wondered about for so long was in the past now. Having sex with Charlie was almost exactly as she had pictured it many times before, but there were also many things she couldn't have imagined—the details that made it real. Ruth recalled the water, the soft air, the closeness of him everywhere, how he smelled like warmth and salt, the feeling of her arm wrapped across the tops of his shoulders, bracing her weight, her palm against the cedar-shingled house, his firm grasp holding her up.

Afterward, in the dark, she'd tried to find the outlines of his face in the light of the moon so she could hold on to the memory, make sure it stuck in her mind, but it was already starting to blur, the sensations mixing together.

There was an air of awkwardness now that both of them were back in the light of the house, clothed. She wondered if he was already going to say it was a mistake, but she didn't want to think about that yet. Nothing about it had felt like a mistake, and while she knew it might later, she wanted to sit within the stolen moment for as long as she could.

"Can I show you something?" Ruth asked, standing.

Charlie nodded.

Ruth grabbed Charlie's hand and felt him wrap it more tightly into hers. They walked back out of the house and toward Diana's studio. Opening the door, Ruth felt around for the switch on the lamp. As she flipped it, the room was filled with warm light, and she climbed up the ladder to the loft. Pulling the bin out of where she had stashed it, she turned to pass it down.

"Here," she said. "Be careful, it's heavy."

Ruth lowered the bin to Charlie, then climbed back down the ladder to the ground. Charlie put it on the floor and held his arms out to support her down the last steps.

"These are the paintings?" Charlie asked, both of them turning to the closed bin. Ruth cracked the lid open and began pulling the canvases out and placing them on the studio floor.

They stood in silence and looked down at Maggie's art.

"You know, I never saw my mom do much for herself," Ruth said as they looked together. "She was always working or spending time with me. She never took any trips. . . . I can't even remember her having many friends."

Charlie didn't respond, and she could feel his eyes on her face as Ruth took in the paintings, the colors, the island seen through her mother's eyes. She knew that in so many ways it was a gift to know this about her mother, to see how she saw the world, but Ruth still couldn't shake the feeling that something had been stolen, and she couldn't help but want more, even if her questions all led to dead ends. Maggie couldn't talk to her about her paintings, about Charlie, about what to do now.

Ruth sat on the ground and Charlie followed, pulling her into him so that she was leaning against his body, encircled by his arms, looking at the paintings on the floor.

Neither of them spoke for a minute and Ruth listened to his heart beating against her back. Finally, Ruth turned so that she was facing him. She leaned in and kissed him, trying to soak in the feeling, and he held her face close, kissing her back.

"I've wanted you for a long time," Ruth said. "I've held on to this hope that in the end it would be you and me. I've always wondered if it would work."

"What did you decide?" Charlie asked. Ruth tried to read what he was feeling in his voice, but this seemed like a version of Charlie and herself she didn't know as well, both of them truly vulnerable—all walls taken down.

"Sometimes I get images of what our house would look like, where we'd drink coffee in the morning," she said. "We would have a dog who liked to sit with us, the walls would be yellow, we'd read the paper."

Charlie smiled, his eyes filling with tears.

"But there's always something blurry about it. I can't fully see it," she said. "I don't get how our lives would fit together anymore. It's like I can't see myself, or I do see someone, but it isn't actually me anymore."

Charlie was nodding, the tears dropping down his face.

"Have you ever imagined it?" Ruth asked.

"Sometimes it seemed like the most . . . right thing, but I always thought you would get bored of me—would want something more," he said. "Sometimes I worry that . . . it's been too long, that maybe there's a reason it hasn't happened after all this time. And now . . . I do love Nadia."

A minute passed in silence.

"What are we going to do?" Charlie asked.

"I don't know," Ruth said, although a clarity was forming within her. She knew she couldn't be with Charlie, couldn't move to Boston with him—that it would be a mistake if she did because she would be jumping into someone else's life, would just be hiding from herself yet again. And she didn't want to hide anymore.

But thinking about their bodies in the darkness, their hands in the car, the look on his face ten years ago when she met him for the first time, and the look on his face now, she doubted herself. She felt this brief window of stolen closeness shutting and felt her heart breaking with it, felt the permanence of the decision. Ruth felt tears on her face too and reached out, poking under the holes around the collar of the old T-shirt he was wearing, finding the indent above the collarbone and tracing her fingers over it, knowing she wouldn't be able to touch him like this again.

"I love you," she said, and all the hesitation she had felt before about telling him was gone. It felt good to say it, for it to be true and for him to know. It felt good to give it to this person she cared about, and only after she said it did she know in her bones that nothing would happen, that he would stay with Nadia, that it would be the right thing. For a brief second, she let the heartbreak hit her, but then Ruth wondered if maybe sometimes, as time passed, he would think about her, think about summer and see her face, the way she might think of his. Maybe when he was old and tired and his joints were sore, he would think about them giggling on a blanket under the stars, their bodies young and their skin taut, sunburned. To know now what they meant to each other, to be able to hold it in this moment—maybe whatever happened after this as time went on, she could feel comfort that somewhere out there Charlie was thinking of her, of the way she used to be. She thought of what her mom said on the stoop all those years ago, that when her first love got married, she would feel sad, and that would be okay.

"I love you too," Charlie said.

"And you love Nadia."

"Yes."

"You fit together," Ruth said, thinking of what she had seen of them all summer, admitting it to herself. "She makes you happy." Ruth felt herself tear up, thinking about their life. She envisioned them walking together, Nadia at Charlie's side, their child sitting on his shoulders, how much sense it all made for them. No matter how much she tried, she couldn't see herself in that place: Charlie's wife, the mother of his children. Ruth imagined then what her life could look like, all the possibilities that were laid out in front of her, and she felt only lightness and a certainty that they were doing the right thing.

"I do love her," he said then, tears dripping down his face.

"I know, Charlie," Ruth said. "It'll be okay."

Back in her work clothes, the wet underwear rolled into a sandy ball in her hand, Ruth watched as Charlie lifted the bin of Maggie's paintings into the bed of the truck and closed the tailgate with a loud bang. They looked at each other across the dark expanse. Charlie was unable to hold her stare, looking down to the ground. Ruth took a deep breath, opened the car door and closed it behind her. The silence of the truck and the darkness reminded her of driving through the night to reach Diana at the hospital back in the spring—how the road had been so empty and quiet, how afraid she had been, until Charlie opened the driver side and started the engine, bringing her back.

As they drove down the dirt road, bumping along in the darkness, Charlie reached out again for her hand, which she grabbed and held with both of hers. They drove like this for a while in the quiet, their palms pressed together. Pulling into town, they drove past the restaurant, and as Ruth looked inside she could tell that it was business as usual, almost as if she had never worked there, the flow continuing, the flurry of waitresses clearing a table, the bartender making a drink all the same, the only difference that she wasn't a part of it.

Charlie parked the truck in the short dirt driveway of the cottage. The lights were out, and Ruth didn't see Lucy's car. She was glad no one was home, and the fact that she was still fighting with her friend made Ruth come back to the lonely reality she had escaped for a few hours.

"Thank you," Ruth said, turning to Charlie. She leaned over the bench in the truck and hugged him, his arms embracing her and pulling her closer.

"Let me help you with the paintings," Charlie said as she pulled away.

"I got it," Ruth replied.

Lifting the bin up the stairs onto the porch, Ruth heard the tires roll over the dirt. Once at the top of the stairs, Ruth turned and watched him pull away. She held up a hand in a small wave, the bin of Maggie's paintings at her feet.

PART 3

August

1

Over the next few weeks, as July turned to August, Ruth didn't hear from Charlie. His wedding was fast approaching, and from her window, when Ruth saw big trucks drive by, she imagined they were heading to Diana's house full of tents and chairs. She still hadn't talked to her dad since the Fourth. Although she came close to calling Joel a few times, when she tried to imagine what she would say, she put the phone down. Louis had been calling her, leaving voicemails, but Ruth didn't listen to them, only watched her phone buzz without answering. Lucy wasn't speaking to her, and while Ruth wanted to apologize, Lucy was always out of the house and didn't even come home at night, sleeping somewhere else. She ignored Ruth's texts, but it all felt like too much to explain in a message anyhow.

Ruth had been hard at work, researching jobs and trying to piece together the article for Ethel, barely leaving the cottage. She was trying to be less critical of herself, although it was difficult to quiet that voice after so many years of believing she was without talent. There were times, when she was in the groove of writing, that she thought she was onto something, but every time she looked back on the work, it didn't seem good enough for *Vogue*, for her tribute to Diana—her goodbye, all the things she hadn't gotten to say. It often took her hours to get a paragraph down, and even still she ended up deleting half of it, but it felt good to at least be trying, even as the deadline closed in on her.

She knew she was burying herself in the work, relying on the tunnel vision of finishing the article so that she didn't have to think about Charlie and the wedding, about Joel and Lucy, about whether or not she was pregnant at that very moment.

There had been a brief window in the middle of July when Ruth thought she was in the clear. One morning she woke up to light pink blood spotting the inside of her underwear, flooding her with relief. But the flow never got heavier and only lasted for a few days, and Ruth's relief turned into confusion and worry again. All of her research online was useless. It said she might be pregnant and the spotting could be from implantation, or that her period might just be delayed because of stress. Maybe she hadn't ovulated that month; it was fairly normal for people to skip periods sometimes. She tried to focus on the last option—her period had never been that regular, so it made some sense.

Each morning she stared at the calendar and counted the days from her last normal period in June. She had had long cycles before, but this felt different. The stress of waiting for it was making her break out in hives on her legs.

She went to the grocery store one day, just to see if they sold pregnancy tests, hoping to put her mind at ease. Her pulse was racing so hard she heard it in her ears as she looked around.

"Hey, Ruth," the cashier called out. "Do you need something?"

Ruth spotted a single pregnancy test on the shelf and stared at it, the sound in the room melting away into a stinging silence. She glanced at the cashier, at the other girls bagging behind the counter. She knew all of them, and something about looking the cashier in the eyes while buying the test made the whole thing too real to Ruth. She imagined the gossip that would spread, imagined it getting back to Louis.

"No, thanks," she said, leaving, breaking into a run once she was on the street.

When she got home she sat on the front lawn, her head between her knees, and tried to comfort herself. She clutched her breasts—they weren't sore. She wasn't nauseous. Her back didn't hurt any more than it normally did. None of this made her calmer.

Every article Ruth read about late periods told her to make an appointment with a doctor and to try to bring stress down in her life. Ruth laughed at both those suggestions. She couldn't remember the last time she went to a doctor. She didn't know how to calm herself down, to be less stressed when she might be pregnant and when there were only six days until the deadline for her article.

The next morning Ruth woke to the sound of birds landing on the privet branch that scraped against her window. The hives on her legs had kept her up, and some of them were bleeding from her scratching in her sleep. Sounds of the fridge closing and utensils rattling in the drawer were coming from the kitchen. Ruth was surprised that Lucy was home. She decided to go downstairs and corner her, apologize, explain everything. Getting up, she went to the top of the stairs and listened, trying to prepare herself, hoping Lucy wasn't running out the door. The smell of burned toast rose up to meet Ruth. At first she thought nothing of it, then suddenly the odor flipped inside her. She barely made it to the bathroom in time to retch, vomit erupting into the toilet. On the tile floor, she stared at the yellow puke afloat in the water and knew she was pregnant.

"Fuck," Ruth said under her breath. "Fuck!" She climbed into the shower and turned on the faucet from her crouched position. Ruth stared at the wall as the water dropped over her and the nausea subsided. Her hands lifted to her breasts and for the first time she felt tenderness at her touch. She slumped against the side of the tub while the water fell on her from above.

The long shower worked to subdue her, and she watched as the dirt and sand from the bottoms of her feet and the dried blood from her legs made rivers of color in the curve of the porcelain tub. She pulled her knees to her chest and felt the water splatter over her body. When she was home alone as a child, long before Maggie's diagnosis, she would get visions of freak accidents happening to her parents—mostly her mom. She'd stop where she was in the house, curl up in a ball, and pray, promising she would be good if her mom came home all right. In that position she'd make deals with herself, that if she sneezed three times in a row, then her mother would open the door right after, and if it was only once, then she wouldn't. Ruth would force the other two sneezes and count it, but still hold the worry in her mind that it wasn't enough, would go into her mom's closet and hold one of her sweaters, smelling the fabric, growing more scared every moment she didn't come home. When Maggie would arrive, groceries in hand, Ruth would hug her and smell the cold air coming off her skin. She'd hold her for longer than usual.

Ruth thought about those prayers now, sitting on the shower floor, curled up in the same way. She wanted to make another one of those magical thinking bargains with God, that if she heard Lucy's footsteps in the next three seconds, then she wouldn't be pregnant anymore, that she had only made herself nauseous with her own worry. Ruth listened, holding her breath, but heard nothing.

She tried to take deep breaths. She thought about Louis, and then she recoiled as the word *father* came into her mind. Father to what? Was she going to have the baby? It was Louis . . . but then the memory of Charlie's body in the darkness, under the water of the outdoor shower, flashed into her mind like a slap. She played through every step of their night together in her head, looking for possible missteps. And although she wasn't able to pinpoint any, she was uncertain, and the possibility that it could've happened with either Louis or Charlie settled within her.

Ruth looked down at her abdomen and tried to see if it was rounder, if it was protruding. As a reflex, she touched the place below her belly button, ran her palm over the soft skin there. She thought back to the way Louis had held her that night, his hand resting on the same place, how comfortable it felt. A pounding on the door pulled Ruth out of her head.

"I need the bathroom!" Lucy yelled. Crawling to the faucet and turning it off, Ruth sat for a second longer in the emptying bathtub, unable to stand. When she did, she felt herself move with an awareness of the difference in her body. She couldn't help thinking of the clump of cells inside her, almost as if it were a tumor, expanding, multiplying, operating without her consent, against her will. The thought made her dizzy. Wrapping herself in a towel, she opened the door.

"I hope there's hot water," Lucy said. For a second, Ruth thought she saw concern ripple over Lucy's face, until she squeezed past her into the bathroom, edging Ruth out. When Lucy returned to the room fifteen minutes later, Ruth was sitting on her bed, still in her towel. Lucy stood in the doorway, staring, before closing the door behind her. The slam Ruth was expecting was replaced by a gentle click.

"What's going on?" Lucy asked, her voice still with an edge in it.

"I'm pretty sure I'm pregnant," Ruth said, staring at the floor.

"How sure?" Lucy asked after a moment.

"Sure," Ruth answered.

Lucy didn't say anything for a long time. Then she started moving, drying herself off and getting dressed. Ruth's heart plummeted. She was alone, she thought, until Lucy opened Ruth's drawers and put underwear and a sundress on Ruth's bed next to her.

"Have you taken a test?" Lucy asked.

"No."

"Okay. I'll be right back."

"I'm sorry we fought," Ruth said, tears falling down her face.

Turning, Lucy gave her a long look. Ruth was unsure of what was about to happen, but Lucy came over and hugged her. Her touch was gentle.

"It's okay. We're gonna figure it out," she said.

Lucy came back with the exact same pregnancy test Ruth had been staring at in the grocery store.

"What did you say?" Ruth asked.

"I just said 'It's mine and also mind your business,'" Lucy said, shrugging.

Ruth peed on the stick, set it on the counter, and went back into their shared bedroom to wait. They each lay silently on their beds, and when the timer that Lucy had set went off, they sat up.

"Do you want me to look?" Lucy asked.

Ruth nodded.

Ruth listened to Lucy's steps into the bathroom, imagined her stooped over the test reading it, her hair obscuring her face. She felt slack, already so tired.

"It's positive," Lucy called out.

Ruth nodded again, this time to herself.

Lucy walked back into the room and looked at Ruth for a long minute while Ruth stared at the floorboards, her mind numb.

"Let's go," Lucy said.

They didn't speak in the car as they drove out to Mansion Beach or on the walk from the parking lot down to the shore. The dune grass swayed behind them as they sat in the sand.

"Louis?" was the first thing Lucy asked.

"I think so," Ruth replied after a minute. "But I don't know." She then recounted everything with Louis and with Charlie, expecting Lucy to grow angry again. Instead, she remained focused.

"I didn't notice the condom break," Ruth said, explaining about finding the piece of latex days later, then about the spotting in July.

Lucy nodded.

"What are you thinking?" Lucy asked after a while.

"I'm thinking that I have no money, I don't even really live anywhere, I think that I'm not a mom. I think that I don't want to be a mom," Ruth said.

"Do you know how far along you are?" Lucy asked.

"I got my last period like June fourth," Ruth said, recounting the math she had been doing in her head for the past few weeks as every day passed. "Eight weeks."

"That's still early. That's good. What do you want to do?" Lucy asked. "Do you want an abortion?"

Ruth blanched at the word. She realized that the old Catholic guilt still stuck with her, circulated throughout her system as she contemplated it. She wanted to shake it off like a bug. It didn't belong there.

"Have you ever . . . ?" Ruth felt herself asking.

"Yeah," Lucy said, nodding.

"When? How old were you?"

"I was . . . twenty. You know I could never take birth control because of my depression. It fucked with my moods. But our condom broke. I went to the appointment by myself."

Ruth looked at her friend and tried to imagine her at twenty, before Ruth knew her. She was struck in that moment by how strong Lucy was, how present in the world she allowed herself to be, and Ruth was nothing but grateful for it. For all that she envied of Lucy, she loved her more.

Ruth thought about her life, about how aimless she had been feeling this summer. Since that day in the water, she had started to form plans, had allowed herself to think ahead to all she wanted to do. She wanted to travel. She wanted to go back to school. The hope that had been blooming inside her felt so new and good and fragile. The idea of those plans falling away and her hope shriveling with them filled her with a fear she couldn't stand.

At twenty-seven she wasn't too young to be a mother, yet the idea of having a baby seemed impossible to her. She thought of that image of Charlie walking down the path, a toddler on his shoulders, and tried hard to consider it, to see it as hers, but she was unable to. She couldn't imagine herself swelling, expanding, and feeling connected to what grew inside her. More than that, she didn't want to. Ruth thought of her mother—how much she gave up to be a mom, how hard she worked. Maggie had been saving up to go to Ireland when she got her cancer diagnosis. She never got to travel out of the country. Ruth had never traveled out of the country either. The pulsing excitement of the unknown, of the choices yet to be made, pushed past any thought of motherhood. She didn't want to be a parent.

"Do you think it's wrong that I'm so old?" Ruth asked. "I'm twenty-seven. Is it like . . . extra wrong to do it now?"

"If it's what you want, of course not."

Ruth was jealous of Lucy's agnostic upbringing and frustrated by her own Catholic conditioning that still showed up, even though she worked hard to rid herself of it. She wondered how different it might have felt as a child to believe in a nonjudgmental God, one who understood you to be a good person who was trying their best.

The anxious voices that had been clouding her head for weeks now silenced themselves, and as she took a deep breath, they were replaced by a resounding feeling of certainty.

"I don't want to be a mom. I don't want to be pregnant," Ruth said out loud, tears filling her eyes and spilling over, falling quickly down her face.

Lucy made the appointment at Planned Parenthood online when they got home. They were able to get her in by the end of the week, which Lucy declared was a miracle.

"August seventh in Providence. I'm shocked they could get you in that early," she said as she hung up the phone after calling to confirm. "They must've had a cancellation or something."

Ruth sighed. Of course the date of the appointment had to be the same day as her deadline for the article. She knew then that she wouldn't be able to finish the piece for *Vogue*—that whatever progress she had made would fall away as the days ticked down until the procedure. She needed to tell Ethel, but the thought of what she would say was too much to consider in that moment. *One thing at a time,* Ruth thought, trying to keep her breathing even—find a hotel room in Providence, book the ferry tickets. Ethel could come later.

Taking a deep breath, she expected a flood of shame for having let everyone down, but it didn't come. She didn't know if it was the adrenaline protecting her, or if she was growing softer with herself.

The only question that loomed over Ruth now was whether to tell Louis or Charlie. The evening before they had to get on the ferry for the mainland, she sat on the porch with Lucy, watching the rain, discussing it.

"I guess I have like this image of an angry man in my head telling me that I killed his baby or something," Ruth said, the rain clinking off the metal gutter. "I don't know if I would be able to handle that."

Lucy nodded and exhaled the smoke from the joint. "I don't think Louis would do that," she said. "But . . . yeah, I get it.

"What about Charlie?" Lucy asked, no judgment in her voice, her tone even and soft.

Ruth felt tears come to her eyes. "I can't," she said, her heart breaking at the thought of the conversation, for a reason she couldn't identify. Was it because it was heartbreaking to see him again so soon after everything that had happened? Or was she scared of his reaction, the idea of hurting him too much for her to handle? "I don't think it's his, anyways."

Lucy nodded. "I really don't think you need to say anything to anyone, by the way. It's your decision."

But later Ruth couldn't get the image of Louis's arm on her stomach out of her head. She texted him and asked if he could pick her up in the dinghy and he replied that the boat was back at the dock in town. Later, after the rain let up, she walked out to the street, her camera in a canvas bag thrown over her shoulder, the damp grass clinging to her feet. The wet roads reflected the streetlights in shining patches of orange as she strode under their glare, and the boats were lit up from the inside as she approached the pier. Couples were playing cards and smoking on their decks. She saw Louis's boat at the end of the dock, saw him sitting on the deck, reading a book and smoking a cigarette with Perry in his lap. The wooden boards of the dock creaked as she walked toward him, and he looked up.

"Hey," she said.

"Hey."

Ruth pulled the sleeves of her sweatshirt down so her fists were balls of cotton. She was nervous.

"You haven't been returning my calls," he said.

"I know."

She stood there unsure of what to do. The words *I'm pregnant* were on the inside of her lips, ready to come out, but she didn't want to say it like that. She imagined every movie she had ever seen with an unplanned pregnancy, the woman showing up like this, saying exactly that. It angered her that she was stuck in a role, in a stereotype, but she couldn't help anticipating Louis's own role in the narrative.

"Will you come on board and smoke a cigarette? You're freaking me out," Louis said, shifting in his seat so Perry had to jump off. Ruth climbed on board, swinging her legs over the side of the bow. Louis pulled out his cigarettes and held them out to her, but she waved her hand, no. She had quit at the beginning of the summer, but really what she was thinking was that she couldn't smoke because she was pregnant. The thought depressed her. She sat down and put her head in her hands.

"Remember when we had sex?" Ruth spoke to the floor at first, then she took a deep breath and looked Louis in the eye. Ruth explained about the broken condom.

"You're pregnant," Louis replied. His eyes were wide, and his knee started bouncing, but his lips were thin.

"I'm not . . . having it," Ruth said in response. "I'm going with Lucy to the mainland tomorrow."

And Ruth felt again the pure resolve that her life would be more fulfilled if she didn't become a parent now, that she didn't yet have the life she wanted, the life she'd want to give to a child if she ever had one.

Louis leaned back in his chair and his body slumped. He took a drag and Ruth braced herself for his response. He kneeled and sat on the floor with Ruth. His movements were gentle, but his knee still bobbed anxiously.

"And you feel good about that?" he asked.

She could tell he was being careful with her. "I don't want to be a mom," she said. "Maybe not yet but also maybe never."

Louis nodded, his eyes on her.

"There's also . . ." Ruth started. "There's a chance it's not yours."

"Charlie?"

Ruth nodded.

"Okay." Louis put his hand on her knee, which she realized was also bobbing—a nervous habit. "Does he know?"

Ruth didn't feel like he was probing. It felt like a friend offering their ear for something hard. "No. I really don't think it is his . . . plus I've already made things difficult enough for him. I want him to be happy."

"I'm sorry, Ruth. I'm sorry this happened."

"It was an accident."

"Can I come with you? What can I do? How much does it cost?" Louis asked. She shook her head and looked at him. It was the first time she really believed the sincerity of what he said at the lighthouse—how they would be good together.

"I'd rather just go with Lucy," she said, adding, "but thanks."

They sat there for a while and Perry walked over, purring, eventually sitting in Ruth's lap, his body vibrating against her legs. Ruth looked up at the stars.

"Do you feel like your younger self? Like do you feel like you're the same person that you were?" she asked, looking back at Louis, who had stubbed out his cigarette in the ashtray next to him.

"He was such an idiot," Louis said. "I get kind of jealous of him sometimes."

"You *were* an idiot," Ruth replied, smiling.

"I know."

"I was an idiot too."

"You were never an idiot," Louis said, shaking his head.

"I say I was."

"It was fun though, right?" Louis asked. "I feel like a lot of people never have that much fun."

Ruth thought back to the swath of late nights, of running in the darkness into the ocean, of looking up at the stars, of the few moments she could break through everything and feel total freedom. They had all happened here.

"You're talking about it like it's over," she said.

"I know," Louis replied, and Ruth nodded in acknowledgment.

"I heard about your job," Louis said after a minute.

"Yeah." Ruth looked out at the water.

"What're you going to do?" he asked.

"I'm not sure yet." She thought about her dwindling money, how the ferry, the hotel, and the abortion were likely to wipe her bank account clean. It was as if her mind was shielding her from that stress, like one more thing would make her crumble, and she needed all the strength she could muster.

"You're not going to leave, are you?" he asked.

Ruth didn't answer him directly. Where would she even go if she left the island? "Do you ever wish you could ask your uncle something?" she asked instead.

"All the time."

"What do you do with the questions?"

"Sometimes I write them down," Louis said. "But sometimes that makes me more sad."

They fell asleep on the deck, Ruth waking only when the sun

rose high enough to make her sweat against Louis's chest. She got up, her footprints leaving marks in the dew on the wood as she climbed over the edge of the bow, back toward home. Before she left, she turned and snapped a photo of Louis asleep in the sun, Perry looking back at her as he meowed.

2

On August seventh, Lucy drove Ruth to Providence in her minivan. Ruth felt like she was experiencing the world slowly, as if through water. Once she'd made her decision, it had been difficult to engage with the outside world, her mind hyper-focused on what was happening in her body. In the city, Lucy had suggested they do something to take Ruth's mind off the appointment in the afternoon, so they decided to go to the art museum at RISD. While Lucy dropped her résumé at the front desk and talked with the woman there about possible job opportunities, Ruth wandered up the stairs and into an exhibit on modern American photography. It was fairly new, but Ruth found it strange that she hadn't heard about it. Ruth had either met or heard of a few of the artists through Diana. It felt like visiting another time as she walked among their work, leaning in to read their names, recognizing some who had come to stay at the house.

When she turned to go find Lucy, she stopped, stunned. Across the room facing her was a photograph by Diana. Ruth walked toward it, as if toward a person she knew well. The photo was of a woman bathing in a river. The form's face was obscured and the water was textured—looked as if it were moving swiftly, the current strong. The woman was solid and unmovable, the water running up the sides of her legs.

Ruth knew the photograph—Diana had chosen it as the cover of one of the books Ruth had helped her produce. It was the first time, however, she had seen it this large or on the white wall of a gallery. She felt guilty about the article then, pictured Ethel looking at her inbox expectantly.

Over the past week, she had tried not to think about the fact that she was letting Diana down by not finishing the article. Now, standing in front of the photograph, she realized she didn't feel that way about it anymore. The article was not the all-or-nothing token of her love for Diana that Ruth had thought it to be, or her one shot to honor Diana by seizing the opportunity she had arranged for her. Diana had loved her, had wanted her to be able to move on, and that was her way of trying to help Ruth, to encourage her to step out of the river. Ruth was doing that now. She was trying hard to do that.

She stood in front of the photograph until Lucy found her and said it was time to get going.

"Will you help me write an email first?" Ruth asked, opening a message to Ethel.

They stayed in Providence overnight, in a hotel close to Planned Parenthood. The next morning Lucy drove them back to Galilee and Ruth stared out the window as the city buildings slowly melted back into green trees lining the side of the road.

When they got on the ferry, she looked around at the crowd on the top deck. The sun was strong and hot, and Ruth realized that it was still high summer. She was almost surprised to see all the people in their bikini tops and sunhats. To her, it felt like the beginning of fall, things moving and changing as they do every September.

Now, as the boat took off, Ruth saw an email from Ethel pop up. She clicked out of it, saving it for later.

The experience in Providence was still reverberating in Ruth's brain, making everything else quiet and out of focus. When they got to the building, there had been a woman outside of Planned Parenthood wearing a sign that said CHOOSE LIFE in red lettering.

She'd shouted something at Ruth as they walked in, but Lucy had covered Ruth's ears so all Ruth heard was Lucy's muffled expletives back at the woman. Ruth imagined she could hear the ocean, like Lucy's hands were two seashells protecting her. Once inside, things moved quickly. Her doctor was a woman in her early forties who insisted Ruth call her Babs, and Ruth only once had to squeeze Lucy's hand out of nervousness in the waiting room.

Afterward, her doctor discussed side effects she might experience, who to call if they did occur, gave her the bill, and sent her on her way. Ruth put it on her credit card, wondering when she would be able to pay it off. Lucy wrapped Ruth in her arms, and they left the building together. As they walked out, Lucy covered Ruth's ears again, but instead of looking away Ruth focused on the woman in front of her. Then she stopped, pulled her camera around, and took the woman's photo. Ruth expected the woman to shout, to become outraged, but instead she stared at her, seemingly somber, seemingly subdued.

Ruth still couldn't stop thinking of the protester, even as she sat with Lucy on the ferry. It was a strange sensation—her worries about pregnancy were now undone, her choices carried out, yet there was an underlying sense of guilt that she tried to examine. What was she feeling guilty about? The abortion itself? That she hadn't wanted motherhood? As the boat bobbed up and down, she sat with that for a moment, watching the woman across from her, who held a sleepy toddler on her chest. She tried to imagine her own child asleep on her chest and could not. She thought of her life, so aimless recently, so lost.

The woman across from Ruth put her nose to the toddler's thin hair, leaned down and kissed the soft cheek, and the child's small arms reached up around her mother's neck, hands clasped there, holding her mother close. Ruth saw the woman smile a small smile for herself, and tears stung her eyes. Looking at the small hands, she could recall as if from the base of her memory the feeling of being small in the arms of her mother, the overwhelming comfort of her hands, of hearing her heartbeat through her chest. Ruth wondered what Maggie must have felt, listening to Ruth's heartbeat as she held her, so familiar, the most familiar in the world.

Ruth thought then of her plans blooming out in front of her, taking shape like flowers in a garden ready for the picking, and she imagined herself sitting among them, the different-colored petals bobbing in a gentle wind. She felt some of the guilt subside, replaced by curiosity and excitement for all the ways in which her life could unfold. She felt a lightness return to her chest, her certainty in her decision unwavering.

"Hey, you okay?" Lucy asked, reaching out to hold her hand, putting it into her lap. The wind was blowing her hair back from her face.

"Yeah." Ruth nodded. "Just thinking about my mom." And for the first time in a while, Ruth felt only warmth at the thought.

The next few days, Ruth spent most of the time in bed. Her doctor had warned her about the strong cramps the first day after, but when those subsided she came down with a heavy cold. For nights her nose was stuffed, her head foggy, and the floor next to her bed was littered with used tissues.

"I'm calling the doctor," Lucy said, standing over her with a mug of tea, asking her about her symptoms. She was still bleeding, although the flow of blood was growing lighter with each day.

"Lucy, it's a cold. I'm fine," Ruth said, not worried. Her body succumbed to the rest she had been denying it for a long time, and slowly she began to feel better, the hives on her legs fading away, the blinders of stress and focus removed.

In her time in and out of sleep, memories passed as dreams

through her mind—her mother's cheek pressed to her forehead as a child to take her temperature, Diana's hair covering her face as she was bent over, examining a tide pool, the feeling of reading on the couch at her mother's side, the innate need to get closer, of Charlie's laugh on the roof of Diana's house in the dark of night.

At one point she felt a hand rubbing her back as she faced the wall, curled up in bed. It was hotter than it had been all summer, and the weak buzzing box fan was doing nothing to cool her. The hand moved from her back to her sweating forehead. She was expecting it to be Lucy's soft palm, but it was calloused, bony, and smelled faintly of cigarettes and fish.

"When was the last time you took your temperature?"

Ruth turned and looked up at Louis.

"What're you doing here?" she asked. "You're going to get my cold. Lucy is already sniffling."

"I've got an immune system you can't break through, baby," he said. His smile looked sad. "I came by earlier, but Lucy said you wanted to be alone. Can I stay?"

Ruth nodded. Louis had never been in her room, but he looked like he belonged there, scooching in on the bed so that he was comfortable. She was glad he was there.

"How was it?" Louis asked, then added, "Sorry, that feels like the wrong thing to say."

Ruth thought about the trip on the boat over, the waiting room, the doctor, the ride back. She thought about how she felt now—like she could breathe.

"It was fine," Ruth said. "I feel good. Apart from the cold."

Ruth propped her pillows up against the wall and patted it, and Louis leaned back so they were shoulder to shoulder.

"Have you found another job on the island yet?" Louis said after a minute of comfortable silence.

Ruth looked at him. Again, she felt and really believed how strong his feelings for her were. She put her hand in his and he clasped it tighter.

"You're going to leave?" Louis asked.

"I think so."

As the days passed and Ruth's cold faded away, she scrolled for jobs on the mainland and applied to some places, but whenever she tried to picture herself somewhere else, she couldn't. She crafted and deleted several replies to Ethel's email. Nothing sounded good enough. Now that she was through the abortion, she could see that she should have said no to the article from the start. She realized now that she hadn't been ready to think of Diana as a monument, as the public would see her: someone to talk about in the past tense without any context of the quiet moments of their life together. What Ruth found important about Diana, the public wouldn't care about—her strange obsession with watching poker, her regret over never having been a librarian, her ability to remember the name of everyone she ever met, her deep love for the ocean, for the island, for Ruth, for Maggie. Someone with more objectivity should write it. Ruth was too close.

Ruth closed the lid of her laptop and looked around the empty cottage. She put on her old running sneakers and tied the frayed laces tight. The sun was strong as she stepped onto the grass. She pulled her baseball hat down over her forehead and headed out onto the road. Walking slowly, she observed people headed out to the beach, the beds of their trucks filled with colorful folding chairs and towels hanging out of the windows to dry. She waved as she passed the sandwich shop, seeing some friends from work. Turning onto Corn Neck Road, Ruth walked more quickly, noticing how the sand of the dunes spilled out onto the asphalt. Looking ahead, the Crescent Bay unfolded and Ruth could see to the corner of the island where Mansion Beach ended and the Clay Head bluffs began. The water was speckled with distant figures jumping in the waves, and the ocean was much calmer than it had been the last time Ruth saw it, but there was a wall of clouds in the distance about to overtake the sun and she felt a strong wind blow off the top of a wave and up onto the road where she stood.

She still hadn't heard from Charlie since their night together, and although she tried not to wonder about what was happening up at the house, it was difficult for her. Charlie had no idea about the pregnancy, or about the abortion. Ruth felt a sense of mourning at not being able to call him, stopping herself whenever she pulled out her phone and typed out a message, forcing herself to hit delete.

As Ruth walked past the town beach parking lot, she stopped and looked at the dunes that her mother had painted. Ruth had been trying to understand why that painting was her favorite—she realized she had even been holding it in her mind as she sat in the doctor's waiting room. Standing in front of the peaks and valleys and watching birds rustle the different bushes and branches, she was entranced. To her left she heard a scuffling and turned her head. Two deer jumped out of the brush and onto the road, crossing the lanes in three quick bounds. Ruth had always loved this spot, the way the thin strip of land cut the beach and the pond in two, the way it was teeming with life, and in that moment she felt more connected to Maggie than she had in years, looking at the same scene, feeling what she might have felt for it too.

Although she and Maggie had chosen different paths with their pregnancies, Ruth had never felt closer to her mother in the years since she died. There was always the ache of loss, the wish she could talk about it with her, that she could hear the warmth of her voice on the phone. But instead of picking at the not knowing, instead of turning it over and over in her mind, Ruth decided to leave it, to think of their lives as meeting in this moment. She couldn't know what her mother might have thought about the abortion, but Ruth knew now what *she* thought, the uncertainty gone, the weight more evenly dispersed and easier to carry.

The thick cloud that had been rolling in overtook the sun, and rain fell like a curtain across the dunes, hitting the pavement in splashes and covering Ruth. She stood for another minute watching the wind pick up, observing how the grasses moved and swayed, then she turned, soaked through but still warm, and headed for home.

When she got there, Lucy's minivan was gone from the driveway. She had left on the one o'clock ferry for a job interview at RISD and was staying the night with an old college friend. Ruth walked through the empty cottage and stood in the center of the kitchen, looking around at the small details of their life—the old stickers and beer labels half scraped off the fridge, the colorful towels hanging like tapestries over the porch ledge. Ruth watched through the screen door as a wind gust blew through, causing them to balloon out and ripple, the scent of spent charcoal from a far-off grill wafting over on the breeze and through the cottage.

Upstairs, she stripped off her wet clothes. Thunder boomed close by, making the lights flicker for a second as more lightning flashed outside. The camera Diana had left her was sitting on her desk, and she had an idea.

The light was soft, low, and gray in the room as she set up the camera on the edge of her desk, bending at an awkward angle, looking through the viewfinder to see where the frame of the shot was. She had never taken a portrait of herself, but in that moment she wanted to capture what she was feeling, who she was right then.

She attached a timer device she had taken from Diana's studio to the shutter and stepped away into the low light coming from the window. Kneeling, she placed herself within the line of the shot, so that only the top of her breasts, her shoulders, and her face would be in the frame. A breeze came in through the screened window, shuffling papers on the desk. Taking a deep breath, she looked into the lens, relaxed her face, clasped the timer in her hand, and heard the shutter close—the sound like a bird taking off from a branch.

. . .

Later that night the privet bushes scraped against the side of the cottage, pushed by the wind whipping across the island in the darkness. The storm had grown heavier throughout the day and Ruth's phone pinged with an alert that all the ferries had been shut down for the evening. When the power went out, she searched for her headlamp in her desk drawer and put it on. The light showed in front of her like a bright hallway as she went down to the kitchen. Ruth gathered the candles she and Lucy kept scattered around the cottage and brought them upstairs. As she lit them, the room was washed with candlelight and although the bushes continued scraping and the wind shook the windows, she was comfortable.

Storms on the island didn't scare her anymore. She liked the way they blew through the town and huddled people together. If Lucy were here, they'd be drinking wine among the candles and doing tarot card readings. Ruth hoped Lucy's interview had gone well. She had said she would call Ruth after dinner to tell her about it, but that had been hours ago. Sitting back on her bed, she pulled the box of photographs over to her and opened it, spreading each photo out on the quilt as she had been doing ever since she received the box.

Her phone started to ring.

Expecting to see Lucy's name on the screen, Ruth was surprised when she saw it was Charlie calling. She hesitated, worried. The phone call dropped as she stared at it, but a few seconds later he called again. This time she picked up.

"Hello?"

"Ruth!" Charlie cried. "Ruth, don't hang up, please, please." Charlie sounded drunk, his words slurred.

"Are you okay?" she asked. "You're not alone, right?" Concern moved through her as she listened to his heavy breathing on the other end of the line.

"We can't get back tonight. The ferries are all down. Nadia's at the house by herself," he said. "I told her, Ruth. I told her what happened. I told her right before I was supposed to leave for this bachelor party, before she was supposed to have her bachelorette at Diana's house. I'm such an idiot."

Ruth was quiet for a second, listening to Charlie's breathing.

"What did she say?" Ruth asked.

"She told me to go," he said. "She shut the door in my face. I tried to stay and talk to her but she told me she needed space so I came here because all these guys were here and now I can't get back and she's in the house alone. Is the power out?"

"Mine is," Ruth said.

"I'm worried about her up there alone." Charlie was crying now.

Over the past few weeks, Ruth had been wondering about whether Charlie had said anything to Nadia, but assumed his silence meant he hadn't. She tried to imagine what he had been thinking, why he had said it at that particular moment. There was a part of Ruth that wondered if it would have been better if he hadn't said anything at all.

"Charlie, where are you? Are your friends there?"

"I'm outside the bar. God, I feel like such an asshole," he said.

"What happened to Nadia's friends?" Ruth asked. "Weren't they supposed to be here for the party?"

"She told them not to come. She said she was sick. She's all alone up there, Ruth. She doesn't know where anything is. Her phone is dead . . . or maybe she blocked me. I need you to go check on her."

"What?" Ruth looked out the window into the blackness. All the streetlights were out. She couldn't see anything.

"Please, I know you don't want to. I need you to do this for me. Please." The desperation in his voice made Ruth intensely jealous for a quick moment, but through his drunken slur was a real sense of fear and urgency that made her heart ache for him.

"Yeah, okay," Ruth said as thunder boomed above the house.

"Thank you, Ruth," Charlie said. "You're . . . too good to me. I don't deserve it." His voice had grown quiet and soft.

"It'll be okay, Charlie."

After Ruth hung up, she considered what she was going to do. Lucy had taken her car with her to the mainland. She could try biking, but the idea of being on a metal bicycle under all that lightning seemed unwise. It was normally a thirty-minute walk up to Diana's house from town. Sighing, Ruth got up, closed the lid of her laptop, and started to gather gear for the hike, blowing out the candles and putting them in her backpack once they had cooled down enough, grabbing her old raincoat out of her closet, and pulling on her beaten-up rain boots.

Opening the front door to the porch, Ruth felt the wind push against it, whipping it open next to her and slamming it against the side of the house. She jumped, then looked out into the black, wet night. The only light came from a single passing car. For a minute Ruth thought about hitchhiking, or walking over to the police station, but then a police car sped past her, blaring blue and red, and she decided against it. She could make it, she thought. In the distance, Ruth couldn't see any lights from the mainland, normally lit up like a string across the horizon.

"Okay," Ruth said aloud to no one. "Let's go."

She walked through the wet grass, the noise of the wind flapping the hood of her raincoat against her ears. As she turned onto the road, Louis came to her mind—she hoped he was okay out on the boat and that Perry wasn't getting seasick. The warm thought surprised her, and she remembered falling asleep on his chest the other night, talking until late, how easy it had felt. The sudden wash of tenderness continued to roll over Ruth as she walked in the rain, focusing on each step.

Lightning flashed, illuminating the slick road in front of her—silent before the thunder clapped loud and close, reverberating in her chest. She considered turning around and heading back inside, telling herself that Charlie just felt guilty, Nadia was a big girl, that she could handle it herself. Then Ruth remembered her first storm up at the house, how Diana had been away at a gala on the mainland, how the house creaked in the wind. Before she knew it, she was walking quickly in the direction of the house.

While Ruth walked, her headlamp illuminated the wet and shining road in front of her. She had been on the island through hurricanes before—it wasn't so uncommon that they would lose power. A strong gust of wind blew against Ruth hard enough that she stopped walking and looked up at the branches creaking above her before running out from underneath them. During the storms the island felt quieter, and in some ways it was when she felt most connected to it. It was just them out there, on top of a hunk of land standing only feet above the ocean. Storms made her remember that.

Town was empty and Ruth could hear the ocean slapping up onto the docks and the concrete. She passed the statue of Rebecca, the rain pouring out of her pot as if the fountain were restored. Her breath grew heavy as she took large strides up the hill toward the house. The trees thinned along the side of the road and were replaced with low bushes that shook in the wind. She felt safer next to them as she listened to the familiar sound of their bodies rocking, the branches scraping against one another. Rain flowed down the side of the street in snakelike rivers, taking rocks and sand with it, forming a deep gully that she accidentally kept stepping into, water getting into her low boots. As she walked, Ruth thought about what she would say when she arrived at the house. Would Nadia even let her in?

She thought about the feeling she had had in Diana's studio on the floor with Charlie—the lightness and the certainty. Did it come because they had finally said they loved each other? Or was it just that it was a conclusion, that there were now no more almosts? She didn't know, and now that some time had passed, a softer melancholia coated their relationship in Ruth's mind, but it was a frame that felt right. The truth was that Ruth didn't feel guilty for sleeping with Charlie. She still felt responsible for his tormented voice on the phone, for the situation he was in now, but when she thought of that night, of their bodies under the water, their hands intertwined in the car, she felt like it had been the right thing.

She didn't want to talk about this with Nadia, and she was

angry that Charlie had left the island, had left this job of explanation to her.

An hour later Ruth turned onto the property, splashing through heavy streams in the guts of the dirt driveway. She was soaked through her raincoat and her feet were covered in blisters from the wet rain boots rubbing against her skin. Walking under the green archway toward the house, she couldn't see even a flicker of light coming from inside—no candles, no flashlights. As she approached, she noticed the chairs covered by a leaking tarp under the beech tree, all of the rain-soaked items that would become their wedding in a few weeks, if it happened. In the cold glow of her headlamp, it looked like a circus had just been broken down, the tarp flapping violently in the wind. Walking up to the new storm door, she opened it, leaning against the glass window of the door behind it. Her headlight illuminated the hallway floor into the kitchen.

"Nadia! Nadia!" she cried out, banging on the front door. Smacking her hand against the glass, the rattle blended in with the wind in the trees and she was worried that Nadia wasn't there, that she would have to turn around.

"Nadia! It's Ruth! Open up!" She almost backed away from the door when she saw Nadia peek her head around the hallway. "Nadia! Open the door," she yelled.

Ruth watched as Nadia walked toward the door and opened it. She glared at Ruth for a long time, silent, her angular features pronounced in the glow of the headlamp, her anger carved on her face.

"Sorry to disappoint you," Nadia said finally. "He's not here."

"He wanted me to check on you," Ruth said. As soon as the words were out of her mouth, she realized they were the wrong ones.

"God—how did I not realize what was going on? This whole time!" Nadia said. "It's so obvious now."

Lightning close by lit up the yard, casting everything in white before thunder shook the house. Ruth heard the plates clink together in the cabinets.

"I brought candles," Ruth said. She was getting herself ready to turn around, although the lightning had grown closer and the storm was starting to worry her more now.

Nadia turned and disappeared back into the house, but she left the door open behind her. Standing in the rain, Ruth contemplated what to do before stepping inside.

3

After Ruth peeled off her raincoat, Nadia wordlessly brought her some of her own clothes. Setting her headlamp against the bathroom counter, she stripped off her wet layers and changed into the dry ones. In the living room, Ruth pulled out the candles she took from the cottage and set them around the table. She went to the kitchen drawer where she knew the matches were kept and went around lighting each candle until the house was aglow, their shadows casting long figures against the walls. Ruth tried to keep moving, to be helpful. She felt Nadia's eyes on her as she walked through the house, and it felt like when she had walked into the Planned Parenthood, the woman's eyes on her behind her handmade sign—exposed and judged.

No one had spoken in a few minutes.

"There are some flashlights down here," Ruth said finally, opening the door to the basement. Since she had entered the house, she'd been waiting for Nadia to snap. She thought of the hurricane boxes upstairs in the attic, but the idea of going back up to where Charlie had kissed her seemed somehow wrong.

"I'll take your word for it," Nadia said from the living room couch. Looking back, she noticed Nadia staring at the floor, the light from the candles flickering. Ruth headed down into the musty basement, her headlamp outlining the filaments from spiderwebs over her head. She searched for the emergency bins that she made Diana put together after Hurricane Irene wiped the power out for three days. Normally, they would have been easy to find, but the basement was filled with boxes and bags. Walking over to one, Ruth pulled the cardboard corner up and peeked in. Inside, she saw photo albums that used to be on the living room shelf. She saw a picture frame and recognized the gold edges. Pulling it out, Ruth held a photo of her and Diana on Ruth's nineteenth birthday. Charlie had taken the picture of them before they had cake. Holding on to it, Ruth spotted the bin she was looking for out of the corner of her eye and returned to finding a flashlight. When Ruth came upstairs, she handed it to Nadia, dust blowing off as it changed hands.

"Okay, well, I guess I can head out now that you're all set," Ruth said, feeling awkward, looking out toward the storm door as it opened and slammed against the wind. Nadia was looking at her over the candles with a gentle, curious stare that concerned Ruth.

"No, stay," Nadia said from the couch, her voice flat. "We should talk."

Uncertain, Ruth sat down on the familiar couch and had to force herself not to bring her feet up to her chest and snuggle into the crevice where she used to spend late nights reading. Instead, she folded her hands in her lap. She felt like she was in church. Looking around the room, Ruth noticed for the first time the wedding dress hanging in plastic on the back of the kitchen door, the big binder on the coffee table with the word *wedding* written across it in cursive Sharpie, and bags of balloons and streamers stacked on the seat of the chair.

Neither of them said anything for a long time and Ruth was wondering how long she would have to wait when Nadia broke the silence.

"You found the boxes downstairs," she said, finally, looking at the photo in Ruth's hand.

It wasn't what Ruth thought she was going to say. "There's a lot of them."

"You're angry," Nadia said.

Ruth paused. It was uncomfortable that they would be talking about Ruth being mad while Ruth knew Nadia had to be seething. Curious, Ruth decided to go with it.

"I don't like change," she replied. Nadia nodded, although she seemed unsure what to do with the comment.

"And you think it was me, right?" Nadia asked after a minute.

Ruth looked at Nadia. She didn't know what to say.

"I mean, I get it," Nadia replied. "But seriously, I'm not that high maintenance."

"Then who?" Ruth asked.

"Lynn has been having a really hard time," Nadia said. "I think her way of grieving is to just . . . avoid . . . right now. She had a screaming fight with Charlie when he said we wanted to get married here. It's been hard for her to be in her house—deal with all of this. Diana was her sister."

Nadia's tone was clear—*you weren't the only one who lost someone*. As Ruth absorbed the comment, she felt shame wash over her. She thought of the picture of Maggie and Diana and the notation on the back, *taken by Lynnie*. She thought of how much Lynn had been off island all summer and in a flash she knew how painful it must be to live in her sister's home, unable to remember in moments whether Diana was there or not. She hadn't considered that Lynn's alterations of the house were a way to avoid this, to move on from the pain of being reminded of Diana. Ruth thought of how she had felt in her own house at seventeen, how she still felt sometimes whenever she was there visiting Joel—that any second her mother was going to call out for tea from her place on the couch or walk through the door, her arms full of grocery bags—how every time she had to remember that Maggie was dead felt like the cruelest realization. She thought then of Joel alone in the house for all these years, how she never asked him if this was something he felt too, if each day he was reminded of Maggie. Ruth suddenly couldn't believe she had ever been upset with him for selling the house.

Looking around again, Ruth picked out more of the trappings of the wedding. She stared at Nadia's engagement ring, at the dress hanging on the back of the door, at the pile of bachelorette decorations gone unused. She wondered if she would ever have anything like that—a big wedding, a bachelorette party, a bridal shower. It all felt separate from her—something foreign, somehow impossible. Nadia followed her gaze around the room, and Ruth thought of the night with Charlie, how she had sat on this couch in his old sweatshirt. In that moment, she became acutely aware that she had stolen something from Charlie and Nadia. The guilt she hadn't felt before seeped through her now.

"I'm sorry," Ruth said, finally. It was a mixture of sympathy and apology, and Ruth was aware that it sounded flat. She didn't know how to begin.

Nadia looked at the pile of stuff, then leaned over for one of the bottles of expensive champagne—Ruth recognized the label—and pulled it out of the chiller that looked like it had once been filled with ice and rose petals but now was a watery pool. Nadia turned to Ruth.

"Want to open it?"

Before Ruth could respond, Nadia was peeling off the foil and twisting the cage around the cork.

Ruth went into the cupboard in the kitchen and reached for two of Diana's favorite champagne flutes she kept for guests. Placing them in front of Nadia on the coffee table, she sat back down on the couch, wringing her hands.

"Are you going to say something?" Ruth asked, staring at the bubbles as Nadia poured the wine and handed her a glass.

Nadia looked at Ruth for a long time, taking occasional sips. Her gaze was blank until she spoke.

"So you had sex," she said, her voice clinical, like she was talking about two people she didn't know.

Ruth nodded.

Nadia was staring at Ruth again. She realized she had emptied her own glass already and reached for the bottle. After offering it to Nadia, who refused, she put more in her own glass.

"Are you two in love with each other?" Nadia asked.

Ruth looked then at the candle flame, focusing on the curling smoke that rose above it.

"Because it seems like you're in love with each other," Nadia said.

Ruth looked up at Nadia and finally saw the pain coming through in her face. Nadia started to cry, turning away and wiping at her tears with her fingertips. Again, Ruth noticed the glittering diamond. She hadn't taken it off.

Not knowing what to do, Ruth lifted her hand to touch Nadia's shoulder but thought better of it. She stopped midair, then dropped her hand back into her lap.

"It's like we love each other but it's gone, you know? It's . . . dead. There is nothing there to live off of. It's just . . . nostalgia now." Ruth didn't really know what she was trying to say, whether she was making it better or worse. She wanted to tell the truth. "I love Charlie, but I love him like I loved him when I was seventeen," she said. "Which . . . isn't enough. It wouldn't work."

"That doesn't really sound like a no," Nadia said.

"I don't want him. We don't want each other," Ruth said. "He wants you. He wants a life with you. We never had that."

Nadia wasn't crying anymore.

"Really, we have nothing in common except for . . . the past, except for this place."

"How do I know this won't happen again?" Nadia said.

"It won't. I know it will never happen again."

As she said it, a heaviness settled within her. Even if she'd already known it was true, the feeling of time having slipped past her was still shocking. The hope she'd had earlier in the summer that so reflected what she felt when she was younger was now displaced, floating, unattached.

"But how am I supposed to trust him?" Nadia asked angrily.

Ruth sighed. "I don't know. I don't know what to say. Charlie is . . . a good person. I know this doesn't make it seem like it, but I really do believe that. People make mistakes."

"Why did you do it?" Nadia asked.

Ruth looked down. "I'm sorry," she said. "I don't . . . regret it, but I am sorry." She continued, "It had to happen. Or . . . it is what happened. And I would be lying to you if I said I regretted it. But we know now that there is nothing more between us."

Nadia leaned her head back against the couch and slumped down.

"It's okay if you hate me," Ruth said. "But please, I'd like to try and . . . be in your life . . . because I'm Charlie's friend," she said. "Don't cut me out. If you can."

"Why would I ever want to see you?" Nadia asked, her eyes closed. "How could I ever see you two talk and not think about this, or not think something was going on?"

"Time, maybe," Ruth said. It was a weak argument, she knew. For the first time, she considered that she might be cut off from Charlie forever. She thought about how few relationships ever really made the transition from love to friendship, how many people gave up on it, seeming not to care in the end whether that person faded from their life altogether. She loved Charlie, but she didn't know how hard he would try, whether it mattered enough to him.

Nadia looked at Ruth, leaned over, picked up the bottle of champagne, realized it was empty, and reached over to the edge of the couch toward the watery cooler for another one.

"Here. Let me," Ruth said, reaching out. Nadia let her take it.

Pouring the wine in the glasses, Ruth started to feel a warm buzzing in her head. She leaned back into the couch.

"What am I gonna do about the wedding?" Nadia asked.

"You think you won't get married?" Ruth put the bottle down.

"I'm not sure," Nadia replied into her glass of wine. "I don't love the idea of marrying someone who cheated on me weeks before our wedding. Would you?"

Ruth knew Nadia wasn't really asking her what she thought, but she considered the question anyway. She didn't know.

Nadia sighed. "I never even wanted to get married," she said. "I mean, I didn't before Charlie. I thought I was going to be moving to Peru and Prague, traveling the world, making art for a while, you know?"

She was looking at the ceiling and Ruth wondered what images of travel crossed her mind.

"You could still travel with Charlie," Ruth said.

Nadia's head rolled to the side so it was facing her.

"You really think I should go through with it, don't you?" Nadia asked, her eyes narrowed.

Ruth thought about what to say. "I just know that he loves you a lot, and it would be a shame to let that go."

"Do you want to get married?" Nadia asked, her face softened from the wine.

Ruth tried to imagine her life again, tried to look forward. Now that the fear of being pregnant had faded from her mind, and the question of her feelings for Charlie was gone, there was a sense of both relief and excitement when she looked into the nothingness that lay before her. Right now, the only thing she felt was a fear of running out of money any day, of how she was going to make her next step. When she imagined falling in love again, she saw herself holding hands with someone, and while her mind snapped back to the feeling of holding Charlie's hand and the gritty sand between their palms, she knew it would be someone else's hand, and that gave her a feeling of both sadness and curiosity. Again, the image of Louis on the boat, the cat in his lap, made her inhale sharply, the emotion attached to him still startling to Ruth.

"Yeah," Ruth said finally. "I think so."

"What about kids?" Nadia asked.

Ruth looked at her lap, feeling as if somehow Nadia knew. Since the abortion, she had been feeling a layer of guilt swim in and out of her mind that she hadn't shared with anyone, not even Lucy. It wasn't that she should've kept the pregnancy. She was firm in her resolution, and the idea of having a child, even now that the threat was gone, made her heart race so quick she thought she was going to cry. The guilt lived in the moments when she was unkind to herself, when she told herself that by twenty-seven she should be in a place to handle a kid, she should have her life more in order, that she was careless. She worried that she'd never be ready to have children, that she didn't deserve another chance. Like she had closed a door forever without knowing it. Maybe it was the wine, but Ruth looked at Nadia and admitted, "I don't know. I really have no idea."

Nadia nodded.

"Do you want kids?" Ruth asked.

"Yeah, I would be pregnant tomorrow if it made any sense," she said, laughing for a second before her face dropped. "I wanted to have kids with Charlie."

"Charlie would be a good dad," Ruth said.

"I know," Nadia replied, sipping her wine. The way she said it was so sure, and Ruth wondered what it must feel like to know you wanted to be a mother.

"What does that feel like?" she asked.

"What does what feel like?"

"The knowing," Ruth said. "How can you *know*?"

"I guess . . . I trust myself to do a good job. I trust the feeling I have when I think about it, it's almost selfish. I just . . . want it."

Ruth thought back to the woman and the toddler on the boat, at her small, private smile. Ever since she found out that her mother never intended to be pregnant with her, she hadn't been able to imagine the joy or curiosity or excitement Maggie might have felt, the small smiles she might have had. Ruth thought of what a *good* mom she was, how it seemed to flow out of her, all of that giving. She thought of Maggie's choice to have her, to not go to New York, and instead of looking at those moments as coated in fear, she considered them in a different light—the pregnancy test, her decision to stay in Rhode Island, feeling Ruth grow inside her. She tried to release herself from analyzing Maggie's motives, considering how she, herself, knew resolutely that she shouldn't become a mother. Maggie must have known with that same certainty that she should be one. It was a choice.

In the morning, Ruth woke up on Diana's couch. The sun had inched into the room, and she was awash in morning light. She was disoriented by her surroundings. The living room looked similar to how she remembered it and she was covered in the usual threadbare quilt that Diana and she had tried to sew new patches in years ago. She heard the sound of dishes in the kitchen sink and was jolted more fully awake at the memory of the night before, noticing the candles burned down to nubs within their glass holders on the coffee table. She was still wearing Nadia's clothes.

What time was it? Her phone had died sometime in the night. Looking out the window, she saw the beech tree had dropped a large limb and the ground was strewn with privet leaves and branches.

"Ruth?" Nadia emerged from the kitchen in a robe.

"Is the power back on?"

"Yeah—everyone's on the first boat over here. I keep getting pictures of Charlie's head in a vomit bag."

"I guess I should probably get home," Ruth said.

"I can drive you," Nadia said. "Just let me change."

The car ride was silent except for Ruth directing Nadia where to go. As they pulled up to the cottage, Nadia turned to her.

"Thank you for coming to check on me," she said.

"Charlie wanted to make sure you were okay." Now that the night was over, she was worried she hadn't said enough to convince Nadia to marry Charlie.

Nadia didn't react.

"Thank you for . . . talking," Ruth said.

Nadia nodded.

"Charlie loves you a lot. You should give him another chance."

Nadia looked ahead, through the windshield, her face without expression, and Ruth felt sorry again for hurting her, felt like she understood her better now. "Bye, Ruth."

Ruth got out of the car, then stopped, her hand still on the door so that Nadia wouldn't drive away. Nadia's eyes were on Ruth's hand.

"Can I take your photo?" Ruth asked.

"What?"

"Wait a second, please."

Ruth ran into the cottage, up the stairs, and grabbed the camera off her desk where she left it the night before. Running back out and back down the front steps, she was surprised that Nadia had stayed. She stopped in front of the passenger-side door.

"Can I?" she asked.

Nadia took a deep breath and shrugged.

"What do you want me to do?" Nadia asked, looking at her now. Her eyes were soft and red.

"Nothing." Ruth brought the camera up to her eyes.

Nadia looked forward into the windshield and Ruth snapped the picture, the sound of the shutter closing making Nadia's head turn.

"What's this for?" she asked.

"I don't know," Ruth replied, although a loose idea was starting to form in her mind. "Thank you."

Ruth stepped back, waved, and Nadia backed out of the dirt driveway into the road.

The car drove away, and Ruth took a minute to look at the cottage from the road. The storm had cleared and although the ground was littered with leaves and twigs, the sun was strong and the sky was a sharp cobalt. Looking up, Ruth felt covered by the blue expanse. Cars drove through puddles and the sound was crisp as if it was happening right next to her. She thought about what she had to do. There was nothing. Sitting in the wet grass, she pulled her camera around, intending to take a picture. She realized she had only one frame left on the roll. It was then that she recalled the mystery photos that had already been taken on the camera when Diana had given it to her. Lifting the viewfinder to her eye, she focused the lens and snapped the last picture: the cottage—where she and Lucy lived.

4

Lucy was the one who told Ruth that the wedding was off.

"I passed Lynn at the grocery store and asked her how things were coming along," Lucy said.

Ruth was sitting on the porch, her computer on her knees, looking back at the email Diana had sent her last Christmas, opening the links to MFA programs, residencies, teaching jobs, and scholarships. Closing the lid and putting the computer aside, she curled over, placing her head in her hands.

"What did she say?" Ruth asked, her voice muffled.

Lucy pulled the rocking chair over toward Ruth and sat, the old wicker squealing as it rocked.

"Honestly, she seemed kind of relieved," Lucy said.

Ruth unfolded her body and looked at Lucy, not believing her.

"I mean, she's pissed." Lucy's eyes bugged out at the word *pissed*. "But I could tell there was a part of her that was okay with it."

"Are you lying to spare my feelings?" Ruth asked.

"Maybe," Lucy said.

Ruth looked at her phone. There were no messages. She wasn't sure what she was expecting, that maybe Charlie would have called to tell her—to confide in her, or to blame her.

"I feel so bad," Ruth said.

She thought of Nadia's tears in the darkness, of how honest she had been the other night.

"I don't think you should," Lucy replied.

"I'm surprised that you would say that."

Lucy shrugged. "I think you were right. I think it was something that had to happen between you two. Who knows, maybe they just decided they needed more time." She paused. "It's okay. You're not a bad person."

"Are you just saying that to make me feel better?" Ruth asked. "Because I feel like a bad person."

Lucy looked at Ruth, her eyes soft.

"Mistakes happen," Lucy said. "You really loved him for a long time." Then she leaned down and put her soft palm on Ruth's cheek. "Plus, I like complicated women."

"I think if I'm being honest, I still do love him," Ruth said after Lucy leaned back. "I just . . . know we don't want the same thing. I guess maybe I know that it wouldn't work, that in the end, it would be a mistake. Did you ever think that we should be together?" Ruth asked, curious.

Lucy looked at Ruth for a while, reached into her pocket, and pulled out her cigarettes. "I saw something special," she said. "But no, I really didn't see that for you."

"Why not?"

"I guess, it just seemed like you would be putting a mask on or something."

They sat in silence for a while, the only sounds the chair under Lucy, the crackle of the burning tip of the cigarette, her whooshing exhalation away from Ruth's face, and the cars driving by on their way to the beach.

"How was your job interview?" Ruth asked.

Lucy bobbed in her chair. "I'm hopeful," she said. "I'm very hopeful, Ruth."

started walking in the direction of the ferry dock. She was still in her pajama shorts and top, but she didn't care. Walking through the crowds, she felt invisible in a way she enjoyed, observing it all as if from the outside, like a ghost.

When they got to the road leading down to the ferry dock, they stepped off the sidewalk and onto the grass. A bachelorette party stumbled by them, the bride in a white bikini top, all of her friends whooping around her like seagulls.

Charlie turned to her and Ruth wondered if this was the same spot where they had first met, the day when she and Diana came to get him that August ten years ago. She remembered standing here, Diana shielding her steel-blue eyes from the sun as she scanned the crowd.

"Charlie will be excited to have someone to explore the island with. I'm usually too slow-paced for him," Diana had said.

Ruth had scanned too, searching the faces of the men that could be his age, guessing which was Charlie. Diana had shown Ruth a picture of him in the house, but she had said it was an old one, that he looked a lot different now. After a few minutes, Diana had pointed, and Ruth tried to follow her gaze. A tall man in a worn T-shirt and frayed shorts emerged from the crowd and headed toward them. The first thing Ruth noticed was his long dark hair, tucked behind his ears, blending into a thick beard. Waving, he smiled and quickened his pace. Dropping his bag on the ground, he pulled Diana into a big hug, lifting her small frame off the pavement while she shrieked with pleasure. Ruth felt young next to him, looking up like a child.

"This is Ruth," Diana said after he put her down. Charlie turned to Ruth then as she held out her hand. But he was already moving in for a hug, this one gentler than the lift that Diana received, which Ruth appreciated. He leaned down, and she felt enveloped by his long arms. He smelled like sunscreen. His touch felt easy, comforting—a complete surprise.

"Hi, Ruth," he said, pulling back and holding her gaze. She felt she had never been looked at with that much attention in her life.

. . .

When Ruth woke up the next morning, Lucy was stil arm thrown over her eyes. It was late and Ruth w she had slept for so long. Her phone had woken her with a missed call from Charlie. Tiptoeing out of the climbed out onto the roof and called him back. H after the second ring.

"Hi," she said. Ruth realized she was nervous.

"I'm getting on the noon ferry. Can I come and sa Charlie asked.

Ruth waited on the front stairs for him. It was day. A taxi pulled up to their driveway and Charlie go ging a big suitcase behind him. After the van drov dropped the suitcase in the grass and came to sit ne the front steps. She felt his body along the side of h had to resist the urge to lean into it.

"Why didn't Lynn drive you?" Ruth asked, afraid swer.

"She's not really speaking to me at the moment," C

"I'm sorry, Charlie."

"It's not your fault."

That Charlie didn't blame her felt like a gift, lik that was true, they could navigate what happened an each other's lives.

"It feels like my fault."

"It's *our* fault, I guess."

Ruth nodded. She was glad that she hadn't told hin abortion, about the possibility that it might've been h was aware, too, that there was now an even wider gu them, one that was likely never to be crossed.

"We're just going to take some time," Charlie sa and me. It's not over and dead, I don't think. I hope."

They sat there in the quiet for a little longer.

"Walk me to the ferry?" Charlie asked.

Ruth grabbed her shoes from next to the front doo

“What’re you going to do?” Charlie asked her now, bringing her out of her memory.

“I don’t know,” Ruth said. “What’re you going to do?”

“I don’t really know either—head home, I guess.” They looked at each other for a long moment and something within Ruth almost reached out again, not wanting to let go. Charlie checked his watch.

“I should get going,” he said, and he hugged Ruth much like he had the first day they met, gently. Lifting her arms, she leaned, felt the soft cotton of his old T-shirt across his back, and smiled into his shoulder.

She watched him walk down the hill and into the line of people boarding the boat. Once she saw him get onto the ferry and disappear up the stairs, she turned to head home. Ruth was halfway to the cottage before she heard the horn blast and knew Charlie was pulling away from the harbor, out into the blue ocean.

It was mid-August and summer on the island was still at its peak, but Ruth felt again like it was the last dying heatwave of fall—the too-hot rattle of something that’s over, like a worn-out car powering down. Walking home, she watched bartenders heading into town for shifts in their restaurant T-shirts, bar rags already hanging out of the back pocket of their jean shorts. It felt odd to be on the island and not be one of the people hustling between jobs, nor one of the vacationers. She didn’t know where she fit in anymore.

Ruth crawled back into the house, packed her laptop and Diana’s camera, grabbed her bike from the front lawn, and started up the hill.

As she walked into Diana’s yard, people were loading a big truck with the chairs and tables that had been meant for the wedding. Slipping through the workers, Ruth snuck toward Diana’s studio. Once she shut the door, the sounds from the yard were extinguished. She took a deep breath.

It had been a while since Ruth had developed a roll of film, but she stood above the bottles of chemicals in the tub, trying to recall the process from when Diana had taught her. Ruth cracked open one of the sealed boxes and pulled out a stack of photo paper. Flipping on the hanging red safelights, she drew the curtains and fastened them together, then pulled down the blackout shades so the room was lit with only the dark glow of the red bulbs.

Ruth grabbed the rubber gloves sitting in the clawfoot bathtub and pulled out the bottles of fixer, stop bath, and developer chemicals. She picked up the developing tanks, wiped them clean of dust, filled them each with a different solution, and got to work.

Feeling trepidation, Ruth settled in front of the enlarger machine, using the easel as a desk, and turned back the roll of the film in the camera, popping it out when it released. Unfurling the negatives in front of her and making cuts, she placed the first short strip in the negative carrier and loaded it into the enlarger. She waited for the machine to warm up, and then the first shot of the roll was finally revealed as the image from the negative was projected onto the easel. It was a photo of Diana.

Ruth spent a moment of intense emotion with the image before she began fussing with the dial on the enlarger, bringing the picture into focus until it was perfect. Loading a piece of photo paper onto the easel, she exposed the photo, the image appearing projected onto the paper only briefly before Ruth took it over to the developing tanks. She quickly placed the paper in the first tray with the developer solution and, over the course of a minute, watched as the image bloomed onto the page, before moving it over to the stop bath, then the fixer, rinsing it in water, and finally hanging the image on the line above the tub.

One by one, Ruth went through the process of developing the film, and each time as she dipped the paper in the chemical bath, Ruth watched the picture take form in front of her. First, the negative space bloomed, then the outlines became the loose forms of the people she loved, before the details of their faces—their wrinkles and eyebrows, their nose rings and tattoos—blossomed on the pages, filling their images in.

As each photo developed, she hung it up to dry on the line above the tub, until in front of her on display was a record of the last year. By now she had opened the curtains, and the light came into the room. She sat on the wooden floor and looked up at the string above her for a long time, taking every photo in.

Lucy asleep in her bed, her incense burning a wispy cloud over her body, obscuring her, the light from the window catching a sparkle of drool.

Louis after he broke into the lighthouse—the sun catching his sunburned cheeks, his eyes squinting against the setting light.

Charlie in front of Diana's house, his smile sweet and familiar—his body turned half away from the camera and half toward Ruth. She stared at this one for a long time.

The woman at Planned Parenthood, her eyes boring into Ruth through the photo, her homemade sign half-visible in the frame. Ruth thought about throwing it away.

There were pictures Ruth took of the dunes, the swaying grasses bent so they caught the bright sheen of the sun; photos of a seagull pecking at the corpse of a dogfish, marbled sand below it; photos of the library and Diana's house that made Ruth choke up.

And the portrait she took of herself—the edges of her face sharp against the light coming in from the window. The wrinkles she knew were developing already caught on film—the lines by her eyes defined and the speckled purple skin under her eyes a clear shadow.

Ruth recognized herself within the picture, could see the way the sun had changed her skin and could identify that wear with the days she spent rolling in sand, biking on the hot pavement, hiking across deep sand dunes. It was all there, the indent on her nose from when she fell off her bike at six years old, the pimples around her chin she couldn't get rid of. She saw herself reflected in the marks and scars, once fresh, now worn in.

But the pictures that stunned her the most were the three photos that had been taken before Diana put the camera in the box for Ruth. Initially, it was difficult to tell when they were shot. The first was of Diana under the beech tree. The leaves above her were dense with shades of purple and she looked damp with sweat, or maybe she had stuck her head under the hose as she often did, and her hair had still been drying. The strands by her ears were darker and slick to her head and her skin looked thin and translucent in the shade of the tree. The shot was taken from under Diana's face, looking up, toward the branches. Ruth imagined the sun glittering through the leaves down onto Diana, could hear them fluttering in a breeze.

In the next photo, Ruth was asleep on the old sheet that she and Diana used at the beach, the sun on her face. This secret portrait startled Ruth and she stared at it for a long time, trying to discern what had been happening in her life when this picture was taken. It felt like holding an old love letter in your hands—the handwriting familiar and the message remembered but all the feeling gone. The day came back to her. It had been last summer, when she and Diana had gone to Mansion Beach with paints and canvases.

"I don't get this," Diana had said as she swirled color across the canvas and waves crashed against the rocks.

"Don't be self-deprecating," Ruth had said. "At least it doesn't look like mine."

"Listen, it's not your medium," Diana said. "You work with the written word."

"Says you," Ruth said.

"Now who's being self-deprecating?"

It had been the first time all season they had spent the day together. They had both gotten so busy. Looking at it now, Ruth couldn't help but tear up at the idea that Diana had maybe already known about the cancer. Then, the tears began to fall harder as she thought that maybe Diana hadn't known yet. She thought of the golden days before they found out about Maggie's cancer—every memory lit up with endless possibilities. In those days, they were rich and lousy with time. They could plan for the future, talk about Ruth's graduation or her wedding as if they'd both be there, as if anyone could make such a promise to be anywhere.

The next shot was painful for Ruth to look at, although she had trouble tearing her eyes away. Diana must have taken it during a doctor's appointment, or she must've made Charlie smuggle the camera in for her toward the end. The fluorescent light cast a shadow over Diana's taut and hollow cheeks. The shading under her eyes was deep and stark. She was smiling—something she never did in a photo unless it was taken candidly. Her hospital gown was loose around her neck, and she was holding one arm above her head—cradling it like a fashion model in a couture spread. Ruth found the photo joyful and garish, sad and beautiful. Ruth hadn't gotten there in time to see Diana when she died, but Diana had taken a picture for her.

Staring at the collection of photographs was difficult, the emotions like a torrent, but Ruth made herself sit and take it in, her face coated with tears. After an unknowable amount of time, Ruth stood up and pulled out the chair to Diana's desk, reaching down to get her laptop out of her bag. Once she started writing, the words came easily as they hadn't all summer, and before too long she realized that she wasn't writing an article just about Diana—it was about the summer of her death, of Charlie, of Ruth herself, of her abortion, of her mother, of all of it.

As she wrote, she felt like she was stepping through the rubble, getting closer to the core of herself, staring herself in the face and not looking away—the grief, the hiding, the shame, her fears, how she had hurt people, how she had hurt herself. The rhythm of the keys and the motion of her hands made her feel strong when she was on an idea, when she stopped analyzing and let the words be, trusting herself to find out where she was going.

She realized it didn't matter whether Diana was the origin of her writing dream or whether it had sprung from within Ruth. Diana had seen her grow up into an adult, had known her better than she was able to know herself, and had given her a vision of what her life could be if she wanted it. It didn't matter how it started, what mattered was what she did with it now, whether she allowed herself to be open to the way she felt when she was writing, whether she leaned into the satisfying ache she felt to express herself, to put words to the images in her head. It wasn't the only path in front of her, but what mattered was that she was willing to consider it, willing to believe in her ability to live the life she wanted.

Ruth kept going as the sun moved across the floor of the studio. She poured herself a glass of water in the old bathroom, drank deeply, and kept writing, ignoring her hunger as it built throughout the day. After typing the last sentence, she felt dazed and slow, calm and empty. The photos had long ago dried, and Ruth scanned them one by one and sent the files to her computer before stacking them in a stolen folder from one of Diana's overflowing drawers.

When she was done and packed, she looked around the studio as if the space had changed. It did look different to her—less impenetrable, more like a part of her own memory. Ruth walked out and shut the studio door behind her. The sun was behind the beech tree and everything had been cleared from the grass. Lynn was sitting on the porch. She lifted her head when Ruth closed the door.

"You were in there a long time," Lynn said, her voice carrying across the yard. She was looking at the beech tree. Following her gaze, Ruth saw the jagged insides where the limb had ripped off from the trunk during the storm. The wood was bright and the colors deep and red like a fresh wound.

Ruth walked over to Lynn and sat on the porch a few feet away from her.

"So, my son is no longer getting married," Lynn said. "And from what I overheard, it seemed to have a lot to do with you."

Ruth looked out at the beech tree, focusing on the splintered and exposed trunk.

"I love Charlie," she said. "I want him to be happy."

"Funny way of showing it," Lynn replied.

Ruth nodded, expecting nothing different than Lynn's coldness toward her. A moment passed. She remembered what Nadia had said—*Diana was her sister.*

"I don't know if I ever said this but . . . I'm really sorry for your loss," Ruth said, her eyes on the ground at first before raising to meet Lynn's.

Lynn was looking at her with direct intensity. Ruth thought she was going to explode in anger for a second before she started nodding.

"Thank you," she said. "It's been a tough year."

"Did she tell you? About the cancer?" Ruth asked.

"Who do you think went to the appointments with her?" Lynn asked. "Until she stopped going, that is."

Ruth thought about that—being the only person who knew that your sister was dying, and she realized she had never understood their relationship. She didn't know what it was like to have a sister—Lucy was the closest thing she had. She wondered what Lynn must have felt the summer that Diana met Maggie, whether she felt left behind in the dust of their love.

Reaching into her bag, Ruth pulled out the box that Diana had given her. Flipping through the pictures, she took out the one of Diana and Maggie at the lighthouse. She passed it to Lynn, who took it, shading her eyes from the sun. Lynn held the photo for a long time and eventually flipped it over.

"Yeah," she said, looking at it for another moment before passing it back to Ruth. "She really was in love with your mom. The one that got away, I guess. Diana was a romantic. I think sometimes it wasn't a good thing for her." Lynn paused. "I probably took that out on you. Actually, I know that I took that out on you. She broke Diana's heart—your mother."

Ruth nodded.

"I don't think she ever got over it, really," Lynn said.

Ruth sat with this information. It was difficult to digest, although she had been staring at the photos for over a month. Ruth thought of Diana's long, unrequited love, of how brutal it was, and how common, to be left with the unknown.

"Are you really going to sell the house?" Ruth asked after a minute.

Suddenly the Lynn Ruth knew came back and she snapped her head in Ruth's direction, raising an eyebrow for a second.

"I'm not sure, Ruth. You want to buy it?" she asked, then she dropped her head into her hands. "Charlie would hate me if I sold it," she said. "But you know—I don't really like it out here anymore. I always thought she was going to leave the house to you. I was actually really surprised when she didn't."

Ruth had never considered that Diana would leave the house to her. If she had, would Ruth have even accepted it? It was what she'd wanted since she was seventeen, to really live on Block Island. But could she walk in Diana's old footsteps? Would it feel like a gift, or would it be haunted, too much of the past Dianas and Ruths touching every surface? Would she be able to move on with her life if she was tied to this place forever?

When Ruth got home, she asked Lucy to read what she had written, handing her the photos and putting the computer in front of her while Lucy lit a cigarette.

Ruth raised her eyebrows at the cigarette inside the house.

"I need to smoke while I'm editing," Lucy said, her eyes already bright with focused attention.

Ruth climbed up onto the roof while Lucy read, smelling the ocean air waft over the island. She could hear the faint clicking of the keys. She had written the piece in such a fugue state that she couldn't think of what Lucy was reading, responding to, whether she should be nervous or not.

She wondered where Nadia was now and how she was doing. She wished she could reach out and ask, although she knew that would be unwelcome. The sun was setting, and Ruth watched the stream of cars returning from the beach. Birds swooped up and over in outlines of black against the sun, headed for the marsh down the street. It was nearly dark when Ruth heard Lucy running up the stairs, her feet heavy against the wooden spiral staircase until she was behind her, tapping her side so that she would move over. Climbing out, Lucy wiped snot across her face. Her eyes were red.

"You made me cry, you bitch," Lucy said.

"What did you think?"

"It needs some structural work, but it's really good, Ruth. I think you should send it to Ethel."

"Thanks for reading it," Ruth said, a thrill running through her.

"Of course."

They were quiet together for a while, watching the red and pink fade from the sky.

Ruth spent the next few days drafting an email to Ethel. She couldn't get past the apology for the article, feeling crazy for asking her to read anything of hers. In the end, she just attached the document and the scanned photographs, deleted the long letter she had been crafting, and typed the message that felt right:

> Ethel,
> There is still no excuse for my inability to finish or even truly start this article about Diana. I should have known it would be too close to home. I've been a bit of a mess. I wrote something, I would love to know if you think it has any merit, although I can't imagine why you would read it after everything.
> Thank you regardless,
> Ruth

After she sent it, she stood up from her chair like she had been zapped. A rippling excitement ran through her and the ferry horn blaring in the distance made her jump. Lucy had left for work already and Ruth had nothing to do. Getting on her bike, she started cycling out of town, toward North Light. She had to weave around families stepping off the sidewalks and crossing the street until she got far enough away where it was just her and the dunes. Ruth could smell the sea spray from the road and hear the crashing of the waves still large from the passing storm.

Looking at the island, she felt the same magical awe that she had felt the first afternoon she had ever spent there in Diana's backyard. She knew now she was going to leave, and although she had no idea where she was heading the unknown was exciting to her. She thought of Diana talking about New York, about how betting on yourself was the thing to help you make it. Now that she had faith that she would figure it out, she could make her life what she wanted it to be.

Coasting down the hill toward the lighthouse, she watched as the curving shoreline came into view, saw a seal poke its head out of the water, pointed upward toward the sky. She thought of the painting in the bin at home of Diana's figure, the lighthouse in the background. Sitting on a boulder, she watched the ocean for a while, counting the seals, watching the seagulls dive among the dunes in the distance. It seemed like months ago that she had stood at the top of the lighthouse with Louis. She decided she would go see him later.

Pulling her phone out to text him, she saw a missed call and a voicemail from a New York number and her adrenaline raced thinking that maybe Ethel had read the piece already.

Ruth called back without listening to the voicemail and someone picked up after three rings.

"Hello, this is Marilynne Dobbs," the woman said. Ruth was confused, although the name sounded vaguely familiar.

"Hi, I'm sorry. I just . . . I just missed a phone call. I think I have the wrong number, I'm sorry."

"Ruth?" the woman asked.

"Yes?"

"This is Diana's lawyer."

"Oh, okay."

"I'm calling about Diana's will."

"What about it?"

"Well, I'm calling to let you know that the probate finally went through. I'm sorry it took so long, but in New York it can often take even longer. I'm calling about Diana's bequest to you."

"Oh," Ruth said again, startled. She had assumed the teal box and the paintings were all that had been left to her.

"Yes, she left you her studio apartment in Bed-Stuy. She had just finished paying it off a few years ago," the lawyer said. "I'm sending you the paperwork soon and I can get you the keys in the mail, or if you want to meet me in New York, we can arrange that as well."

The waves were crashing against the rocks, and it was hard to hear Marilynne.

"What did you say? Bed-Stuy?" Ruth asked.

Marilynne was silent for a second before laughing once. "It's a neighborhood in Brooklyn. In New York City."

"She left me . . . an apartment?" Ruth was stunned.

"Yes, hon. You're a homeowner! I'm sorry that I have to run but like I said, look out for those emails. We'll talk soon."

Marilynne hung up and Ruth sat on the log, shocked. Another seal lifted its head out of the water close to the shore, and his dark eyes looked right at Ruth.

A feeling she couldn't understand was moving through her now. The idea that Ruth had somewhere that was hers, somewhere solid, where she could go each night, shut the door, and be secure, was slow to pierce through her years of shared spaces, of instability—it was difficult for Ruth to understand that it was true, hard for her to imagine what it could mean.

Ruth started to worry that she didn't deserve it, hadn't earned it. So far, she'd thrown away all the chances anyone had ever given her—why was Diana betting on her again? If she had known Ruth wouldn't complete the article, would she have changed her mind and not given Ruth the apartment?

The discomfort of the thought seeped throughout Ruth for a minute, the shame returning, and her email to Ethel now seemed wrong. Through the discomfort, though, there was a different piece of her that felt a blooming relief and curiosity, a realization that the constant pressure of just making ends meet could now be released. She wondered what that might feel like, what space in her life it would create as she tried to shake the shame that still lingered. Diana had loved her. She had thought of Ruth as her own daughter. Her love was not weak or conditional. It was strong and believed in the best of everyone. Diana's love was still pushing her.

Another seal emerged from the water, tossing its body on the sand and up the beach. The golden hour light was glistening off its wet skin and casting the ocean in its sheen. If Ruth squinted, she could see the mainland in the distance. Seagulls whirred around the lighthouse, their figures only specks of black against the sky. The air brushed over her body, fresh off the ocean. Ruth took a deep breath. She had another realization: She could sell the apartment and use the money to stay on Block Island. Looking around her now, sadness moved through her. How could she ever leave this place?

Ruth thought of how many times she had traversed the island—thought of her body rolling in sand, running down a dune path, the water hitting her legs—she could see herself everywhere here. She knew she would come back if she left, but that it would be different. Her place here, once so carved into stone, might get swept away like sand at high tide. The rhythm of the island would continue without her as soon as Ruth stepped out of it. Could she let go of all that?

Ruth tried to imagine the apartment. She had never seen it, but had heard Diana talk about staying there before, whenever she was in the city for work, and Ruth suddenly understood that this was the place her mother was meant to move into all those years ago, the place that Diana had made beautiful for her arrival, the place that Maggie never saw. She knew that this was Diana's final gift to her; she was giving Ruth a fresh start. As she looked into the fading light and tried to make out lights on the mainland across the darkening ocean, Ruth made a silent promise to Diana that she wasn't going to waste it.

5

Ruth knocked before she opened the front door, but there was no response. Stepping inside, she leaned down to calm Hank as he ran toward her, his butt wiggling. The house was filled with cardboard boxes, the flaps still raised. Ruth walked into the kitchen and peered over the top of one on the counter. It was filled with pots and pans and loose cutlery. Most of the furniture had sticky notes on it—some said *Ruth?* and others, *Goodwill.* It had been almost a year since she had been inside her childhood home. While she had made her peace with Joel selling it, she hadn't known how she was going to feel, whether seeing her and her mother's things in boxes would hurt her in a way she wasn't expecting.

She had left most of her own belongings on Block Island sitting on the side of the road outside of the cottage with a sign written on journal paper that said *Free.* There wasn't much to get rid of—some books that she had read enough times to memorize and the rusted bike she had bought in June. In the end, she left the island with a few clothes, her computer, her waitressing clogs, her journals, the photos Diana left her and the ones she developed, the camera, and the bin of her mother's paintings. The taxi driver at Galilee had muttered under his breath as the both of them tried to fit the bin in the back seat of the car. Eventually they were able to close the door, and he drove her to Joel's house.

Walking toward her old room, Hank following her and licking the backs of her knees, Ruth peeked inside. There were a few boxes on her bed and on the floor, but it was otherwise untouched. Turning, Ruth thought she heard voices in the backyard. For a second, she worried she was interrupting something, then became curious about who might be at the house on a Sunday afternoon.

"Hello?" Joel called out from the back. "Who's that?"

Ruth still hadn't talked to her father since their fight on the phone over a month ago. She didn't hear him get up, so she walked through the house to the back screen door and opened it, pushing against where it always slipped off its tracks. Hank ran out toward Joel from under her legs.

"Hey, Dad," she said.

Joel looked sheepish. He had a cup of coffee next to him on the glass patio table they bought together at Ocean State Job Lot a few years ago.

"Hey, kid," Joel said, standing up.

Ruth waved her hand, motioning for him to stay sitting. The sound of the metal chairs scraping against the concrete subsided after they both were settled, and then there was silence.

"Did I interrupt something?" she finally asked, thinking about the voices.

"Oh, no," he said. "I was just on the phone with Sarah and Bill."

"Oh." Ruth nodded.

"I've been calling them since you stopped answering me, seeing if they saw you around town—if you were okay."

Ruth thought back to seeing Sarah and Bill in the restaurant the night she got fired. She felt the old guilt return that she had pushed him so far away that he needed to learn about her life through someone else.

"I'm sorry I didn't call you back," Ruth said. "I was angry with you. I felt lied to."

Her father nodded. She could tell he was about to change the subject, to deflect his own pain and move on without mentioning it again. Ruth hastened to keep talking, the words she had been thinking about on the ferry flowing out of her now.

"I felt like I didn't know Mom anymore," she said. "I felt like I didn't know Diana." Saying it now, it felt silly to her, that she would think that she could know everything about these women, or about anyone. "I thought that Mom made a mistake in having me, that maybe she regretted it," Ruth said.

Silent tears dripped down Joel's face. Hank whined and tried to lick them off, standing on his hind legs so his snout could reach Joel's cheeks.

"No," he said. Ruth waited for more, but after coughing and petting Hank, all he could manage was "No, never. Not possible."

Ruth knew that he would say that, and she believed him, but there was still a part of her that felt she would never really know how much her mother thought about New York, about Diana. It didn't have to be one or the other, she had decided. It was like how Ruth knew that not having a baby was the right thing for her, but sometimes she'd found herself wondering what her life would have looked like if she hadn't had an abortion, how big her belly would be by now, or what would've happened if she had held on to Charlie. It wasn't a yearning for something that didn't exist, but a curiosity about the things she could never know, the paths that she didn't take.

Maggie could have wanted Ruth more than anything and still have thought about what her days might have looked like in the city, whether her clothes would have been artfully covered in paint, whether she ever would have sold a painting, whether she and Diana would have lasted, whether they would have lived in Diana's house on the island, going for walks on the beach and picking up the perfect stone for the line of rocks they might have kept behind the sink. There was no way that Ruth could know if these thoughts haunted her mother or if they comforted her, or if she thought about things like that at all.

Ruth decided that they would have been a comfort to Maggie. She knew she was choosing this for her own benefit—that there was no way to know how someone else thought about the narrative that you both shared. She decided that it was okay for her to pick this thought, that it could be a comfort to her too, if she imagined the two women thinking of each other fondly, holding space for the memories of each other, and for Ruth to be a part of it, as if she was holding both of their hands while crossing the street.

"I was angry with you for sending me away," Ruth said.

"I'm sorry." Joel's voice was only a whisper.

"You sent me to Diana because of how much Mom loved her."

Joel stared at the glass table for a minute.

"I thought if you couldn't have your mom, maybe Diana would be a close second. I didn't mean to make things hard between us. . . . I just thought she would be better for you than me." He sighed as if he was getting frustrated, but Ruth understood. She knew her father, for all he might feel within himself, found expressing his emotions very difficult. The selflessness of the act made Ruth ache at the time she had spent angry with Joel for sending her away, for the way she allowed herself to drift from him.

"Maybe I was a bad dad to send you out there like that," he continued. "Maybe I should have tried harder. You were just so . . . broken, and I didn't know what to do."

As he said the word *broken,* Joel turned to Ruth, his eyes full of anguish.

Ruth tried to remember herself during those few months after her mother died and before she got to the island. It was blurry, like her mind had scrubbed out some of the pain, but she could still picture her dark room, how she barely left her bed. It was the first time she wondered how scary that must have been for Joel.

"I think you did the right thing, Dad," she said, knowing it was true.

"I miss Maggie a lot, you know."

Ruth thought of the way she assumed he was avoiding his wife's cancer, how after every treatment he would try to distract Maggie with some news about the car or a sports team, how her mother sat there, tired from the chemo, only half listening, and how Ruth had judged him as unfeeling. Ruth realized now that those offerings were what Joel had, were the ways he must have distracted himself from the pain, that he was doing his best. She was sorry that she had never asked him about his grief, that she had been too consumed with her own.

"Can I show you something?" Ruth asked. Joel was dabbing his eyes with the piece of paper towel from under the coffee cup, the brown stains mixing with his tears.

Hank followed her, sniffing at the bin as Ruth carried it out to the deck, stepping sideways to fit through the door. Cracking open the lid, she lifted out a few of the canvases and placed them on the table. Joel stood.

"What're these?" he asked.

"Mom's paintings."

They looked at them together for a while.

"She was really good, right?" Ruth said.

Her father nodded, more silent tears dropping down his tired face. He held each painting reverently in his hands before placing it down and picking up the next, until he had seen everything that was in the bin.

"There are some boxes of Mom's stuff for you," Joel said after a long stretch of silence. "I left them in your room."

While Joel went out to the store to get things for dinner, Ruth went back to her childhood room. Opening the boxes on the floor, she combed through the contents—books on teaching, some of her mom's summer dresses, and a collection of winter coats. On the top of the pile was a red ski coat, and pulling it out, it brought Ruth back to a memory she hadn't thought of in a long time—sledding with her mom down at the high school, the sun setting behind the barren trees, throwing reds and oranges across the day-old snow. It was crusting over with ice, and so Ruth and Maggie were going fast down the sharp hill next to the baseball field. Ruth remembered how they sat together in the pink plastic toboggan, her stomach dropping as they picked up speed, the scream of delight leaving her mouth like it was coming from deep within her tiny chest. She remembered her mother's arms around her, how at the bottom of the hill they kept going, almost running into the chain-link fence, so that they had to bail out of the sled, rolling over into the hard snow. She remembered her mom lying in the snow, laughing, her breath condensing above her face, tears streaming from her eyes, how Ruth had wiped them away with her small purple fleece mittens and asked to go again.

Holding the old coat and looking it over, Ruth saw the fabric was thick with dust and small spots of mold. She coughed, and she set the box aside to throw out. She hadn't envisioned being able to part with anything, but there was peace that came with letting some of her mother's things go.

Turning to her bed, Ruth saw a small, unfamiliar Tupperware box, cobwebs in the lip where the latches were. Ruth shook them off her fingers as she pried it open. She was wary of opening another box, of how much could be revealed so long after someone's death.

She recognized them immediately, like a prick to a nerve in the back of her mind. The small baby clothes were still soft as Ruth picked up the tiny sweater that her mother had made for her, the hat, the small boots, all hand-crocheted. Admiring the bright colors and the careful stitching, she wondered how she could have ever doubted that her mother wanted her, could have ever ignored her mother's artistic talents when, really, there had been signs everywhere. Ruth wondered then what it must have felt like to make something for someone you hadn't met yet, someone so close to you—the closest someone could be and yet still unknowable. She wondered at what point in her pregnancy it all felt real to Maggie, whether crafting the small clothes had been a way of welcoming Ruth, of threading together the realization that she was going to be a mother, one stitch at a time.

Later, Ruth was grilling corn out in the backyard while Hank chewed on a stuffed octopus at the base of the stairs, growling, when an email notification popped up on her phone. Ruth clicked it and saw Ethel's name. She closed the grill lid, stepped away, and read the message.

> Ruth,
> I'm also sorry that the article didn't work out. I can't say I was pleased with how everything occurred. It would've saved us some scrambling on our end to know that you weren't ready to write about Diana. That being said, I understand. I miss her too.
>
> I read what you sent me and I looked at the photographs. While I don't think we can use it here at *Vogue*, I really encourage you to keep with it. I left some comments on the structure and some editing that I think would take it to the next level. There's a lot of power in this piece, and the photos are something special. Keep working. I've included a list of places I think you should send it when you think it's really ready. You can tell them I suggested you send it.
>
> I hope to see you at Diana's exhibition opening in December.
> Ethel

She put her phone back in her pocket and felt the thrilling pulse of possibility pass through her. She wanted to get started editing as soon as possible. Ruth heard the horn of the ferry heading out to Block Island sound in the distance. She wasn't on that boat.

Later that night after helping Joel pack things up in the house until late, in her old room, she shut the lid of her laptop, her eyes blinking in the darkness. She had emailed a few restaurants and bookstores nearby the apartment in Bed-Stuy to see if they were hiring, was looking into a teaching program she could complete online, and had downloaded an application for a writer's residency up in Vermont for next summer. Each time she sent an email or an application out into the world, she imagined what her life might look like on that path, and each time she felt like she could see her future unfolding in so many different ways, but instead of doubt and indecision at the unknown leaving her stuck, she felt only propulsion and possibility.

Ruth turned her lamp on, blinding herself momentarily. It had been a long time since she had stayed the night at the house. In the morning, Joel was going to drive her to the station in Connecticut, where she would take the train into the city. After Marilynne had learned that Ruth had only been to New York once before, she'd promised to pick her up from the station and bring her to the apartment.

"Are you sure you want to live here?" Marilynne had asked. "I could connect you with a good Realtor. You'd make a lot of money, for sure," she said.

Ruth was scared that she would feel unmoored without the finite landscape of the island around her, worried she would be bored and stranded by the lack of nature, but she trusted Diana, and her curiosity overrode every doubt. She liked the idea of who she might become there, that it might be someone she couldn't yet imagine.

When Marilynne sent Ruth the documents for the apartment, there was a note from Diana that accompanied it.

Ruth,

I left you the apartment in New York. I know you love it on Block Island. You will continue to love it there. I think this will be good for you.

Love you always,

Diana

What Diana didn't write in her note, but what Ruth had come to understand, was there was a part of Diana that had wanted Ruth to live in the apartment so that it would feel as if there was a piece of her mom there too.

Her eyes now adjusted to the light, Ruth stared at her mother's bureau against the wall, still crowding the room. Standing, she walked over and pulled on the old swollen wooden drawers, trying to be quiet as she yanked them open. Ruth ran her hand over the wool sweaters as she used to when she was a teenager. Nothing had moved. It all looked the same as it had ten years ago. Ruth hesitated, her hand over the fabric, until finally she picked one of them up, unfolding it and holding it out in front of her. The sweater had a faint musty smell that was new to Ruth. The folds that had been worn into the fabric from sitting for so long were already beginning to smooth out as it hung in front of her. Then, in one quick move, she thrust both arms into the drawer and pulled the sweaters from it, dropping them all into her open suitcase next to her feet. Looking from the pile of her mother's clothes and back to the empty drawer, she felt a thrill run through her. Things didn't need to stay as they had been anymore.

6

Marilynne opened the door for Ruth after driving her through unknown streets and helping her lift her few things up the three flights of narrow stairs.

"You'll get good exercise," Marilynne said, her face coated in sweat and blooming red.

The key took some shimmying in the lock but after a few seconds Ruth heard the click and Marilynne pushed the heavy metal door open. It was a one-room studio, but the apartment was wide and the ceilings were high. One wall was lined with windows, so that the sun drenched the wooden floor and reached across to the bed along the far side of the apartment. Stepping into the center of the room, Ruth tried to find traces of Diana. In the far corner there was a wooden desk, similar to the one on Block Island, with scraps of paper pinned to a board above it. A rack stood next to the bed, empty except for a yellow raincoat. The walls were bare.

"Okay," Marilynne said. "Remember that the documents I sent you have all the ins and outs of the apartment. There's a good Vietnamese place at the end of the block if you need to eat like right away. I've been there before. . . . And, well, let me know if I can do anything more to help."

Ruth knew the last part was only Marilynne being polite. The ride from the station to the apartment had been disorienting for Ruth and she was glad she had someone to usher her in, otherwise she was sure she would've gotten lost.

"Thank you so much," she said.

Marilynne nodded and handed Ruth the key. "Bye, hon," she said, waving and closing the door behind her.

Ruth listened to the sound of Marilynne's heeled boots on the steps. As they faded, Ruth took in the apartment, the sounds from outside swelling into a din of traffic. Cookware was stacked on the exposed shelves above the stove, and linens were rolled neatly on the top of a bureau by a small door that Ruth thought must be the bathroom. The bed was made, a quilt folded on top of a checkered duvet. It looked like Diana could've been there only last week. Ruth pushed off her shoes by the heels and stepped out so she was barefoot on the wooden floor. The air was stale and she pulled her hair up into a high bun, feeling the sweat at the base of her neck as someone on the street below laid on their horn. Walking over to the large window, she searched for the latch, pushing it open so that a hot breeze flowed into the apartment, along with the sounds from outside—crisper now.

Her phone buzzed. Messages from Lucy and Louis popped up, wishing her a happy twenty-eighth birthday and asking to see pictures of the apartment, asking if she had heard back about any of the jobs she applied to yet, if she liked her neighborhood. For a second, Ruth's heart ached as she missed them, even though Lucy already had plans to come down before she started her new job at RISD in September. Ruth wondered then what Charlie and Nadia were doing in that moment, whether they were together. There was still a big part of her that itched to call him, to show him the apartment and hear his voice.

She allowed herself to feel another wave of heartbreak at really letting him go before she took a deep breath and released it. Walking over to the desk, running her hands across the grain of the wood, she imagined getting up each morning, making coffee, and sitting down to her computer to write, and she felt a deep belief in her ability to create there, maybe even something great.

The wind came in through the window, cooling the sweat on her neck, and Ruth lifted her head, her eyes catching the bin of her mother's paintings. Crossing the room, Ruth cracked the lid open and pulled out the painting that her mother had gifted to Diana—the one that Ruth loved the most. Flipping it over, she read the inscription in her mother's handwriting a few times over—*Happy birthday, June Baby!*

And Ruth decided that Maggie was wishing her a happy birthday in that moment too. She let the feeling swell within her, filling her up, allowing it to spill over into a few small tears that dropped onto the back of the canvas. She traced the texture of the old paint with the gentle tips of her fingers and felt both women with her in the new place. Walking around the apartment, she searched the walls until she found the flat head of a nail protruding from the space above the bed. Ruth stepped onto the soft mattress and leaned forward so that the lip of the canvas caught the edge of the nail and held it. Ruth steadied the painting, and then, stepping off the bed, she walked into the middle of the room and turned around.

ACKNOWLEDGMENTS

It takes so many people to believe in you, to advocate for you, to speak about you in rooms where you are not, to put their talent, skill, and expertise forward on your behalf in order to bring art into the world and to bring a novel from spark to shelf. Please know that I consider myself the luckiest woman alive that so many people offered their incredibly valuable talents and time toward this novel.

I'd like to thank my agent, Stephanie Cabot. Her fierce assuredness and ample encouragement kept me moving toward my dreams. I am a woman who worries, but her clear-eyed, candid, and calm approach to this business made me stronger. Thank you, Stephanie, for reading my novel and seeing what it might become. Thank you for taking a chance on me and changing my life.

To my kind and brilliant editor, Clio Seraphim. Thank you for loving the characters of *June Baby* with your whole heart and talking with me about them as if they were real. Editing this novel with you was the most creatively fulfilling, stimulating, and truly enjoyable experience I've had as a writer. What a privilege it is to get to "book club" books with you—discussing fiction with you is like being a fish out of water and getting dropped back into the ocean. Thank you for swimming in the world of this novel with me, for your generous patience, for understanding me, and for guiding me toward a better novel. I know I am not only a lucky woman to work with you, but I am a lucky woman to know you.

Thank you to Jenna Bush Hager, who offered her impeccable editorial eye and beyond impactful voice toward shaping and uplifting this novel. I feel so honored that you chose *June Baby* to represent you in Thousand Voices. Thank you for shining your powerful spotlight on artists and authors. You make dreams come true!

Thank you to Julia Plant for her strategic planning, deft coordination, and cheerful encouragement throughout the publishing process.

Thank you to my magnificent team at Random House: Maria Braeckel, Milena Brown, Madison Dettlinger, Michelle Jasmine, Caitlin McKenna, Alison Rich, and Leila Teijani for sharing your boundless talents, creativity, dedication, and support in bringing this novel into the world. You are truly a dream team.

To the amazing book production team: Rebecca Berlant, Melissa Churchill, Jennifer Rodriguez, and Sandra Sjursen, for your razor-sharp eyes and creativity.

To the book cover designer, Rachel Ake, and the artist who painted the cover image, Whitney Knapp Bowditch, for creating the most beautiful book cover imaginable that so well captures the spirit of Ruth's journey and Block Island itself.

To my dearest James, who has believed in me since our first date, and who supports me in my adventurous dreams. You make me stronger, and you lift me up. I'm so glad it was you.

Thank you to my parents, Chrissy and Phil, for raising me to be a reader, for supporting my unconventional path, and for being a safe and loving place to land when the world's chaos is consuming.

To my first-ever editor and dear friend, Karin Krisher. Thank you for being the very first reader of *June Baby*. Our conversations are among the most enriching in my life. Thank you for opening the world of creativity to me.

To Christy and Becca and to their families. This novel would truly not exist if you hadn't hired me and brought me into the world of Block Island with so much generosity of time and spirit. I treasure you two and your friendship, and am thankful for every day spent in your company. Thank you for letting me haunt the Darius kitchen, for sharing meals, for housing me, for playing the bird game, and for lending your support among your community. It means the world.

To my brilliant friends Alex and Katherine, for sharing your talents, your ears, and your creative support. Thank you for your love, time, and care throughout this journey. To Amber, who always believed in me. To Laney, for your steadfast enthusiasm.

To the restaurant community in the Seacoast, you are a group of the hardest working, most creative, wackiest, kindest, and unique individuals. Thank you for all the staff meals, shift drinks, pep talks, tacos eaten over the trash can, laughs, and lessons.

To the many educators who encouraged me throughout my life and made me believe that I had a talent worth fostering, especially Mrs. White, Tom Payne, and Ann Joslin Williams.

To Block Island, for enchanting me, for inspiring me, and for healing me.

ABOUT THE AUTHOR

SHANNON GARVEY received her MFA from the University of New Hampshire, where she taught undergraduate classes. She has published short fiction in *The Saturday Evening Post*. She grew up in Rhode Island and now lives on the rocky New Hampshire coast. She researched *June Baby* during many years of waiting tables in tourist towns and her time working on Block Island.

shannongarveyauthor.com
Instagram: @shannonmgarvey
TikTok: @shannongarveyauthor
Substack: @shannongarvey1